Since his first rousing encounter with horror fiction at the age of thirteen, Leigh Blackmore has been obsessed with the genre.

After working on *The Australian Horror and Fantasy Magazine*, he edited and published its successor, *Terror Australis* magazine (1988–92). His macabre verse, essays and bibliographies have been widely published in Australia and overseas, and his horror review columns appear in the magazines *Skinned Alive* and *Science Fiction*.

While pursuing his interests in activism and magick, Leigh Blackmore has a day job in book distribution and is a sometime bookdealer in horror and occult fiction. He lives in Sydney.

For Diane —

edited by Leigh Blackmore

TERROR AUSTRALIS
The Best of Australian Horror

Pat, buddy & favourite
correspondent

Hope you enjoy the
read (& tell your
friends!)

Warmest regards
Leigh

CORONET BOOKS
Hodder & Stoughton Australia

Compilation copyright © 1993
by Leigh Blackmore

First published in Australia in
1993 by Hodder & Stoughton
(Australia) Pty Limited
10-16 South Street
Rydalmere NSW 2116

National Library of Australia
Cataloguing-in-Publication entry:

Terror Australis : best of
   Australian horror.
   ISBN 0 340 58455 6.
   1. Horror tales, Australian.
   2. Short stories, Australian.
   I. Blackmore, Leigh
A823.087370803

Printed and bound in Australia
for Hodder and Stoughton
(Australia) by McPherson's Printing
Group, Victoria.
Typeset by Egan-Reid Ltd,
Auckland, NZ

CORONET BOOKS
Hodder & Stoughton

Contents

Acknowledgements

A long roll-call, but an honourable one: While it's not possible to mention every individual who has lent moral and/or practical support, I can't possibly neglect to thank: Justin Ackroyd & Slow Glass Books, Vicki Adams, Mike Ashley, Jello Biafra and Alternative Tentacles Records, Michael Birch, Stephen R. Bissette and TABOO, Robert Bloch, Terry Brown & Brett Garten of Land Beyond Beyond, Ramsey Campbell, Bede Carmody and THE GLEBE, Steve Carter and CHARNEL HOUSE, Clive Barker, Bill Congreve, Jon Cooke and TEKELI-LI, Philip Cornell, Stuart Coupe and MEAN STREETS, Keith Curtis, Syd Deadlocke, Kevin Dillon, Terry Dowling, Dennis & Kristina Etchison, John Gaspar and all at Galaxy Bookshop, Rob Hood, Van Ikin and SCIENCE FICTION, Mike Jeffries, ST Joshi and the US Lovecraftians, Kerry Kennedy, Kings Comics, Pamela Klacar, James Larsen, Gayle Lovett and Gaslight Books, Brian Lumley, Jock McKenna, Terry Mackrell, Marc Michaud and Necronomicon Press, Doc Martin, Chris Masters and *EOD*, Minotaur Books, Mark Morrison, Adele Moy & the NSW Writers Centre, Steve Paulsen and AUSTRALIAN SF WRITERS NEWS, Barry Radburn (wherever he is), Keith Richmond, Nicholas Royle, Antoinette Rydyr, Jon Sequeira, Colin Steele, Graham Stone, Kurt and Anne Stone, Simon Taafe, Steve Smith and Comic Kingdom, TERRORZONE, Whitley Strieber, Bronwyn Tonkin, Ursula Vaneed, Lindsay Walker, Neil Walpole, Richard Whittington-Egan, Rod Williams and SKINNED ALIVE; all at Black Rose, Jellyheads, Jura Books and TOPY CHAOS; the many readers of TERROR AUSTRALIS magazine (whose hunger for horror provided essential impetus to this project); the many contributors to the magazine; (needless to say) all the authors whose work is included in the present volume; and of course, the people at Hodder & Stoughton Australia—Joan Tasker, Jane Gillman, Jenny Nagle and especially Bert Hingley, without whose vision and enthusiasm, this collection of fictional nightmares would not have become a reality.

INTRODUCTION:
THE UNEASY CHAIR
by Leigh Blackmore

Speaking of the unspeakable

Most of us spend our lives seeking safety and comfort. Horror, by contrast, is about the profane pushing at the bounds of the sacred, pushing where some readers might prefer not to go. Horror is not meant to make us feel safe.

Paradoxically, the discourse between horror writer and horror reader *is* a safe way of exploring threatening issues from the comparative safety of the armchair—not by any means a comfortable, easy chair—let's call it an *uneasy* chair. Settled in our uneasy chairs, reading horror, we have the opportunity to confront frightening issues mentally and emotionally. Horror offers us danger (to a point)—the paradoxical excitement of the taboo, the thrill of the edge; it deals with the outer limits of consensus reality, takes us into the realms of the unacceptable, of the forbidden. But horror fiction does more than simply offer the *frisson* of thinking about the unthinkable: it speaks about the unspeakable.

Horror sees that 'in the midst of life we are in death . . .'; it kicks over the rotten log of consciousness, and takes delight in describing what's crawling around in the usually unacknowledged underside. Readers of horror are akin to Doubting Thomas pushing a finger into Christ's wounds—their attitude is: 'Don't just tell me—show me. I want to experience it'.

Horror, politically, is the most potentially radical fictional mode. It is the eternal rebel; in our *fin-de-siecle* consumer culture (the Situationists' 'Society of the Spectacle'), by its very nature it works to break us out of our 'reality-tunnel', our preconceptions about self and the world. Horror deals with the irruption of the irrational or the supernormal into the everyday. Like sf, horror can extrapolate from current trends in technology and sociology; but it rarely fails to deal as well with the numinous—inherent in it is a degree of ethical seriousness which many fail to appreciate.

These are exciting times for the horror genre, of which Clive Barker has said 'there are no limits'. He means that, of course, in terms of the subject matter that can be explored. But we needn't think that the abandonment of limits in terms of theme also means we can neglect style, plot, and interior logic, as is often the case with the idea-driven horror written by inexperienced writers. The successful horror writer knows that he or she must do more than just impart a creepy idea, or relate a gruesome episode; that the horror must be intimated and foreshadowed through suggestions that unsettle or disturb the reader. The willing suspension of disbelief, even more so than in other forms of speculative fiction, like sf, is an essential ingredient of the best horror.

Horror in Australia: the past

What are the cultural sources of our horror? By contrast with England, for instance, which has a *past* (old gods, druids, pagan rituals, Guy Fawkes), Australia's atheist/materialist culture (its equivalent social icons might be the barbecue, Melbourne Cup, the Gay and Lesbian Mardi Gras) has often been dismissed as raw, shallow, lacking in sophistication. 'We live on a placid island of ignorance in the midst of black seas of infinity, and it was not meant that we should voyage far': so wrote H.P. Lovecraft in his classic cosmic horror story 'The Call of Cthulhu'. While Lovecraft's words were meant metaphorically, if applied to the lingering Australian 'cultural cringe', they could be taken literally. Fortunately this attitude is now largely moribund, consigned to the historical dustbin along with the colonialism that engendered it. We increasingly understand that our landscape, our flora and fauna, our social conditions are all unique, and therefore we have a unique position from which to comment on the world at large.

If until now there has been a sense of having to count Australia's horror achievements on the fingers of one hand, that merely reflects the disdain that has been accorded horror until very recently. Horror fiction everywhere has, to paraphrase Oscar Wilde, been a sort of 'genre-that-dare-not-speak-its-name'; while its mass popularity has never been in doubt, its cultural 'legitimacy' is only gradually being acknowledged; this has been inevitable due to its willingness to ask uncomfortable questions about our internal and external reality.

The horror genre has shared these difficulties with all literature produced in this country; the historical process whereby the Australian identity has striven to assert itself against its colonial heritage and the tyranny of distance; to come to terms with its multiculturalism and the white man's position as intruder on a culture far older—that of the Aboriginal people. These are truisms of Australian literary theory, and show themselves in the early literature that can be classed as horror.

Australian ghost stories are often of the 'Bush Gothic' school—traditional bush yarns with supernatural elements tacked on. Aboriginal traditions have not really been absorbed into white culture even now; they offer many unexplored avenues for fiction (though a token flirtation with the mysteries of the Dreamtime has been made in such motion pictures as *The Last Wave* and *Kadaicha*).

Horror in Australia: the present

Sf fanzines and semi-professional magazines thrived in Australia from the mid-1940s onwards, but the real surge in Australian sf activity can be dated to the 1975 World Science Fiction Convention, held in Melbourne. It was not until the 1980s that the horror genre could be said in any sense to have begun to flourish in Australia. Discounting Don Boyd's *Futuristic Tales*, which published a few Lovecraftian yarns but leaned heavily to sf, the first magazine devoted to the horror genre in this country was Barry Radburn's *The Australian Horror and Fantasy Magazine* (*AH&FM*) which ran six issues between 1984 and 1986. *AH&FM* was a brave attempt at a local magazine; though nearly half the content was by overseas writers, at least they were originals not reprints, and *AH&FM* did offer for the first time a regular local forum for new Australian horror fiction.

Phantastique, a horror comic funded by a government unemployed-youth training scheme, ran four issues during 1986 but ended when its grant ran out and its graphic content caused it to be banned in three states. Editor Steve Carter continued his graphic horror explorations on an underground level with *Charnel House*, now in its fourth issue.

A number of writers and artists involved in *Phantastique* went on to found the team that produced *Terror Australis* (*TA*) magazine, which took up where *AH&FM* left off. *TA*, while running lead stories by overseas names, for the first time gave most of its space to original Australian horror and dark fantasy stories. It published three book-sized issues between 1987 and 1992, and made possible the present anthology. Only the occasional genre piece saw print outside the specialist sources (for instance 'The Howling at Bentmoor Castle' by Michael S. Christian (*Campaign*, July 1987), notable only perhaps for being the first of a new subgenre which could be termed 'Gay Gothic').

In the yet more specialised area of horror film fandom, the horror/exploitation fanzine *Crimson Celluloid* managed a few issues, on the back of regular horror filmfests at innercity Sydney cinemas. Then it was back to underground shlockzines like *Mondo Gore* and Steve Bedwell's rock-magazine column *Dr Steve's Splatter Chatter* until the advent of the slick and cynical Melbourne-based exploitation zine *Fatal Visions* (now past its twelfth issue). *Terrorzone*, a glossy cinematic zine aimed at the teenage market, folded after three issues in 1992.

Locally produced horror comics have included the one-off *Family Slaughter* and Chris Sequeira's Gothic chiller series with a vampire theme, *Pulse of Darkness*, and Neil Walpole's *The Fright Stuff*. Mark Morrison kept fans in touch with his late-eighties fanzine *Scratchings from the Crypt*.

The Canberra-based *Order of Dagon* newsletter, begun in 1988 by David Tansey, moved to Melbourne under the editorship of Chris Masters in 1990, and as *EOD* magazine has provided a fertile ground for the development of contemporary Australian horror. Masters has since published two issues of *Shoggoth*, a small press magazine devoted to Lovecraftian horror.

Collections and novels were restricted to independent publishers. In 1986 Dorothy Michell issued her *Australian Tales of Ghost* (sic) *and Fantasy* (described in one cover blurb as 'a collection for those who want to read good stories without being overly terrified'), and *Further Australian Tales of Ghost and Fantasy*. The literary quality of these was not high, but their reprinting since attests to their commercial success. Another collection, *Pale Flesh: Stories of the Macabre* by B.J. Stevens, appeared in a tiny run in 1989 and was quickly out of print.

A few horror novels began to emerge, though none was exceptional. Again, while many sf and fantasy writers have achieved professional prominence, no professional Australian writer has yet made a major impact with a novel marketed as horror. Bruce Kaplan's *Jenny's Dance* (1989) and Huw Merlin's *Dark Streets* (1992) were both self-published; the former far superior to the latter, a not altogether successful attempt to mesh crime, horror and sf themes. Richard Harland's *The Vicar of Morbing Vile* (1993) is a literate and amusing Gothic in the spirit of Peake.

Currently we are seeing a huge increase in the success of juvenile-audience horror: with, for example, Judith Clarke's *The Boy on the Lake: Stories of the Supernatural* (UQP, 1989) and *Strange Objects* by Gary Crew (Mammoth, 1991), and further anthologies for teenagers—Penny Matthews' *Spine-Chilling: Ten Horror Stories* and *Hair-Raising: Ten Horror Stories* (both Omnibus Press 1992).

In 1991, growing academic interest in the Gothic impulse evinced itself in a one-day course offered by Sydney University's Continuing Education Program—'*After Dark: A Day-time Study in Terror*'; and in February 1992 in the conference held at the State Library of NSW—'Imagining the Darker Self: Australian Gothic in Literature and Culture'. Intelligent reviews and criticism of the horror genre can be found (apart from *EOD* magazine) in Rod Williams' *Skinned Alive*, an irreverent and irregular Queensland journal; and in Van Ikin's respected *Science Fiction*.

In 1992 came the first adult anthology of horror stories to be seen in Australia—Bill Congreve's *Intimate Armageddons* (Five Islands Press), a small-run book which should definitely be sought out by fans. Single-author short story collections of horror are on the horizon, with Bill Congreve's *Fade to Black* and Terry Dowling's forthcoming collection.

Australian horror: the future

And so we come to the volume you hold in your hands. Not least of the joys of editing this collection has been the opportunity to bring together writers from both the sf and horror streams of speculative writing in this country, and to bring together seasoned professionals with writers rising from the small press pack. Here are the finest horror stories I have been able to find. The writers included here are not pulling any punches, and the range of themes is wide. These are tales to please the casual reader and the connoisseur.

As to Australian content, not all the tales are set in this continent. I have included, for example, tales set in Malaysia, and in the USA. But all are examples of an Australian sensibility and the collection as a whole pushes a little further into forbidden territory. These writers have grown up on a diet not only of the horror classics (Poe, Blackwood, Bierce, Machen, Lovecraft), but of Stephen King, Clive Barker, Joe Lansdale and other hotter up-and-comers. There are, I venture to say, plenty of hot up-and-comers amongst them. And in all of them, despite inevitable overseas influences, you will find a unique Antipodean flavour and a quality that eloquently equals the calibre of horror fiction published anywhere.

So brace yourself in your uneasy chair. And in just a moment, when you turn the page to enjoy the first delicious tingle of fear, be terrified. Be shocked. Be horrified. Above all—be entertained.

CATALYST

by Leanne Frahm

Light touches of pearly white mist kiss Gary's cheeks, leaving tiny flakes of moisture that coalesce and run like pale fire down his face. He feels them, feels the weight of his now-sodden clothes, but the feeling is like the faint distraction of a lonely echo, unsubstantiated. He tramps solidly through puddles that have formed on the cement footpath like grey reflectionless shards of metal. He has stopped running; it was beginning to wind him. He clutches the knife in his pocket.

A riot of shrubs and ornamental trees crowd the footpath, their branches drooping under the weight of slow fat drops from the mist and drizzle that descends from the dark, overcast evening. The foliage fades and reappears according to the vagaries of the vapour and Gary's mind accommodates it, fading in and out of reality. The knife is his anchor. The elastic band around his brain twangs with every step.

A thick hedge of hibiscus bushes with sagging scarlet buds sprays his arm as he brushes past; poinsettia petals tumble lightly in a blood-red shower. He has come a long way. This suburb is strange to him.

He shakes the flowers off with a hot shiver and comes to a place where the hibiscus stops, replaced by a long concrete driveway that leads to a low stucco house, reminiscent of the Mediterranean. Gary stops too, staring

down the slight slope at it. The lights of the house are ablaze, guardians against the twilight, and through the arched floor-to-ceiling louvre windows he can see a woman clearly.

She is sitting in a large straight-backed chair, her legs crossed, forming a comfortable lap in which her hands are busy at something white, visible against her dark clothes. His look of blank intensity vanishes and he leans against a nearby lamp-post, staring through the swirls of mist at the house and the woman.

A pale wash of flickering colours crosses her face and the whiteness in her lap. She is in front of a television set, its back against the wall facing Gary. Concentrating, he can hear a muted gobble of sound from it.

The driveway leads to a detached garage with the doors open, revealing it to be unoccupied. An empty garage. The elastic likes the word 'empty'. It pulses the word around Gary's brain as it stretches and contracts; *empty, empty, empty.* And then; *no husband, no husband, no husband,* at first with just the tiniest flicker of doubt, a lazy yellow question mark that follows it for a few circuits, then fades, zig-zagging into the blacker depths of his mind.

Gary feels the knife become electric in his pocket.

Gary has not had an easy day.

In the afternoon, while peering, hunched forward, at the PC screen, he felt a heavy hand on his shoulder. He looked up into the oiled granite face of John Perkins, his supervisor. Perkins made Gary nervous. He reminded him of a school teacher who had used that same expression of coiled contemptuous anger to intimidate his students. It had worked when Gary was seventeen, and it still worked now he was twenty-seven and hanging tenaciously on to a job he wasn't suited for, but was desperate to keep.

There was just the hint of a lift to one side of John Perkins' mouth as he nodded for Gary to follow him into the corridor. Gary nervously wiped his hands and stood, feeling a coldness in his chest that had nothing to do with the air-conditioning.

Perkins was abrupt. 'You're retrenched,' he said, his voice loud in the stillness of the deserted corridor.

Gary felt the cold change to a heat that rushed up to his throat.

'Why?' It was inane, but he was having trouble focusing his eyes on Perkins' chest, and it was all he could manage to get past his tongue.

'Company policy,' said Perkins, moving closer and seeming to loom over Gary.

Gary tried to think fast. He felt his hands rubbing the sides of his pants, fought to control them. This was not how he should be handling this. He should be meeting Perkins' stare with a confident expression and a light laugh, like the other men in the department would. He should be arguing smoothly and efficiently, using words as his father did, adroitly and cleverly, tying Perkins into a knot of contradictions.

But his face was stiff and the words wouldn't come and Perkins' eyes were little, close-set augers that drilled into his skull.

'But look,' he said, and was appalled by the whine in his voice. 'Look, I'm only half-way through that night course. When I finish it . . .' He was going to say that when he finished it, he'd be much better at his job, but that stuck in his throat, because he was suddenly, frighteningly, unsure that he would be any better.

'Sorry,' said Perkins casually. 'You can pick up your pay at the front office. Two weeks in lieu.'

That's it? thought Gary wildly. That's *it*? Finished, just like that? 'That's not bloody fair!' he managed to stutter, halting Perkins who was already striding away.

Perkins wheeled slowly, like an ice-breaker in heavy seas. He stared at Gary and his lips curled.

Gary's fear changed, becoming a tight ball of rage that bubbled in his stomach. He wanted to smash that unyielding boulder with its gash for a mouth, but it was too big. He knew he could pound on it for a week and make no appreciable difference to the scorn that emanated from it.

He turned abruptly, away from it. Two of his workmates were peering round the doorway, watching. The mouth of one of them twitched, and as he passed, they nudged each other.

His face aflame, he hurried down the corridor, away from them, and when he came out into the street a short time later, he found the drizzle had begun.

The woman rises suddenly while he watches, puts the whiteness, which now looks like some sort of cloth, on the arm of the chair and goes to a door beyond Gary's sight, but when she opens it he realises it is a single pane of glass. She stands just inside the open door and he can hear her clearly.

'Puss, puss, puss,' she calls in that false high voice that people use only for cats and babies. The elastic band now has a new sound and it pulses joyfully; *puss, puss, puss*. But no cat comes.

The woman returns to her chair and resumes her position, leaving the door open.

For the first time that day Gary's eyes glisten with mirth at his unbelievable luck . . .

He was home early, but no one seemed to notice. His sister was living with them temporarily while separated from her husband and her two children bellowed and screamed in the lounge. The noise buffeted him as he came through the door. His mother was trying to quiet them while his sister, his mother informed him, took a bubble bath to unwind. His mother looked harried.

Gary nodded, relieved to find his father not yet home from his game of golf. He would go to his room, find some peace, try to decide whether to confess his retrenchment tonight or let it ride for a while. But before he could do this his father entered, and Gary felt his legs turn to jelly.

'What's the matter?' his father said, staring at him, and his mother looked up apprehensively at his tone. She sent the children up to their room and they went, big-eyed and without protest.

Gary's father's gaze was locked on his son's face. Gary felt himself redden, in awe of the magic of the man who could take one look at him and know whether he had got a bad report from school, whether he had damaged the car's bumper, whether he had lost his job . . .

'You've lost your job,' stated his father flatly, contempt flicking from him like a snake's tongue. His usually smooth voice was rough, and Gary knew he had had a bad round, followed by 'a few drinks' to compensate. He felt the old familiar fright unfurling like a flower's petals in his stomach. He tried to tamp it down, but it grew inexorably.

'Yes,' he said, smiling sickly. 'The company needed to retrench some employees, and being last on . . .'

'Oh Gary,' his mother breathed, her eyes pained. Gary wished desperately that she would have the sense to leave the room, but it was too late.

'Shut up,' said his father tonelessly to her. 'I obtained that job for you—once again,' his father went on, addressing Gary now. His voice held that lilting pedantry that signalled danger. Gary nodded, sweating at the unfairness of it; a retired doctor shouldn't do this. Professional people, for God's sake, should be above this. His father was continuing. 'How a son of mine—of *yours*—' he flung at his wife, 'could prove so incompetent, so spineless.'

'Gary does his best,' his mother interjected as Gary knew she would, and he wanted to hit her, to shut her up, because she knew what was coming, what *always* came when his father was in this mood, but prescience paralysed him.

'I said shut up,' said his father conversationally, slapping his mother across the face so casually it was like ballet. Gary choked on a sob as his mother gave a little surprised bleat and tottered backwards.

There was silence from the upper levels of the house, where his sister, with a sixth sense developed over the years, was no doubt hiding with her children. No help from that quarter.

And none here, thought Gary miserably, unable to move, watching with sick fascination as his father warmed up verbally like an athlete before a race. It was strange, but his father reminded Gary so much of John Perkins and the teacher and numerous others who had given Gary a life in which his guts were perpetually filled with lead.

He was musing on this when he first felt the elastic band slipping around the inside of his skull. It made a distinct slithering sound as it did so, and he touched his brow in surprise. It came to rest exactly encircling his brain, and was oddly comforting.

'Call your son a *man*, you useless bitch?' his father was shouting. His mother muttered a reply, too muffled to be heard clearly. Gary turned and walked to the kitchen where his mother had been preparing vegetables for dinner. The knife's blade was white with dried potato juice and a shred of bright orange carrot skin was curled on the handle. He picked it up and wiped the blade on the dishcloth. The elastic moved round and round like a dog circling for comfort. When the knife was clean he walked back to the lounge.

'Shut up,' he said loudly.

His father looked at him, and at the knife. He wasn't a big man, but the resemblance to John Perkins was truly striking. The knife shook in Gary's hand. He glanced at his mother who was still sniffling, while she stared vacantly at the floor. Gary waited for their dismayed screams.

His father laughed.

Even his laugh sounded academic and professional. It was a startling sound in the silence of the lounge and it caused the elastic to throb. His father walked over to him, plucked the knife from his hand and back-handed him across the face. Gary felt something break in his mouth and tasted copper. He ducked past his father and into the hall.

'Get out of here,' his father called, sounding highly

amused, and threw the knife after him. It clattered, glinting brightly, across the tiled floor.

Then there was a sound like a baseball driven into a taut cushion and his mother gave a series of faint hiccupping moans. The elastic was squeezing now in earnest and he groped for the knife.

When he left the house he began running, aimlessly, in the rain that now mingled with a white oncoming evening mist.

Gary slides noiselessly across the yard towards the open door. His spirits lift. There is no sign of any cat to forestall him, and if he keeps to the bushes the woman won't glimpse him through the louvres.

He comes to a brick-paved patio where the door is open. The sounds from the television are loud and disjointed. They are crowd noises, screams and calls, with an excited commentator's voice shouting over them. It is a game of some sort. The noise is almost overwhelming, and he wonders how the woman, sitting directly in front of it, can stand it.

He stops just outside the open door where the angle doesn't permit the woman to see him yet. He pauses to picture accurately the coming scene, so that he will be prepared for every eventuality.

The woman will scream. There is no doubt about that. But the sounds from the television and the distance from neighbouring houses will take care of that. The elastic band jumps and squeezes almost painfully when he thinks of the screams and his throat becomes clogged at the thought, the fullness of anticipation, as it does when he thinks about sex.

Yes; he will leap through the door with the knife raised and the woman will start up and scream in fright. Perhaps she will flail at him in desperation, but she will be plump and soft, and then, when he is ready, the knife will flash . . . Gary's body shudders violently. He can hear her screaming already.

He leaps through the door, his eyes finding the woman's and locking onto them. He hears her screams, loud, piercing and full of terror.

Except that she is not screaming. The sounds are only coming from the television. The woman is still sitting, looking up at him enquiringly. Her mouth is a faint, polite smile. Her hands are still busy with a needle in her lap. Gary looks at his hand, upraised, the clean knife blade reflecting brilliant flashes of light from an overhead fluorescent light. It's there, she can't *miss* it. He can feel his mouth twisted into a threatening grimace. What's the matter with her?

'Yes?' she says to him.

Yes? Yes?! Gary has seen that sort of smile before. The smile of the middle-aged reserved lady. The ladies of the school committee, the ladies of his mother's gardening club. They all use that same reserved, polite smile. It is bred into them. 'Yes?' they say, smiling at him.

And now this woman looks up at him and says, 'Yes?'

His arm remains locked in position, menacingly, with the anticipated actions unable to continue until the right signal comes from the woman; a terrified scream, or a series of them. But she's not reacting. An angry bafflement descends on Gary, masking the excitement and converting it to rage. He pulls his arm down in a sequence of jerky movements and brandishes the knife in front of his chest. The jerky movements don't cease, they transmit themselves to his torso, then to his legs, as he stands in front of the television, almost tap-dancing in his agitation.

'Yes?' she says again, quite relaxed, legs still crossed, doing some sort of embroidery on the material in her lap. He can see patterns of pastel flowers and is repelled by their cloying ripeness. The needle gleams too, like the knife, lancing slivers of light up and down through the fabric.

Rage is bubbling inside his head, but the woman has drawn an invisible shield around herself with her courteous smile and disregard of his threats.

The television behind him emits an even louder and more prolonged cheer, and he realises with relief that this is part of the problem. The unending crowd noises are distracting him, upsetting him. He can concentrate better if they stop.

'Turn that thing off!' he half-screams, dismayed to find his voice so high and hoping she won't notice. He waves his free hand behind himself at the set, skipping sideways so she can see what he's referring to.

Her hands continue to busy themselves with the embroidery.

'Look,' she says, 'there's a slide volume control just below the station selector. Just slide it to your left.' Her voice is neutral and competent.

Gary feels his eyes rolling and sweat breaks out on his forehead. He wants to yell at her to do what she is told, but what she says sounds so reasonable; he is, after all, much closer to it than she is and it's the quickest way to silence the distraction. Above all, he still has the knife. With a quick swipe he shuts down the noise, reducing it to the muted roar of waves on a distant shore. He wheels round, knife waving, ready for her screams. Now she *must* have realised that she is in deadly danger.

'Thank you,' she says.

Thank you. Gary feels his knees become bubble-gum. He watches her clip a piece of thread with her teeth, and swiftly and efficiently thread another piece of bright scarlet thread, with which she begins to sew in flashing stitches. He feels very much like crying.

Nothing has happened. Nothing is happening. It was a mistake. A shockingly leaden tiredness settles over him, and he turns towards the door.

'Wait,' says the woman. 'Don't go yet. Sit down.'

She gestures to a divan near the door, across the room from her. The elastic is completely loose now and it allows Gary to slump unthinkingly onto the seat, the hand holding the knife, still firmly, dangling between his knees.

He looks across the room at her. And finds her smiling broadly at him.

'So,' she says. 'What's the problem?'

It is only his acute embarrassment at the mis-aligned situation that prevents Gary from laughing. Has he found a woman who's a social worker at heart? *The* problem. As if there was only one? And where were the social workers when his family needed them? He wants to tell her that, wants to scoff at her and her sympathy. In fact, the jumble of thoughts rekindles some of the fire he felt when he leapt through the door and he grips the knife hard, but he sees her smile change as he looks at her, and the words die in his throat.

She doesn't care at all about his problems. She is aware that there was only one satisfactory solution to his problems tonight, and that involved her death, a vision of bloody spray and hacked flesh. Her smile is intrinsically triumphant, and for a second it frightens him.

He shrugs and looks away from her. At the carpet, at the wallpaper, at the bookshelf in the corner with its motley collection of books.

'You men have it so easy,' she says loudly.

He looks at her in surprise, but she is frowning at her work where her fingers are flying, dragging red ribbons behind them in convoluted coils and loops. A mosquito has landed at the corner of her jaw and is digging in. He waits for her to brush it aside, but she seems not to notice.

'What d'you mean?' he mumbles, as much to cover the sea-shore noise and fill the void in the rest of the room as anything else.

'Well, you can just explode, can't you?' she says.

Gary shifts uncomfortably. The pressure is seeping away now, but an explosion. That was how it felt, yes.

'It happens all the time. "A man can only take so much,"' she quotes, and a thin note of mockery has entered her voice. 'A few upsets, and you can go crazy with an orgy of bloodlust and murder. It's practically *expected* of you.'

'Hey,' says Gary, stung. 'I didn't *do* anything . . .'

'But you wanted to.'

The simple observation is so accurate that Gary is defenceless. The mosquito is plumping now, its abdomen taking on a reddish tinge. It makes him feel uneasy, this second-hand acquaintance with her blood. He turns the knife over and over in his fingers.

'*I* can't do that,' says the woman after a silence.

Gary looks up. 'Do what?'

'Explode. Rampage. Kill. Ladies don't do that.' She pauses to examine her progress critically. 'No. We just sit here, putting up with all the frustrations, petty and large, the disappointments, the fears. Sit here, sitting on them.'

Gary shrugs again. There is little he feels he can say in reply to this.

'No,' the woman murmurs, once more intent on her work. 'Middle-aged women don't do that. *Men* do, it's in the papers all the time. Look at the Hoddle Street massacre; and afterwards, he takes a camera-man around to reconstruct it, so there are no details the viewer can be unsure of, as if it was a cooking demonstration . . .' She shakes her head in wonderment.

The mosquito is bloated now, looking like a large red mole on her cheek. Gary is fascinated by it. As he watches, it lifts off, sated, and hovers for a moment, its movements slowed by the extra weight of the blood. Quick as a flash the woman spears it with her needle. Gary jumps. He didn't think she was even aware of it. She holds it up to the light, the needle embedded in its middle, examining the pulsing ruby abdomen clinically.

'We get angry too, you know.'

She squashes the mosquito on the cloth on her lap, leaving a crimson stain across its whiteness. There is a satisfaction in her movement that Gary does not like.

'Yes, well,' he says hesitantly, and starts to rise.

She looks at him and pins him to the divan with that look.

'We can't go seeking violence, like men can,' she says. 'Like you can.'

'Look, it was a mistake, just a mistake,' says Gary. He

feels very weary. If only she had been frightened, just a little bit, it would have been different. Then he would have felt like a god; now he just feels like a fool.

'However,' she continues, utterly ignoring his statement, 'sometimes violence comes to *us*.' She bites off another piece of thread.

Gary shakes his head tiredly and rises. It's time to go, he thinks, all ambition evaporated, all dreams dust . . .

'Look,' the woman says. Gary turns to find her holding the piece of cloth out to him. She is still sitting. Gary stands indecisively for a moment. He wants to go, desperately, before the husband returns, before the police are called. Mostly he wants to go to hide the shame of failure yet again. But he owes this woman some sort of amendment for what he did and what he failed to do.

He walks over, the knife loose in his hand. She tightens the embroidery for him to see clearly. In the centre, in the middle of a bouquet of blue flowers and pink garlands, is a rapidly and crudely sketched dagger, done in jagged scarlet stitches. At the tip is the smear of blood from the mosquito.

Gary peers at it. It has a primitive power that he finds hypnotic. He realises that she has been working on this while he has been in the room, and the realisation reawakens the emotions with which he had entered the room. The elastic stirs sluggishly and he swallows a sudden rush of saliva.

Meanwhile the woman has been talking while he looks at her work, and gradually her words come together in a pattern that catches his attention.

' . . . totally removed from violence, expressing our repressions in arts and crafts. Then, one day, violence is brought into our houses, through our doors. You do it; you bring violence to us. You become a catalyst. And we are glad.'

Gary steps back, uncertain of the huge expression in her eyes, eyes with gentle laughter-lines at the corner.

'Because then everything becomes all right for us, too.'

She whips away the cloth, and he sees her other hand is grasping a pair of sewing shears in her lap. He remembers the knife in his hand, but woodenly. It is too late. She has lunged with the speed of a big cat and his gut is on fire.

He staggers back. His legs crumple without feeling. He is on his back on the floor, the knife still caught in a hand spasmed into paralysis, just like his legs. He can see the handles of the scissors protruding from his stomach but can't move to remove them and the pain snaps the elastic band and sends it flying into a vortex of darkness.

His head is near the television set and over the wash of crowd noises a commentator's tinny voice is breathless with suspense and revelation.

'Remember,' says the woman gravely, standing over him, '*you* invited *me* in.'

She has her large blunt-pointed needle newly threaded, this time with a deep distinguished green, and she kneels by his side. Her expression is joyous as she bends over the taut canvas of his body.

Later, while the blackness ebbs and flows through his mind, he hears the television set being clicked off and her footsteps leaving the room. Hearing is all that is left to him; she has closed off all other sensations. Hearing and pain. Such pain. Even her delicate stitchery can't reform the mutilated nerves.

The crowd noises are now silent. With his last coherent thought, he wonders what game they have been playing.

THE DAEMON STREET GHOST-TRAP
by Terry Dowling

I first heard of the Daemon Street ghost-trap from Jarvis
Henry on the day after he lost his aide of six years to an
interstate posting.

I was doing my Honours year, and the retired academic
had been giving some honorary lectures and a completely
optional series of seminars on perceptual anomalies. I enjoyed the classes, participated readily in the discussions,
and received an invitation to stay back after the three
o'clock meeting on that momentous Friday. Jarvis Henry's
words were gently spoken, but they exploded in my mind.

'Jack, I wonder if you would like to accompany me this
evening to see a Renfeld ghost-trap in Daemon Street?'

We'd all heard the news of his assistant's departure, so I
spent the next hour daring to hope I was being considered
as a replacement for the job—the Sorcerer's Apprentice.

All through the class, I watched Jarvis (as he preferred
to be known), his bushy eyebrows flicking about on that
pink, scrubbed-looking teddy-bear face, studying the
small blue eyes for some sign. But no. He seemed jovial,
excited, and determined to leave me in suspense.

While he listened patiently to a question from Megan
Hatford, I reviewed all I knew about the Sorcerer (our
name for him), trying to distinguish fact from rumour.

This small neatly-scrubbed-looking man in a worn tan
suit, for all his qualifications, had made a name for himself

searching out ghost-traps and spirit-foils across the world.
He'd already examined forty-seven, but as I was later to
discover, the one in Daemon Street had always been the
one he most wanted to see.

When the class finally ended I approached him.

'I'd love to . . . Jarvis,' I said, as though the previous
hour hadn't existed, only his invitation.

'Good man,' he replied, then spent ten minutes with me
talking about the visit.

All through the next lecture I thought about what Jarvis
Henry had said relating to Daemon Street. I looked out of
the window at the fading autumn light, hoping my friends
wouldn't mind me cancelling our plans for this evening. As
I tried to take notes, Jarvis's words kept coming back to me.

Daemon Street. What a name. What a rare joke.

For a start, he suspected it was a real ghost-trap, not
just a foil for keeping ghosts away like the Baxter's stair-
case-to-nowhere, or the Talbot's Blank Door, the false Red
Room at Cromer, the Rot Bottle or the Blackfriar's Eat-
Yourself Spiral Maze. According to Jarvis's most reliable
source, the Crane residence in Daemon Street probably
had token versions of those too, but it was the doorless
room in the centre of the ground floor that had Jarvis so
excited. It was not a modification, Jarvis had said, not
some afterthought added later, but part of the house's
original design. Someone had set out to catch and hold
something.

I marvelled at it too. It wasn't just that someone had
had the determination and commitment to give over a
dining-room-sized space to catching a family ghost. There
was also the healthy respect that kept the succeeding generations from breaking the thing open and putting it to
more immediate use. As Jarvis said, it took a strong haunting tradition, recurring manifestations, to do that.

These people believed.

I arrived at Jarvis's office in the Whiting Building at six.
It was a brightly lit room, with the same twinkling, neatly
scrubbed quality that Jarvis had. Amid the drab functional

greys of filing cabinets and bookshelves, there was a collection of small curios and talismans.

I took the sound equipment and cameras Jarvis handed me and we went down to his car in the staff carpark.

'I wish I had time to show you more of the Private Listings, Jack; the Bellerton and Dutton breakdown released last year, the Getier monograph. You only got to browse them in class and you would be interested. Oh, I am so excited!'

There was no need for the street directory. Jarvis had plotted the route in advance, had no doubt driven down Daemon Street many times just to look at the house. He put some of the heavier things on the back seat, gave me the Pentax to hold, and started the engine.

'It's a real one, Jack. I am convinced!' he said as we reversed out of the carpark.

'Are there many fakes, Jarvis?'

'Oh yes, Jack. It's like mazes and topiaries. You make their existence public and everyone wants to see them. They become tourist attractions, even status symbols. The fakes soon appear. It's understandable with the television shows and magazines paying so well for coverage.'

While Jarvis discussed the next week's parking arrangements with a university security guard I had time to savour what was happening, to glance at the traffic moving under a chill blue evening sky, and know that this was a special time.

I was the Sorcerer's Apprentice. For tonight at least, I was it.

To my knowledge Jarvis had seen two fakes: the Garden Trap at Higgs, and the Wentletrap-in-a-Well at Barstow. Campus talk had it that he had exposed many others, always in the same urbane, thoroughly civilized way, always avoiding legal action with his celebrated and quite damning line: 'There is nothing for me here.'

'How did you persuade Mr Crane?' I asked, wondering why he had never been able to visit the Daemon Street site before now.

'Ah, Jack,' Jarvis said, turning left and heading towards the city. 'Ever since I heard about Tesserley Crane seventeen years ago I've been trying to get in to see it. Phone calls and letters every other month for a while. Polite refusals every time. He's a widower, but one of his sons, Bradlan or young Roderick, or Tesserley himself, would point out that publicity wasn't wanted. I promised discretion but they refused. Every other month became every other year. Now this phone call. The old man claims he has trapped a ghost—a Renfeld Four—and apparently he's going to breach the room. He invited me to be there.'

'A Four?' I said, deciding to show my ignorance up front.

'Yes, Jack. You've heard me mention Eugene Renfeld's GHOSTINGS: A TAXONOMY in class. Remind me to show you the extracts I have, if you like apprenticing for me.'

And he winked. I definitely saw him wink.

'It's a limited edition, published in 1934. Very much a vanity press thing; none of the respectable publishers would touch it. The mutual friend who first told me about Crane's room also mentioned that Crane has a copy and, from what he says, probably believes in Renfeld's four types. This is a marvellous opportunity if this is the case.'

I went to comment but Jarvis spoke first.

'Forgive me, Jack, if I leave it to Crane to tell you what the four kinds of ghosts are. I'm hoping to hear how the old man handles it, and your detachment may be useful. I'm even thinking he may have been a student of Renfeld at some time. But you may remember the concept of the Red Room. I mentioned it at our first class when I showed my slides of Cromer.'

'Yes, I do,' I said, trying to remember what I had heard in class, and what Jarvis had told me that afternoon.

'Well, Renfeld fixed on that as the best way to hold the ghost. I'm thinking that the room in Daemon Street is a Renfeld trap.'

'A Red Room?'

'Yes.'

We turned into Parkhill, then did a sharp left into Makinson.

'What's the reasoning there, Jarvis?'

'It's straightforward, Jack. Blood memory, I should think, though I prefer to leave that sort of theorizing to people like Renfeld. Honorary lectureships are worth a degree of circumspection. Off the record though' (and again there was a wink) 'the ghost essence once occupied a living body. Whatever life is—or was—is drawn to that colour. Red and darkness. Renfeld gives ten cases in my extracts from GHOSTINGS where Red Rooms attracted and neutralized Fours.'

The car's headlights fell on a metal sign fixed to the brick wall of a corner terrace house: Daemon Street. I was startled by the archaic spelling.

The Crane house was halfway down the street. A large three-storeyed dwelling, it was set back behind some pin oaks, appearing smaller than it was because of even larger houses closely adjoining it on either side.

The evening had turned cold. The pin oaks shook in the sudden chill wind, and the warm light spilling out of the stained-glass fantail above the front door was a welcome sight. Through the ragged, autumn-stripped trees we could see more light falling from the long shades of the first-storey windows.

A butler answered the door, a dour sallow-skinned elderly man in formal black, who admitted us to a lit hallway. At the end of the hall, a stairway went up into darkness. The rest of the ground floor was in gloom.

'Mr Crane is upstairs, gentlemen, if you would be so kind. First door on the left. He is expecting you, of course. Dinner will be in twenty minutes.'

Both Jarvis and I had been studying the panelled wall to the right of the staircase.

'That's it,' the butler said, and moved off towards the kitchen at the back of the house.

We left our gear on a hall table and found Crane waiting for us at the door of an upstairs drawing room.

He was a tall, gaunt, bespectacled man in a mulberry-coloured lounge jacket and dark trousers, who was so pale and ancient that he made Jarvis seem robust and youthful by comparison.

Crane was in his early eighties, but even allowing for the rough usage of years his haggard appearance had to be the result of some affliction, though Jarvis clearly had no knowledge of it. He gave me a look of puzzled surprise as we were ushered into the large room which combined the functions of a study, library and dining room.

It was a splendid room, obviously loved and much lived in, occupying most of the first floor. Deep, comfortable armchairs were set before a crackling fire; high bookcases reached to the ceiling, holding thousands of volumes; a chandelier and fine crystal bent the firelight into sudden brilliant flecks and glimmers. To one side, a mahogany dining table was laid for three.

'This is very good of you, Mr Crane,' Jarvis said when the introductions were completed.

'It's a pleasure, Dr Henry. Andrew and I keep to this part of the house while the boys are away.'

He asked me to pour sherry while he and Jarvis discussed the house, which the Crane family had lived in for generations. I joined them by the fireside, waiting for Jarvis to steer the conversation on to the subject of the room.

It didn't happen, not then. Andrew called us to the table and served soup and croutons followed by a casserole. Crane ate sparingly, then settled back with his eyes closed as if he had fallen asleep. There was no sound other than the crackle of the fire and the tick-tick of our eating utensils.

Just when I felt that Jarvis would suggest we return another time, the old man's head came up and his eyes flashed with new life.

'I am doing the right thing!' he said. 'The story bears telling and I've procrastinated long enough.'

He spoke in a vigorous, forthright voice, as if the conversation had been proceeding all along.

'I chose you, Dr Henry, because you make no coin out

of this. Like me, you are the genuine article, and you remind me a little of Eugene Renfeld as he's been described to me. Set your recorder going, Mr Obern.'

Our things had been brought upstairs, so I placed the machine on the table and switched it on. Crane nodded with approval.

'I have trapped something, a ghost, a horrifying and utterly cruel Four, the very worst of them. Downstairs is a closed room. You passed it when you came in. Tonight, with your help, we shall breach the room. Then you will re-write the books, Dr Henry, should you have the courage. Or you will, Mr Obern, because it's a sensational new viewpoint. But, like poor Renfeld, and like my forebears, you will have the story and the truth, and that seems the very least I owe myself and my family and my faithful Andrew here.'

Andrew created a silence by serving sherry, then went back to reading a book by the fire.

'Why are you doing it, Mr Crane?' Jarvis asked when the silence became unbearable. 'Why you?'

The old man sipped his sherry, then cleared his throat.

'Do you know of the Alderson house at Port Savine? Of Janie Alderson, the woman who for years added to her house, room by room, believing that so long as she kept adding new rooms, new corridors, that a ghost would not kill her? It's somewhat like that here. We have auspicious relatives all over the world, Dr Henry. In law, in politics, in commerce, and the arts. We're well represented, quite wealthy, and long-lived.

'It fell to the Daemon Street Cranes to safeguard the rest, you see. Some forebear rightly divined that our family was especially prone to the destructive force of ghostings; so he established this house. At first, the occupancy was rotated among less accomplished, less promising cousins, for a handsome stipend and the privilege of living here rent-free. They had nothing whatever to do for it, they could just live their lives peaceably, so long as the room remained intact. It was a powerful family superstition.

These are more enlightened times, but I suppose I'm still the poorer line of the family.' He laughed.

'But it's coming to an end?' Jarvis said.

'Oh yes. It's time. The Cranes can fend for themselves.'

'Your sons don't wish to keep up the tradition?' I said.

'Partly correct, Mr Obern. I live alone but for Andrew here.' Crane gave an unreadable frown, one that might have hinted at recalcitrance and obduracy in Bradlan and his younger brother, Roderick, but which might have meant other things too.

'But it's more to do with something I have discovered, some research I've carried out on the Daemon Street Cranes.'

'May we ask what that is?' Jarvis said.

'I wish to tell you. My father discovered that a great percentage of the Cranes who resided here in Daemon Street —men, women, young and old—all died of what is commonly diagnosed these days as carcinogens. Living here, they fell prey to cancer in all its hideous forms.'

I could see why Bradlan and Roderick Crane had left. The rumour alone would be enough to set me packing.

'I had difficulty verifying much of this, of course. Cancer is very much a modern discovery by that name. But the coincidence was striking, especially in view of the Crane longevity elsewhere. Naturally my father suspected the ghost-trap downstairs, some deleterious by-product of its working through the years.'

I glanced at Andrew sitting with his book by the fire, looked again at the ruined man at the head of the table but could not bring myself to ask Crane if he were suffering from cancer.

Jarvis spoke carefully. 'You suggest that such disease is ghost-related?'

'It's more than that.' Crane poured us both more sherry and stood up, indicating with a gesture that we should join him at the fire.

Jarvis and I sat down in two of the deep armchairs, but Crane remained standing.

'It occurred to me shortly after my father's death that ghosts had to be homotropic in every sense. They only have half-life energy to draw on, sometimes very weak and fleeting, sometimes remarkably powerful and enduring. But it seemed natural then that the ghost would be directed to that end—which may account for conditions like possession and schizophrenia. Or, failing that, they would seek the strongest material things we ever own, houses, rooms, objects, as fixing points. But people first. They would try to get back to people first; relatives, friends, the impressionable young, unsuspecting tenants, doctors at the bedsides of dying patients.'

'Hence your closed room,' I said, welcoming the fire of the wine, relying on the act of drinking it to keep me from being too impatient.

Jarvis, however, seemed the very soul of patience, relaxing back in his chair, as if prepared to let Crane talk all evening.

I hadn't learnt the Sorcerer's ways yet. I was impatient to see the room, to break it open and look upon what Jarvis had probably seen many times.

Crane began to move slowly to and fro in front of the tall bookcases. He laid a finger on the spine of a red-bound volume.

'This is Renfeld. He classifies the ghost as four types—according to power vectors and how they manifest the tropism. Do you know Renfeld, Dr Henry? Mr Obern?'

'Of him,' Jarvis said. 'Yes. I don't have my own copy, and I have never read it. Only extracts.'

'This will be yours soon,' Crane said. 'I'll see to it. No! Here! Take it now.' And he passed it over.

Jarvis accepted it, his mouth open in amazement at the unexpected generosity. Crane gave him no time to express his thanks.

'The Ones, Renfeld suggests, and I believe him, are the barest echoes, all non-specific residues. Premonitions and *frissons*. The conviction of something under the bed. The *déjà-vus* and *cauchemars*.'

'*Cauchemars?*' I said, and instantly recalled the French word and regretted the interruption.

'The nightmare, Mr Obern. The ghost as nightmare. Intruding into our consciousness when the mind is at rest and vulnerable. Most spectres are Ones. Quite weak, ineffectual, diluted, just as many personalities are average, undynamic. Very tenuous life-echoes.

'The Twos are more powerful versions of these, still subjective experiences, private, solitary things, phenomenological rather than phenomenal, but more defined. With characteristics and features, identities, behaviour. You would agree, Dr Henry? Most ghostings, over ninety-five percent, are Ones and Twos. There is never anything to find; it all happens within the perceiver. Objectively, they do not harm us overly much.'

Jarvis nodded, encouraging Crane with attentive silence.

'Exasperating for you two,' Crane said, and smiled weakly. 'The only haunted house is the self.'

'The Bogeyman,' I said, giving in to the flush of the sherry, needing to speak.

'The very worst of the Bogeymen, Jack,' Jarvis said, and I appreciated his use of my name. 'The ones children take with them when families move house.'

'Absolutely,' Crane said. 'Renfeld's Threes, on the other hand, mark the cross-over. The subjective experience becomes the phenomenal one, measurable at last. External manifestations. Recordable bumpings and groanings. Visible signs and stigmata. Traceable energy surges. With enough power for the ghosting to sustain itself out-of-body, haunting a space, a locality, a house, a closet . . .'

'A sealed room?'

'No, Mr Obern. My sealed room is not where a ghost would ever *want* to be. It's where it is forced to be. By techniques which are not completely understood but which were discovered by chance and refined by repeated effective use. Cargo cult empiricism. A cause and effect.'

'Mr Crane's point, Jack,' Jarvis said, 'is that with a Three, the ghost haunts the artefact rather than a person's unconscious, and different individuals will experience the ghost both subjectively *and* objectively, and with the same characteristics.'

I didn't say anything. The wine was making me eager and I was coming over as foolish. Thankfully, Jarvis didn't seem to mind.

Crane continued. 'The Four is the really dangerous one. It has enough power to haunt a house for many, many years, a whole town or neighbourhood, a lake, a beach, but it aims that power at a living person, directs all of its force to returning to an in-life state.'

Jarvis leaned forward in his chair.

'What are you telling us, Mr Crane?'

Crane stopped pacing. 'Just this, Doctor. The ghost-trap in this house has been catching ghosts since my great-grandfather's time.'

And killing you with cancer, I thought. Jarvis too was busy trying to fathom what Crane had told us. The room downstairs was full of Fours?

'You are opening it tonight, Mr Crane,' Jarvis said. 'Tell us again why that is.'

'I am dying, Doctor, as you have guessed. I am riddled with cancers, and I know I have less than the few months the doctors have allowed. It will be sooner, I know. Much sooner.

'The Fours are not common, but statistically many exist. The Fours in our ghost-trap here at Daemon Street have all been focused there and neutralized long ago, "consumed in the panelled darkness of the Red Room". I love Renfeld's writing, don't you? Except for one that arrived three nights ago and prompted my call to you, and the one I believe will appear tonight when the room is breached.

'I want to share my family's legacy now. People resist the idea of ghosts because they sense the harm; they seem to know intuitively that the ghostings accrue about the preoccupied and the sensitive among us. They come so quickly to any receptive person, bringing physical harm not just psychological. It takes courage to think of the discontinued identities trying to get back in, trying to be bodies again, trying to be people, trying to be what they cannot be. But they cannot stop.

'Tomorrow Andrew will deliver all my papers to your office at the university, Dr Henry. My other legacy to you; the legacy of the Daemon Street Cranes. We've done our share of ghost-hunting. Let the others try.'

'Your sons will sell the house then?' Jarvis asked.

'My sons are abroad, Doctor. They want no part of this. And why should they? Why should anyone bring ghosts together, work at such a task, bear such a burden and die for it? It's better that we disregard these displaced forces, let them remain free radicals sullying our more susceptible moments. Acknowledging them focuses their energy, directs it. It is folly.'

'Is your ghost-trap a Red Room, Mr Crane?'

The ruined old man smiled and moved away from the bookcases. 'Why don't I show you? Come, gentlemen. And Mr Obern, if you and Andrew would be so good as to bring those heavy crow-bars by the hearth; we will need them. This is a momentous occasion.'

We left the cosy room and went downstairs to the blind wall at the end of the entrance hall. Crane switched on the lights as we went, far more lights than were needed. The lower floor was ablaze with warm yellow light when we reached it.

Then he began feeling the panelled walls, striking panels to find joists and sections.

'Some sealed rooms have spy-holes which, of course, render them useless,' Crane told us. 'Modern ones are totally sealed but have light-fittings and video cameras inside so the interior can be lit and observed. None of that foolishness here. This room has not seen light for one hundred and sixteen years. It is the no-place.'

'Is it furnished?' Jarvis said.

'Oh yes. In a sense,' Crane answered. 'With enough people-things to draw the Threes and Fours.'

The last words prompted a thought, one that suddenly

grew to worry me in this overlit corridor.

'You said a Four arrived three nights ago, Mr Crane. Is it in there now then?'

Crane looked at us again in a wholly unreadable way, giving a strange lop-sided smile, his long hands planted on the panels like two parchment spiders. He reminded me of a creature about to spring, or of a thief listening for the fall of tumblers in a hidden wall safe.

'The Four is in the trap, Mr Obern. But it will not harm you. It is otherwise engaged. Its days, too, are numbered. But another will come when the walls are broken. If this troubles either of you, please . . .'

'No, Mr Crane,' Jarvis said. 'Jack and I wouldn't miss this.'

'Good. I doubt the exercise would be advisable for me. Or for Andrew. Mr Obern, if you would strike here, here and here,'—he indicated the spots with his white spider hands—'we can begin to make the breach.'

I struck where he said, struck again and again until the panelling split and could be wrenched back, exposing some joists which formed a door that had never been finished as one. Jarvis took some photographs.

'In the middle of the room, Dr Henry, there is a table. On it is a large porcelain bowl.'

'A water-trap!' Jarvis cried. 'Your ancestor used a water-trap?'

'Initially,' the old man said. 'It's basic and it works. Please, when the wall is sundered, shine that hand-light on the bowl immediately. Mr Obern can then bring those other lights in from the hall. The room must be lit.'

Jarvis began taking photographs again while I pounded at the wood, shattering more of the panelling, ruining beautiful old timber that would have cost a fortune now. I had cleared the false door from this side. Only the inner panelling remained. I found I was trembling with anticipation and fear looking at it, aware only of the broken wood and the steady flash of Jarvis's Pentax.

Obviously the whole south wall had been fitted as a

pre-fabricated section, with the outer panels added once
the frame was bolted in place. It must have cost a great
sum; the finishing was flawless, a true fourth wall, not just
a partition.

'This is your moment, gentlemen,' Crane said. 'Andrew,
goodnight to you. It's time you were out of this. I am in
good hands.'

Jarvis and I were surprised to see the men embrace, to
see the tears of a painful and final farewell on their faces.

'Bless you, Mr Crane,' the butler said. He made no further fuss, just nodded a goodnight to us, took up a small
suitcase, and went out of the front door.

It had a sense of unreality about it, how suddenly it happened. It seemed comical in its intensity and abruptness:
the embrace, the door opening, the windy street beyond,
the click of the lock.

Jarvis went to speak but did not.

'Let us continue,' Crane said. 'And thank you for for-
bearing with your questions. We can proceed.'

I struck the inner panels a resounding blow, turning my
anxiety into hard action. I struck and struck until the timber burst, and stale chill air engulfed me. I swooned a little
at it, trying not to breathe, and kept up the blows, while
Crane stood to my left and Jarvis took his pictures.

'Stop!' Crane hissed, and suddenly there was a parchment claw closing on my shoulder. I froze, stopped
mid-strike, and lowered the crow-bar.

'What is it, Mr Crane?' Jarvis said.

The hand relaxed its terrible grip.

'Not yet!' the old man said. 'Proceed! Proceed!'

Again I put my fear into the blows. Like someone whistling past the graveyard or shouting at the devil, I made my
big brash noises to hide the deathly silence, to distract me
from the dread I felt growing within.

Splinters flew, whole sections of shattered oak fell in-
wards. I hit and pounded and pole-axed any part that
resisted, until only the joists stood and the sealed room
was no longer any part of that.

'Bring the lights!' Crane said. 'Light everywhere!'

In my haste, I dropped the crowbar so it clanged against the wooden floor. Jarvis helped me set up the portable floodlights. We aimed them into the room and switched them on.

We saw striped wallpaper, polished wainscoting and panels, a featureless plastered ceiling. There was a wooden chair by one wall, with a book resting on the chair. On the mantelpiece of the blind fireplace directly opposite there was a clock with no hands. In the middle of the room was a narrow wooden table and on it a large white bowl.

'It's not a Red Room!' Jarvis said, but the words were lost as Crane gasped, gave a soft cry of agony, and staggered against the wall. His face was a white mask, as if all the skin had yellowed cords underneath suddenly drawn tight. His hand was on his chest.

'Mr Crane!' Jarvis cried.

In a moment we had him, holding him steady between us, trying to ease him away from the trap to a chaise-longue we saw near the front door.

'I can take it,' he muttered, breathing deeply. 'I can do it.' Then: 'It's all right now. Dr Henry, examine the room.'

Jarvis did so, while I brought in yet another light. Crane sat in the hall while we moved about the panelled space.

'It's not a Red Room,' Jarvis said to me. He moved to the bowl, empty of water for the best part of a century. 'This is not painted red either.'

Behind us, Crane had recovered and was climbing gingerly between the joists of the door frame, throwing long distorted shadows about the room as he came to us, crossing a floor unused before our intrusion.

'No, it isn't,' he said, looking as if he would collapse at any moment. Jarvis steadied him.

'You said there was a Four here.'

'There is. Now there is. And other ghostings. They know what I am doing. And they are vicious and blindly angry things. Powerful, vicious and quite desperate. They want to live again so much. A tropism . . .' The old man paused, grimaced.

We held him again. Jarvis got the room's wooden chair
and we sat him in it. He nodded his thanks, then looked up
at us.

'You know the story of Dorian Grey?' he said, panting,
obviously in great pain. 'The painting ages while the man
lives on.'

Jarvis nodded. 'Of course.'

'Yes,' I said, seeking the connection.

Jarvis leant in close. 'Are you saying, Tesserley . . .?'

'Not Tesserley,' Crane gasped. 'Not Tesserley. I am
Roderick, the youngest. I am thirty-two.'

We stared at eighty-two, ninety, and more; at wasted,
diseased parchment. At the mouth working to speak. At a
dying man.

'Tesserley, Bradlan . . . died full of ghosts. Both filled up
. . . choked with them. *We* are the ghost-traps! We never
knew. The room only focuses them; they leak out into us.
The Fours become living tissue. That is what cancer is,
what ghosts become. So many of us . . . so full of ghosts. It
happens more quickly once you know. You cannot stop
thinking of it, drawing them to you . . .'

Jarvis stood wide-eyed beside me, saying nothing, but
understanding as I was just beginning to.

'The room was never it at all,' I said, marvelling and horrified at the same instant.

Roderick Crane seemed not to hear.

'You only have to know, to think of them, to focus them
somewhere.' His voice was very soft, filled with his agony.
'Then you cannot stop them.' He gave a ratcheting, bleat-
ing laugh. 'But the irony! We destroy them only by dying.
And now I have Tesserley and Bradlan both. Now I have
them.'

'Here?' I cried, needing to be sure.

'Oh yes, I have them now,' Crane said, at the edge of
death, and jerked a thumb up to his chest.

'In the Red Room!'

THE WOLVES ARE RUNNING
by Paul Lindsey

They picked up three at the railway station and another two at the bus shelter. Keyte put them in the back of the truck. The whole business was much easier than he had imagined. He went back to look for the third, but there was nothing.

There was no cover. Most of the buildings had gone. He walked round, kicking the rubble, moving debris and iron sheeting. Nothing. Just the two. He climbed back in and slammed the door.

'Two?' Danno said. 'Thought it was three. Just two?'

'That's all. I've looked. Only two.'

'O.K. Shifts change in half an hour. Let's go.'

'Five's enough.'

Danno yawned. He wasn't smoking tonight, but the smell of fruit chewing-gum filled the cabin. He rested his arms across the steering wheel and gazed past the wipers at the rain sweeping across the street lighting.

'Yeah. Five's enough,' Danno said. 'What're they like?'

'Nothing special. Tired, bewildered, hungry.'

'Hungry's right.'

'Come on. You promised, Danno.'

'Okay, okay. I promised.'

He started the truck. They drove back through the town to the Compound.

'There's one more out there.'

'Danno, the shift changes in fifteen minutes. A night's sleep, or a medal? You want a medal?'

The streets were empty. Keyte could hear the tyres smacking the rain against the tarmac. Every street light was on, a few of the shop neon signs were still flashing, but no people. He wasn't used to it yet. There were a lot of dogs, hunting in and out of the buildings for food. The truck scattered a pack of them running near the Compound gates. Danno blasted the horn, and swore.

'Bloody mongrels. They're hungry too, eh?'

'We're all hungry, mate. Food, bed. That's all I need.'

There were the usual checks at the boom. Keyte climbed out and stood beside Danno facing the wall. They both leaned their hands up on the high white line while Security searched them, looked under the truck, inspected the locks on the rear door of the truck and sprayed inside the cabin. At least, Keyte thought, it fixes the smell of gum.

'How many?' The trooper scribbled on his clipboard.

'Five.'

'Right.' He spoke into his radio. 'They're ready now.'

The cabin stank of spray. Danno coughed.

'Now for the nice part, eh?'

'Danno,' said Keyte, 'just drive. Go gently. Remember? An early night?'

The Adjutant's office was a bleak, single-storey brick building. Floodlights shone for thirty feet round the perimeter. Each window in the Adjutant's office was barred. One wide steel door faced the Compound, and incorporated a communications system. Danno parked the truck by the door. Keyte jumped down and went to the intercom. He pressed the button.

'Alpha Foxtrot with five,' he said.

The iron door hummed and opened. A wave of warm air swept into the night. Keyte remembered how cold he was. Better to be cold than in there.

Three Night Police came out. The tall one held out his

hand for the keys. No one spoke.

'Hey!' Danno whispered. 'See him? Sharman. He did the Cathedral Group last week. Cool, real cool.'

The Night Police opened the back of the truck. Keyte heard a whimpering. Danno heard it and looked at him.

'Bit late for that now,' said Keyte.

Two Night Police clambered in. There was a scuffling sound, followed by a sigh.

'Out. Quickly. All of you.'

Five children stood in the drizzle, screwing up their eyes in the bright flood-lighting. The men jumped down, and began to separate the group. Without being told, the children put their arms above their heads and walked to the brick wall.

The tall man who had taken the keys tossed them back.

'Fine,' he said. 'That's fine. You're right for Decontamination now.'

Danno climbed back behind the wheel.

'Come on, Keyte. Keyte!'

As he heaved himself into the passenger seat, Keyte saw the children taking off their shoes. The girl had canvas boots, and she was taking a long time undoing the laces.

Decontamination was at the east perimeter of the Compound. The truck took forty minutes to be cleaned. No one could go inside because of the chemicals. You sat and waited till the indicators flashed green. The truck would reappear on the rollers, pushing through the thick, pliable doors.

'It's like a bloody car wash,' Danno said.

For a short while afterwards there was a sweet pungent smell. Mercaptopurines, Keyte guessed. Vile and toxic.

They sat in the waiting bay, too tired to talk. Danno lit a cigarette. Keyte thought about the children. What would they do with them? That girl with the canvas boots, for instance?

The bay door opened and Sharman came in.

'Keyte. Which one of you is Keyte? Adjutant wants you.

And you! Can't you bloody read? Put out that cigarette.'

Danno stubbed the cigarette on his heel, and shoved it in his tunic pocket.

'But the shift . . .'

'Adjutant's office. Now. Doesn't like to be kept waiting, does he?' Sharman pushed the door open wider and stood there smiling. He's enjoying this, thought Keyte.

'I've got Keyte here, sir.' Sharman spoke into the intercom.

They went inside. The corridors were carpeted and pleasantly warm. There was no noise other than the air-conditioning. As he walked down the corridor, Keyte could hear people moving about inside the offices. There were neatly painted signs on all the doors . . . Section Commander, Duty Officer, Store Requisitions, Operations Room. Towards the end of the corridor they passed a sign that read 'Adjutant'. Keyte paused.

'Not there, sonny,' said Sharman. 'Keep going.'

The Interrogation Room was at the far end of the corridor. Another intercom was set in the wall. Before he pressed the button, Sharman turned and grinned at Keyte.

'Worried, are you, Keyte?'

'Get stuffed.'

'Sharman with Keyte,' he announced.

Keyte knew that something was wrong before the door opened.

The Adjutant sat behind a large table. Behind him were the two Night Police who had taken the children from the truck. The five children sat on a bench fixed to the opposite wall. They had their hands above their heads, with their wrists tied to a long metal bar two feet above. Their heads lolled on their shoulders. They made no sound. Someone had taken off their tunics. Two were stripped to the waist, and Keyte saw the Wolf tattoos on their chests. The girl was at the far end. They had left her blouse on. Her feet looked dirty on the clean carpet, with mud between her toes and grimy, ragged nails. One of the boys coughed.

The Adjutant closed the folder in front of him and looked up.

'You're Keyte?'

'Sir.'

'Daniels was Duty Driver?'

'Sir.' Keyte was sweating.

The Adjutant had all the information. He did the rosters. Sharman would have told him. So why didn't he get to the point?

'Three at the station. Two at the bus shelter. Right?'

'Yes, sir.'

'Not three?'

'No, sir.'

'Operations are certain that three were at the shelter. Did you search thoroughly? Follow procedures? Daniels looked too?'

'Ground Search routine for Collections states drivers must not leave vehicles unattended, sir.'

Conjure te, Adjutant! Bloody Operations, sitting at their screens collating phantoms. Get them out in the night and see how they go, finding spectres in the ruins. There were only two, for God's sake.

'Sharman here saw six escape from the Cathedral. Tonight was regrouping, but we lost one. At the bus shelter, Keyte.'

'There were only two, sir.'

'Sharman?'

'They won't tell us, sir.' He looked at the children. 'Besides, scanning shows high antibody levels. They'll all be dead by the morning.'

'And if the one out there hasn't been eating? Has normal antibodies? What then? We can't chance it. Sick, dying, alive . . . I want them all for Disposals.'

The Adjutant slapped a paper-knife noisily on the desk top and stood up.

'There it is, Keyte. You get that last one. You and Daniels, go and find him. At first light. And check with

Operations first. They'll have a trace by now. Should be easy, just the one.' He walked towards the door.

'Sharman, you can take these now. I'll be in my office. But no noise, thanks. I must insist on there being no noise.' He paused with his hand on the doorknob.

'And, Keyte.'

'Sir.'

'It's special, this job.'

'Sir?'

'The one out there, the boy.'

'Yes, sir.'

'You see . . . they could be wrong . . . but they say it's your boy.'

He closed the door quietly. Keyte could hear Sharman and the Night Police moving the children off the bench towards Disposals. Sharman held the girl by the back of her blouse, and looked at Keyte over her shoulder.

'You heard him, Keyte. Operations. Look smart about it. We've all got work to do, eh?'

The cursor on the large screen on the wall in the Operations room blinked continuously. A gentle, fat man with spectacles and a courteous manner took Keyte by the elbow.

'The black pigment used for the Wolf tattoos came from a drum of contaminated waste. We picked that in the first few weeks, before they started getting sick. Radioactivity. Some of them still don't realise. Their leaders never told them.' He smiled.

'Of course, the fewer there are, the easier it is for us. The clusters made counting almost impossible to begin with. You can imagine. Everything shows on our screens.' The fat man sighed.

'There's only this one left now. You know, there were three at that bus shelter. One left just before you arrived. It was you, wasn't it? Last night? On Collections?'

'Yes,' Keyte said.

'Well, you missed him by minutes, I'd say. No idea why

he left the regrouping like that. They're usually quite pre-
dictable. Must be sick. Or suspicious, eh?' He took his
spectacles off and polished them.

'But where is he now? I suppose that's what you need to
know? Eh? He took his spectacles off and polished them.

'Yes,' Keyte said. He noticed that the cursor on the
screen was beating more regularly than his own pulse, and
wondered what it signified. He told the man.

'You see . . . this last one . . . he's my son.'

'Oh dear,' the man said. 'I am sorry. This sort of thing is
bound to happen. How very disturbing. Does Control
know?'

'It's their idea,' Keyte said.

'Well,' the fat man said uncertainly, 'Control knows
best. Perhaps if you try to remember that they were canni-
bals?'

'I'll try,' Keyte said.

'Look. There he is,' the man said. 'There, back at the bus
shelter again. He hasn't moved for some time. He's probably very sick by now. Shouldn't be too difficult to collect,
I'd imagine. I wonder how he disappeared from the moni-
tor? Must have one of the first tattoos. Their signals would
be fading a little now, especially if they're sick.'

'Yes, I suppose so,' Keyte said. 'I'd better go now.'

'Goodbye,' the fat man said. 'Hope it's not too awful.
The boy, I mean.'

'Thanks,' Keyte said.

'Last time I drive for you, mate,' Danno said. 'Two
bloody shifts in twenty-four hours. What is this? Get up
Sharman's nostrils, did you?'

The rain had stopped. Pieces of rubbish and paper were
tumbling across the pavements. They eddied in shop door-
ways and slapped into the speeding truck. The dawn light
was yellow, the sky overcast.

'No more after this, Danno,' Keyte said. 'It's the last
Collection.'

'Need to be,' Danno said. 'Need to be.'

They saw him lying curled on the seat inside the shelter. When the truck stopped he didn't move. Keyte got out and walked across. Control was right. It was the boy.

His face was thinner, paler than Keyte remembered. Hunched in sleep, the anger and the wildness had gone. He saw the serene face of a child.

Keyte went back to the truck.

'Orange zipper job?' Danno leaned out of the window. Two men were required to fill an Orange bag, and all their strength was needed to heave it up into the truck.

'Think so. Look, Danno . . .' Keyte turned away. He couldn't explain.

They put on their gloves, laid the garish bag on the ground in front of the shelter, and rolled the body into it.

'Very bloody ferocious I'd say, this last one,' Danno said. He zipped the bag closed. They heaved it into the back of the truck.

'Bit quiet, aren't you , mate?'

'Tired,' Keyte said. 'Very tired.'

The engine roared. Danno swung the truck round in the empty street. Keyte heard the sack roll in the back. He wanted to sleep. Sleep without dreaming.

Disposals took the Orange bag. Sharman was there, standing behind the Adjutant who seemed pleased. Danno went with the truck to Decontamination, and Keyte walked across to Married Quarters.

She was still in bed.

'You're very late. Something special, was there?'

He took off his clothes and lay beside her. She was warm and comfortable. He couldn't look at her.

'Yes,' he said.

He lay beside her. Hands on his chest, he looked at the ceiling, searching for words. He was so tired.

She turned her face to look at him.

'You've never done a double shift on Collections before,' she said. 'Must have been special.'

'The Cathedral Six,' he said. 'We found five. Then we

had to get the last one. That's why.'

'Yes?' she said.

'It was him. The boy,' Keyte said. 'He was at the shelter. He looked so peaceful. Just lying there.'

She turned from him in the bed and buried her face in the pillows.

'Don't cry,' Keyte said. 'Please, don't cry.'

CHAMELEON
by Sharon A. Hansen

Murphy shuddered. He shook from his head downwards like a dog just out of water. Christ, he thought, something's stomping on my grave. His mouth went dry and he bent his head as he convulsively tried to swallow.

'Hey, Murphy!'

Murphy looked up as a harassed-looking police sergeant planted his broad frame in front of a relief map and pointed to a particular section.

'You'll be taking Long Gully, the caves and Fredricks' shack again, Murph. Curly's coming in now and you'll pair up with him again. Mick and Sandy will be on the ridge above you. Keep ten-minute checks on the walkie-talkie . . . and don't take any chances. You know the score. I'll tell the others as I check them.'

The wiry-haired, short man with the sad brown eyes nodded and bent over his gear. He heard familiar footsteps behind him. He kept on working.

'G'day, Murph. Just in time, eh? Reckon we might cop it lucky today. Got a funny feeling. What d'ya reckon, eh?'

The smaller man straightened and breathed deeply. He looked very tired. The slightly nasal voice belonged to Curly Temple, so nicknamed for his prematurely bald pate. In the past, those who should have known better had laughingly called him 'Shirley' and were flattened for their effort.

Curly was a big man, but like many large men he was light on his feet. A capable bushman and a good shot, Curly was a good mate to have at your back when you faced the unexpected. Murphy could count on Curly (even if he was thought to be a bit soft in the head by a few hard cases in town) providing he could keep his mouth shut when necessary. He considered Curly's question.

'Depends,' he said slowly. 'Depends on what it is. If it's on the move during the day, it could be anywhere. It was on the move again last night and fed again.' He swallowed quickly. 'And it could be layin' up somewhere. We've got more blokes comin' in today that know what they're doing, anyway. Someone's got to get lucky and get a shot at it. It hasn't left the district. It's got to be somethin' we haven't seen before, too. I just know it.' Murphy spoke quietly as both men checked their equipment.

Satisfied that everything was in order, the nuggetty Murphy nodded to the sergeant and led the way to his battered ute parked outside the hall. He placed the gear in the tray, taking only his Winchester into the cabin. Curly followed suit.

They waited until two men nearby waved to them and headed out in a four-wheel drive, and then they backed out on to the road and drove after them.

Nearly five minutes passed without an exchange of words in the cabin before Curly broke the silence.

'What happened last night, Murph?' He removed his hat and wiped around the lining with a khaki handkerchief. Both had seen better days. His bright blue eyes studied the impassive face of the driver. 'Didn't hear. Was scared I'd be late. Blasted alarm didn't go off.' He replaced his hat, gave his nose a wipe on the rag, and leaning forward, shoved it in his back pocket. He looked sideways again at his silent friend. 'Bad, was it? Sheep, calves . . .?'

All he received from Murphy was a silent grimace. Curly's voice was whisper-soft as he screwed up his face.

'Oh Jeez, oh Jeez, Murph. Who was it this time?'

'No good asking Him!' exploded Murphy. 'He wasn't

around when the Graham kids were slaughtered, or poor old Fredricks either. What we need is the bloody army in here. Flush the bastard out like them old boar hunts. He's still around. I can feel it. He's laughing at us.' His voice lowered again. 'May Dixon . . . last night it was May.'

He swung the ute viciously to the side of the road to avoid a bad patch.

'It's gotta be someone we've seen. May's place was locked up tighter than a drum, but she opened the door herself. And she musta trusted him. It used shears or somethin' on her after. You know of an animal that uses shears?'

'But you've been calling it "It", Murph,' Curly's voice jerked out. 'And you said it fed last night.'

'I know it!' Murphy hit the steering wheel with his fist. The smaller man's face was like granite, except for a muscle quivering in his jaw. 'I've tried for days to tell myself it must be some sort of large animal escaped from one of them travelling shows and the owners didn't want anyone to know. That's happened before. But it's not. It goes on two legs. It kills and eats like an animal. And it covers its tracks so well that the black trackers can't get a good line on it. They're scared, too. Reckon it's somethin' from the Dreamtime, somethin' bad.'

He glanced in the rear-view mirror, then swung the ute off the bitumen onto a dirt road which headed towards thick green hills with rock escarpments scarring their heights. There was silence again.

What was being hunted was on the bush cot in Fredricks' shack. It was thinking. It was the first time it had been back in the shack since Fredricks' body had been stumbled over and identified the previous month. Now the police were looking for the man who had taken over Fredricks' identity; who looked enough like him to collect the old man's pension for a year; who was suspected of killing the old man and who didn't bury the remains deep enough.

It wasn't worried. It didn't intend to use Fredricks' face again. Last night was enough. It was after something warm for the nights to come, tinned food for a backpack and anything else it could carry.

It had stayed longer here than in any other district. At first it had only hunted the smaller animals. 'Curse those kids,' it thought. 'If they hadn't seen me at that calf I wouldn't have got the need so soon. Stupid animals. That's all they are, just two-legged animals with no fur. Think they're somethin' special. Well, they learnt they're not!'

It had its own name once, a long time ago, a lot of identities ago. And a face of its own. It had been named Hunter Street, a fine-sounding name for a boy-child deposited on a doorstep in a city. No family wanted him. He did not 'fit in'.

At the tender age of nine, Hunter Street overheard this remark and decided to make himself fit. He changed. He changed into the image of a boy named Arthur, who was believed to have run away. When Arthur's body was found, it was Hunter who had to run.

By the time he was fourteen Hunter had gained a great deal of survival knowledge and developed superlative acting skills. His gift had become a way of life.

The first time he killed, and enjoyed it, was after he was given a lift in a car by a seemingly solicitous man whose intentions were to be more than a friend to the lad. Hunter killed quickly but not cleanly, and the smell of blood triggered a 'difference' in him. In the years following, 'he' became 'it', no longer regarding himself as being herd-human. He became a predator of great skill.

It left the shack, silently threading its way through the trees, heading north towards Long Gully. After ten minutes, it paused and took one last look back. Two small figures were going into Fredricks' shack.

'Yes,' it thought, 'there's time.' It squatted and waited patiently.

'Phew,' groaned Curly. 'Something's dead in here.'

Murphy looked around. The shack had changed since

yesterday. Not just the stench, but the feeling of the place. Though the door had been jammed shut when they forced their way in, something had been here. The hair on the nape of his neck lifted. The cot had been stripped of blankets. Murphy felt the old mattress. There was still a vestige of warmth and here the smell was the strongest. He grabbed for his walkie-talkie.

'Mick? Murphy here. It's been in the shack. It's close. Could be heading for the caves or cutting through the gully. Watch yourself. Murphy out.' Curly was watching him.

'We nearly walked into it, Curly. The damn thing was here.' He walked to the back lean-to, then retreated, treading on Curly's toes. Curly had caught sight of something that had been crudely butchered. All questions died in his throat.

Murphy swung his backpack around and pulled at a cloth-wrapped bundle—a shotgun. He inserted two cartridges into the barrels and rammed more cartridges into his top pocket. With the walkie-talkie slung round his neck and the Winchester over one shoulder, the shotgun was carried in the safe position. The pack remained on the floor.

'We're heading towards the ridge, Curl. It could head down the gully and cut through, or it could head for the caves or the ridge. Close in to five paces back and no talking from here on in. And watch your back. It could double around through the rocks when we get to the north of the dip.'

Curly nodded silently, his genial face abnormally grim. He trod softly and surely in Murphy's wake, rifle slanted sideways and down.

Murphy halted, one hand held palm outwards at his side. He sniffed the air. There was very little breeze, and even though the day was still fresh, he could feel the threat of the day's heat.

There were no tracks to follow on the ground or traces of injured vegetation, nothing to denote the quarry's passing but the smell. Murphy sniffed again. He tilted his head one way, then the other. Nearly seven minutes had passed in silence since they left the shack. He was still smelling the musky foetid odour, the cloying stench becoming stronger now. Was it coming from behind the rocks at the bottom of the escarpment?

He half-turned to Curly and patted the air away from himself. Curly nodded that he understood and backed off, then turned to cover the rear. Murphy sidled towards a granite outcrop about twenty yards from the head of the gully. One moment he was still in sight of Curly. Then he was gone.

Curly eyed the trees. If it came from the side or behind it would use the foliage for cover. No rocks here. He was concerned for Murphy, but he knew if he closed up with him, Murph would sound off. 'Most prey is stalked from behind,' he'd say. 'Not the front.' But Curly knew that his little mate would be the one who'd face the danger first. Murphy was a tough little coot.

Curly considered what Murphy had said. Someone from the district? Nah. Murph must be wrong. He knew everyone in town and even if there were some roughies in the timber-cutters, they wouldn't hurt an old lady or kids. Nah. Gotta be an animal of some sort. It's gotta be.

There was a furtive rustle among the leaves at the gully side. Curly's rifle was steady as he waited. If it was what they were hunting, it wouldn't make deliberate noise, now would it? It could be Sandy or Mick cutting down from the ridge, couldn't it?

A hand appeared, sidling round the trunk of a fat stringy-bark. Then a face peered at Curly.

'Murph? Whatcha doin' . . . I thought you were up ahead.'

Curly came closer and what looked like Murphy moved a lot faster. The shocking realisation stunned Curly. His surprise was short-lived. He grunted deeply once, twice, then folded himself over his stomach, pitching face forward onto the dry undergrowth.

Above his body, the being tensed as it heard the voice from Curly's walkie-talkie. It kicked twice to turn the body on to its back. It smiled. It would answer the call, in person. It donned Curly's coat and hat. It headed back towards the gully. It didn't bother with Curly's rifle.

Murphy was still using the walkie-talkie, glancing upwards as he spoke, giving the news that Curly failed to answer. He downed the aerial, and slinging the set around his neck again, checked his shotgun. Curly didn't play games. Something was wrong.

Murphy's gut exploded with a hot searing wave as he saw the figure approaching from the rear. Then he felt a cold emptiness. He acted naturally. He waved and beckoned, turning half towards it. The little man exhaled slowly and drew in a deep, deep breath. His face twisted as the smell and the footsteps came closer.

'Hey, Curly. I think we'd better chuck it in, mate. We'll join up with the others. We can do this section again tomorrer.' He turned fully round to face the figure, but what was shambling towards him wasn't Curly. The coat was his, and the hat, but it wasn't quite his old mate.

It gave a parody of a grin like the rictus of death and leaned forward.

Halfway down the ridge above, Sandy and Mick heard the shot, and not getting any answer from the walkie-talkie, made fast time down the rest of the way into the gully.

They found the body of Curly first. His open eyes had an expression of surprised innocence. There was no mutilation apart from the gaping wounds in his chest.

'Must be after Murphy.' Their shouts of warning to Murphy were answered but the voice didn't sound like his.

They found Murphy. Backed up against a tree, shotgun still aimed at something on the ground, and Murphy was crying.

'It got Curly, didn't it? It musta done . . . it pretended . . .'

The two newcomers recoiled when they leaned closer over what was still wearing Curly's hat. The hat didn't disguise the face any more. It was man-shaped and mewled words at them still, even though the shot had found its mark in Curly's coat.

As the three of them watched, the face blurred, forming into new features and smoothing out, over and over, into different personalities . . . young and old, male and female . . . animalistic . . . a lifetime's trail of death.

The putty-like blob above the blood-spattered coat reformed to that of Curly again and the mouth tried to form words, but the sound of a shotgun blotted out any voice as it blotted out any features.

Murphy shuddered.

MABUZA'S PLUM
by Eddie Van Helden

Today I could not catch a cockroach.

I look at myself in the mirror. The sore on my left cheek is growing larger. Or is it my face that is growing thinner? Anyway I touch the skin around the red puckered edge of the sore and I can feel the skin move and slide around as if it is no longer connected to anything underneath. This is intriguing I think. I open my mouth. I count them. One. Two. Three. Two's company and three's a crowd I say to myself and hear someone laughing and realise it is me. Anyway I look at those three and all the holes around them and I touch one and it moves backwards. It is afraid. I grab it with my thumb and first finger and push it forward and back, forward and back, and it comes out. Plop! Just like that. I hold it up and see it is blackened at the root like the others. It looks like a little bean. I drop the little bean in the cup.

I touch the skin around the sore again. I play with it like I'd play with a piece of jelly. It wobbles. Then the skin silently tears and a piece comes off into my hand and underneath it is red and juicy like a plum. I wish I had a plum now. A red juicy plum like the ones from Mabuza's orchard. I bring up my hand to my lips, to my mouth, and slip the piece of skin in. It feels like a Mabuza plum skin. Only thicker and more rubbery. It is slippery. I swallow

48

and it slides down my throat. I look at myself in the mirror again and feel, then see, my hand coming up to my left cheek. Those bastards, I think. I'm going to live. And I tear off another piece of skin.

HANTU-RIMBA
by Dr John Hugoe-Matthews

1. ZAINUL

Fatimah was a flirt. Selfish, tough, unscrupulous, she flaunted her unusual beauty and inborn powers to a point where she enjoyed fomenting jealousy between her many real and would-be admirers, often to a degree where killing was avoided only by the frantic efforts of the *Penghulu*, the village headman, and his spiritual advisers.

She abused the holy men and the matchmakers who tried to find partners for her according to tradition.

In a deep rural Malaysian village she was considered a menace to the peace and quiet of the community. The simple existence of a Kampong housewife was not for her. Eventually she chose a passing trader, a powerful, boastful type who succumbed to her charms and asked the *Penghulu*'s permission to marry her.

Impressed by the man-of-the-world behaviour of the applicant, and glad to get rid of the young woman, consent was given and they were married. After the ceremony the couple departed, as far as the villagers knew, never to return again. 'For which mercy Allah be praised,' intoned the holy men.

Fatimah had chosen well. Zainul her husband was as avaricious and as ruthless as herself and listened willingly to the project she put before him.

'In my Kampong lives Mustapha, an old man due to die

anyway,' she told him. 'He used to be a trader, Padi planter and landowner. He is a miser, hoarding his wealth and living alone. Though all men think he is poor, he has a fortune hidden.'

'Real money?' the man gasped.

'Yes. I used to go to him often at nights to amuse him. I know where his treasure is hidden. Money, silver and gold, is beneath the fireplace.'

'You mean?' Zainul anticipated her.

'Yes, I do mean,' the young woman responded. 'We can get it. He lives alone outside the Kampong on his own Padi land. His shack is strongly built but there are cracks in between the planks.'

'How can we get in without rousing him and possibly the whole Kampong if the house is strongly built?'

'We don't.' Fatimah pointed to a heap of items she had collected in readiness, sure of her husband's agreement. 'It is easy. We make him come to us. We use the hollow reed to blow powder through the cracks in the wall. It is worse than sniffing chilli powder. He is bound to come to the door and rush out for fresh air to breathe.'

'The powder is that potent?'

'Yes. A few inches in the tube, blown into his bedroom. He'll come out all right, then you catch him.'

'Then I tie him up while you find the treasure. It sounds simple enough.'

'No. You kill him. He must not survive to say that he has been robbed by us.'

'Just as easy; I break his neck,' Zainul proposed.

'No. You strangle him or suffocate him with a pillow to make it look like heart failure,' Fatimah ordered.

'You must have been planning this for a long time, my woman,' the man said admiringly. 'The method is perfect.'

'I've spent a long time thinking it over. I needed the right man. Now I have found him, Zainul, do not fail me.'

'The treasure is as good as ours already,' Zainul boasted but at the back of his mind was the fear that this clever woman might have similar designs on himself so she could keep the fortune for herself.

The operation proceeded smoothly. Fatimah's powder drove the old man gasping into the open air. Zainul seized him and pressed his skinny face and neck deep into a soft pillow. There was wiry strength in the aged body, so he took a long time to die.

This way of dying was significant. Had the end been quick such as by stabbing knife, head-crushing blow or broken neck, the victim's *Semangat* or 'soul' that lives on after bodily death would have emerged untroubled to wander around the world benignly in search of another home. But with the slow demise this soul had to fight for survival, knowing its body was being murdered. So it was transformed into a vengeful spectre, an evil Hantu, as are the ghosts of murdered people.

'*Selamat jalan*,' said Zainul derisively quoting the farewell greeting to a man going on a long journey.

There was a thunderous roar like the crack of doomsday; the screams of tormented souls, the rushing sound of wild rivers and growling surf, a gust of cyclonic wind, a stench like a thousand rotting corpses and finally a cataclysmic upheaval that shook the earth around them—a requiem for the killing of Mustapha and the birth of something evil.

'Wha-a-a t was that?' croaked Fatimah.

'A Hantu is born, a terrible one,' the killer quavered. 'Let us get far away from here before it turns on us and destroys us.'

'But the treasure?'

'What good is treasure to bodies ripped by vengeful ghosts?' the man urged. 'Hasten, before it is too late.'

They fled the place in panic, never to return.

The soul of Mustapha, angry at the insult of murder, now a marauding man-killing spectre, one of the major Hantu, was homeless. Such beings reside close to the borders of Hell; others find refuge in hollow trees, cracks in rocks or in the graves of their earthly bodies, emerging from time to time for their sustenance of blood. The hour of dawn was approaching; he needed a home. A large *Angsana* tree stood near. It was old and would have a hollow stem. Eaten by insects, decaying with age, it would still stand for many more years. The new arrival had found a convenient place to enter and rest, to leave the world in peace.

2. MOHKTAR.

The ordinary man-in-the-street needed a mediator to advise him in his dealings with the mysteries of the spirit underworld and in the forces of inanimate nature which, if he hoped to live in peace and prosperity, he had to propitiate at all times.

Such practitioners were called *Bomohs*. Their range of activity extended from the benign village herbalist, the soothsayer, the adviser in agriculture and family matters, to the awesomely malignant. These shaman-type witch-priests were wholly evil as was the magic they practised. As exorcists they had the power of calling up the horrendous spectres of the underworld and turning them loose to cause death and destruction.

Mohktar, the *Bomoh* of Mustapha's village, was basically benign. He practised therapeutic magic combined with treatment with herbs. He was also *Pawang Buang*, a 'thrower out', an exorcist skilled in calling up evil spirits which infect human bodies causing diseases. He had a good record of successful cures.

His technique was traditional. Within the confines of his *Barisan*, a white circle painted on the ground using clay and powdered bone, he would begin to work. The object of the *Barisan* was to prevent the intrusion of evil *Djinns* which could interfere with his work of summoning the evil spirits to leave the body of his patient. His own body was covered with amulets at all vital places.

Using traditional phrases from the Koran, *Jampi-Jampi*, incantations dating from prehistory, and the *Bahasa Hantu*, the language of the ghosts, he would call up one *Djinn* after another from the body of his patient until he found the offender and threw him out.

He was successful but the rewards were small. He had an ambition which he admitted to no one. It was to own his own personal ghost to do his bidding. To find his own *Hantu-Raya*. Then he would be rich.

One day, riding his bicycle some twelve feet away from a tree, he fell off as if he had ridden head-on into the solid trunk. He landed in a heap, severely shaken. Ali, a friend who was riding a little further away, was not affected, but stopped to watch in amazement.

'*Ajaib sa-kali!*' the fallen cyclist expressed his bewilderment. His trained mind at once turned to witchcraft. 'I wonder . . .?'

He remounted, retreated a short distance and repeated the same course. This time at exactly the same place, but this time prepared for trouble, he was only forced to swerve violently.

'What is the matter, Mohktar?' Ali was frightened.

'This place is haunted. I came too near to something which took offence and pushed me away. You were not so close so nothing happened to you. Somewhere here, a Hantu has its resting place.'

'It could be so,' Ali agreed. 'Let us leave it in peace.'

'That big *Angsana* over there would be a fine home for one,' the *Bomoh* said. 'I must return and investigate sometime.'

'Take care, my friend,' Ali warned, 'some of these ghosts are man-killers as you know. Why not let him alone?'

'I must be sure.'

'You do what you like, may Allah protect you. I shall warn the whole Kampong so that all can steer clear of the place.'

'That you must do, Ali, for the safety of the others,' the *Bomoh* agreed. 'But I must find out the truth.'

That night, dressed as *Pawang Buang*, armed with his protective amulets at every vital point of his body and carrying a jar of paint for the *Barisan*, Mohktar approached the suspected tree.

In spite of his precautions and the chanting of the *Jampi-Jampi* he began to shiver feverishly.

He was certain—the *Angsana* tree. The massive trunk could be hollow, a suitable home for a spectre. He watched a faint luminescent haze, visible due to the brilliant moonlight, spiralling from a crack in the rugged bark—the Hantu was emerging!

Free to wander, the spectre would search for blood. Caught unprepared, Mohktar was ill-protected. Frantically he painted his *Barisan* as near to the *Angsana* tree as he dared. Though the Hantu could not pass the white line, the witch-priest might inadvertently allow some part of his body to extend beyond it and be trapped. He intensified his incantations. Should the shimmering haze begin to materialise into definite shape he was doomed.

Until that moment he had a chance of survival.

The deep, moonlit shadows between the trees seemed to be full of ghosts whispering.

'Your time has not yet come! In the name of *Shasta* and *Sinnoget* who carry the tortures of Hell to the land of the living, go back!'

Deep in the hollow nest the Hantu roared in angry protest. He was hungry and wanted freedom.

Mohktar wondered what kind of Hantu it could be. Male? Like *Hantu-Rimba*, the jungle spectre who could take many forms, such as a tiger or leopard. Or female? Like *Hantu-Pontianak*, a ghost who flew through the air with her belly open and intestines hanging free.

He had no means of knowing at this stage. The witch-priest was in danger and only the *Barisan* protected him.

Eventually, with reluctance, the spectre withdrew completely.

Mohktar then inserted a length of hollow reed into the crevice from which the haze had emerged. He plugged the mouth of the tube tight with the mixture used to paint his *Barisan*, and finally plastered firmly around the point of insertion, overlapping with a wide margin. Having securely sealed off the still-protesting Hantu, he was in a position now to converse.

'Tell me, who are you?' the witch-priest began. He used the *Bahasa Hantu*, the language of the ghosts acquired after years of study in the Thai jungles.

'I lived in the body of Mustapha bin Oman,' the spectre replied, 'a man and a woman murdered it. I am hungry for blood and vengeance.' Further grumbling. 'Let me out of here.'

He had won! The Hantu was controlled. Weakened, but triumphant, the exorcist relaxed. He intoned his thanks.

'Praise be to Allah for my deliverance.'

As Islam strictly forbade such dealings with the spirit world he could hardly continue his thanks to include the fulfilment of a lifetime's dream; he now had his own *Hantu-Raya* which he could use for his personal advancement.

Fully aware of the powers of the being he was proposing to control, well aware of the terrible risks of failure, he decided to try.

'Have patience,' he soothed the angry ghost, 'in a little while I will find food for you.'

Daily he inspected the tree, examining the reed to ensure there was no leakage and to coax the spectre into an amicable relationship. He reviewed his armoury of protective amulets, replacing some that were deteriorating and adding others more potent. He journeyed deep into the Thai jungle to find his old master and learn even more powerful incantations.

At last he was confident. The Hantu was hungry and wanted blood. But from where could the witch-priest obtain it?

By coincidence, the choice of victim was easy.

3. ACHMET.
Faridah was pretty, unmarried and at the height of her nubile womanhood. Achmet, a merchant who dressed in silks, was rich, fat, old and ugly. He desired Faridah. Syed was young and handsome compared to Achmet, and poor.

He loved Faridah, who returned his affection. Faridah's parents were undecided and frustrated by Faridah's rejection of Achmet but tempted by his wealth. So they resolved to seek impartial advice.

All concerned agreed to abide by the decision of the regular matchmakers, of which group Mohktar was an automatic member. Bribed heavily by Achmet, they gave a verdict in his favour.

Faridah rebelled.

'If I cannot have my Syed, I have no desire to live,' she screamed, 'better to die unwed!'

She then rushed and flung herself over a cliff-edge which dropped down into a narrow gorge, screaming the name of her beloved. Had she fallen the full distance she would have certainly been either crushed or drowned, but a protruding bush half-way down caught and held her firmly. She was rescued, tearful and muttering promises to marry Syed in the spirit world.

It was decided that the girl was insane. But Achmet had no use for a crazy wife, though Syed said he would marry her anyway.

The parents, sympathetic and badly scared, agreed to let their daughter marry Syed and began the arrangements. Immediately Faridah miraculously recovered.

Achmet the silk merchant, furious at the way he had been tricked, sought the advice of his friends, including Mohktar.

'Can anything be done?' he moaned. 'If only that accursed youth could disappear, die or be stricken with some foul disease.'

Mohktar made an offer. This man was the opportunity for which he had been waiting.

'Something can be arranged,' he promised, 'but it will cost you a lot of money.'

'You promise me? How much?'

'One thousand Ringgits and a parcel of rich Padi land.'

'That little?' the wealthy merchant gasped. 'It is yours if you succeed.'

The witch-priest cursed himself for not asking for twice as much, but amended his claim: 'the money first as there will be expenses, the land when all is accomplished.'

'It is agreed,' the delighted Achmet burbled as he began to count out the money, 'get to work as soon as you can.'

Mohktar, the village *Bomoh*, now acting as *Pawang Buang* and covered with double the usual number of amulets, approached the *Angsana* tree. He wore a shirt on which were painted quotations from the Holy Koran denouncing evil spirits, and incantations in ancient languages long unspoken by any other than those involved in the world of ghosts. On the ground he drew his *Barisan* of double width, then made the first move to unlock the frightful powers he had imprisoned.

It was necessary to leave the safety of the *Barisan* to cut away the plug sealing the hollow reed, but he quickly returned to the protective circle.

The moon was fading; another hour or so would bring dawn. Orang Bunian, a friendly little Hantu watching in the tree-tops, stirred the branches though there was no wind. The kind of awakening a deadly spectre would appreciate.

Steadily intoning his *Jampi-Jampi*, Mohktar watched the foul-smelling haze emerge from the hollow reed to the tune of a hideous growling like a pack of hungry dogs.

'Allah give me strength!' The witch-priest found time to break the barrier of his incantations as he watched the haze thicken, writhe, stiffen and materialise into the shape of an enormous tiger—*Hantu-Rimba*—hungry for his first taste of human blood.

It was critical. One weak spot in that protective *Barisan*, one misquoted or omitted *Jampi-Jampi*, one inch of living body extending across the barrier and Mohktar himself by sheer propinquity might be the first victim to the spectre's blood-lust.

But the *Pawang* won.

'There is blood for you,' the instructions were issued, 'hot strong blood from a sturdy youth, enough to satisfy your first need. You will find him where the river bends, tending his fishing traps. Go now and devour.'

The *Bomoh* waited in the safety of his *Barisan* long enough to give his *Hantu-Raya* ample time to find his victim, then emerged and entered the Kampong to chat with his friends. After a few hours they were joined by a small group of terrified villagers reporting the death of young Syed. One sufficiently coherent witness told the story.

'We were approaching the place where Syed traps his fish, to see what he had caught and perhaps buy some,' he related. 'Dawn was well broken, but suddenly darkness such as I have never known descended on us . . .'

'So dark and evil you could feel it,' another added.

'A choking wind like burning sulphur,' said a third.

'Screams of human pain and horrible snarling like wild pigs fighting over a sow,' the first man filled in.

'What happened then?' gasped the excited witch-priest.

'A huge form in the shape of a tiger that glowed bright in the darkness appeared and carried poor Syed into the jungle. He was screaming, the tiger was snarling, and we heard the crunch of jaws as the beast tore the limbs from his body,' one terrified spectator ended the story.

'Undoubtedly a Hantu, probably *Hantu-Rimba*,' Mohktar said, trying hard to suppress his satisfaction. 'To have gone to his aid would have been certain death. Syed was a well-loved youth and will be badly missed. I suggest we . . .'

He stopped, his eyes bulging in astonishment. The little group watched an approaching figure.

Syed!

The young man came closer, sensing their alarm.

'We thought you were dead,' breathed Mohktar hiding his disappointment and alarm with difficulty. What had gone wrong? 'You seem troubled. Is anything wrong?'

'Something terrible has happened,' the youth began in a hoarse whisper as though frightened of being overheard. 'I have long suspected that my traps were being robbed. This morning I went down early to watch. A man came and began to open them. I meant to go down and catch

him but instead . . .' He recounted the story already told
and continued. 'Who he is I do not know, but this I know, I
am lucky to be alive. It might have been me.'

Angry that by simple chance his target had escaped, the
Pawang Buang was still pleased with his experiment. It
proved he had mastery over the horrendous spectre. Now,
well-fed, it would be in a good mood and quite happy to
return to its home in the *Angsana* tree. But Mohktar
would have to appease a disgruntled silk merchant and
there was no way of predicting whether the Hantu would
provide an immediate rerun if Achmet demanded it.

In the security of his *Barisan* the witch-priest intoned
his incantations, waiting patiently as he called his *Hantu-
Raya* to rest. Bird-song greeted the morning, bright-
coloured butterflies decorated the flowers, ants covered
the rugged trunk pursued by hungry lizards and mason
wasps carried their pellets of red clay to build their nests.
Mohktar contemplated the speed and skill of these ingen-
ious insects.

'My Hantu has been away too long,' the witch-priest
murmured, 'the sun is already much too high for his safety.
I wonder what is wrong?'

'Come quickly before the sun's heat burns you,' he
urged the dawdling monster.

But the *Hantu-Raya* did not want to return to his tree
yet. He would prefer to retire into the gloomy depths of
the jungle and rest in the shade of some cavern until he
could emerge again in the evening. But the magic spells
chanted by his master compelled him. Resentfully he
moved closer in obedience.

The witch-priest intensified his *Jampi-Jampi*. The sun
became overcast and the same foul stench developed as
the Hantu stood before the *Angsana* tree, for its nature
was eternally malignant.

Slowly the ghostly tiger began to dissolve into its vapor-
ous form, a spiralling rope of thick haze. Watched and
urged by Mohktar the haze entered the tubular wide-
open reed and began to disappear. The *Pawang* grinned

wickedly at the success of his powers.

Suddenly the writhing haze reversed its progress and started to re-emerge, returning to its materialised shape of angry tiger. *Hantu-Rimba* was reshaping!

In a flash of understanding the *Pawang* knew what had happened. One of those accursed mason wasps must have blocked the tube with its clayey pellets!

The problem was, how far down?

The other difficulty was, how to cut it free and escape the anger of the Hantu waiting outside the safety of the *Barisan*? He might have a chance; the ghost was not yet fully formed.

Only the front half had emerged, its throat roaring curses in the *Bahasa Hantu*, impatiently waiting complete formation of the hind parts. The *Pawang* had only seconds to act.

He had no choice either.

Screaming incantations, calling on Allah, the *nabi*, Jesus, the Lord Krishna and other deities, Mohktar raced from the safety of his *Barisan*, crossed the few feet to the *Angsana* tree and hacked away frantically near the base of the hollow reed. The loosened section came free and from it rolled the mason wasp's nest, a solid lump of red clay.

The entrance now clear, the witch-priest hurled himself back to safety as the last bit of the hind limbs of the Hantu took definite form.

It was a battle of wills. The horrendous roaring of the spectre as it tried to break the barrier of the white line, the screaming of the *Jampi-Jampi*, the rattling of protective amulets; till finally, reluctantly, the *Semangat* of old Mustapha dematerialised, flowing and spiralling back into its *Angsana* tree refuge.

Limp, drained in body, soul and spirit, Mohktar the village *Bomoh*, the exorcist, performed his final duty.

Praising all the deities he had called upon for his deliverance, he once again sealed the tube with white clay.

But this time with a difference.

He knew he had had better luck than he deserved. He wanted no more of it. He would return the thousand Ringgits and tell Achmet to find another murderer. He cut the tube off level with the surface of the tree trunk and applied his plaster thickly and widely, effectively sealing the Hantu for a long, long time.

He looked at his handiwork.

'Let it stay . . . for ever,' he murmured.

LOSING FAITH
by Louise M. Steer

It was a fine clear April day, so everyone in Gilead came to watch the hanging of Goodwife Cruff. Arriving at the scaffold, the old woman stared at those who had been her friends and neighbours with a look of mild astonishment and disbelief on her face. Her gaze rested on Goodman Emerson, who was there with eight of his nine children (his goodwife was at home with her latest baby).

'So you even brought your wee bairns, Caleb Emerson, to gawk at this poor old woman who did no wrong but to help your goodwife. Satan's curse on ye and yourn!' She stood still and let them put the noose around her neck without struggling.

The preacher said to her, 'Goodwife Cruff, do you repent?' and she answered him defiantly. 'I repent that I ever left England with the likes of you, Enoch Matthews.'

The noose tightened and her body jerked into the air with a choking sort of sound, her feet kicking helplessly. Faith Emerson, third daughter of Caleb, stared with horrified fascination, as Goody Cruff's face turned blue and her eyes bulged out of her head and blood ran out of her nose and mouth. Somewhere, an owl hooted, even though it was broad daylight. Pastor Matthews declared the witch to be dead and her body was tossed into the sandy flat by the river—unhallowed ground which they called Potter's Field. Nothing would grow there but a few sparse weeds.

63

The old woman was the first corpse to be buried there.

Every night after the hanging, Faith lay in the narrow trundle bed at the foot of her parents' big bed, where she always slept, afraid to shut her eyes for fear of seeing the old woman's blue and swollen face. Over and over, she heard the old woman's curse on her father and her family.

Faith had known old Goody Cruff, a widow who lived nearby. When Faith's mother had been struck with the childbed fever after birthing William two years ago, the old woman had nursed her with soup made from her own chickens and an evil-smelling concoction made of willow bark, blue mould scraped from an old cheese and some forest herbs which had no Christian names, only Indian ones. Goodwife Emerson had recovered, although her husband Caleb said it was the Lord's will, nothing to do with old Goody's stinking potions. Later when the old woman refused to sell her farm to her neighbour Goodman Powell, the goodman's best cow died of an unknown stomach ailment. His goodwife whispered to Goodwife Emerson that it was a clear example of witchcraft. Had not the cow been perfectly healthy the day before it died? The whispers reached Pastor Matthews who decided that old Goody must be tried. Caleb Emerson gave evidence at her trial, saying that she was known to make potions out of heathen substances which smelt so evil they must be the Devil's work.

Night after night, seeing the old woman in her dreams, Faith could not escape the feeling that a great wrong had been done for which someone must pay. When Satan finally came to her, she was not surprised.

It was after her fourteenth birthday in May, a warm Friday night, which she knew from the warnings of the preacher to be the night of the witches' sabbath. She could not see his face in the darkness of her room as he crouched over her, a huge, looming, black shape, smelling of sweat and piss. He was covered in thick hair all over, just as the preacher had described. She could not see if he had hooves, but his feet felt hard and horny. He appeared to have no horns on his head, but she was afraid to touch him in case they were hidden in his hair. It was so quiet she could hear her mother gently snoring in the big bed above her.

Satan crouched over her in the trundle bed, putting one hand over her mouth so she could not cry out. With his other hand, through her nightgown he squeezed her breasts, still not fully formed, although her women's courses had begun a few months earlier. His hand moved all over her body. She started to feel a strange tingling which she had never felt before. She felt wet between her legs, but not the same sort of wetness as when her courses moved. He moved his hand lower, thrusting his hand between her legs, poking his fingers into the secret space hidden there. It hurt sharply and she jerked her legs convulsively. Grunting softly, he moved away and troubled her no more that night.

All next day, Faith was sore and trembling. She could not concentrate on her chores. She went to bed early but even in sleep, she could hear the voice of Goodwife Cruff chanting crazily *Satan, Satan, Satan . . .*

Every Friday night after that, he came to her, running his hands over her body and poking his fingers into her. She never felt the warm tingling feeling or wetness between her legs again. Instead, she felt terror that someone would discover that Satan had chosen her for his mate. She believed she must be very bad to entice him to her, that it was her fault for not paying attention to her father's Bible readings and the preacher's sermons at Assembly. If she paid more attention to her chores, it would not have happened. Now it was too late to stop him; he was too powerful for Faith. Her only hope was to hide her secret in order to avoid hanging.

A few weeks after Satan began his visitations, he became more adventurous. Faith knew what he was doing; once she had seen two of their dogs mating in the farmyard before her mother threw a bucket of water over them. Now her mother lay asleep, oblivious, while Satan held one hard, furry hand over her mouth to prevent her crying out as he entered her. The pain was excruciating; she felt as though he was forcing a red-hot poker inside her. She was afraid he would split her apart. As he rutted against her, she lay rigid, her fingers clenched. Her fear seemed to excite him and his movements became harder and more urgent.

In the morning, she saw that the sheets, her legs, her nightgown, were all streaked with blood. It was not the time for her courses. She was too afraid to ask her mother or sisters what it could mean, so she cleaned herself up and went into the forest, taking a basket with her in case she found mushrooms. She would have to be back before sunset, the start of the Sabbath, but that was hours away.

Away from Gilead, Faith felt peace. She sat on a log and saw a squirrel scrambling along a branch of an oak tree. It was too early for acorns. A blue jay cried out above her head. Everywhere, flowers were bursting from the ground or in the trees. She felt much closer to God here in the forest than she ever did at the Assembly Hall in Gilead. This was probably the sort of wicked thought witches might have. She did not care.

She decided to pick some bluebells for her mother; she could see a patch nearby. Standing up, she heard footsteps behind her. She froze. How could Satan know where to find her? It was not even Friday.

'Hullo, Mistress Faith', she knew the voice well. It belonged to Samuel Quincey, who lived on the farm next to the Emerson farm. Samuel was the second son, about sixteen or seventeen. All the girls in Gilead admired Samuel. He was tall and blond, a good worker, always ready with a laugh or a joke to help a neighbour.

'You startled me, Master Samuel! Creeping up behind me like that!'

'You looked so deep in thought, I was not sure if I should disturb you.'

'I was only thinking about going to pick bluebells for my mother. She works so hard and she is not so strong after the last baby.'

'You're a thoughtful girl, Mistress, I've always thought so. Would you like some help with the bluebells?'

Faith blushed. 'I, I'm not sure if it would be seemly— alone in the woods.'

'I won't tell anyone. I like to come walking in the woods sometimes, if I can get away from the farm. The New World is so beautiful, so much like England and yet, different somehow. I don't think we spend enough time just looking at the world.'

'Pastor Matthews would say we should have our thoughts on the things of God.'

'Didn't God create the bluebells and the animals of the forest? What did he make them for, if not for us to enjoy? The spirit needs more than words in order to be fed!'

'Why, Master Samuel, I do believe you are a free-thinker!' Faith knew she was being bold, but she felt free, here in the woods.

Samuel looked worried and sat up, a bluebell in his hand. 'You won't tell anyone, Faith, will you?' he said urgently. 'Please?'

Faith thought of her own secret, so much more shocking than Samuel's. 'Of course not, Samuel.' She spoke his name hesitantly. What a beautiful name. 'I agree with you, about the beauty of the forest. I don't really know what a free-thinker is. I just know the Pastor doesn't like them. But sometimes I think he does not like anything of this world.'

Samuel smiled at her. How gentle his smile was, how soft his hair. Faith wished more than ever that Satan had not spoilt her. But, who would know unless she told? Maybe, if Samuel liked her enough, she could get right away from Gilead.

'It's getting late,' said Samuel. 'It will soon be sunset. Let me carry the basket for you. I'll walk you to the edge of the forest.'

They walked in silence for a while. Faith was flooded with happiness. She was walking with a young man, the sun was shining and she had a basket full of bluebells. Whatever else happened, she would treasure this moment for the rest of her life.

At the edge of the forest, Samuel stopped and turned to her. 'You'll have time to get back home before sunset. God-speed, Faith. Would you like to meet again next Saturday?'

She could not speak, but answered with her eyes. 'God-speed, Samuel,' she whispered before taking the path to her home. Every Saturday afternoon after that, she could forget for a while the shame of her Friday nights.

One July afternoon, Samuel asked Faith to go with him when the time came. She flung her arms round him and said, 'I hoped you would ask me! I'll go anywhere with you, dearest Samuel.' He returned her embrace for a moment and then gently disengaged himself, taking a few steps backward.

'We must be careful not to take the path of sin, Faith. We cannot go to Boston yet. I must speak to your father about our betrothal. And my father too.' They walked home, taking care to keep at arm's length. With Samuel, she felt clean, like a maid again.

Summer faded into autumn. Her walks with Samuel became even more precious. Soon, it would be too cold and dark to meet in the forest. Men and women were not allowed to sit near each other at Assembly, which would be their only chance of meeting.

At the same time, Faith became gradually aware that her clothes were getting tighter. Her breasts pressed against her bodice, which was tight under the arms. She had to let out the drawstring of her skirts nearly the whole way, because her stomach jutted out. She did not need to ask her mother what this meant; she did not want to tell her mother about her visits from Satan.

After one Sunday Assembly, Goodwife Quincey, Samuel's mother, said to Goodwife Emerson as Faith stood beside her, 'Your Faith is getting to be a fine figure of a woman, isn't she? Let us hope she has not adopted the sin of gluttony.'

Faith blushed and ducked her head, hoping the Goodwife did not see that her eyes were brimming with tears.

Her mother replied, 'Faith has a healthy appetite, but no more than she deserves. She's a great help to me now that her sisters have married. Godspeed, Goodwife. Come along, daughter.' She started walking back to their farm, Faith beside her, the other children trailing along. Her brothers walked with her father.

Goodwife Emerson did not mention the conversation with Goodwife Quincey, but she began paying closer attention to Faith. Her mother, worn out by drudgery and childbearing, tired easily and the household chores fell to Faith. She was finding it more difficult to do them, falling asleep as soon as dinner was finished and always being out of breath. At night, in bed, she could feel the muscles in her belly rippling and if she ran her hands over her belly she could feel strange bulges across the surface. She hoped that she would die soon. Her only consolation was that Satan no longer attended her. It did not matter; she could never marry Samuel now, when she had been defiled by Satan's curse.

Christmas in Gilead was a solemn celebration, similar to the regular Sunday Assemblies. The people had their major celebration on Christmas Eve, resting on Christmas Day as though it were the Sabbath. They did not exchange gifts, because this was a heathen custom. Everyone in the Emerson household spent several days before Christmas Eve making their preparations. Her father killed a couple of geese and the women plucked and dressed them. Her mother made her famous pumpkin and sweet potato pie; these were almost the only vegetables available at this time of year. Faith made bread and bannocks, ready to feed any visitors that may come by after the midday meal.

Samuel came with his parents to visit the Emersons. Faith stayed in the kitchen. She was afraid to see Samuel. He would see the marks of Satan's curse. She could not bear that. The Quinceys sat in the parlour while Faith, listening in the kitchen, thought they would never leave.

Just before they left Samuel came through the kitchen where Faith sat at the kitchen table, pretending to peel a potato.

He spoke first. 'Happy Christmas, Faith.'

She nodded her head but kept her eyes down.

He tried again. 'I have missed our walks, Faith.'

'I am too busy for such things.' Her voice was a whisper. 'My mother is not well and there is such a lot to do in the house.'

'Maybe you will be looking after your own house one day.'

'I fear not. I do not wish to marry any man. I must look after my mother.'

'I'll not give up so easily. Look. I have a present for you.' He held out a small wooden box. 'I made it myself.'

She did not take the box. He placed it on the table. It sat there between them. She looked at it. The box was made of hickory wood; the lid had the initials F.E. picked out in poker-work.

'I put your initials on it, so that you would know it was for you.'

'I can't read, not even the Bible.'

'I'll teach you one day when we go to Boston.'

'I'm not going to Boston with you or anyone. I must stay here. I've told you.'

'I won't listen to you, Faith.'

'I think you should go now.'

'Think about what I've said, Faith. It will soon be spring again.'

He turned to leave. 'Godspeed, Samuel.' She put the pokerwork box in her apron pocket. It was the first gift anyone had ever made especially for her. She put her hands to her face to muffle the sobs that she could no longer stifle.

She did not see Samuel for the rest of the winter. Once or twice, he came to visit her parents, but Faith kept out of sight. She no longer went to Sunday Assembly. Her mother told anyone who asked that Faith was feeling poorly, although she did not ask Faith why this was.

It was nearly March now; the winter snows had started to melt and a few early snowdrops appeared. Faith did not see them; she no longer left the house. One Sunday, she was sitting alone at the kitchen table when she felt a great gush of something hot and wet between her legs. Her skirt and apron were soaked with water. She struggled out of her chair to go and change her clothes. As she went to the bedroom, she felt a hard pain tear across her stomach. Her eyes watered but she did not cry out. She lay on her trundle bed in her shift, clenching her teeth as more pains came. She wanted her mother to come but was terrified that she would. Where was her mother? Where was anyone? They must return from Assembly soon. She had no idea of how long she lay there on the bed. She was sucked into a vortex of pain, aware of nothing but the waves of agony that seemed they would split her in two. Suddenly, she vomited yellow bile and felt an uncontrollable need to push. She leant down and felt a small downy head between her legs. Satan's spawn! She pushed with her utmost strength and the baby slithered out in a mess of blood and slime. It did not cry; the cord was twisted around its neck and it was blue. The afterbirth quickly followed. The pain vanished as abruptly as it had come. Faith felt nothing but enormous relief that it was over. She did not know what to do with the baby, so she left it on the sheet, still attached to the cord, closed her eyes and fell asleep. For once, she had no nightmares; she slept in a cocoon of oblivion.

Someone was shaking her awake. The room was in darkness. Her father loomed like a giant, his face eerie in the light of the candle he carried.

'Get up! Do not make a sound.' He tossed a wrap to her. 'Cover yourself.'

She looked down. Her nightgown and the mattress were still stained with blood but the baby was no longer there. She got up with difficulty, pulling the wrap around

her. The entire house was in darkness and everyone else
was asleep. She followed her father to the yard. She saw a
small deep hole and beside it, a little calico drawstring
bag, stained slightly with blood.

'Put the bag in the hole,' said her father. 'Do not open it.'

The bag was heavy in her trembling hands. She opened
the drawstring. What could it matter now? She did not
care that the baby would not have a Christian burial. It
was only Satan's spawn. Faith put the bag in the hole and
scooped earth over it. She did not cry.

When she had finished, she was allowed to bathe. Her
mother, who had been sitting in the darkness of the
kitchen, gave her a clean nightgown and a draught to stop
the bleeding, while her father burnt the old nightgown and
the bloody bedclothes. She was to move into the attic by
herself and she was to do no housework for six weeks.
They would tell the community she had a fever.

Exhausted by her labours, it did not occur to Faith to
wonder why her parents were helping her instead of pun-
ishing her for her sins.

Not everyone in Gilead accepted the news of Goodman
and Goodwife Emerson as to the health of their daughter.
For one thing, several of the goodwives noticed that Faith,
on her return to Assembly, was much thinner than she had
been. Calculations were done as to how long it had been
since she had been declared to be too ill to go to Assembly.
Wasn't that the same amount of time that she had been
gaining weight? The goodwives spoke to Pastor Matthews.
He told Faith's parents that, in order to quell the foul ru-
mours about their daughter, they must consent to her
being examined by Goodwife Brody, the midwife.

Goodwife Brody announced that Faith had been with
child and had been delivered of the child. Where was the
child now? Faith's parents denied all knowledge of her
condition. Hannah Brody, the midwife's daughter, remembered that she had seen Faith walking in the woods with
Samuel Quincey. Pastor Matthews and Goodman Emerson
went to see the Quinceys. Samuel denied ever touching

Faith. He swore that he had always considered her with
honour. He was so clearly shocked by the questions and
the midwife's findings that the Pastor decided he must be
telling the truth.

The Pastor and Goodwife Brody questioned Faith in
front of her parents. Her denials were slow, halting, her
hands twisting in her lap, her head hanging so that she
could not meet her parents' eyes. As she sat there, trying
to find the words that would make them leave her alone,
her little brother John ran into the room. 'Mam! Dad!
Come quick! Tray has dug something up in the yard!'

'Just some old chicken bones, I expect,' said Goodman
Emerson smoothly. 'Dogs are always burying bones to
chew later. I'll attend to it.'

'Let me come with you,' said the Pastor, equally
smoothly. 'I'm sure Faith could do with a rest to settle her
nerves.'

Faith could stand it no longer. 'Don't look, don't go out
there!' she cried. 'I'll tell you what you want to know! Just
don't look!'

'What will you tell us, Faith?' The Pastor oozed sympathy and understanding.

'The Devil, Satan, he made me do it, with him, on the
witches' sabbath eve. I couldn't make him go away, I
couldn't tell anyone. I don't want to hang! And then the
baby, it was dead, I didn't know what to do. But the Devil
told me what to do and I did it. Leave Samuel alone! He's
good, he's the only one who is!' Faith sobbed and no one
moved to comfort her.

'I think I'd better go outside and see what the dog has
found,' said the Pastor.

After a short trial, at which no one spoke in her favour,
Faith was found guilty of witchcraft and of child murder
and sentenced to hang.

It was April again, but the day on which she was to die
was cold with a light drizzle. Faith stood on the platform,
looking at the people who had once been her friends, her
community. Her parents were there, heads bowed, in an

attitude the others assumed to be grief. Samuel Quincey was not there, although the rest of his family was. Faith thought of all those witches' sabbaths with Satan prodding her. She knew who Satan really was; she had known since that dreadful night he made her bury the poor dead baby. She had only protected her father because of her brothers and sisters; who would look after them if he was gone? Who would believe her? It was better this way. Soon she would be free. She smiled quietly, remembering the previous night when Pastor Matthews came to her cell, preaching repentance. She spat full in his face, laughing as he left in a hurry. She thought of Goodwife Cruff and her curse. Had that curse been the cause of all her troubles? She doubted that the Goodwife had wanted to hurt her this way. To curse properly, she decided, you must make the meaning plain and wait for the right moment.

She saw the faces of the people of Gilead, some avid for the hanging, some shamefaced, some there because it was expected. It would be better for all of them if she was out of the way, forgotten, buried like her poor little baby.

The hangman was about to put the noose around her neck when she cried out, 'A plague on you people of Gilead that will not help a child in need! A plague on all of you here today! My Lord, give me a sign that my prayer is answered!' She did not know if she was praying to Christ or Satan; she hoped someone would hear her cry.

As the noose slipped about her neck, the sun broke through the clouds, a field of blue spreading as the clouds melted away. She kept her eyes on the sun, feeling herself becoming smaller and smaller until she was nothing more than a speck of dust, a mote of air, floating in space, free of the ties of earth.

They cut her down and buried her in Potter's Field.

The records show that the townsfolk of Gilead were decimated by a mysterious plague the following summer. The river which supplied water to the town was thought to be poisoned, but no one knew why. One survivor, Hannah Brody, claimed to have seen Goodwife Cruff and Faith

Emerson dancing with the Devil at Potter's Field, but the community had lost its taste for witchfinding. The few survivors thought that her vision was all the more reason to abandon the accursed village of Gilead for a more fruitful site upstream. As for Samuel Quincey, it is known that he stole one of his father's horses and left Gilead for Boston on the day that Faith was hanged. The records are silent as to whether he arrived.

OPENINGS

by Robert Hood

The words were directed at Tom; he knew that, and
though he wanted to rush past, eyes determinedly focused
on the distant traffic, curiosity stopped him.

'Pardon?' he said.

'I have terrible powers in me!'

'Terrible powers?'

'Terrible!'

Tom nodded, gripping his briefcase tightly. A pigeon
flapped by his head, like a page of newsprint caught on a
wind he couldn't feel. 'What do you mean?' he asked, letting his eyes scan the old man suspiciously; the derelict's
grey beard seemed as little a part of him as the baggy
brown trousers.

'I mean I can do things.' His lips didn't move, Tom
thought; and saw the derelict as a puppet worked by some
unseen hand. 'I've got to go,' he managed, stumbling one
step away, then tottering back again. A pair of teenagers
passed behind him; he heard one say, 'Deros!' and snicker.
Not me, he wanted to tell them, I've got a suit on!

'If I want to I can open up the world,' the man persisted.

'Open up the world?' Tom caught a whiff of some strong
smell. What was it? Cheap grog probably, but Tom thought
something nastier. A petrochemical by-product perhaps.

'I can create openings.'

What in God's name did he mean? Tom thought, and

76

would have mocked him; but the memory of this morning's breakfast conversation crossed his mind, and he saw Lou sitting opposite him, sipping coffee.

'He made a pass at me, Tom! You've got to get rid of him.'

'I can't just fire him, Louise.'

'Why not? What are you waiting for?'

'The right opportunity. You know; an opening, an excuse. But he's fastidious, never puts a foot wrong. If I complain about him, it looks as if I'm at fault, as if I'm being petty.'

'You're his boss, Tom.'

'But people like him.'

They did too. They liked him a lot. Bryant Derrick was tall, suave and everyone thought of him as both competent and likeable. Everyone except Tom and Louise. He wanted Tom's job, Tom knew that; he also knew the bastard would get it eventually. Tom didn't like his job, but he couldn't afford to get dismissed. The advertising industry was tight at the moment, the openings just weren't there. Tom had to wait, and to be safe, Derrick had to go.

'I can give you the opportunity,' the old man said.

'What are you talking about?'

'You know.' The man giggled.

'You mean you'll get rid of him?'

'I'll give you the opening. The rest is up to you.'

The pencil Tom was using suddenly broke. He cursed and tossed it across the room. It rebounded off the wall and then rolled out of sight under a row of cupboards. 'Damn!' he muttered. He got up to see if he could still get at it, decided it was too much trouble to try, and headed toward the supply cabinet instead. It was made of brownish metal, about two metres high, and tinny-looking. Inside it, he knew, there were four shelves covered in pens, pencils, liquid paper bottles, reams of paper, a dozen different types of fastener, rubbers and Letraset. He swung the door open, reached toward the pencils and found nothing there, nothing except a vast black hole. Chill and terrible stenches leaked out from the darkness, and, although he couldn't see anything in it, he had the impression he was standing at the doorway to a space that went straight ahead, downwards, left and right, not just for a couple of metres, but forever. He slammed the cabinet door shut and stood staring at the brown metal surface.

'Good God!' he muttered. After a moment he cautiously opened the door a crack.

'Leave it open, mister!' a voice whispered. 'I won't bite.'

Tom began to turn away, planning to run or hide, anything; but the airy voice, which was resonating in his blood, spoke again:

'Don't be such a wimp! I'm here to help.'

'Help?' whined Tom.

'You wanted an opening. Is this an opening or what?'

The literalness of the idea hit Tom hard; he staggered toward the cabinet. As he reached his hand out to steady himself it was suddenly wrapped around the door handle. He yanked it open. 'It's not possible,' he said.

'Anything's possible, if you know what to ask.' Tom couldn't see the speaker, although the voice seemed to come from very close by.

'Who *are* you?'

'*What* am I, you mean?' the voice said, and added, 'I'm a Good-Luck Pixie,' as matter-of-factly as if it were saying, 'A salesman.'

'A Good-Luck Pixie? You're kidding me?'

'Would I do that?'

'I don't know. Would you?'

'Of course not. My whole purpose in Life, or whatever you'd like to call it, is to be helpful. Fibbing would hardly be helpful, would it?'

Tom went from wondering whether he was on *Candid Camera*, to whether he was dreaming, or even going mad. 'Pixies, of any kind, don't exist. They can't! You can't be speaking to me from a bloody great hole in my stationery cabinet. Magic's just hokum. It violates the laws of thermodynamics, or something.'

'Probably does. But who cares? Look, can we talk about something else? Metaphysics gives me indigestion.'

Oddly enough, perhaps because the Good-Luck Pixie sounded a little like a bloke he'd known in Tech, Tom suddenly didn't feel too skeptical or scared. Fat and ugly Henry Ridner had been intellectually aggressive, but ineffectual in action. Tom had sussed him out as someone to listen to, but not too closely. He had never been afraid of him, though others treated him with kid-gloves. And he'd always given Tom the impression he was much more than he seemed.

'What are you doing in my supply cabinet then?'

'*He* put me here.'

'He?' queried Tom carefully. 'Henry Ridner?'

'Henry Ridner!' The Good-Luck Pixie sounded annoyed. 'What's Ridner got to do with anything? Hey, did you know Henry Ridner's head of military intelligence these days? Pretty funny, eh?'

'Military intelligence? Why's military intelligence put you into my cabinet?'

'They didn't.'

'Who did then?'

The Good-Luck Pixie huffed and its voice shifted subtly in tone and emphasis so that it sounded like the voice of an old man.

'The derelict,' it said. 'Who else!'

'*If I want to I can open up the world,*' *the derelict had insisted.*

'*Open up the world?*' *A strong smell. Cheap grog, or petrochemicals.*

'*I can create openings.*'

Tom narrowed his eyes. 'You were sent by the derelict?' he asked.

'He's my pimp. Just a channel, though without him I couldn't open a cupboard door, let alone a doorway to hell . . .'

Tom breathed in suddenly. 'This is hell?' he asked, pointing into the darkness.

'Just a figure of speech. This is a much nicer place than hell; big and scenic, a nice place to get lost in. And that's precisely my point. You want to get rid of this Derrick character, right?'

'Um, sure.'

'But you don't want to actually get rid of him yourself, eh?'

'Get rid of him?'

'So, bring him here to me. Give him a shove. I'll do the rest.'

'You'll . . . get rid of him?' Tom pondered, considering the possibilities. 'But if he just disappears, I might get blamed. If he was last seen with me.'

'He won't just disappear. I'll create another opening and he'll appear again, but not quite in pristine condition. Don't worry, for God's sake! I'm no amateur.'

'Sure, but what do *you* get out of this?'

'Hopefully some lunch. I haven't eaten for over a decade. I'm starving.'

Tom went out and bought the Good-Luck Pixie half a dozen Big Macs. He tossed them into the abyss, then shut the door quickly.

Derrick sleazed in like someone who wanted to sell him the office. 'Did you want something, Mr Mitchell?' He smiled compliantly. Tom scowled.

'Yes. Sit down, Bryant.'

He watched as his marketing assistant slid into the nearest chair. Every twist of Derrick's body, every turn of his head, seemed to exude an air of insolence. Hate ballooned in Tom like a bad case of flatulence. 'I want you to answer a question honestly, Bryant. Do you think you can manage that?'

'Of course, Mr Mitchell.'

'Are you after my job?'

Tom felt gratified when Derrick's lips twitched. 'Am I after your job? I don't know what you mean.'

'Of course you do. I want an honest answer. Whatever it is, it won't leave this room, I promise, and it won't affect your chances of promotion. It's a personal question. If you like I'll pretend for a moment that I'm not your superior.' Tom put a lot of emphasis on the last word.

Minute spasms wriggled across Derrick's cheeks and under his eyes. When he finally looked squarely at Tom, he was almost squinting. 'Naturally I anticipate promotion.'

'But would you stab me in the back to get it?'

'Of course not.' He smiled again.

Tom smiled too. 'That *is* nice to know. A great relief. On your way out, would you get me a black pen from the cabinet?'

Derrick stared, momentarily defiant. Then he stood, smiling falsely, turned his back on Tom and opened the cabinet. Tom leapt from his chair and before Derrick had time to register the abyss within the cabinet, Tom had shoved hard against his back. The darkness swallowed Derrick up.

Even though he could see nothing, Tom stood staring into the gloom and thought he heard the distant sound of chewing.

At ten to five Tom's secretary Ellie rushed into his office. She was pale and breathing heavily. 'Mr Mitchell,' she said, 'have you heard about Bryant?' Tom's heart thudded but he just shrugged. 'He's been killed!' Ellie whispered.

'Killed?' Tom registered shock, but before he could control it, the shock became a smile which he transformed into a grimace instead.

'Yes, sir. A car crash near Circular Quay.'

'He was in his car?'

'No, sir. A car rammed him against a pylon.'

'A pylon?'

'He was crushed.'

Tom thought about it, then sighed. There was both
great relief and vague terror in the sigh. 'What the hell was
he doing near Circular Quay?' he said.

That night Tom dropped Derrick's death into the conversation as though it was only of passing consequence.
Louise looked genuinely shocked, which surprised him;
and when he queried her reaction, she shook, passing a
trembling hand over her forehead. 'I know I spoke against
him . . .' she stumbled.

'You said you hated him.'

'I know. But, my God, Tom. He's dead. I wouldn't have
wished that on him or on anyone.'

Tom stared into his plate of designer fettucine, following its curves with his eyes, like a puzzle. 'Well, he's out of
the way,' he said.

For a while Tom felt guilty, especially in view of Louise's
compassion. When no police enquiries were made, and no
one cast a suspicious eye in his direction, or remembered
that Derrick had not been seen actually *leaving* Tom's office, Tom began to relax. He'd wanted to tell Louise all
about it, about the pixie especially, but when he tried, he
found he couldn't. She might hate him for it. Worse, she
might think him mad. Secretly he hoped it had all been
some sort of phantasm; that there'd never been anything
but stationery in the supply cabinet. But he couldn't bring
himself to look again and went for several days giving it a
wide berth.

On the following Thursday Ellie opened the door of the
supply cabinet before Tom could stop her. He cried out.

'Mr Mitchell, are you all right?' she asked. Tom coughed,
embarrassed. There was no darkness in the cabinet; only
pens, reams of paper, cartons of Letraset—and half a dozen
Big Macs, still in their styrofoam containers.

'Something caught in my throat.' He coughed again.

'You eat too much takeaway food,' said Ellie.

That night, after making unsuccessful advances towards Louise, who had been singularly unresponsive of late, Tom padded down the hallway into the kitchen. He couldn't understand what was wrong with her. They had married two years ago, the end result of a passionate affair that had broken up both their previous marriages. Tom had idolised her body and craved her devotion; it had made him proud to bring her along to company outings, to see her lusted after by the other men and envied by the women, knowing that she was his and that neither the men nor the women could have her. But in the last three or four months she had become sadder, less passionate. Sure, things had improved slightly in more recent times, but since Derrick's departure Tom had felt a barrier come between them, as though she suspected his part in the marketing assistant's demise and could not bring herself to condone it. She was distracted, obtuse, with none of the joyful camaraderie he had anticipated.

He opened the fridge door and reached in. The internal light has blown, he thought, then realised that the darkness was thicker and deeper than it should have been. And it smelt of petrochemicals.

'You know what's wrong, don't you?' the Good-Luck Pixie said.

'What are you doing in my fridge?' yelled Tom.

'Making a sandwich! What do you think? Now answer my question, mister. Do you want to know what's wrong?'

Tom made an effort to calm his mind. His naked flesh shrank from contact with the darkness within the fridge. 'Wrong? Wrong with what?'

'With your female.'

'My . . .' Tom spluttered. 'Leave Louise out of this. I don't want you even *thinking* about her.'

'She's forlorn and grief-stricken. Anyone can see that. Sure, she'll get over it, but how does it feel to know your wife was screwing Derrick, eh?'

'What?' The accusation made Tom want to lunge at the Good-Luck Pixie; but he couldn't see the creature. 'What are you talking about?'

'Think about how she took the news. Think about how she's been treating you since Derrick came on the scene.'

Tom did. In an instant he remembered many things. Tuesday last.

'I'm really tired, honey. I had a tough day,' she says, pushing his hand from her breast.

'Seeing you in that dress always makes me horny. You know that. You only wear it to get me going.'

'I was out shopping, that's all.'

'Come on. Not in that dress you weren't.'

Reaching for her, touching her bare shoulder, slipping the strap down so the top of her left nipple and the rounded curve of flesh on which it sat emerges from silky concealment.

'I said no!' She slaps his hand and jerks away, scowling.

Tom frowned. 'It's ridiculous. She wanted *me* to get rid of *him*.'

'Did she? She said she did. But did she mean it? Maybe she knew you wouldn't, and was saying those things to cover her tracks. Maybe she was secretly screwing him, turning him into a rival for your bed, as well as your job.'

'Impossible!'

'You wouldn't want to be thought a fool, would you? Maybe you'd better consider the possibility.'

Tom was silent.

'I'm only trying to be helpful,' the Good-Luck Pixie added.

'Did you fancy Derrick?' he asked Louise next morning, hoping to catch her off-guard. She blanched, nearly dropping her coffee into her lap. 'Did you?' he persisted.

She looked up at him, eyes pleading. 'What?' she said weakly.

'Did you fancy Derrick?'

A scowl moved across her face, then she thrust the

chair back and stood up. 'That's in very bad taste, Tom!'
she said, and left the room.

Later, when Tom found that the door to their walk-in
cupboard had become a gateway to someplace else, he
didn't tell Louise, hating her for having betrayed him with
Derrick. Instead, he followed her as she went to the walk-
in to put her coat away; then he shoved her from behind
with a short, sharp kick.

She reappeared next morning on the pavement in front
of the building where she worked. Someone said they'd
seen her plummet from a tenth-storey window. Tom was
in his office at the other side of the city when it happened.
He was, of course, shattered by the news.

Ellie proved to be a great consolation. She helped him
home, ministering to his shock with all the altruism of the
self-interested. His advances she regarded as another
symptom of grief, an understandable expression of the
depth of his feelings. But she did have hopes that she
might eventually replace the deceased Mrs Mitchell in his
affections, especially as Tom cuddled her well into the
night, drifting toward sleep with his face against her stomach.

'I've always liked you, Ellie,' he muttered, 'but my wife
was in the way. If I'd only known she was having it off with
Derrick, we could have got together sooner.'

Despite herself, Ellie jerked upright. 'With Derrick?' she
yelled. 'The bastard!'

'What?' Tom was forced awake by her sudden movement.

'I was going with Bryant before he . . . before he . . .'
She remembered what had become of him and it damp-
ened her indignation.

'Before he was squashed?' Tom finished, annoyed to
learn that Derrick had had Ellie too.

She began to cry.

Tom calmed her with caresses, and percolated coffee to

steady her nerves and his frustration. Later they sat on the bed sipping Irish Cream and sharing betrayal. 'I thought I loved her,' Tom said, 'but it was all a con.'

'Yeah. Me too.' She looked at him seriously and sucked on the edge of her glass. 'How'd you find out?'

A pixie told me, he thought. But he said: 'Tuesday week. She met him. They went to a hotel room for lunch, I suppose.'

'Oh.' Ellie looked puzzled; no doubt she thought the evidence rather slim.

Tom shrugged. 'I got suspicious and I had her followed.'

'But she couldn't have been having lunch with Derrick on Tuesday. He was in Melbourne that day. The Marketing Conference.'

This time Tom jerked upright. His mind was racing. The Marketing Conference? I forgot. My God, she couldn't have seen him. What a relief! I should've known she wouldn't be chasing a drip like Derrick. Suddenly the blood drained from his face as though someone had cut his throat. 'It was a trick! The bastard! He lied to me!'

'Bryant?'

'The pixie!' Tom jumped up and grabbed Ellie's naked shoulders. 'I killed her, Ellie, as surely as if I'd stabbed her. And she didn't do it! She didn't do a bloody thing!' He turned, yelling toward different parts of the room. 'Bastard! Show yourself! Come on! I'll have you!'

Ellie crawled over to the other side of the bed, looking for her clothes.

'Where are you going?' Tom screamed. She didn't answer; instead she bolted for the nearest door, which happened to be the en-suite bathroom. It slammed behind her. But Tom was close on her heels. He wrenched open the door and found himself hanging over an enormous black gulf. Rage turned to terror; he scrambled backwards frantically, finding a toe-hold in the shag of the bedroom carpet. He pulled himself up.

'That was close,' said the Good-Luck Pixie. 'You'll have to be more careful.'

'Bastard!' screamed Tom, tears of grief and fear dribbling down his cheeks.

'You were willing enough to believe it.'

'You lied to me!'

'That's a bit strong. I just asked a few questions, that's all. I only wanted to help.'

'Help? You lied about everything. You want to kill me.

'Would it help?'

'I'll get you for this. I'll slice you up into little bits.'

'You're letting your sense of the dramatic get the better of you, mister. I'm well out of your reach. How are you going to get me?'

Tom knew how. The pixie had said: *He's my pimp. Just a channel . . . though without him, I couldn't open a cupboard door let alone a doorway to hell . . .*

That was how Tom would get the pixie: find his pimp.

The old man was where Tom had first met him, on a bench beneath an arthritic oak that seemed, unreasonably, more withered than it had been three weeks earlier. Not the old man though. He looked like nothing had changed, as though he'd been waiting for Tom to return, patient and unmoving.

'Said I'd create openings,' he chuckled.

Tom glanced around. It was nearing midnight and, miraculously, there was no one else in sight. A train rattled by on the cliff-like viaduct above the park, heading into the City Circle. There were people in the distant, dimly lit carriages, but they'd never recognise him, even if he could be seen.

'Was I right, eh?' The derelict began to stand, to shuffle toward Tom. 'Was it terrible or what?'

Tom shoved him back so that he fell heavily onto the bench. 'Just sit there,' Tom growled. Chill spidered across the bare skin of his face. 'We've got to talk.'

'Sure, sure.' The old man nodded absurdly, like a doll with a wonky neck-spring. 'Didn't you like my magic?'

'It's not *your* magic I'm interested in.' Tom stood over him, so that he couldn't escape; he shook his head to dislodge the buzzing that had started there. 'I know whose magic it is. That bloody pixie's.'

'What's the difference?'

'That pixie's stuffed me around. It tricked me into killing my wife, and I don't intend to let it get away with it.'

'Yeah?'

'Get it! Bring it here! I want the snivelling little bastard in front of me, so I can carve it up into Good-Luck Pixie rashers . . .'

The old man reached up and touched Tom's coat. 'But I can't. You see, it's not allowed to come into the world just as it pleases. There are rules. It has to be brought.' He grinned.

'So bring it!'

'I can't. Sorry. Maybe you should take it out on me.'

'You?' Tom didn't want to do that, but as the man spoke, he felt the will drain from his arms and legs. Sight popped and crinkled, as though too much blood was flowing into his head.

'The pixie's not in this world, you see. But I am. I'm a sort of harmless image really, a skin to hold it prisoner. But at least I can get things done for it.'

Tom screamed.

'There's no need to get upset, mister,' said the old man, in the pixie's thick windy voice.

Frustration swamped Tom's ability to think. His limbs took control and in a moment he'd drawn a heavy, long-bladed knife from his coat. A moment later he'd plunged the knife into the derelict's chest and was ripping downwards as though gutting a fish. It was surprisingly easy; it didn't feel like there were any bones in him. Before Tom could breathe out, he had opened up the old man from his neck to his groin in one violent slash.

Then something—a heavy, embodied blackness—leaked from the opening.

It was big and solid, more like a second body than

the mess of intestines and blood that should have been pouring out from the wound. It spread impossibly, rising up in the midnight-grey air and becoming more ghastly as it grew to twice, maybe three times the size of the derelict. It sprouted growths: a head like a lump of raw meat (with a mouth so full of teeth it looked as if it wouldn't close without ripping away half the face); snaking tubes of flesh that ended in sores or mouths or phallic protuberances; limbs and appendages in irrational abundance. Its slitted, red eyes washed over the park and everything they touched seemed to waver and fade.

It stretched. 'At last,' it said. 'Free at last.'

'You lied about everything!'

Tom couldn't move; his body felt drained. Instead he watched as the pixie's unpixieish eyes turned. It reached out. Grabbed him.

'But what do you get out of this?'
'Hopefully some lunch. I haven't eaten for over a dec-ade. And I'm starving.'

'I never liked hamburgers,' the creature said. And began to feed.

REMORSELESS VENGEANCE
by Guy Boothby

To use that expressive South Seas phrase, I have had the
misfortune to be 'on the beach' in a variety of places in my
time. There are people who say that it is worse to be
stranded in Trafalgar Square than, shall we say, Honolulu
or Rangoon. Be that as it may, the worst time I ever had
was that of which I am now going to tell you. I had crossed
the Pacific from San Francisco before the mast on an
American mail boat, had left her in Hong Kong, and had
made my way down to Singapore on a collier. As matters
did not look very bright there, I signed aboard a Dutch
boat for Batavia, intending to work my way on to Australia. It was in Batavia, however, that the real trouble
began. As soon as I arrived I fell ill, and the little money I
had managed to scrape together melted like snow before
the midday sun. What to do I knew not—I was on my
beam-ends. I had nothing to sell, even if there were anyone to buy, and horrible visions of Dutch gaols began to
obtrude themselves upon me.

It was on the night of the 22rd of December, such a
night as I'll be bound they were not having in the old country. There was not a cloud in the sky, and the stars shone
like the lamps along the Thames Embankment when you
look at them from Waterloo Bridge. I was smoking in the
brick-paved verandah of the hotel and wondering how I
was going to pay my bill, when a man entered the gates of

the hotel and walked across the garden and along the verandah towards where I was seated. I noticed that he was very tall, very broad-shouldered, and that he carried himself like a man who liked his own way and generally managed to get it.

'I wonder who he can be?' I said to myself, and half expected that he would pass me and proceed in the direction of the manager's office. My astonishment may be imagined, therefore, when he picked up a chair from beside the wall and seated himself at my side.

'Good evening,' he said, as calmly as you might address a friend on the top of a 'bus.

'Good evening,' I replied in the same tone.

'Frank Riddington is your name, I believe?' he continued, still with the same composure.

'I believe so,' I answered, 'but I don't know how you became aware of it.'

'That's neither here nor there,' he answered; 'putting other matters aside for the moment, let me give you some news.' He paused for a moment and puffed meditatively at his cigar.

'I don't know whether you're aware that there's an amiable plot on hand in this hotel to kick you into the street in the morning,' he went on. 'The proprietor seems to think it unlikely that you will be able to settle your account.'

'And, by Jove, he is not far wrong,' I replied. 'It's Christmas time, I know, and I am probably in bed and dreaming. You're undoubtedly the fairy godmother sent to help me out of my difficulty.'

He laughed a short, sharp laugh. 'How do you propose to do it?'

'By putting a piece of business in your way. I want your assistance, and if you will give it me I am prepared to hand you sufficient money not only to settle your bill, but to leave a bit over. What's more, you can leave Batavia, if you like.'

'Provided the business of which you speak is satisfactory,' I replied, 'you can call it settled. What am I to do?'

He took several long puffs at his cigar.

'You have heard of General Van der Vaal?'

'The man who, until lately, has been commanding the Dutch forces up in Achin?'

'The same. He arrived in Batavia three days ago. His house is situated on the King's Plain, three-quarters of a mile or so from here.'

'Well, what about him?'

Leaning a little towards me, and sinking his voice, he continued: 'I want General Van der Vaal badly—and to-night!'

For a moment I had doubts as to his sanity.

'I'm afraid I haven't quite grasped the situation,' I said. 'Do I understand that you are going to abduct General Van der Vaal?'

'Exactly!' he replied. 'I am going to deport him from the island. You need not ask why at this stage of the proceedings. I shouldn't have brought you into the matter at all, but that my mate fell ill, and I had to find a substitute.'

'You haven't told me your name yet,' I replied.

'It slipped my memory,' he answered. 'But you are welcome to it now. I am Captain Berringer!'

You may imagine my surprise. Here I was sitting talking face to face with the notorious Captain Berringer, whose doings were known from Rangoon to Vladivostock—from Nagasaki to Sourabaya. He and his brother—of whom, by the way, nothing had been heard for some time past—had been more than suspected of flagrant acts of piracy. They were well-known to the Dutch as pearl stealers in prohibited waters. The Russians had threatened to hang them for seal-stealing in Behring Straits, while the French had some charges against them in Tonkin that would ensure them a considerable sojourn there should they appear in that neighbourhood again.

'Well, what do you say to my proposal?' he asked. 'It will be as easy to accomplish as it will be for them to turn you into the street in the morning.'

I knew this well enough, but I saw that if he happened

to fail I should, in all probability, be even worse off than before.

'Where's your vessel?' I asked, feeling sure that he had one near at hand.

'Dodging about off the coast,' he said. 'We'll pick her up before daylight.'

'And you'll take me with you?'

'That's as you please,' he answered.

'I'll come right enough. Batavia will be too hot for me after tonight. But first you must hand over the money. I must settle with that little beast of a proprietor tonight.'

'I like your honesty,' he said, with a sneer. 'Under the circumstances it is so easy to run away without paying.'

'Captain Berringer,' said I, 'whatever I may be now, I was once a gentleman.'

A quarter of an hour later the bill was paid, and I had made my arrangements to meet my employer outside the Harmonic Club punctually at midnight. I am not going to say that I was not nervous, for it would not be the truth. Van der Vaal's reputation was a cruel one, and if he got the upper hand of us we should be likely to receive but scant mercy. Punctually to the minute I reached the rendezvous, where I found the Captain awaiting me. Then we set off in the direction of the King's Plain, as you may suppose keeping well in the shadow of the trees. We had not walked very far before Berringer placed a revolver into my hand, which I slipped into my pocket.

'Let's hope we shan't have to use them,' he said, 'but there's nothing like being prepared.'

By the time we had climbed the wall and were approaching the house, still keeping in the shadow of the trees, I was beginning to think I had had enough of the adventure, but it was too late to draw back, even had the Captain permitted such a thing.

Suddenly the Captain laid his hand on my arm.

'His room is at the end on this side,' he whispered. 'He sleeps with his window open, and his bed is in the furthest corner. His lamp is still burning, but let us hope that he is asleep. If he gives the alarm we're done for.'

I was too frightened to answer him. My fear, however, did not prevent me from following him into the clump of trees near the steps that led to the verandah. Here we slipped off our boots, made our preparations, and then tip-toed with the utmost care across the path, up the steps, and in the direction of the General's room. That he was a strict disciplinarian we were aware, and that, in conse-quence, we knew that his watchman was likely to be a watchman in the real sense of the word.

The heavy breathing that came from the further corner of the room told us that the man we wanted was fast asleep. A faint light, from a wick which floated in a bowl of coconut oil, illuminated the room, and showed us a large bed of the Dutch pattern, closely veiled with mosquito curtains. Towards this we made our way. On it, stretched out at full length, was the figure of a man. I lifted the net-ting while the Captain prepared for the struggle. A moment later he leapt on his victim, seized him by the throat and pinioned him. A gag was quickly thrust into his mouth, whilst I took hold of his wrists. In less time than it takes to tell he was bound hand and foot, unable either to resist or to summon help.

'Bundle up some of his clothes,' whispered Berringer, pointing to some garments on a chair. 'Then pick up his heels, while I'll take his shoulders. But not a sound as you love your life.'

In less than ten minutes we had carried him across the grounds, had lifted him over the wall, where we found a native cart waiting for us, and had stowed him and our-selves away in it.

'Now for Tanjong Prick,' said the Captain. 'We must be out of the island before daybreak.'

At a pre-arranged spot some four or five miles from the port we pulled up beneath a small tope of palms.

'Are you still bent upon accompanying me?' asked the Captain, as we lifted the inanimate General from the cart and placed him on the ground.

'More than ever,' I replied. 'Java shall see me no more.'

Berringer consulted his watch, and found the time to be exactly half past two. A second later a shrill whistle reached us from the beach.

'That's the boat,' said Berringer. 'Now let's carry him down to her.'

We accordingly set off in the direction indicated. It was not, however, until we were alongside a smart-looking brig, and I was clambering aboard, that I felt in any way easy in my mind.

'Pick him up and bring him aft to the cuddy,' said the skipper to two of the hands, indicating the prostrate General. Then turning to the second mate, who was standing by, he added: 'Make sail, and let's get out of this. Follow me, Mr Riddington.' I accompanied him along the deck, and from it into the cuddy, the two sailors and their heavy burden preceding us. Once there the wretched man's bonds were loosed. They had been tight enough, goodness knows, for when we released him he was so weak that he could not stand, but sank down on one of the seats beside the table, and buried his face in his hands. 'What does this mean?' he asked at last, looking up at us with a pitiable assumption of dignity. 'Why have you brought me here?'

'That's easily told,' said the Captain. 'Last Christmas you were commanding in Achin. Do you remember an Englishman named Bernard Watson who threw in his lot with them?'

'I hanged him on Christmas Day,' said the other, with a touch of his old spirit.

'Exactly,' said Berringer. 'And that's why you're here tonight. He was my brother. We will cry "quits" when I hang you on the yard-arm on Christmas morning.'

'Good heavens, Captain!' I cried. 'You're surely not going to do this?'

'I am,' he answered, with a firmness there was no mistaking. The idea was too horrible to contemplate. I tried to convince myself that, had I known what the end would be, I should have taken no part in it.

A cabin had already been prepared for the General, and to it he was forthwith conducted. The door having been closed and locked upon him, the Captain and I were left alone together. I implored him to reconsider his decision.

'I never reconsider my decisions,' he answered. 'The man shall hang at sunrise the day after tomorrow. He hanged my brother in cold blood, and I'll do the same for him. That's enough. Now I must go and look at my mate; he's been ailing this week past. If you want food the steward will bring it to you, and if you want a bunk—well, you can help yourself.' With that he turned on his heel, and left me.

Here I was in a nice position. To all intents and purposes I had aided and abetted a murder, and if any of Berringer's crew should care to turn Queen's evidence I should find myself in the dock, a convicted murderer. In vain I set my wits to work to try and find some scheme which might save the wretched man and myself. I could discover none, however.

All the next day we sailed on, heading for the Northern Australian Coast, so it seemed to me. I met the Captain at meals, and upon the deck, but he appeared morose and sullen, gave his orders in peremptory jerks, and never once, so far as I heard, alluded to the unhappy man below. I attempted to broach the subject with the mate, in the hope that he might take the same view of it as I did, but I soon found that my advances in that quarter were not likely to be favourably received. The crew, as I soon discovered, were Kanakas, with two exceptions, and devoted to their Captain. I was quite certain that they would do nothing but what he wished. Such a Christmas Eve I sincerely trust I may never spend again.

Late in the afternoon I bearded the Captain in his cabin and once more endeavoured to induce him to think well before committing such an act. Ten minutes later I was back in the cuddy, a wiser and sadder man. From that moment I resigned myself to the inevitable.

At half past six that evening the Captain and I dined

together in solitary state. Afterwards I went on deck. It was a beautiful moonlight night, with scarcely enough wind to fill the canvas. The sea was as smooth as glass, with a long train of phosphorous light in our wake. I had seen nothing of the skipper since eight bells. At about ten o'clock, however, and just as I was thinking of turning in, he emerged from the companion. A few strides brought him to my side.

'A fine night, Riddington,' he said, in a strange, hard voice, very unlike his usual tone.

'A very fine night,' I answered.

'Riddington,' he began again, with sudden vehemence, 'do you believe in ghosts?'

'I have never thought much about the matter,' I answered. 'Why do you ask?'

'Because I've seen a ghost tonight,' he replied. 'The ghost of my brother Bernard, who was hanged by that man locked in the cabin below, exactly a year ago, at daybreak. Don't make any mistake about what I'm saying. You can feel my pulse, if you like, and you will find it beating as steady as ever it has done in my life. I haven't touched a drop of liquor today, and I honestly believe I'm as sane a man as there is in the world. Yet I tell you that, not a quarter of an hour ago, my brother stood beside me in my cabin.'

Not knowing what answer to make, I held my tongue for the moment. At last I spoke.

'Did he say anything?' I inquired.

'He told me that I should not be permitted to execute my vengeance on Van der Vaal! It was to be left to him to deal with him. But I've passed my word, and I'll not depart from it. Ghost or no ghost, he hangs at sunrise.' So saying, he turned and walked away from me, and went below.

I am not going to pretend that I slept that night. Of one thing I am quite certain, and that is that the Captain did not leave his cabin all night. Half an hour before daybreak, however, he came to my cabin.

'Come on deck,' he said. 'The time is up.'

I followed him to find all the ghastly preparations complete. Once more I pleaded for mercy with all the strength at my command, and once more I failed to move him. Even the vision he had declared he had seen seemed now to be forgotten.

'Bring him on deck,' he said at last, turning to the mate and handing him the key of the cabin as he spoke. The other disappeared, and I, unable to control myself, went to the side of the vessel and looked down at the still water below. The brig was scarcely moving. Presently I heard the noise of feet in the companion, and turning, with a white face no doubt, I saw the mate and two of the hands emerge from the hatchway. They approached the Captain, who seemed not to see them. To the amazement of everyone, he was looking straight before him across the poop, with an expression of indescribable terror on his face. Then, with a crash, he lost his balance and fell forward upon the deck. We ran to his assistance, but were too late. He was dead.

Who shall say what he had seen in that terrible half minute? The mate and I looked at each other in stupefied bewilderment.

I was the first to find my voice. 'The General?'

'Dead,' the other replied. 'He died as we entered the cabin to fetch him out. God help me—you never saw such a sight! It looked as if he were fighting with someone whom we could not see, and was slowly being strangled.'

I waited to hear no more, but turned and walked aft. I am not a superstitious man, but I felt that the Captain's brother had been right after all, when he had said that he would take the matter of revenge into his hands.

A GIFT FROM GEHENNA
by B. J. Stevens

I

Autumn turned to one of the coldest winters on record. It was a time of dying. Sparrows huddled under the eaves of houses. Some would never see another summer. Sleet and exhaust fumes and biting winds filled the days of those in the city. For some it was but a passing misery; for others misery and pain were on the way.

Doctor Mildan was several hours off his forty-sixth year. Iron-grey hair sat tightly curled on his wide head and, capping a heavy brow, perched eyebrows that would have made Brehznev envious. Below these spiky growths, Mildan's dark eyes showed no trace of past youth. His neglected career in physics had years before been replaced by a loving affair with 'the bottle.' Now, with one minor heart attack behind him and the warm hand of sobriety by his side, Mildan was slowly getting his life into order.

Long since ostracised by his science colleagues, Mildan lived frugally on the proceeds of his numerous patents involving electrical components that used less power. His garage workshop-cum-laboratory at the back of his modest suburban home was a criss-cross of narrow pathways. Old workbenches squatted under the bulk and clutter of old machines and devices of dubious usage.

Flies winged lazily outside in the sun, occasionally tapping on the grimy, sack-covered windows of the work-

shop. An air-conditioner hummed. Mildan's long fingers fluttered over the dials of an energy-displacement device sitting amid the mess on a small workbench. Then with sweaty palms he pressed down on a studded cylinder and held his breath. Nothing happened. He exhaled slowly.

Suddenly there was a bright flash. Then a loud bang. Mildan's heart pounded as if trying to escape from the bone bars of his rib cage. A fly-blown bulb above the bench flickered on and off several times. The Doctor blinked rapidly, wiping away trickles of sweat from his forehead.

Then a thunderous crackling filled the workshop. The overhead bulb burst. The air snapped with static electricity; a low hum began and the air clogged with the smell of burned ozone.

Silence.

It was several moments before Mildan had the courage to move. In the gloom he picked his way through the narrow walkways until he came to the fuse-box. The sack-covered windows behind him let little light reach the back wall. Shadows huddled thick.

He reached shakily for a torch on a shelf. He did not want to look back into the gloom because he felt he was no longer alone.

Silence.

With trembling fingers he fumbled with the torch; dropped it. In a half-panic, he tried reassuring himself that there were no sounds of movement behind him. His eyes were squeezed shut as he bent down and patted the floor at his feet until he found the torch. He gripped it fiercely, praying amid rising panic that he had not heard anything shuffling along the floor.

Mildan rose slowly. He had a fleeting thought of something huge close by also rising to its feet. Wet, sticky hairs clung uncomfortably to the nape of his neck. He poked the button on the torch. The beam flickered uncertainly, grew in strength and went out. Mildan sobbed as he feverishly shook the flashlight. It flickered back on. The beam dimmed and then came to its full strength. With nerves screaming, Mildan spun around and fed the beam into the hungry darkness. Nothing. Bending down he flashed the beam under the benches. Shadows cringed. He breathed heavily. Moving across to the fuse-box he checked the board and found everything in order. The bulb had simply blown. He fetched another from a shelf and replaced the old one at the other end of the frayed cord. The gloom scuttled away.

Mildan looked down at his machine and noticed a wisp of bluish smoke rising from the cylinder casing. He bent down to see how much damage had been done. As he stooped he heard a rustling near the far wall. Mildan jerked upright and spun around.

At first he noticed nothing. Then a slight shifting of the air in front of him caught his eye. He tilted his head, studying it for a moment. Then gaining courage he stepped forward to peer more closely. Little specks, like dust motes, danced in the air at chest level.

The Doctor walked around a bench and approached the anomaly from the other direction. He was more curious than scared, and immediately decided on an experiment. He held a screwdriver near the dancing motes and quickly passed the metal end through the area. Nothing happened. He passed it through again, this time more slowly. The screwdriver was sucked out of his grasp. To his astonishment it had simply vanished into the patch of air.

Over the following days, Mildan lost many bits and pieces while experimenting with his strange patch of air. He had been doing a lot of thinking and had nearly filled a pad with calculations. Except for the occasional patch of colour the patch looked no different to heatwaves rising off hot bitumen. Although the oddity was not much to look at, it was only too clear to the Doctor what he had inadvertently caused. Somehow he had managed to breach some fundamental law of physics and had opened a kind of dimensional hole.

Mildan's curiosity had been greatly aroused. The scientist in him had spoken and he knew what had to be done.

He planned to experiment on himself by following the screwdriver through to wherever it had been taken.

II

There are places cold enough to blister the flesh of humans; places where lashing winds shriek down sheer-walled valleys. In such places the grunts and howls and squeals of the hunter and the hunted merge with the roaring of the seas and the laughter of vast shapes unseen in the night.

The trap had been sprung.

And a force with great patience waited for the prey.

III

Gaunt and anaemic, the old man leaned against the grimy, inner-city alley wall. He gasped as his stomach knotted and his mouth began to slowly fill with saliva. He hung his head and gagged as stomach acids, like sluggish waves, lapped around the ulcer in his duodenum. It was playing up badly today; and the drinks he had downed earlier had not helped. He swallowed his saliva; the sour taste of bile receded. He breathed shallowly, reshouldered his bag of dirty laundry and trudged to the end of the alley. Here the laundromat squatted amid a run-down part of the inner-urban sprawl.

In recent years the thin man had often had to remind himself that he was Jack Wilder, ex-radio personality. Washed-up was more like it. Faded and wrinkled like last week's laundry. Wilder had long since accepted that his excessive use of alcohol had driven his friends from him and had alienated him from his family. He mumbled at nothing in particular. He stepped over a rather larger dog turd outside the wash-house and shuffled inside to find an empty machine.

God knows, he needed a drink. His gnarled, purple-veined hands shook as he loaded a machine and fed it some coinage. Then he stepped back on to the side street.

Today his unemployment benefit had arrived. This

meant he could stock up on his favourite cheap port. The
cracked-faced clock on the nearby council chambers
showed Wilder that his clock at home had been fast. He
cursed. The bottle store across the road would not open
for twenty minutes. Wilder normally timed his laundry
chore to the opening of the liquor store. He knew there
was nothing to do but wait.

Two doors down the hill was a second-hand bookshop
he frequented. Wilder tried to ignore the sour, oily taste
rising up his throat. He crossed the road to the bookshop.
The place was musty inside and dust motes floated in the
autumn sunlight filtering weakly through the smudged
front window. After a few minutes searching the shelves
he selected a cheap, dog-eared paperback and approached
the counter. Wilder handed it to the cashier, an obese
woman with a perpetual cough. She was a surly one, this.
Not accustomed to pleasantries. She looked at the cover
of Wilder's book, frowned, looked at the price, frowned
again and shoved it into an old, ironed paper bag. He fumbled in his pocket for the money. He cursed inwardly as
she refused to be handed the coins. He placed them on the
counter, turned and left the shop. As he stepped into the
street he heard the woman sniff loudly. He felt sure it was
directed at him.

Outside a light rain had started. Wilder spat onto the
sidewalk. His spittle was flecked with blood. Then hunch-
ing up against the cold he trudged back across to the
laundromat to wait for the bottle shop to open. When his
washing was finished he gathered it into the bag, and with
a grunt he shouldered it. After stopping to pick up three
bottles of port he began the walk up the hill to his tiny,
cold inner-city bedsit.

He sat for a while wishing he had some company. But
had there been any, he probably would have wanted to be
alone. He unscrewed the cap of the port and upended it
for several long swallows. He coughed once and wiped his
mouth with the back of his hand.

Wilder knew that the pain would come later, but right

now the alcohol was pure bliss. His watery gaze settled on the solitary row of paperbacks on a brick and plank shelf.

An hour later, Wilder looked at the empty bottle clutched in his fist. He sighed. The bottle reminded him of himself, open yet empty.

Autumn wind came in through a hole in the boarded-up window of his little bathroom. There was one thing Wilder was sure of, there was no escaping it. The pain would come soon. The weekend might not come for him but the pain sure as hell would.

Wilder staggered to his feet and donned a second over-coat. He swallowed bile as he snatched up another bottle of port. The pain was not far away. But he thought another drink might make it more tolerable.

He left the bedsit. Turning away from the direction of the bookshop and the laundromat, he made his way down the other side of the hill towards an overgrown vacant lot. There he could drink and think and feel pain alone. As he started down the hill a siren screamed somewhere across the city. Wilder hunkered into his coat away from the cold. He unscrewed the cap off the port, swallowed some and began to weep the tears of a lonely, bitter and scared old man.

IV

Doctor Mildan stood still and sniffed the air. A faint throbbing like an earth tremor came from under the surrounding terrain. A sun so weak it might have been covered in muslin cloth lay close to the horizon. It seemed like twilight. Mildan felt the chill air wrap itself around his face and exposed throat. He shrugged to shift the rucksack on his back to a better position. Turning slowly he tried to get a better view of his surroundings. Smells assailed his quivering nostrils; smells that seemed somehow familiar yet he could not place them. A roaring like breakers on a stony beach sounded from some distance, but the Doctor could not tell from which direction it came.

He turned to face the small sun and noticed it had risen

higher above the horizon. Daybreak. He could see his surroundings more clearly. As he started toward the roaring,
Mildan noticed the ground was spongy to his tread. Water
squelched around the ankles of his tramping boots.

The sun rose, its light revealing more of the landscape.
Mildan found himself in what appeared to be an ancient
battle-site. The ground was pocked with miniature ponds
and lakes. Dotted amid these were tiny, metre-high hill-
ocks. At their crests, blackened, stunted trees grew at
oblique angles. The place had so much an air of desolation
that he was sure that nothing could live in it.

As the roaring grew louder Mildan grew more cautious.
It was fortunate that day was breaking, allowing him to
see the pit before he stepped into it.

Kneeling down he heard the roaring. It was coming
from the pit. All at once a rush of air brought an overpow-
ering stench. He gagged and lost his balance, to fall
heavily onto the moist earth at the edge of the pit.

On climbing to his feet he felt a tugging. The tugging
was growing in strength. His curiosity had turned to fear,
and he tried to back away from the pit. His feet dragged. A
backdraught was sucking him toward the edge of the hole.
Mildan fought against the tugging but was powerless.
Slowly he was drawn to the brink. Then with a cry that
seemed to be snatched from his throat and dragged down
the hole, he toppled over the edge to follow his voice.

He bounced and rolled and slid down a long, winding,
muddy tube. The roaring of the breakers grew louder and
was joined by low gurglings and growlings. Somewhere
during his bruising descent the rucksack was wrenched
from his back. Then after an interminable age, he saw light
below him, and landed with a thump on a low mound of
soft earth.

His sight was fuzzy and his head ached from many
knocks.

Shaking some of the giddiness away, Mildan looked
confusedly around. For a moment he dared not move. He
fully remembered feeling in his workshop that he had not

been alone. But the sensation did not return. So, with caution, he gained his feet and stepped down off the dirt mound. He found himself in the middle of a large, circular, concrete enclosure. He slowly turned full circle and discovered he was completely shut in by high, inward-sloping walls. Set at intervals and about chest-high were barred openings set into the slope. The Doctor walked timidly toward one of these. As he neared it he felt his flesh begin to prickle. He stopped. The sensation ceased. When he resumed walking so did the tingling. It was like a very mild electric shock—strange, although not unpleasant.

The roaring had died away but it was replaced by other sounds. Mildan swallowed hard and ground his teeth together. The new sounds were such as people in great pain would make. Wails and moans, punctuated by screams, slashed the air. Another gust of foul air was pushed up his nostrils. He wanted to vomit. More screams sounded and the air was filled with a low hum; a deep sound that nauseated him. Feeling a wetness on his top lip, he wiped it away and realised his nose was bleeding.

He took several steps closer to the nearest barred opening. A headache was growing behind his eyes. The closer he got to the opening the more Mildan felt like something was opening up inside of him, making him vulnerable. His senses were reeling, yet still he approached that barred opening. His nose was bleeding profusely as his eyes became accustomed to the gloom within. Something resembling a human in a grey cloth writhed within the opening and the shrieks grew closer together. Then wetness, like thick water, splashed out of the barred opening. It covered his face and chest, and a putrid smell sent him reeling backwards. The spattered wetness on the front of his jacket was blackish blood.

Again he felt the tugging. His will was exhausted. He did not struggle. The ache behind his eyes was unbearable. He gnashed his teeth and flecks of spittle dribbled from the corners of his twisted mouth. Blood from his nose dribbled down to merge with the blood on his throat and jacket. The tugging grew stronger. He saw the hole into which he knew he was being dragged. A sob escaped his parched throat. Yellow vapours issued up from the depths of the pit. Swaying amid this were glistening, black, eel-shaped things that appeared horribly alive. He teetered on the brink. Just as he was being sucked down the hole, Mildan felt as if he was being slowly scalped with the blunted edge of a shell. He cried out in despair. Then with the feeling of falling a great distance, he passed out.

V

Mildan regained consciousness with an aching back and the smell of stale port assaulting his groggy senses. His eyes refocused and he saw an old, gnarly man with a huge, purple-veined nose leaning over him, arm outstretched, wearing a concerned look on his stubbled face.

The Doctor shook his head and glanced around apprehensively. To his left he saw mounds of bricks marking the grave of shops that used to stand on the vacant lot. He realised with relief that he was not far from his home. He had no idea how he had come to be in the lot. But all theories aside, he was safe back in his own world. A quavering voice butted in on his muddled thoughts.

'Hey, mister, are you all right?'

'Huh?' Mildan looked back up at the man standing over him. 'What? Oh, yes. I'm fine . . . thank you.'

'You must have had a fall. Here, let me help you up.'

For a moment the Doctor cringed, trying vainly to dodge the gnarly man's breath which reeked of alcohol. Mildan remembered his own days as an alcoholic and he felt a familiar nausea rise within him.

'Here. Take my hand,' said the old man.

Mildan grasped and was swung easily to his feet.

'Thank you . . . very much.' Mildan smiled with embarrassment. 'I must have had a dizzy spell.'

'Name's Jack Wilder. Couldn't have you lying down there in the . . .'

Wilder's face seemed to drain of colour, and he became

rigid. Mildan noticed the eyes roll back in their sockets and his rescuer began to tremble violently. Looking down, Mildan saw their hands were still clasped. He winced as Wilder's grip tightened. It was only by using both hands that he was able to free himself. He stared into the old man's frightening face and wondered what was happening.

'Christ!' he swore half-aloud. 'Don't tell me the old drunk is having a seizure. That's all I need.' Mildan was about to reach out to help Wilder when he noticed the man's pupils roll back into place. The trembling stopped.

Mildan waited, ready to catch Wilder if he fell. Then the old man regained his composure. The only thing different about him was a strange grin playing about his mouth. Wilder's eyes were not smiling, only his mouth. Mildan saw the irony in the reversed situation. It was his turn to ask if Wilder was all right.

'Well, Mr Wilder. You seem to have had a mild turn. How are you feeling now?'

Wilder stared blankly for a moment. 'What? Um . . . how are *you* feeling now mister . . . Mr?'

'Mildan,' the Doctor smiled wanly. 'I'm all right now, thanks.'

They looked for a moment at each other before backing off a step.

Wilder exhaled loudly. 'Shit! I feel funny myself. Guess I'd better take off home for a rest. Seems like I've come over tired all of a sudden.' He moved past Mildan and wandered through the lot, towards the hill leading to the city centre.

Mildan watched, then held open his hand to look at his palm. He looked again at Wilder staggering up the hill, then glanced back at his hand. His eyes narrowed and again he began thinking strange, jumbled thoughts.

He knew he had to somehow get rid of the anomaly in his workshop. He had no idea of where he had been; or indeed if he had in fact been anywhere other than inside his own head. Whatever this thing that had happened in his life was, he knew with a certainty it was mentally and physically dangerous. As he stood in the lot watching the old drunk reach the top of the hill, Mildan knew he was through tampering with his last experiment.

His back was sore and he felt cold. He remembered the moans and the shrieks from a place that might or might not have been real. He shivered and pulled his jacket closer around his chest. A cold stickiness slid through his fingers. He glanced at his hands and his stomach tightened at what he saw. With a glint of cunning in his eyes, Mildan began walking quickly home. He did not wish to be outside when night fell over the city.

VI

Wilder sat on the floor of his bedsit. Rain beat against the iron fence outside his bathroom. The smell of the shit that filled his trousers hung in the closeness of his little hovel. The pain of his ulcer throbbed dully inside his gut. He knew that was the least of his worries. He had all three lights on in the bedsit, while sitting, shivering. There was no way he was going to look away from the door. Wilder was deathly afraid, but did not know of what.

He sat for a long time in his own filth. The third bottle of port sat unopened on his cluttered sink. Somewhere outside amid the rain and rubbish bins a dog barked. Wilder jerked in fear. His feet felt numb and he heard a whimpering which he mistook for the dog until he realised it came from his own throat. He hugged himself tightly and sat very still on the hard floor. A bulb flickered and went out with a pop. A second one over the sink blinked off. Wilder rocked back and forth and stared at the door. A solitary twenty-five watt bulb glowed weakly over his bed. But he was not going there; oh, no, not there. The corners of the room were thick with shadow. Wilder knew that if he moved . . .

For the second time that day he began to weep. Tears rolled down his grizzled cheeks. His thoughts were spinning. 'Don't let me sniff. Please don't let me make a noise. I want to clean myself . . . not go to bed. I know, I know. You'll be okay, Jack. Just don't move.'

The tears filled his eyes. This time they were not the tears of a bitter, lonely old man. They were those of a little boy sitting alone, terrified of the dark. But this little boy's mother would never again be there to comfort him. Ever.

VII

For several days, Della Brackett had been feeling off-colour. She had connected this to the kindly man with the shaggy eyebrows. Della sat in her lounge, wet hair felling across her pretty face. With her knees tucked up under her chin she hugged her ankles. Slowly, Della mentally recounted the events leading up to the present.

She had finished her shift pulling beer at 'The Rose of Australia' and had picked up some groceries. She recalled walking down the hill to her place when the bottom of the grocery bag split, letting the contents spill to the footpath. It was then that the eyebrow-man had trotted across the road to help her. It came back to her in a rush. The man had helped her home with an armload and passed her the items to place on her porch. Della remembered that the man's hand had, by accident, momentarily touched hers. Thinking back, she wondered if it had been by accident. Her thoughts skirted the memory of the event and she remembered now. It was right then that she had felt a little giddy, had felt her stomach constrict.

Della pushed her drying hair from her eyes and focused on her floor rug. She knew now. That was when her body had altered its rhythms. She looked at her fingernails, and became alarmed. They were getting long and she had cut them only the day before. More importantly, she had just completed her cycle and it was happening again. It was almost as if her first period had never happened. This one was unusually heavy and she was having to swallow painkillers to ease the cramps. Her body-clock was running haywire.

By piecing things together, she knew it had something to do with the eyebrow-man touching her hand.

Della was not afraid, simply concerned about what was

happening to her. She rose from the couch and dried her hair in readiness for her evening shift at the pub.

Feeling irritable and stiff from the heaviness of her second cycle, she decided to catch a bus the short distance to work. Two women sat opposite, on the facing seats, glaring at her. Her gaze dropped from theirs to her lap. She jumped involuntarily upon realising she had been sitting with her dress pulled up and her legs spread apart.

Christ! she thought. What the hell is happening? What am I doing? She pulled the dress down over her knees and stared out of the window.

At her stop she hurriedly stepped off the bus and stood still, facing away from the bus until it pulled away from the stop. Her mind reeled. Never, ever, had she behaved like that before. Looking around, she saw no one was watching. So, deftly, she slipped her hand up under her dress and readjusted her pad. She cringed. God, she was wet. Things were getting serious. Her sense of smell had heightened enormously and it seemed to her that she must reek of her menstrual blood.

'Oh, shit,' she moaned half-aloud. 'I can't go to work like this.' Looking at her watch, Della saw that she was early for her shift. So she sat on the bus-stop bench to think things out. Making sure she crossed her legs, she also crossed her arms as if for protection. Thoughts came to her mind. Protection from what? What the hell is happening to me? C'mon Dell, girl. Get it together here.

Her eyes narrowed as her gaze settled on a brick wall across the street. Della was aware of the graffiti before she began to read it. She looked away for a moment before looking quickly back. Her eyes focused and she read the short statement: 'You won't last long, Della.' Her heart thumped against her ribs. She reread the scrawl: 'You won't last long, Dennis.' Her shoulders sagged in relief. She double-checked. Yes, it did say Dennis.

Della put her hands between her legs and pressed her thighs together. This action somehow gave her a little security. A bus pulled up, disgorged its meal of passengers

and moved off. Della noticed nothing, her thoughts in tur-
moil. She squeezed her thighs tighter about her slippery, wet
hands.

A young couple with dreadlocks walked past and
laughed at something. Della did not want to look up at
them in case she was the object of their mirth. She pic-
tured their amused look as they saw her sitting alone at
the bus-stop; heard the cruel undertones beneath their
laughter as they exchanged secret whispers about her
bleeding onto the pavement. Della felt that if she did not
move, her shoes would fill with blood. She was terrified
and wanted to run home, crawl into her bed and hide. She
could not understand why she was feeling this way. It was
so unlike her to feel paranoid and afraid and, what was it?
Yes, vulnerable.

Gathering the reserves of her inner strength, she com-
posed herself and got to her feet. She saw that her hands
were bloody, as if she was experiencing some weird stigmata where the palms bled. Holding back a sob she leaned
against a fence post. Then, gathering mental strength, she
walked swiftly back home.

Della had already made up her mind to check out the
eyebrow-man. Although having no idea what she was going to do, or any notion of what she could possibly say to
him once they met, she was damned well going to think of
something.

VIII

Three weeks had passed since Mildan had returned from
what he felt was a province of hell. He was more sure than
ever that he had been somewhere real; as real as anything
in his world.

With increasing frequency the Doctor was experiencing
what he had come to term 'The Gehenna Effect'. His normally inquisitive mind had lately been filled with
trepidation. He was becoming alarmed at being alone in
his own home and was frightened to sleep with the lights
off. The television bothered him more than he cared to

admit. And he was coming to the realisation that his bath-room—especially his shower and toilet—scared the bejesus out of him.

Whenever he sat on the toilet it would give out strange gurgling, growling noises. He had long given up on the notion that it was nothing other than faulty plumbing. The bloke he had called in had found nothing wrong with the system.

Worst of all, he had felt forced to shower down at an inner-city sauna house. There was no way now that he would shower in his house. The first time Mildan had showered after waking up in the vacant lot with the drunk leaning over him, he had felt something brush featherlike against his naked buttocks then ever so gently run its nails up and down the length of his back. Mildan had jerked forward with a sob, hitting his head on the shower nozzle, desperately trying to wash lather off his face. With eyes screwed shut at the sting of shampoo, he felt a hooked nail explore between his buttocks.

He had shrieked with fear, struggling to keep his balance. He spun around. While in mid-turn he felt the talon thing slide lower. Then with a flick it scratched a bloody line down to his clenched anus. Mildan roared with rage and terror. He lashed out with both fists, flailing the misty air of the bathroom. The last of the soap left his eyes and he opened them, flicking his head wildly from side to side. Red spots appeared before his eyes. Then, fighting to gain control of his convulsing reflexes, he found he was alone in the room.

He had been violated and his body reacted by trembling uncontrollably. Suddenly tired, he let his head fall on his chest. Tears of rage and helplessness came. Through his tear-soaked eyes, Mildan noticed a thin trickle of blood running down his thigh and across his foot to mix with the water running down the plughole.

IX

Wilder trudged up the road with another bag of laundry.

He had the look of a haunted man. Bags under his eyes made him look years older than he was. His eyes were veined road-maps from lack of sleep and his hands had a permanent tremor. Weight had dropped off his frame, leaving him emaciated. This suited Wilder just fine, because he had lost his appetite. What he had thought was really bizarre was that he had not touched a drop of alcohol since that first, sleepless night in his dingy bedsit.

He was about to take his short cut through the alley when he happened to glance across the street. He blinked several times to be sure he was seeing correctly. Wilder was never sure lately that what he saw was real or imaginary.

He looked again at the man across the road. This time there was no doubting his eyes. 'The bastard,' he hissed. 'That's the fucker who did this to me.' He gripped his bag tightly, and with strength that surprised him, he strode purposefully across the road to confront Mildan.

The Doctor was looking in a shop window. He heard a screech of brakes and the curses of an irate motorist. Turning, he saw the cause of the hassle: Wilder. Mildan immediately knew what was coming. He had been half-expecting it.

He had, for the past few days, been thinking of the drunk, and of the girl he had helped, and was certain he had brought back some kind of effect in his body. The Gehenna Effect. Wherever he had been, something had reacted with his body chemistry. Something that was similar to an electric charge. Mildan had remembered how Wilder had reacted that time in the lot. He recalled the blank stare the girl had given him outside her house. They had both reacted strangely to his touch. He had been wondering how to meet Wilder and how to approach the girl. At last he had the chance with Wilder.

Mildan's brows knitted with concern when he saw the angry look on Wilder's face. He noticed how purposefully the older man stepped onto the sidewalk.

'Funny,' thought Mildan. 'He doesn't look drunk... looks more sober than I do.' His thoughts were interrupted.

'I want to talk to you, you bastard,' Wilder snapped, dropping his bag of laundry on the ground. He pushed Mildan roughly against the shop's plate glass window.

'Wait. Wait!' Mildan shouted defensively. 'Just a moment. Before you do anything. Let me explain.'

'Make it good . . . and quick,' hissed Wilder, his eyes sparkling with anger.

'I've been looking for you, too,' Mildan blurted.

'You have?' Wilder's eyes narrowed with suspicion.

'Yes. Let me explain a few things to you.'

'Such as?'

Mildan looked up and down the road. He noticed a beer sign hanging outside a pub on a corner. 'Please. Let's not talk here. Come with me to the pub. I'll buy you a . . . port?'

'Don't drink,' Wilder replied tersely. Having said this he looked almost pleased with himself. Then his look of suspicion returned.

'You don't dri . . . What?' Mildan's eyes widened. 'But just the other week. I saw . . ."

'I said I don't drink,' Wilder growled. 'Don't you listen?' He unhanded the Doctor and stepped back.

'Yes. Yes,' Mildan stammered. 'But how about we go to the pub for a squash or something? It will be quieter there and we can talk. I'll explain everything. All right?'

Wilder hesitated as he studied Mildan's face. He noticed that the younger man seemed somehow scared of something. It was as though he carried a mental burden he wanted desperately to unload. Suddenly Wilder felt a kinship with Mildan.

'All right,' he said picking up his laundry. 'You can buy me a squash.'

Mildan looked relieved as they both walked towards the corner pub.

X

For Della, the past two weeks had been filled with a series of mishaps. She had experienced some frightening sensations. But her fingernails seemed to have stopped their abnormal growth. Also, her period had run its course. But it had left her weak. The bouts of paranoia still occurred, but she had learned to control them by forcing herself to think before reacting. She told herself over and over that there was no graffiti actually directed at her. But the strange sensation of that experience was something that she would not soon forget. But now things seemed to be settling down. She hoped it was a permanent thing.

It was opening time and Della had laid out the pub-counter mats. She had flicked a switch to turn on the card gambling machines, and was just organising her cash register float, when she heard her first customers enter the saloon bar.

Looking around, Della's eyes locked with the Doctor's. They stood for a moment gaping at each other.

'You!' she said loudly, setting her mouth in a hard line. 'You are just the prick I've been looking for.'

'Listen to me,' said Mildan. 'There are three of us here with the same problem. You must believe me.'

Della scowled, her anger momentarily subsiding. She looked from Mildan to Wilder. 'Jack,' she asked, 'you want some port . . . say, are you with this guy?'

Jack's face showed his puzzlement. He looked at Mildan, then back at Della. He wiped his sleeve across his dry mouth and coughed.

'Well, I'll be damned,' said Mildan. 'Well! Things *have* turned out fortuitously. I . . .'

'Stop the shit,' said Della. 'What is this?'

'Yeah,' Wilder echoed. 'What is this, Mildan? Have you done something to Della?'

'Shut up! Both of you,' Mildan snapped. 'I said I would explain and I will. Miss . . . Della, have you got a few minutes to talk with us?'

Della looked around the empty bar. 'Yeah, I guess so.'

'A squash, please, Del,' said Wilder.

'A squash, Jack?' Della's eyebrows lifted.

'Yeah, Del. Given up the bot. I sure as hell don't need it anymore.'

Della stared at Wilder for a moment. Then turning to Mildan she said: 'Squash?'

'Please,' he said nodding.

'I'll make it three,' said Della. 'I gotta hear this.'

Mildan explained. 'I am an inventor, and the fact is that one of my experiments went wrong. It was to do with electricity.'

He left out the unbelievable parts, and finished his story the same time as downing his squash.

Della and Wilder stared at him for a moment. Della cleared her throat to speak.

'So you think this effect is just temporary? You *think*?'

'I'm sure of it,' Mildan lied.

Two men walked into the bar. Della looked up. 'Gotta go.' She hesitated. 'You sure it's only temporary?'

Mildan nodded.

Della moved away to the bar.

'I guess I have been feeling better by the day,' said Wilder. 'I don't feel as tense as I did a couple of days ago. You think maybe this effect of yours is weakening already?'

'Maybe,' Mildan admitted.

Della came back and sat looking at Mildan. He did not meet her gaze.

'I'm sorry. Really,' he said quietly.

'I know,' she replied. 'Well, you know where I work.' With that she rose and walked back to the bar.

The men parted outside the hotel. Mildan watched Wilder cross the street. He noticed there was more of a spring in the older man's stride. It was certainly a different man to the one he had seen three weeks before. Mildan pulled up the collar of his overcoat, put his hands in his pockets and began to walk home, thinking about how the Gehenna Effect altered individuals in different ways. He wondered whether what he had seen on the other side had been an hallucination, or if in fact there had been another side. His thoughts returned to the frightening experience in his shower. That had been real enough. Mildan shivered in the winter air as he trudged home through the traffic.

Jack and Della had agreed to meet at her place to discuss further the strange events that had so recently changed their lives. He sat facing her. They each held a steaming hot coffee and were relaxing with their legs stretched towards Della's bar heater.

XI

A vast shape shifted across a forbidding landscape. It was no longer patient. Now it was time to eat.

Mildan sat in bed reading a slim book on frontier physics. He looked up sharply toward the end of his bed. Something weighty had put pressure there. He could see nothing. Suddenly, something unseen and very sharp reached under the blankets, ripped open his pyjama trousers and grabbed his testicles.

Mildan screamed as the pressure was applied. The lights flickered once then went out. He screamed again as something monstrous, invisible, turned him onto his stomach. His head was pushed down hard onto the mattress. He began to suffocate.

Huge, firm boils on the creature's hide began bursting at its growing excitement. The massive, twin penises glistened as they slid greasily out of their sheaths; and droplets of pre-come dangled wetly from the tips of the black knobs. The creature grinned with what it had for a mouth and a long-toothed appendage slid out of its throat. It began to lick its food up and down the length of the struggling prey's small body. The penises quivered at the thought of the taste within.

Sensing the weakening struggles of the food under it, the creature allowed the prey to breathe. Mildan gasped and sucked in deep breaths through his sobs. Then the unseen thing inserted its penises into Mildan—split him wide open—and began a long, slow violation. It felt no need for haste, for it had all night for pleasure. Mildan had been dead for some time before the predator began to eat him. A short while later the creature looked up from the bloody, stripped carcass. Its throat appendage flicked out and licked its face, leaving behind a slick film. It huffed loudly through its nose slits and turned towards the glass french doors of the bedroom. Judging the size with its sensors, it saw it would have to squeeze out. The bed groaned as it lumbered off. Glass shattered and part of the bedroom wall crumbled as the thing left the house.

Several moments later, the lights in Della's flat winked out.

JOHNNY TWOFELLER
by Kendall Hoffman

That dangerous bastard, O'Flynn, had arrived back in town. It seemed like the locals would have to harden themselves for yet another trial of hell-raising and wild debauchery after weeks of peace and quiet. The big Irish roo-shooter had returned again to enliven and colour the drab monotony of our outback shanty town.

It was a midsummer Saturday afternoon with the temperature hovering around forty degrees Celsius in the bar-room shade when Frank drove up. He arrived from an easterly directly, driving the same beat-up, four-wheel drive Toyota wagon which was his living quarters and transport when he was last in the area. At that memorable time, after a typically riotous occasion, he had travelled away towards the setting sun and into the desert, leaving us locals somewhat bewildered as to the reason for this unlikely direction. Kangaroo targets were sparse out there and no place for a proshooter whose livelihood depended on the number of animals he took. But apparently O'Flynn had been on the scent of more exciting game, of whose nature we had no knowledge.

Charlie Boswell, the publican, was drawing a couple of frosty ales when he saw a dust cloud approaching from about four kilometres of spinifex-covered flatland. It could only have been some uncanny sixth sense that prompted him to say without looking up, 'Here comes bloody O'Flynn.'

'Yeah?' gasped Billy Jones, looking shocked. He stood with three other part-Aborigines at the bar, all sipping beers. They seemed to accept their host's prescience without question. Billy muttered to his mates, 'Tho't we seen the lasta that bastard. Hope he jest passin' through.'

The bar-room was probably the coolest place in town and the natural attraction at weekend for thirsty stockmen from surrounding cattle runs, eager for company and a weekly break in their lonely lives. The hotel's clients included men from the Aborigines' permanent camp which sprawled along both banks of a dry creek bed about a kilometre out of town. The population there was made up of under-privileged people, ranging from full-blood black to pale yellow, and at the hotel's bar that day they prevailed in numbers over a sprinkling of scruffy whites.

Shortly after the publican's prescient remark, O'Flynn's wagon came to a rowdy stop in the parking yard alongside other dust-covered vehicles parked there. We were standing at the open window, attempting to diffuse the smoky air in our lungs with the hotter, but purer stuff outside.

'Struth! He got a sheila wid him!' exclaimed Bandy Bob Maddigan. 'A bloody black un would ya believe?'

And he had.

O'Flynn bounded out of his wagon, banged the door shut, raced around the smoking front-end, reefed open the off-side door, and out hopped a most gorgeous example of feminine beauty. The girl, black as printer's ink, wore a white shift covered with red spots, a red band around lustrous, wavy hair and she had a wide, white-toothed smile. Her feet were bare and dusty.

'Holy Jesus!' exclaimed Bob at my side. 'Look at that vision.'

O'Flynn towered over his lovely friend and his sandy hair and beard contrasted starkly with her black splendour. He took her gently by the elbow and steered a course towards the cool shade of the pub's interior.

Conversation, which had previously dulled the senses with its persistent monotony, almost ceased entirely. All eyes were riveted upon the Irish giant and his shapely companion as they came through the batwing doors.

'Guudday, Frank. How ya doin'?' the publican greeted, breaking the silence, his piggy eyes fixed on the curvy body of O'Flynn's delightful friend.

'Never better, Charlie, ol' mate,' answered the roo-shooter, smiling broadly, his wide Irish face alive with pride. A massive arm draped around the shoulders of the black girl, he said, 'Want ye all ta meet me misses . . . Fellers, this here be Misses O'Flynn.'

There was complete silence for a full minute as everyone tried to digest the utterly improbable information, until Boswell, compelled by common courtesy, stammered, 'Yer *wife*, Frank?'

'Yeah? . . . Now why not may I askee?'

Boswell gave a slight shrug in the face of O'Flynn's challenging stare, noticing the sparks of hostility beginning to appear in those sea-blue eyes—a sign that everyone in the bar-room knew to be the start of trouble and to be avoided at all costs.

'Hey, Frank! Congratulations!' shouted a bearded ringer who was almost as large as the two-hundred-and-seventy-pound kangaroo shooter. He grabbed O'Flynn's bulky fist as it opened with pleasure and shook the hand with firm sincerity. This gesture fortunately broke the tension and the smile returned to O'Flynn's freckled face as the others came forward with similar sentiments.

'What's her name?' asked one of the drinkers. 'What do we call yer missus?'

'Jesus bloody Christ! . . . I tól' ye . . . She's Misses O'Flynn. That's what ye call her. Nothin' more, nothin' less, okay?' He looked over at Boswell, 'Now Charlie, you got a room we kin have, private like? We got some restin' ta do an' all. Bin travellin' all away from Cunnamulla where we got hitched. Done proper, too. Done by a Roman Catholic priest. Till death do us part, he say. So if I ever catch any bastard lookin' at her lustful like or that, I'll break he's bloody legs.'

Boswell picked a long rimlock key, tagged number three, from the wall rack and said, 'She's the third on yer left, along the passage upstairs, Frank . . . She's a double, right?'

They didn't appear again until noon when they were seen to descend the stairs huddling close and enter the dining room.

In the absence of O'Flynn and his new missus, there was a lot of speculative talk regarding the beautiful bride and how the roo-shooter had managed to come by such a prize.

'It ain't bloody likely they let 'im take her from the tribe,' one full-blooded Aborigine said, a ready-rubbed durry dangling from the corner of his thick lips. Another agreed, 'She's a Wombi, bet ya life, an' them never let a whitey near one o' they.'

The last speaker was a bloke I had relied on before to supply me with expert knowledge on Aboriginal folklore. I considered him a valuable contact; a source from whom I had obtained authentic details for my previous writings. So I called him over to my table where I sat alone. Tossing a five-dollar note on the table, I said, 'Get a coupl'a pots, Gerry, and join me. Got some things to talk about, okay?'

After we had both taken the ceremonial sip, I asked, 'What you know about this new lubra, sport?'

Gerry Blake, who was from the Creek Bank camp, wiped froth from his mouth with the back of a big black hand and asked back, 'You wanna pay me, boss?'

'Of course. If it's worth anything.' I laid a ten on top of the beer change he had placed in front of me and looked over at him with enquiring eyes.

He said, 'Reckon she a Wombi. Almost sure, 'fact. She got high tits an' thin lips like Wombi gin. They all pretty, an' blacker un us boongs.'

'Yeah, so what? . . . That ain't worth a ten. What's special about a Wombi? Never heard of 'em.'

'Dey hab debil debil men. Mebbe one, mebbe ten. Plendy magic. Could be they send Bitamulla. He leader. Or mebbe Johnny Twofeller . . . Plurry bad boy, him.'

'You reckon O'Flynn stole off with that black girl? Elope they call it. She seems more than satisfied with the deal. Don't look like he forced her, eh?'

'No matter, Wombi feller . . . Kill, kill. Right, wrong.'

'Where do they hang out then, these wild magicians?'

Gerry gave a tired shrug and said, 'Most longa desert. Sometime far, sometime . . .' He demonstrated with open palms held close together.

I shoved the money to him and said, 'Thanks, Gerry. There's about five dollar wortha info still owing. Keep her on the slate. Maybe I'll think of something else.'

Sipping at the rest of my beer which had become blood-warm, I reflected on Gerry's words, jotting the pertinent highlights into my notebook. I then took a sitting-up nap, which I often did when that edge-of-desert heat joined hands with a certain quantity of booze.

When I woke up it was evening, and most of the blokes were either in the dining-room or down at Nick's.

There are two places to eat in town; the pub, or at Nick the Greek's, three doors up. Most of the bar patrons favoured Nick's because he was cheaper; also he dished up some really nice Mediterranean food.

Mrs Boswell was behind the bar washing glasses and humming an old 1940s war tune.

'Enjoy your nap?' she asked.

I told her, yes, and said I would be dining at Nick's because I had just given that black bastard, Gerry, most of my day's spending money and I had to be careful with my budget.

Returning from Nick's later on, I was about to re-enter the bar-room, when I noticed a Myall bloke building a small fire with twigs from a nearby dead wattle. He was in the empty tract of flat land across from the pub which the locals affectionately called 'The Park'. He was pretty well naked and his black skin glistened with an oily sheen.

The crescent moon, close to the eastern horizon, hung like a stationary boomerang, laying on the countryside such a ghostly effusion that I felt a twinge of fear as I looked at that mysterious black figure reflected in the eerie moon-rays.

Back at the bar, I ordered a beer. A few of the afternoon's patrons had returned and some late arrivals had drifted in from outlying stations. One bloke, who had returned from the Creek Bank camp, was my informant Gerry Blake, and when he saw me enter, he came over, his eyes twinkling with excitement.

'You want yo' five dollar owin' now, boss?' he asked, a little cheekily, I thought.

'Shoot,' I said.

'Tha' blackfeller out buildum fire, he Wombi.'

'I coulda figured that out for twenty cents.'

'He name, Johnny Twofeller . . . Him debil debil bad . . . Him come gettum Flint.' He finished the announcement with a self-satisfied leer, then added, 'We square now, hump.'

I wanted to ask him more but without the extra dollars I knew his lips would remain sealed. Also, I decided, a little knowledge could be a dangerous thing, but a lot of it may very well be disastrous. So I told him, okay, thinking that a fool and his cash are easily parted, but remaining courteous, aware that old Gerry was holding a lot of worthwhile information which would soon be priceless, inherent knowledge which was becoming scarce as the white influence dissipated the age-old Aboriginal culture.

I carried my beer over to a table directly under a low sash-window; firstly, because a faint breeze had come up with the moon, and secondly, because it gave me a perfect view of the park and its sole occupant.

It was an extremely small fire that the Myall had built, no larger than a breakfast cup and saucer, and at first I assumed that he was cooking a meal; a rat perhaps or even a fieldmouse. But after watching for a few minutes and studying his movements carefully, I concluded that he was enacting some weird kind of ritual.

The Aborigines' corroboree dances have many unique steps and movements which, on reflection, I sometimes wonder if they do not invent on the run. I also speculate as to what strange, symbolic messages they are designed to express.

The native was performing (what appeared to be from the white man's viewpoint) mumbo-jumbo. He was uttering a weird, babbly tirade at the fire, all the while feinting towards it and hastily pulling back. Or circling it, sometimes with movements indicative of fear, as if it was an adversary, like a dog sparring with a snake. He then adopted a semi-squat pose, facing the fire. With arms held wide and fingers splayed, his head moved rapidly from side to side while an unholy gibberish issued from his mouth. Continuing the ritual, he stooped low over the small flames, all the while moaning and wailing with blood-chilling passion as his body writhed and juddered in pure frenzy.

I watched him complete this series of actions three times before I glanced across the bar-room and noticed that O'Flynn and his wife had returned and taken over a small table along the side wall.

Charlie Boswell had replaced his wife on duty behind the bar. He was now serving O'Flynn with two big beers which the locals call 'pots' but seldom order now because of the price.

The black girl had changed and now wore a vivid, low-cut red dress. Her eyes, reflected in the overhead neon, were large with what I thought to be fear, or nervous doubts. The delicate muscles around her jaw-line were tensed. Her hair, wavy and crow-black, hung neatly over straight, proud shoulders. She began sipping the froth from her newly acquired beer with a timid, self-conscious movement.

O'Flynn's hands fondled the dusky wrists of his pretty wife across the table, hindering her attempts to drink her beer. They were thus occupied when the Myall made his entrance. I must have missed seeing him leave the fire by seconds.

Mrs O'Flynn let out a half-scream as her eyes rested on the almost naked figure standing at the bar-room doorway. The beer glass in her hand fell on the table, splashing amber liquid over its surface.

O'Flynn, seated with his back to the entrance, sprang to his feet and was at her side in a flash. He wrapped his brawny arm about her shoulders in a comforting, protective gesture, saying, 'Wha' the bloody matter wid ye?', still not seeing the object of her alarm but evidently feeling her terror.

She pointed a trembling finger towards the doorway, and O'Flynn raised his eyes to see who was standing there; a reminder that there were still big debts to pay.

All the coloured patrons seemed to be aware of the Myall's identity as they edged uneasily away from their favourite bar positions to the far end, out of possible personal danger. The white men remained in their places wondering what strange drama was about to happen.

The Myall moved forward slowly, approaching O'Flynn, stooped with possessive concern over his wife, his giant hand almost concealing her from view. Then, in his own lingo, the menacing native let out a string of invective towards the girl, the tone of which indicated a berating of the highest order. The tirade continued with ever increasing vehemence until she uttered a galah-like scream of frustration, or shame, collapsed her head into nest-formed arms on the table-top and began to sob pitifully. Her whole body trembled with agitated emotion.

Frank O'Flynn stood in a trance-like state, amazed at the native's fearless temerity. But when his wife collapsed, he was jolted out of his daze as if he'd been hit with an electric cattle prod. He yelled, 'What ye bloody well talkin' boot, ye uncouth nigger? Get oot o' here 'fore I break ye atwain.'

The native continued with his rapid, unintelligible, but obvious denunciation, oblivious to O'Flynn's words.

The Irishman's massive, freckle-covered arm swung up from somewhere near his bootlaces in a vicious arc of impending destruction. His fist settled with an almighty thud on the Myall's left ear, stunning him with its brutal impact.

The stranger, previously referred to by my informant as Johnny Twofeller, lay in an almost naked, bundled-up heap at O'Flynn's dinghy-sized boots.

The Irish giant turned his attention to his distressed wife, switching his mood instantly from that of a crazed killer to a comforting husband. The hushed silence brought to an end the immediate excitement. The men relaxed with their ales again, re-forming into groups to debate the remarkable events of the evening.

The Myall raised himself slowly onto all four limbs, shook his shaggy head and looked about in confusion. A trickle of blood dribbled with snail-like pace from his swollen bottom lip and hung there. He was of slight build, approximately one hundred and fifty pounds, maybe five foot seven tall, and all steel-rope muscle. With all of O'Flynn's size, he probably carried half the Myall's weight in fat. But natives don't fight with fists, not this Wombi boy, anyway; this fellow reckoned it was the exact moment to beat a hasty retreat. He jumped to his feet, let out a hearty vocal expression close to the right ear of O'Flynn and galloped for the bar-room exit.

I still sat at the window table, with my second 'slated' small beer, recording events as they happened. I watched the Myall slink back to his fire and squat before it in apparent lengthy meditation. Glancing towards the newly-weds' table, these two were enjoying each other's company over their previously interrupted drinks.

Gerry, my informant nonpareil, approached with a conceited smile, touting further knowledge in advance for the petty price of drinking silver. 'She's gonna happen now, boss,' he said as if he was announcing the next fight at the Festival Hall, 'Big ting 'bout ta happen . . . Wanna buy ol' Gerry beer for tellin' next move?'

'You're conning me, sport,' I said, 'but I'll buy you a grog, even so. Nothing more's gonna happen. Show's over.'

'Betcha not. Show's 'bout ta start. That whitey Flint bloke, he gonna get liddle shock.'

Two more beers were added to my slate and we both touched glasses. As far as I was concerned it looked as if 'more money down the drain' was to be my new philosophy. What the hell! Hard come, easy go.

The babble of voices which had resumed five minutes before was cut like a skinning knife-slash to silence.

The Myall was standing where he had stood earlier with the same arrogant stance, the same contemptuous look. Only this time, there was a whip about his shoulders.

With an incredulous gasp, I jerked my gaze back to the little fire and saw him still there, hunched over the red embers and moaning that low, monotonous dirge.

Even as I watched, the fellow outside leapt to his feet, the moonlight lighting up his shiny body as he pranced around the fire in eerie gyrations, howling at the crescent moon like a dingo bitch on heat.

I looked again at the native inside and had to hastily re-assess my opinion that he carried a whip. The thing he held now by the scruff of the neck was an oily black snake, its jaws opening and closing revealing ivory-white fangs through which a forked tongue darted, testing the air-waves. As it writhed and squirmed against the glistening black skin of the native, the reptile's form was hard to distinguish against the man's similar shade, except for small movements which occasionally exposed its red underbelly.

There were *two* Myalls to be sure. Identical twins? How could that be? But whatever—they were there. One singing an esoteric lament outside, the other a few feet away, sporting a snake for a collar.

The snake-carrying Myall advanced towards O'Flynn's table with glazed eyes, and as he came near he spoke again to the girl. But the tone this time was one of supplication. No one but she knew what he said, but we were all spellbound by the sound of the words, by the passion in the message they conveyed, by the magic that incensed the air.

She responded with the sign of negation, shaking her head from side to side.

The message was given and answered at once. That should have been the end of it, but O'Flynn, in his egocentric way, taunted the black man as he was about to give in. He spluttered as he lunged forward, 'I'll break yer laigs wid wan swipe o' me harnd, ye bastard. Won't be so karnd a' las' tame, fer sure an' all.'

But this time the Myall skipped back a pace, and the head of the black snake came out from where it nestled against the native's cheek. It hit O'Flynn's thick wrist before the fist could complete its arc, driving a set of white fangs deep into the tensed sinews, squirting poison into the luckless Irishman to paralyse his hulking frame.

Charlie Boswell, who always kept a loaded sawn-off shotgun under the bar, and often produced it to quieten down rowdy and boisterous revellers, grabbed it now and fired on the snake.

The blasting report shattered against the charged airwaves, and, whether it was concussion or fright from the snake bite, O'Flynn fell back with the howl of an enraged warrigal, then crumbled in a deflated heap on the floor. Mrs O'Flynn screamed repeatedly.

The Myall simply vanished with the impact of the blast and the snake followed.

I glanced through the window towards the park and was rewarded with perhaps the most singular sight I may ever witness. Still performing by the fire, but with his movements slowed down and trance-like now, the original native seemed to be exerting his will on the flames as they rose higher and higher in a slender column structure, until they reached over the man's head and appeared like a golden totem pole. He began circling the eerie flame and conversing with it in a strange tongue, resembling no other Aboriginal dialect, or indeed, no language that I had ever heard.

As I watched, I slowly came to realise that there were two native forms performing around that weird fire, their movements and gestures so perfectly co-ordinated that I questioned whether I was having double vision.

Back in the bar-room, Mrs O'Flynn had stopped screaming, but even over the general hubbub I could hear the unnatural congruity of those vocal sounds from the park, unsure whether they came from one voice or two. Even more spectacular was when the two dancers moved closer and closer together, until, with illusionary deception, they merged into one.

Being conscious of Gerry Blake, among others, watching beside me, I gasped, 'That's damn uncanny. Did you see that, mate?'

Gerry was grinning broadly as he answered, 'No trobble, Johnny Twofeller. Him kill, kill first, den him go.'

As Gerry predicted, Johnny Twofeller vanished, disappearing into the column of fire with abrupt suddenness. But his voice continued for a while, as if lost or abandoned in the ether. And as it faded into a supernatural distance, the flame pole was gradually losing height, sinking towards the ground like water leaking from a badly holed bucket, slowly sagging until only a small heap of glowing coals remained. The fading of the vocal sound corresponded to the diminishing flame. Then it could be heard no more.

In the confusion of laying out the big Irishman's body (having found it to be truly dead) and of radioing frantically for the Flying Doctor Service, Mrs O'Flynn quietly slipped away without anyone immediately noticing her absence.

At Roma an autopsy was performed on O'Flynn's deceased body. The medical verdict was that the man had succumbed to a massive heart attack. There was no sign of fang marks on his arms or wrists, no snake poison in his blood.

Although I eventually squandered more bribe money

than I could afford to discover more about that mysterious desert tribe, and, in particular, its magical member, I was only to find out what I already knew; having created an illusion of bi-location, the Wombi emissary deserved his name—Johnny Twofeller.

IN THE LIGHT OF THE LAMP
by Steven Paulsen

It blazed—Great God! . . . But the vast shapes we saw
In that mad flash have seared our lives with awe
                              — H.P. Lovecraft, 'The Lamp'

I

Peter Briggs and his girlfriend, Jocelyn Harris, stood shivering in the cobbled lane behind a small group of shops. 'Back at two', read the scribble on the brown-paper bag taped to the stairwell door.

'He's out, damn it!' said Jocelyn, pulling a crocheted shawl about her shoulders.

'Yeah,' said Peter. 'We needn't have rushed to catch that bloody train after all.' He glanced at his watch and shrugged. 'Half an hour. We've got to score, so we'll just have to wait.' He ran his fingers through his long, lank hair, freeing some of the knots that had got tangled in.

'Well it's too damn cold to hang around here, man. I'm freezing. And look at those clouds, there's rain on the way. Let's go and browse in the shops.'

They left the lane, the cold wind driving them out, and circled around to the front of the shops.

The buildings were old and dilapidated, superseded now by the all-in-one complex on the highway that had by-passed them twenty years ago. They huddled around the mostly quiet railway station; grimy, dull and forlorn.

Peter and Jocelyn passed one uninviting doorway after another: an espresso bar where dark-eyed men were playing cards, drinking thick black coffee from tiny cups; a derelict shop, its windows daubed in spray enamel with the words WAIT FOR WHEN THE STARS ARE RIGHT; the pizza shop, above which their dope dealer lived; a dingy bookstore displaying yellowed volumes of poetry by Justin Geoffrey; until finally they paused outside a cluttered bric-à-brac shop where boxes, furniture, bolts of cloth and other merchandise were precariously stacked up against the inside of its grimy window, hiding the interior.

'This'll do,' Peter said, trying to peer into the shop through the maze of oddments. Inside the shop was relatively warm, but the air was tainted; damp, dusty and aged. The only illumination came from a single fly-specked light bulb suspended from the ceiling. It was dim, so dim in fact that shadows obscured much of the stock, while parts of the shop were in darkness. The old, chipped glass sales-counter, smudged with countless fingerprints, was deserted.

They peered into the gloom. Objects of unrecognisable shapes were hung and stacked all about. In one corner there were huge earthenware jars and amphorae, while from the walls trophy-mounted animal heads watched them with ominous and fiery lifelike eyes. Behind the glass counter they could see hundreds of tinted-glass apothecary phials stacked in a tall rack.

'Let's look around,' suggested Jocelyn, strolling over to the nearest table and examining the objects laid out on it. Peter moved to another table and began picking through a selection of brass ornaments, suppressing a sneeze as he stirred dust with his movements.

Something tickled Jocelyn's ankle and she shivered uncomfortably. Then, as she tried to move away it grabbed her ankle. She screamed, kicking her foot free, and a loud staccato screech from under the table made her scream again and run to Peter's side.

'Peter . . .' she managed between sobs, 'there's something horrible under there.'

He loosened her grip on his arm and went to where she had been standing. Striking a match, he took a deep breath, bent over and thrust the flame below the table.

'It's a monkey!' he cried. 'It's cool, come and have a look. It's only a monkey.'

He struck another match and they both peered under the table. There, in a bamboo cage, sat a large-eyed, scrawny monkey with its head tilted to one side. It was laughing at them, revealing a shiny gold front tooth.

'Ah, he's cute,' Jocelyn said, placing her hand into the cage, patting its head. 'Hello there, boy.'

Peter laughed. 'A minute ago you thought he was horrible.'

Suddenly the monkey swivelled its head and lunged at Jocelyn's hand. She snatched it away as his jaw snapped shut. 'He tried to bite me!' She stood up. 'Let's go, I don't think I like him after all.'

She followed Peter to another table, casting backward glances into the dark recess she knew contained the strange gold-toothed monkey. She felt uneasy and slightly suspicious about this place. Catching up with Peter, she noticed the counter was still unattended.

Peter stopped before a tall brass water pipe. 'Far out! Hey Joss, get a load of this hookah will you.'

'Oh, wow.' Jocelyn stared at Peter's find. 'Isn't it great? I wonder how much they want for it?'

'*Salaam*, young *Effendi*, young Madam.'

Peter and Jocelyn spun around. Jocelyn gasped. Peter took hold of her hand. Before them, stood a tall, swarthy hook-nosed man, dressed in flowing robes and a turban. He was smiling but his eyes held an unnerving glint.

'In answer to your question, Madam, two hundred dollars is the price for the hubble-bubble. Hand-tooled by Tso Tso craftsmen. A bargain, don't you think?' His words oozed politeness, but a mocking tone seemed to deny servility.

Jocelyn raised her eyebrows at Peter.

The man smiled, his top lip curling up in one corner.
'Can I show you something else? Some trinkets perhaps,
or a talisman?'

'It's cool,' said Peter. 'Just looking, man.'

'Just looking,' repeated the shopkeeper. 'Then please
allow me to draw your attention to some very special merchandise.' He strode to a table in the middle of the shop,
easily avoiding the obstacles that cluttered the gloom.
'These items are bargain-priced, 'on special', I think you
say. For a very short time, just for you *Effendi*, everything
on this table is priced at a mere five dollars.' He gave his
curled-lip smile, bowed and moved quietly away to stand
behind the counter.

'Junk,' whispered Jocelyn, the urge to leave growing in
her.

'You never know,' Peter said as he began to sift through
the unusual assortment of paraphernalia. 'There could be
something good in here.'

Every so often he paused to examine one of the curios
or trinkets: an octagonal piece of thick red glass; a multi-
faceted black-red sphere suspended in a lidless box; a
rusty dagger with a serpentine blade; a sheaf of hand-writ-
ten parchment fragments in Latin; a cloudy jewel-like orb
about the size of a tennis ball. Finally he paused a bit
longer over one particular object, admiring it, looking at it
from different angles.

'Hey, look at this, Joss.'

Looking up from tracing the dust with her feet, Jocelyn
said, 'Come on, Pete, let's go. Dealer-Bob'll be back any
time.'

'Yeah, okay, just look at this first.' He held out a tar-
nished metal object.

Jocelyn glanced at it, disinterested. 'What is it, Peter? A
teapot or something?'

'It's an old oil-lamp, I think.' Peter ran his fingers lightly
over the surface of the metal body. 'You know, like
Aladdin's lamp. Yeah, listen'—he shook it—'You can hear
the oil sloshing around inside.'

Jocelyn smiled crookedly, then giggled, her heavy mood lifting briefly. 'Maybe there's a *genie* in it—let's polish it and see.'

'Maybe there is,' said Peter, pretending to be serious, 'it looks really old. Look, it's even engraved with runes and hieroglyphics. I think I'll buy it.'

'Don't be silly, we can't afford it. Besides, it was probably made in Taiwan last week.'

'I don't care if it was, I'm still going to buy it.'

'Well, just make sure you've still got enough to pay Dealer-Bob! And hurry up.'

Digging into the pockets of his threadbare jeans, Peter counted five dollars in coins onto the counter. The shopkeeper nodded, verifying the amount, but Jocelyn was already leading Peter from the unusual shop. As she opened the door, a shaft of cool sunlight broke into the shop, revealing an empty bamboo cage under a nearby table. Peter closed the door without either of them noticing it.

When they left the man laughed aloud, his gold front-tooth glinting, catching the light from the feeble light-globe.

II

Sitting, polishing the lamp later that night in their small, bare living-room, Peter Briggs marvelled at the quality of the workmanship as the grime and tarnish came away. It looked just like he had always imagined Aladdin's lamp would look: a squat, oblong teapot stretched to a spout at one end with a handle on the other.

Jocelyn had soon lost interest in the lamp and was now sitting cross-legged on the floor, preparing a joint on a Cheech and Chong record album cover with the marijuana they had bought from Dealer-Bob.

The lamp gleamed in Peter's hands as he gave it a final buff with a soft cloth. It was more the colour of gold than brass; but for five dollars that was impossible.

'I think I'll light it,' Peter said as he pulled the wick from the spout with a pair of tweezers.

'Do you have to, man? The damn thing'll probably smoke and stink out the room, or even worse, what if it blows up or catches fire or something?'

Peter laughed. 'It won't blow up, and that's just the Brasso you can smell.'

'You can't be sure. It mightn't be safe. Anyway, I just don't like it. It makes me uncomfortable. You can light it if you like, but I'm going to bed if you do.'

'Aw, Joss, don't be like that.' He put the lamp on the coffee table and got down on his hands and knees, nuzzling his face into her small breasts.

'Careful, you nearly spilled the dope.' She squealed and pushed him away as he playfully took her nipple between his lips through her thin cotton kaftan.

'Peter, I mean it!'

'Okay. I won't light it.'

'Thank you.'

Outside, a flash of lightning suddenly flared brilliantly, illuminating the stark room. Jocelyn gave a little gasp, gripping Peter's arm tightly. Moments later there was a violent peal of thunder that rattled the windows in their frames.

'Wow!' exclaimed Jocelyn, putting her hands over her ears.

'Jeez, that was close.' Peter got to his feet and returned to his armchair. 'Looks like we're in for a doozie storm.'

'I don't like storms.' Jocelyn went to the windows and pulled the blinds down over them. Thunder rumbled deeply in the distance and the light in their room flickered off and on.

'Well let's light this then. It'll make you feel better.'

Peter leant over and picked up the reefer and a box of matches. He sat back and lit the oversized cigarette, inhaling the smoke deeply before he passed it to Jocelyn.

'Anyway,' Peter said as he exhaled the smoke, 'there's nothing to worry about. The chances of actually being hit by lightning are billions to one. And even if . . .'

He was cut short by a flash of lightning so bright it illuminated the room through the blinds. Then the lights went out, plunging the house into darkness, and an enormous crack of thunder pounded against the windows.

'Peter!'

'It's all right Joss, hang on a second.' A match flared. Peter cupped it in his hands. 'There.'

'Have we got any candles?'

'Not that I know of; no candles, no torch, no nothing. Ouch!' Peter shook out the match and blew on his burnt finger.

'Well do something.' There was a note of panic in her voice.

He struck another match. 'I suppose I could light the lamp . . .'

'Light the lamp, then.'

'But you said . . .'

'I don't care what I said, just light it.'

He leant over and picked up the lamp from the coffee-table, putting the burning match to it. The flame sputtered for a moment then stabilised. The light the lamp gave off was surprisingly strong, lighting up the room with a warm, steady brilliance.

'There,' Peter said smugly. 'That's done the trick. See, it doesn't smoke and it hasn't blown up after all.' He placed it back on the table. 'Look, it's even better than a candle would've been.'

But Jocelyn wasn't listening. Instead she was engrossed in something across the room.

'Peter,' she said slowly, shakily, holding the joint up in front of her face, 'what's in this stuff we're smoking? I think I'm hallucinating.'

'It's just grass, what . . .'

Then they both stared dumbfounded, for now Peter saw it too. All around them the walls of the room had come to life. Wherever the light from the lamp fell, images and scenes were forming before their eyes. Except where shadows fell on the walls; there the scenes were empty, incomplete, like an unfinished jigsaw puzzle. Pictures formed and faded before they could properly make them out as they both stared incredulously.

Then the kaleidoscope sensation began to ease and a scene slowly began to come into focus. Before them lay a wooded slope leading down to a flat riverbank. Around them stood dark green trees, tall and majestic. It was as though they were looking out from a glade on a forest hillside. Peter could almost smell the freshness of pine, of dew, feel the subtle, ghostly sensation of a breeze brushing lightly against his face. The storm that had moments before thrilled him was now forgotten.

'Look!'

Jocelyn pointed as the figure of a boy came into view by the dark river. He stopped, looking towards them, then slipped from sight behind some trees on the bank of the river.

The scene twisted out of focus, shifting, changing, until another began to appear.

Peter took Jocelyn's hand in his. 'It's the lamp . . .' he whispered huskily, 'not the dope. I can feel it.' He turned back to the images.

Before them now stretched a boundless white-blue landscape. High mountains of ice and stone thrusting out from immense frozen plains. Peter felt drawn towards them; fascinated and enthralled, he imagined he could step into the scene. Holding his arm before him, fingers out-stretched, he shuffled towards the icy panorama on the wall.

Jocelyn reached out and took his other hand in her own, subconsciously holding him back.

He reached the wall and placed his fingertips against it, holding them there for a second or two. Suddenly he withdrew them with an audible sharp intake of breath.

'What's wrong?' hissed Jocelyn.

Peter removed his fingertips from his mouth and blew on them. 'I thought they were burning, but they're cold.'

'This is weird, Peter! What's going on? What do you mean, "it's the lamp", huh? I think I'm freaking out on this stuff!' She threw Peter's hand aside and covered her face with her own as she began to weep.

'Don't cry, Joss. I'll show you. Look . . .'

Peter snuffed the lamp out with the side of the matchbox, throwing the room into a darkness which amplified the howling wind and driving rain pounding against the windows, cascading from the overflowing gutters. Peter lit another match and held it up. The images were gone from the walls.

Jocelyn watched him as he relit the wick. In the light of the lamp, the familiar blank walls were being replaced by the shifting patterns of a new scene forming. The recently present sounds of the storm receded into the darkness outside like a dying echo.

A time-worn city jutting from the sands of a vast desert came into focus out of a misty blurred image. Some of the ancient buildings and walls were half-buried in the ever-moving sand dunes, while others, at the whim of the wind, had their crumbling forms fully exposed.

But the image was fleeting, melting back into the swirling sand and mist before they could take in any details. Even as this nameless city disappeared, another scene was already beginning to form.

A moonlit hillock appeared before them in the distance, and the scene seemed to grow as if they were falling into it. Closer and closer it came, until at last they saw movement on it; a tiny dancing creature which they recognised as the gold-toothed monkey from the curio shop.

The animal raised its head, lifting its face to the moon, and began to grow before their eyes, growing with impossible speed, and at the same time its shape began to change. In a matter of seconds its size had doubled and its features were taking on human aspects. They recognised it as the swarthy shopkeeper, his hands on his hips, his laughing head thrown back, a contemptuous sneer on his face. And still he grew and changed, his arms elongating, his hands replaced by huge pincer-like claws.

'I don't like this at all,' Jocelyn said timidly. 'How can a lamp do this?' But whatever she might have said then remained unspoken as she tried to comprehend the horror before her.

The creature's face (the thing now resembled neither monkey nor man) was stretching and changing colour. Finally the shifting ceased and the fiendish horror raised the long blood-red tentacle that had once been its face toward the moon and howled; a howl that Peter and Jocelyn felt rather than heard, a howl that clawed at their hearts with icy fingers.

Then the scene blurred, changing again.

'I can't take this, Peter!'

But Peter failed to acknowledge Jocelyn at all. He stood motionless, transfixed, oblivious to anything other than the new scene now on the wall.

Steaming, mud-covered and wet, a mighty Cyclopean city of spires and monoliths and confused geometry seemed to stretch interminably before him. Water poured from its black ramparts and queerly angled towers, and green slime oozed thickly down its pre-human edifices and walls, as though the city had suddenly burst into the sunlight after aeons at the bottom of the sea.

'R'lyeh,' whispered Peter without knowing why, for the word had formed itself and come from his lips of its own accord. He had the impression of many distant voices chanting monotonously and somehow he knew he had uttered the name of the dank, black city.

A movement high above the rest of the buildings caught his attention. He looked towards it. An immense gate or doorway had opened in the high citadel at the centre of the city, revealing a mighty cavern, so dark Peter could only imagine what it contained.

But even though he could see nothing, Peter *knew* something was there; something huge, something moving, something ancient . . .

Then they saw it.

Bloated and lumbering, it squeezed its rubbery mass through the immense gap and slopped itself into the sunlight. It was an obscene green scaly thing, sticky with ooze and slime. The tentacles around its kraken-like face writhed and whipped, and it lumbered forward on four-clawed feet.

The chanting became ominously audible, and although the guttural words themselves meant nothing to either Peter or Jocelyn, in response the *Thing* seemed to increase its speed over the carved monoliths and masonry of the city. Then a hideous stench, not unlike putrid seaweed and decaying fish, permeated the room.

The guttural, monotonous chanting continued, louder and louder. In a voice hardly louder than a whisper, Peter joined in the mesmerizing chorus.

'Dear God,' screamed Jocelyn. 'What are you saying? What's going on? Stop it, Peter. Put the lamp out!'

The gelatinous, bloated monster stopped and fixed its malignant gaze on Peter and Jocelyn. Leering, awful eyes pierced them as it moved with uncanny speed, slavering and groping towards them.

'Put it out, Peter!'

But Peter hesitated, turning back to look as the slobbering, rampant horror filled the wall with its unnatural bulk. And in that instant, a monstrous dripping, rubbery member lashed into the room and plucked Peter from where he stood.

Screaming, spittle spraying from her lips, Jocelyn dived for the lamp and clasped her hand over the flame. In the lamp's dying flicker, a nauseating sucking sound came from beyond the wall and she looked up in time to see Peter's limp form enveloped in a writhing mass of slippery tentacles.

Then the room went dark. Even the sounds of the wind and the rain roaring through the house could not blanket Jocelyn's shrieking.

III

The police patrol car cruised along the deserted street at little more than walking pace. A flurry of rain filled the beam of its headlights. Occasionally, a yellow glimmer of candle or lantern light shone from one of the blacked-out houses.

Constable Rex Whatley stopped the patrol car and peered through the downpour at a narrow Victorian-style house. He pulled the car over to the kerb and switched off the engine. The windscreen wipers clunked as they came to rest, and the heavy rain beat loudly on the metal roof.

'This's the place, Sarge,' he said. 'It's difficult to see if anything's going on from here.'

'Yeah,' said Sergeant David Finch. He picked up the heavy-duty police flashlight from the seat beside him. 'Grab your torch, Rex.'

A disturbance had been reported by neighbours (it sounded like a violent domestic) and the two officers had reluctantly left their warm station-house to check it out.

Splashing through the water in the flooded roadside gutters and the puddles along the footpath, they reached the front porch. Sergeant Finch knocked loudly on the door and it swung open a little, unlatched, but there was no reply from the darkened house. Finch motioned Whatley around to the rear, then knocked again, louder. There was still no reply.

Cautiously, he let himself into the house, holding his breath while he listened. No sound. When he breathed again a foetid smell assaulted his nostrils. He switched on his torch and moved cautiously into the lounge-room. He shone his light around, noting a plastic bag full of marijuana on the floor and other drug paraphernalia on the mantelpiece and coffee-table.

Over by the wall he noticed a pool of slimy liquid splashed across the floor. As he approached it the offensive smell became stronger. He screwed up his nose in distaste.

Another light flashed across the room, and Constable Whatley appeared.

'The house seems empty, Sarge. Phew! What stinks in here? It smells like someone's left a dead cat in the corner.'

'Something rotten's been spilt on the floor over there,'

said Finch. 'Dirty bloody druggies.' He shone his torch on the illicit drugs. 'Looks like they shot through in a hurry.'

The portable radio on Finch's belt crackled to life with their call sign.

'Richmond-203 responding,' he said.

'Roger, Richmond-203,' replied a tinny voice. 'Code 12 and 16 on the corner of Belrose Avenue and Centre Road. Ambulance *en route*. Can you attend?'

'That's just around the corner,' said Whatley.

'Affirmative, D24. We're on our way.'

IV

Run! Escape! were the only coherent thoughts in Jocelyn's terror-seared mind.

She fled from the house, vomit dribbling from her chin, oblivious to the rain, feeling no pain in her burnt right hand. Retching, gasping for air, she ran down the street, still clutching the lamp.

At the end of the street Jocelyn paused, confused. She realised she was still holding the lamp. Cold dread gripped her and she flung it away into the darkness. Somewhere in the back of her mind she heard a thud as it struck the ground, and she ran.

She ran blindly down the centre of the road, into the middle of an intersection.

A horn blared. Brakes screeched. Headlights illuminated Jocelyn's wan, hollow-cheeked face. Her eyes wide, unseeing. There was a thud. Pain. Everything went black.

Somewhere in the distance Jocelyn could hear voices. She began to pray to herself. She had not said a prayer since she was a little girl. This one was for Peter, but somehow she knew he was beyond God's help.

She began to tremble, gibbering quietly to herself, unaware of the rain, the approaching siren, the flashing blue and red lights.

The two policemen made their way through the inevitable onlookers. Sergeant Finch went to the distressed driver and Constable Whatley went to attend the injured girl lying on the road. He could hear an ambulance approaching the accident.

The girl was lying quietly, the side of her face grazed and bloody, her lips and chin flecked with spittle and vomit. It looked to Whatley as though her leg might be broken. He reached out to wipe the girl's face clean.

Jocelyn was wondering how God could possibly allow such a horribly evil creature to exist? But her contemplation was broken by the sight of a tentacle, its wet suckers pulsing, reaching for her face.

'Put it out!' she screamed. 'Out!'

She struck out at Whatley, her nails drawing blood from his cheek as she lurched away from him, scrabbling on her hands and one good leg. Gibbering and mumbling.

'The monkey's not a monkey. It's a man, but it's not really a man, it's a, a . . .' She began to sob. 'Oh, help me. Dear God, help me. Got to destroy the lamp. Find the lamp.'

Jocelyn reared up as they reached her, thrashing, screaming the words in their face as they restrained her. Her voice breaking.

'Find the lamp!'

All she could finally manage, as they held her, were gut-wrenching sobs. The last thing she said was, 'The lamp is a door.'

The two policemen exchanged glances.

Finch shrugged.

Whatley shook his head. 'The things these stupid kids do to themselves with dope.'

V

The next morning, eleven-year-old Jamie Bonnar wheeled his bicycle from the garage on his way to school. The storm had passed during the night, but it was cold, his breath coming out in visible clouds.

He scooted his bike down the drive, avoiding the puddles of rain-water. But as he threw his leg over the saddle some burnished thing on the front lawn caught his eye and he stopped.

Jamie laid his bike on the ground and squelched across the lawn to retrieve the curious object. He recognised it immediately as a Middle-Eastern-style oil-lamp. What a find! It was made of brass, chased with obscure symbols and patterned scrolls. It even appeared still to have oil in it. And it was on his own front lawn!

He glanced about, wondering where it had come from, wondering if he had been seen. There was nobody in sight. Quickly, he took it around to the back of the house, to the cubby he and his mates had built behind the garage.

When his eyes adjusted to the dim light inside the ramshackle hut, he put the lamp in their secret compartment in the wall; behind the plywood where they kept their cigarettes and matches. It would be safe there for now.

Tonight, after school, they could try it out . . . light it and see if it worked.

FEELING EMPTY
Christopher Sequeira

Robert Freemont was amazed to discover he no longer had the headache. It had dissipated quietly, and in its place was the sweet calm of his senses operating with their normal acuity. The headache, which had frustrated all his attempts to lose himself in his work during the day, had slithered away sometime in the last half-hour, while he had been crying.

He felt silly now. His original reasoning had dictated that he deal with his misfortune as some sort of cause-and-effect matter; something to be looked at as 'wife and daughter leave me versus my ability to continue life without them'. This now seemed incredibly foolish and an act of conceit.

The pistol he had bought yesterday to kill himself with no longer gleamed as if with some cold beauty. He picked it up to be certain and, yes, its weight and touch were now intimidating, not reassuring.

He stood up and pressed the balls of his palms into the small of his back, tightening his back muscles as he made little circles with his hands, increasing the pressure quickly. He then flung his arms out quickly with a long shuddering stretch, put the gun away in a bedside-table drawer and pulled the afternoon newspaper over from the corner of the bed with one hand. He raised his face upwards for a moment and glanced at his lamplit image in a mirror, wishing for a comb.

He flicked through the newspaper with disgust and finally arose impatiently. He pulled on his coat with one hand as he walked to the door, and rummaged in his shirt pocket with the other. A short gasp of annoyance escaped his lips as he left the hotel room in search of something to occupy his mind, and now, in search of cigarettes as well.

Dinner smells chased one another amongst the neon as Freemont trudged through Chinatown. His stomach remained numbly loyal to his numb mind. The neon grew more sparse and he slowed down at a group of cheap dirty cinema-houses.

He was willingly deceived by the face of a woman on a poster which dully echoed the visage of some adolescent companion. He lied to himself that he was only going inside to see if poster and old friend were one and the same. He exchanged notes for a small blue ticket, curious that he felt no discomfort at the paranoid idea that someone he knew might chance to see him patronizing such a place.

For the first few minutes he felt excited and hungry but after about half an hour the sensation of arousal had become as much a phantom as the odours of Chinese cooking. His mind was buoyant yet inert, only bobbing up and down with any sense of time and place in the gaps created between the short films when blackness bubbled into the cinema.

He looked at his watch as he raised his face, sticky with sweat, from the vinyl of a seat. He was only mildly surprised to find he'd been fully stretched out asleep on a row of seats near the back for more than three hours.

Something in the air had changed. He felt that perhaps that was what had woken him, so he sat up quietly. It was more than just the style of film now flickering in front. Apart from himself, only about a dozen others were in the theatre, men and women sitting next to one another in a group in the centre of the front row. They murmured occasionally to one another in confident, clipped tones, yet there still seemed that quality of reverence about them he would have associated with sex-film watchers.

Though it was similarly grainy the screening was not of a sex-film now. This film reminded Freemont of nothing so much as a documentary; stilted holiday footage, seeming to transpire with agonizing slowness, repetitive shots lingering for indulgent periods of time. A half-hour passed with scenes of apparently only one location, a temple of some kind set in a tropical jungle. Undecorated and bland, it looked to be constructed of long rounded slabs of blackish rock, criss-crossed at the corners like the tree-trunks of a log cabin, decreasing in size as they stepped up to a pyramidal apex. Relief from this imagery came in the dubious form of a Eurasian-looking man in an ugly green sarong, whose purpose in the film seemed only to be to provide observers with a sense of the scale of the gigantic structure.

When the scene switched to night shots of the same site, Freemont still refrained from leaving for a few moments. But then he stood up and ran out past a surprised door-attendant while a voice was raised behind him, because he thought he'd seen the stone logs undulating like awakening snakes.

When he awoke in his hotel room the next afternoon it was too late to go to the bank. He hadn't been able to find his wallet so he unzipped his suitcase, put the pistol away and took a credit card out of a leather folder. He hesitated over his wife's photograph, but pushed his black thoughts aside and himself out of the hotel room. A couple of streets away he was able to use the card at an automatic teller machine that chirruped at him with what he felt was suspicion. He snorted audibly at it for both his own benefit and that of the fish-eyed man standing behind him.

There were fish-eyed people and undulating logs all about him in the bar he finally settled in, but every time he looked up from the swamp of his glass and the smoke of his ashtray, they vanished, replaced by yuppies and veteran drinkers who laughed behind their hands at Freemont, the-Man-whose-wife-had-left-him. When the blurry ideas collided he giggled. He wondered if his wife had thought his trouser-snake was too small.

Later, his thoughts clotted, he shuffled down an unfamiliar street with enough money for a cheap meal. Turning in one direction, he then reversed in his tracks as an odour hooked him. Now, food normally too exotic for his ale-bloated gut seemed attractive, perhaps a necessary jolt to his insides, something he could *feel*. He couldn't remember really *feeling* anything for hours.

The slight, smiling proprietor bowed jerkily under fluorescence and ushered him to a tidy, linoleum-floored cafe-seat. Ten or twelve other diners faced each other across scattered tables and laminated menus; chewing, chatting and smoking.

The host's idiot-grin almost caused Freemont to guffaw, as the little man failed to make the menu comprehensible to English-speaking ears. After fumbling with his money Freemont consented to sampling the day's 'SPESHAILE'.

Pushing aside one steaming bowl that reminded him too much of dead insects, he ate with an inebriated lack of discretion from a plate of thick grey ropy noodles. He was uncaring of the signs the owner was making that he wished to close for the night; clearing dishes from other tables and pulling the door to. When he finally pushed his bowl away empty, Freemont stretched back in his chair, casting his eyes about for a toothpick. He patted his gurgling stomach and lamented to himself that he wasn't capable of faking a hearty belch.

The owner appeared in front of Freemont, his silly smile now replaced with an open mouth as he uttered a series of short, high, singing sounds, gesticulating with his raised hands in slow, deliberate movements.

The other diners all turned and stood behind the small man, staring at Freemont, who only now noticed that under the Asian's filthy apron was a green sarong. Freemont didn't even have time to whimper his wife's name as he saw the scraps on his almost-empty plate writhe and form into slippery black eels, before his eyes bulged and the creatures began to tear and rip him from within.

THE NICHOLAS VINE
by Ann C. Whitehead

'Hello Bill, it's us. We were sorry to hear about Casey.'

'Fred and Dawn, thanks for coming.' William Carson, Bill to his friends, continued to jumble in that new hushed voice. Of course, the names changed, but the voice and the greeting was the same each time. 'Thanks for thinking of us, we need our friends around us now.' There was that tinge of relief again.

Nicholas watched the steady procession up the pathway with bewilderment. Where had they all come from? There'd been no sign of family for years, and his parents' friends had gradually dropped away when the fights began. And why, now, had he suddenly become Casey again?

With each group of visitors came a fresh outcry from Joyce Carson. Then a rush of sobs, mutterings of support, mumbles of apologies, and always that undercurrent of relief.

But of course they were relieved. The fights were over, the coldness had warmed. There was no oppression in his absence; his parents surely felt he was somewhere nearby.

He looked down at the vine and smiled, remembering when he first suspected its truth.

He'd grabbed the stem with both hands and pulled, using all his strength to tear its roots from the earth. They had snapped, twanging from the ground with enough

force to throw him backwards. Yet the moment he had released the vine, its roots had slid back into the small round
holes. When its tendrils had begun to wind around the tree
again, he had pushed himself up and dived, grabbed again
to wrench it away. That's when he had found the thorns.

He could have sworn they weren't there before, but
now they jagged into his hands with a viciousness match-
ing his own frenzy. Refusing to let go, he had watched
blood drip onto the stem, seen it slide down and disappear
into the roots. The vine had pulsed. The thorns had
swelled. He had dragged both hands away, looked up at
the tree and mumbled an apology. He'd done his best.

Casey's obsession with the she-oak had begun when he
was five, when they told him it was planted the day he was
born. He'd stare, seeing it so much taller than himself, and
imagine how he'd grow when the time came. But he didn't
grow much, and he never understood the medical explanation. He became Nicholas instead of Casey, as if the
longer name made up for his puniness. Or was it because
only a pet had a pet name? He knew his father blamed his
mother; he understood that much from the eyes sliding to
her when the doctor explained about chromosomes. She
denied guilt, but her eyes would shift during these denials.
Over the years she stopped denying and began to look at
him with less love, less sympathy. Pity became resentment. Sometimes he sensed dislike. So he'd stand for
hours and watch the tree.

After his twelfth birthday, as he grew older but no taller,
the fights began. His mother and father, screaming, throwing things, juggling accusations. He wanted to tell them he
didn't blame them, but he was afraid if he did, the blame
would be shifted to him. His fourteenth birthday was during one of the long cold silences. It was around this time
he found the vine growing from the tree's roots. He
watched, fascinated by the swiftness of its growth. Until
he noticed the she-oak had stopped growing. He pulled
out the vine every month for a year. It was a stand-off. The
tree wouldn't grow, the vine wouldn't stop.

It was after he found the thorns they decided to go on holiday. He didn't want to go, but it was to be the start of a new start. Yet the silences grew longer and colder; ice-picks chipping away, digging into cracks and forcing them apart. When they came back the tree was withered and small, almost totally covered by the vine. Nicholas reached out to tear it away, remembered the thorns in time and ran for the axe. He fought with his mother and father, trying to make them understand. If he could get rid of the vine all would be well.

'The tree's dying and the vine's prettier anyway. Look at those lovely little flowers,' Joyce Carson had cried.

'What about the thorns?' Nicholas screamed. 'They're what's killing my tree.'

'There's no thorns on that vine,' Bill Carson snapped, ignoring his wife's warning look.

'But they were there before we went away. I saw them. Remember when I cut my hands?'

'There's no thorns, Nicholas, we know how you cut your hands,' his father said tightly. 'It's about time we got this out in the open.'

'But the vine's killing my tree.'

'If the tree dies you might find something better to do than stand staring at it.'

'Perhaps if his father took him out occasionally he would have something better to do,' Joyce shouted.

'Please, don't start. Listen to me, just listen for once,' Nicholas had begged.

But they wouldn't listen. His father's polished black shoe thumped down on the head of the axe, holding it against the vine stem while he shoved Nicholas against the dying tree. Nicholas could feel its coldness through his jumper. He tried to move, to break out of the coldness, but he could feel the vine stem pulsating as it held him there.

'You didn't have to push him so hard,' his mother screamed, and placed both her hands against the father's chest to shove him away.

When his father knocked her to the ground, Nicholas

grasped the axe and swung at the vine, but the axe slid across the stem and bit through his father's polished black shoe. Blood oozed up from the shiny leather. Bill Carson bit down on his lip and stared at Nicholas in shocked silence. The vine throbbed; Nicholas could feel it through his body. He could feel himself growing. He smiled.

Joyce Carson stepped in front of her husband, between him and the vine. Nicholas saw the fear in her eyes and smiled again as he clenched the axe tightly, trying to show that he'd protect them. She moved, slowly at first, holding out her hand, palm upward. Her fingers beckoned. He frowned, not sure what she wanted. Her eyes slid from him to the axe. He sighed with relief. She wanted to help him save the tree. But when he held out the axe she flinched. He turned it to offer the handle. She knocked it aside as if afraid to take it from his hand. His father stepped back from the vine, still staring, still silent. But it was a different kind of silence. This time he was not caught in the vacuum between his parents; this time the silence was directed at him. His head and shoulders dropped as they unloaded their guilt. Joyce put her arms around her husband and quietly led him to the house.

Nicholas heard the key turn in the lock. The vine couldn't move; why were they trying to lock it out? He turned away from their backs to look at the tree. It was grey, dead. While he watched, it crumbled to ash and the vine shrank to a small plant no higher than his knee. He bent to study the tiny red flowers and touch a curling tendril, careful of the thorns. Slowly, carefully, he used both hands to reach into the vine. The thorns had disappeared. He parted the bush, staring down into its depths. The tree was completely gone; all he could see was a dark patch where it had been. Or was that a reminder of his father's black shoe?

He backed away and ran up the path to hammer on the door. It remained closed. Out of breath, he leaned forward, resting his head against the heavy oak door while he whispered a plea to come in. The door was cold against his face, as frozen as their silences. He slid downwards, sat with his back against the cold wood to stare at the vine bush, listening to the faint mumble of voices from inside. It's time to send him away, the voices agreed. That was the first time he heard the tinge of relief in them.

He stood slowly, walked down the path and stepped into the vine.

Joyce stood by the heavy oak door, her husband's arm around her waist, and watched the last of the mourners depart. She clapped a hand over her mouth to disguise a smile, wincing at the stab of guilt, telling herself she was relieved because it was all over at last. She meant the funeral of course. Family deaths were hard on everyone. Parents expected a child to outlive them. Even sickly, difficult ones like their darling Casey. Of course, they should have seen it coming, but the doctors had told them Casey's only problem was his lack of growth. They knew better; they'd seen him change over the last three years. His obsession with that vine. It was all part of his sickness. But they'd cared for him until the last, they could take pride in that. How could they have possibly known he would kill himself, and in such a dreadful way? She looked at the vine, at the bright red flowers waving softly to her in the breeze. It seemed to have shrunk to half-size. It was no more than three and a half feet tall now, much the same size as Casey. She shuddered, remembering his body, the cuts, the paleness, the axe near his head, the outstretched hand curled around the vine stem.

'It's all over now.' Bill pulled her closer. 'We'll have to get rid of that vine, it'll always be a reminder.'

Joyce turned restlessly and moved away from Bill, rejecting the extra heat of his body. The night was unnaturally warm. He grunted and rolled over, chasing her across the bed. Joyce bit back a rush of tears. She'd cried enough, there was no sense in tears when they didn't help. Of course, it was natural to still feel depressed; it was just a week since Casey's death. She sighed loudly, irritated by

Bill's grunting snores, and climbed out of bed to wander
through the front door.

The path was hot under her bare feet, so she stepped
onto the lawn, wriggling her toes in the thick grass with
each step. Her glance flicked to the space, the brown
patch, left when Bill had removed the vine. He'd ripped it
out without much effort, and had marvelled at the shal-
lowness of its roots. But he'd thrown it on the mulch heap
by the vegetable garden, promising to take it away as soon
as he had time. She knew she wouldn't feel at ease until it
was completely gone. Though perhaps it wouldn't help,
she was continually drawn back to this bare patch of
earth. Her glance became a stare.

A small bush, no more than a foot high, was growing in
the centre of the patch. She moved closer, knelt to study
the bush. Her hope of a renewal of the she-oak disappeared when she saw the tiny red flowers. A rustle behind
her, the sound of a breeze blowing through leaves, made
her turn. She whimpered, and cowered away.

The figure was dressed in a long, flowing robe. The
walk was slow and hesitant, as if the feet, hidden by the
fluttering robe, became rooted to the ground with each
step and must be dragged loose. The sound of movement
was a rustle of leaves. The head turned continually but
gave the impression of being night-blinded. Thick brown
hair hung almost to the ground. It was still and dark, more
like a covering of bark. The figure moved into a spill of
light from the open door, and Joyce realised the gown was
a fall of shiny green leaves. The pale face turned, catching
the light. Joyce whimpered a denial and scrambled to her
feet.

He turned to look at her and smiled, but the smile didn't
touch his eyes. They were oval and half-slitted. The irises
were a bright red. He held out both hands, beckoning for
her to come to him. She saw his arms were covered in
bark. She cried out and stepped back into the vine bush. It
slid around her, trapping her legs, the tendrils sliding upwards and around her body, growing along her arms,

pushing through her hair. Nicholas moved closer, widening his arms to encompass her. As he held her, muffling her screams against his bark chest, the tendrils sprouted inch-long thorns.

He held her for the rest of the night; watching, bewildered, the procession of people, listening to them calling her name. None marvelled at his growth, not even Bill Carson when they found her body next morning. He didn't pay any attention to the vine.

But Nicholas knew his father would remember sooner or later, probably tonight when he was alone and had time to think.

Nicholas smiled and settled back to wait.

THE KEEPER
Geoff O'Callaghan

'Play "Combat"—I dare you to play it across the cemetery. Tonight.'

'Meet you there then. In full camo gear,' you said.

'I'm going to be "Nemesis" this time. You'll have to hunt me. Don't forget your paintgun.'

'Or your goggles, smarty.'

You rose with the moon, creeping from your bed on padded feet, listening with one ear to Dad's snoring, accompanied by Mum's treble. The thick drill camo shirt felt good to your touch as you slipped your thirteen-year-old arms into its slightly over-large sleeves, folding them back carefully, step by step to neat pseudo-muscles as wide as cigarette packets above the elbows. You buttoned it up along that thick central ridge before tucking it neatly into the trousers that wrapped around your toes under the woollen socks.

Paintgun and goggles in hand, you set out to meet the challenge of the night, slipping on Ninja feet across the squeaking floorboards and down the stairs to where she waited, gleaming silver across the silent lawn. Boots took time to lace in the silent nether world, and fear of being late gave wings to your feet as you pedalled across the town on your unlit BMX bike.

His braces gleamed across his teeth as you rode up. A cigarette glowed in his clawed hand.

'You're late.'

'Gimme a cigarette. Had to wait until they were really asleep, didn't I?'

'Mine don't give a bugger where I am.'

He walked his bike into the moonshadow of the rain trees that marked the boundary of God's acre, and you followed, putting your Kawahara alongside his where it could not be seen from the road.

Rows of monuments stood silently moonlit. Awed by the quiet majesty, you stood side by side, brothers in arms—two tiny soldiers against the quiet legions of the undisturbed dead. His fair hair hung over his eyes which you remembered as blue, eyes that now looked black against the painted stripes of camouflage. He flashed his gleaming braces at you in a last smile before heading into the forest of stone.

'Give me five minutes.'

You nodded, and watched him depart, running zigzagged into the labyrinth while you checked the reservoir of paint slugs in the pistol. The moon darkened, and you looked up, concerned to see the thickness of gathering clouds. Perhaps it would not be so bright a night, after all.

And now it is nearly time for you to begin the game.

A beacon shatters the darkness as the police patrol passes. You flatten yourself behind the tree, watching as the long spotlight probes through the tombstones. You are not seen, and the car hums away, but your heart thuds against your chest. The thick shirt is marked now, with the impression of leaves, some dirt, and the cloying perspiration that breaks out as the patrol car leaves. It is time to leave. Time to hunt.

Carefully now, you slide forward, and to the right. He could have doubled back, ready to ambush within the first few rows. You feel the slightest hint of fear, but are not really scared of graveyards, tombstones, or the rising dead. At thirteen, you are a man, a warrior, unafraid of the dark, or of phantoms, spectres, vampires. Nobody believes in them any more, least of all you, the fearless, the brave.

The gravestones lie neatly, row upon white-washed row, among paths cleaned and worked over carefully by the council. Only the Old Section lies in ruins, overrun with grass and trees, not touched or cleared because of a long court battle by environmentalists to save 'Our Heritage'.

Carefully scouring row after row, methodically checking each line of stones, you reach the conclusion that he is in that Old Section—possibly waiting on the branch of a native tree for you to pass below, and even now watching and grinning as you come closer and closer to his shady redoubt. He always was a cunning little bastard. Like the time he wet the classroom chalk, then froze it. It all fell to pieces in the teacher's hand. Or the time he raided the drink-dispenser at the local garage with a rubber tube and a can-opener.

You know he's a good enemy—your best mate. He'll be careful, real careful, and when you're right in his sight he'll jump you from behind with a blood-curdling scream and a 'SPLAT' that tells you you've lost the game, and then you'll both roll in mock combat on the grass until, winded, you both lie there, and your lungs will pump hot air, until he says it's your turn to be hunted.

You roll quietly across the dividing strip of earth into the no-man's-land of long grass and trees. Looking up, you see no silhouettes against the sky, so you edge to your crouch and survey the dim forest of native trees ahead. Scattered here and there are dipping tombstones, old iron fences, and grave-markers. To one end is the blocky shape of Morgan's Crypt; last resting place of a succession of bearers of that name, with sufficient money for a fashionable form of burial in the last century. But who remembers grocers when they have transpired their earthly shifts? Little now remains but a heavy stone door repaired at council expense after some drunken high-jinx several years ago, and four stone walls, topped by a concrete slab.

You edge forward, gun at the ready, head low, looking high into the trees. A low branch crosses your gaze, and you see a chance to climb. Silently, and with great care, you lift yourself above the ground, higher and higher, until you reach eye-level with the roof. The top of the crypt is covered with leaves. Slits below the roofline admit air and some light, but not enough to penetrate the interior blackness. The door, normally closed, yawns open.

He must be inside.

A quick circle of the crypt from a distance reveals no waiting ambush. It would be so like him to wait for you to enter, and then to slam the door on you from outside, but you are wise to that trick.

A small puff of smoke curls from one of the slits, covering a smokers' cough. You grin. He'll be waiting within, puffing away at a cigarette, and when you appear, he'll ask what took you so long.

In the darkness, you gather your paintgun for the final assault. Sneaking up behind the heavy door, you are ready to pounce. Already, you can imagine the splat of the paintball against your shirt as he sits waiting for you. You ready yourself.

You leap!

He is waiting for you, spread-eagled against the back wall, arms held high, feet spread out, ready to leap at you as you fire first.

SPLAT!

'Got you!'

He coughs painfully and you look closely at him, moving forward towards your friend in the light from the door.

Iron spikes have been hammered through his hands and feet, nailing him cruciform to the wall. He is still alive, because, although another spike has been rammed through his mouth, pinning his head back so that his shining braces gleam above the obscenity, he whimpers and his eyes plead for mercy, bulging outwards in the same terror that you feel as you turn, just in time to see the great stone door slamming shut behind you.

For a few moments, you can only see the glow of the cigarette which lies on the floor. Then, as your eyes get used to the darkness, the slits near the ceiling admit enough light to reveal me to you.

I stand, five spikes in one hand, hammer in the other, waiting to place you beside your friend.

While he cannot scream, you can, and do.

OUT OF THE STORM
by Rick Kennett

The destroyer found her in the middle of the Indian Ocean, drifting bows down from out of a storm that had killed three other ships. Binoculars trained on her from the warship's bridge confirmed that she was *HMAS Barrinji*, a minesweeper-corvette missing for nearly a week. The destroyer sounded her siren and fired a blank shot.

No response. *Barrinji*, silent, dead, rolled to the troughs and crests, her bows lifting sluggishly, dipping deep. The ropes from the empty lifeboat davits trailed in the water. The canvas flap of the door to her bridge slapped against the woodwork.

With her guns swinging through their arcs, the destroyer circled, then came abeam. Those on the bridge and lining her decks saw the ugly black gash behind the four-inch gun on the foredeck of the little ship. Grapples were thrown, clanking, catching, and *Barrinji* was boarded.

The first man to hit her deck clambered down, forward to where the bomb or shell had struck behind the gun. What remained of the gun's crew was already black and drying, draped over the splinters of the deck and merging into the blast mark across the front of the bridge super-structure. At the bottom of the hole, not far below, oily water oozed around twists of jagged metal; and in odd, quiet moments something down there made soft bumping noises.

170

The others who boarded climbed upward to the tilted quarterdeck or down deep into the engine-room and boiler room; over hatch coamings and into echoing steel alleyways, finding no one. The wireless office, crew's space, lobbies, lockers, messes, wash-places, small-arms magazine, officers' quarters were all deserted.

The hatch leading to the bo'sun's store was shut and dogged watertight. The leader of the boarding party, Lieutenant Dixson, stood beside it. He said, 'What's it sound like?'

The seamen had already pressed their ears against the steel, hearing only their own breathing. Someone thought there was a faraway tap-tap behind the silent hatch. But none of this was said to Lieutenant Dixson, whose beard and close-set eyes seemed to fix his expression with a permanent 'What did you call me!' look, regardless of the occasion.

A Leading Seaman spoke cautiously, 'Sounds dry behind it, sir.' He stood aside.

Dixson bent to the hatch and listened. 'What about the seams and rivets in this bulkhead?'

'Dry, sir. Bone-dry.'

'Hmmm.' He could hear nothing that sounded like sea sloshing around in there, though there was perhaps a rhythmic tap-tap somewhere in a muffled distance. 'Everybody get back to the last compartment and close the hatch behind you.'

Being neither heroes nor fools, the seamen did as they were told. Dixson, as the officer in charge of the boarding party, eased off the hatch's bottom dog-iron. He gripped the locking-wheel central of the hatch and jerked it counter-clockwise, then kicked against the steel just above the coaming. No sudden wetness glistened on the bottom edge so he eased off the remaining dog-iron and inched the hatch open.

An electric voice crackled across the water. 'What's it look like, Number One?'

Lacking a loud-hailer to reply, Lieutenant Dixson had to shout through cupped hands to his Captain as the destroyer steamed slowly down *Barrinji*'s port side. 'Complete derelict, sir! Boilers stone-cold! Engineer says about eight hours for a head of steam! All dry aft of the gyro compass room bulkhead! It's buckled and been shored up pretty rough! I'm having it redone!' He hesitated, glancing at the front of the bridge superstructure. 'A steam-hose would be appreciated, sir!'

'Understandable.' The figure holding the microphone on the destroyer's bridge nodded, turned and spoke to others. The warship's engine-room telegraphs clanged flat notes on the still sea air and she slipped away from *Barrinji* at increased speed, to circle with the asdic pinging the depths. It was unhealthy not to keep moving in these waters.

Dixson watched her glide away, all too aware of being a sitting duck. Except for the four-inch gun which was smashed and rendered useless, *Barrinji*'s only weapon was a 40mm Bofors anti-aircraft gun on the boat deck aft. That and two 20mm machine-guns mounted one either bridge-wing. The four-inch, he decided, could be . . .

He jerked about, startled by a sudden hollow hammering inside the dead ship. He relaxed. It was the damage control party reshoring the gyro compass room bulkhead. He turned his attention back to the four-inch gun sitting askew and jammed on its mounting, its breach-block shattered by the same blast that had shattered its gunners. It would have to be cut up and ditched, which would help bring up her bows. They'd need that extra freeboard if *Barrinji* was to be steamed back. He tried not admitting it to himself, but he was unhappy with the knowledge that if they did get her underway he would have to captain her. He'd often dreamt of a command of his own, but this was a nightmare he'd not counted on. Down below the hammering abruptly stopped.

For a second Dixson thought the hatch had given way. He recognized the thought to be an actual wish. But there was no crash, no shouts, no gush of in-rushing sea. A moment more and the hammering started again. He looked out over the near-sunken bows. Luck was with them. The sea was calming.

For what it was worth, someone said a prayer before the steam-hose was turned on.

The job was done hastily without further ceremony, the Captain not wanting his destroyer delayed with a hose-pipe draped over the side for any longer than necessary. Neither radar nor asdic were returning echoes, but the sea was now unusually flat and the sky clear. They were the perfect targets.

In the Captain's Cabin aboard *Barrinji*, Lieutenant Dixson sat himself down at the desk. In front of him lay a framed photograph face-down. He picked it up. It showed two naval men dressed in tropical kit, short-sleeved shirts and shorts. One was a Lieutenant-Commander of average height and build, who looked about forty, despite his boyish curly hair. The other man was younger, a Lieutenant, rather lanky with a thin face and fair, receding hair.

With a shock Dixson realized he knew this man, had trained with him at a shore-station before the war. But he could not remember the man's name. Nevertheless, the black and white photograph was a horrible coincidence. He dropped the photo back face-down, wishing he'd never picked it up.

He turned his attention to the boarding party's reports. There were fuel-oil estimates, fresh water reserves, provisions, ammunition, then there were the general reports about the condition of the ship as found: boiler room safety-valve wide open; primer-pins pulled from the depth-charges on the quarterdeck (an Abandon Ship procedure so they don't explode as the ship goes under); all life-jackets gone; sextant and log-book gone; code and recognition signal books gone, probably dumped (another Abandon Ship procedure). In fact, everything pointed to the orderly evacuation of a sinking ship.

But then *Barrinji* didn't sink.

Someone had noticed that both anchors were missing, and with them fathoms of chain, tons of weight which, Dixson told himself, might partly explain *Barrinji*'s miraculous survival. But without engine-power and a hand on her helm, he knew the little corvette should've broached to on the first storm wave and been rolled under. Strange.

There was a knock on the cabin door.

'Come,' said Dixson; he was expecting the Engineer with a report on the pumps. No one entered. 'Yes, come in.'

Nothing happened.

'Damnation!' Dixson stepped to the door and wrenched it open.

In the lobby outside stood the lanky, thin-faced man from the photograph. The figure was shrouded in black, a cloak of darkness that made the thin bloodless face seem to glow. The apparition wavered to and fro like tossing flotsam. Then it suddenly swelled toward Dixson, bringing with it a cold dampness, until its face was pressed close into his.

'*Leave!*'

Dixson stumbled back, hit the chair and fell. He was on his feet again in an instant, but there was nothing now in the doorway. Feeling strange and shaky he peered into the lobby. It was empty.

He ran up the companion-way to the bridge and looked wildly left and right.

'Who came through just then?'

The seaman sweeping up smashed glass and the quartermaster tending the wheel fixed the officer with stares of surprise.

'Beg your pardon, sir?'

'Don't come the innocent with me, Tyler!' Dixson snapped, slightly shrill. 'I'll have you on report!'

'Sir, no one's been through that door,' said the man with the broom. 'Not since yourself, sir, five minutes ago.'

The Lieutenant glared at one man and then the other as

if daring either to make the slightest conspiratorial twitch. 'Mind your helm, Tyler!' He banged the door shut.

The Captain's Cabin was still empty when he returned. Nothing waiting, wavering, dark. But the lobby, an enclosed space between cabins, was cold and smelt unnaturally damp.

The circling destroyer had given those aboard *Barrinji* a sense of security, something they needed as the afternoon brought more blue skies and flat seas. The weather had made them nervous, and noticeably the most nervous was Lieutenant Dixson who had suddenly developed the habit of glancing over his shoulder at nothing at all.

Except for some pumping which had had no effect on the ship's bows-down attitude, work was proceeding well. The anchor chain winch had been unbolted and was about to be manhandled over the side. Oxy-cutting gear had been ferried over by motorboat and the demolition of the smashed four-inch was well advanced. A tarpaulin had been stretched over the punched-in deck.

'Steam pressure's building satisfactorily,' said the Engineer above the hiss of the cutting torch. He paused a moment, wiping his hands down his overalls before adding, 'Got the dynamo running now; there's power in the ship.'

Lieutenant Dixson acknowledged this with a stiff nod. 'How's that bulkhead? Will it take the strain once we get underway?'

'It should if you don't take it too quick; four or five knots should be all right. There's no leaks, and the new shoring's holding up. But there's something knocking against that bulkhead, just every now and then a series of taps in the flooded compartments.'

'What do you think it is?'

'I wouldn't like to say.'

'Neither would I,' Dixson replied. He glanced behind him. Nothing was there. 'Bloody strange this ship, don't you think? The way she survived that storm with this sort of damage and no crew; the way everything points to the abandonment of a sinking ship. And then the ship doesn't sink. Bloody strange.'

'I wouldn't have expected a ship damaged like this to survive that storm, no.' The Engineer had wondered about that, of course, though right now he was wondering why the First Lieutenant was talking as if accusing the ship of something like deception. 'Just lucky, I suppose.'

Lucky, said Dixson to himself. Then, to the Engineer, 'As soon as they're finished with the anchor winch, detail a couple of hands to dump those depth-charges. Without their primer-pins they're just so much amatol waiting on the quarterdeck for the first stray bullet. We won't be lucky forever.'

At that moment the winch went over the side with a mighty splash and a cheer. The bows came up, though not by much. Half an hour later they came up more in a series of little jerks as the four-inch gun went over in four or five large slag-edged pieces. This also put the rudder and screws deeper into the water, at the same time bringing into view a jagged hole blown out on the port bow. Some oil oozed, some flotsam drifted out. They waited and watched, but nothing more emerged.

Only later, when there was steam pressure and the Engineer had intoned the formula, 'Ready to proceed, sir,' did anyone notice the ship's clocks. On the bridge, in the officers' quarters and Captain's Cabin, in the engine-room, boiler room and wardroom, all these eight-day pieces had stopped at precisely six minutes past six, and no amount of winding, tinkering or swearing would make them work.

At sunset *Barrinji* turned to the south-east to begin a five-knot waddle to Geraldton, a small port on the West Australian coast and at three hundred miles the closest harbour. Three to four days were estimated for the voyage, weather permitting. And if things got too rough there was always the destroyer's motorboat slung in *Barrinji*'s port-side davits.

'Bitch to steer,' said Quartermaster Tyler, struggling with the wheel. The comment was uncalled for, despite its truth, though Lieutenant Dixson said nothing. He stepped out onto the port bridge-wing to watch the destroyer, cut black against the afterglow, racing into the west on her search for *Barrinji*'s crew.

Night closed in over the little ship as she plodded on with only the brilliance of the stars to light her way and magnetic compasses to guide her. The wind keening through the empty window frames sounded like lost voices or a woman's crying, but hardly ever like the wind. It blew cold against the men at the engine-room telegraphs, the quartermaster wrestling the wheel, and the young signal-man standing at the back of the bridge in the dark.

Just before the ten o'clock change of watch, Dixson went out again onto the bridge-wing where the wind was coming from the sea and sounded that way. The foredeck below was a large triangle of shadow, flat save for where wind rippled the tarpaulin. All he could see of the bows was white water nudging waves aside. He looked astern, past the single squat funnel, past their motorboat in the davits, past the mine-sweeping derricks on the quarter-deck to the wake.

At five knots *Barrinji* was hardly churning up the water, making the wake hard to see, making it difficult to determine any dog-legging. What he could see of the wake seemed straight enough, yet the more he looked the more he thought there was some indefinite shape trailing in the wake . . .

'Callaghan!'

The young signal-man came scuttling up out of the dark. 'Sir?'

'Lay aft. See if we're dragging something astern.'

'Aye, aye, sir.' The youth slid down the ladder to the main deck.

Dixson ducked back onto the bridge. 'What's the helm feel like, Tyler?'

'Nothing different, sir,' said the quartermaster. 'Heavy handling, but that's nothing unusual.'

Dixson grunted, stepped to the opposite bridge-wing and looked aft. He thought he saw Callaghan at the stern rails, standing beneath the derrick booms which were crossed over each other like the resting hands of the dead. But it was hard to tell what was what among the paravanes, derricks, cables and winches. Besides, it was dark. And was that thing still in the wake? It was hard to tell.

'Callaghan!'

No one answered, nothing moved on the quarterdeck. Then he thought he saw a face briefly around the funnel. One of those manning the Bofors gun? He wasn't sure. He wondered about the face, and wondered why he wasn't certain who it'd been. But who else could it have been? And where the hell was Callaghan?

'Callaghan!'

Again nothing happened.

Dixson put his head around the bridge flap. 'Stop both . . . no, belay that!' He turned again as the bridge ladder rattled. Young Callaghan came up slowly, hesitant, looking confused which is what made Dixson hold back from upbraiding him. Instead he asked with a sense of foreboding, 'What did you see?'

Callaghan shuffled his feet and was unable to meet the officer's eyes as he said, 'There's, there's nothing back there, sir.'

Dixson peered aft. The water did appear empty now. Yet he was sure he'd glimpsed something. 'All right. Get to the galley and fetch us up some cocoa.'

Dixson watched Callaghan descend the ladder again, not so sprightly this time. Another long look aft showed nothing. He shrugged and wondered why Callaghan had lied.

Fifteen minutes before sunrise *Barrinji* went to Dawn Action Stations. Her three guns swung through their arcs, waiting. But the sun came up in a clear sky over a smooth sea to show an unbroken horizon.

The ship's clocks took no notice of time as watch followed watch throughout the day. It was six minutes past six aboard *Barrinji*. A story circulated that somebody had altered one of the clocks. Yet later it was found still showing six past six . . .

Late that afternoon a seaplane droned out of the north on an apparent interception course. Long-barrel binoculars were raised to see the red ball insignia on the wings and fuselage. The plane came on at a steady speed, too high for their guns, closing until even those without binoculars could see the pontoons beneath its wings. A seaplane this far out could only mean a cruiser somewhere close by; 10,000 tons of brutal steel which might come prowling over the horizon at any moment.

'Stop both!' ordered Dixson.

The engine-room telegraphs rang. *Barrinji* lost way and stopped, small and quiet, showing no wake now. The plane's shadow flickered over the ship.

'He must be blind,' someone whispered on the bridge.

But the plane droned over them, and five minutes later was a fading speck in the south.

'I'm taking out a ticket in Tatts when we get back,' said one of the telegraph-men and, on orders from the Lieutenant, pushed his lever forward again to SLOW AHEAD.

Dixson sat down on the Captain's stool at the back of the bridge as the wind picked up through the windows.

Just lucky, I suppose, he recalled the Engineer's words of the previous day. *A strange sort of luck*, he went on thinking, *to survive a storm and lose a crew*. He couldn't help but think the word *unnatural* better described *Barrinji*'s luck, and wondered what exactly he meant by it. Thoughts linked to thoughts, leading his mind unwillingly back to that wavering dark thing in the lobby. *Leave*. He'd been unable to deny to himself the reality of it the way he wished he could; at the same time he was unable to comprehend its reality. *Leave*. Why leave? *Barrinji* had proved a lucky ship so far for himself and his men, if not for her original crew.

'Lucky,' he said softly.

'Beg your pardon, sir?'

Dixson almost jumped. But it was only Chief Bosun's Mate Frood (the Buffer) standing beside him in the gathering shadows, doing his job as an ad hoc officer for this particular watch.

'Lucky,' repeated Dixson.

'About the plane, yes, sir.'

'About everything, Buffer. The plane, the calm seas, lack of enemy attention, the way she survived that storm damaged like she is and with no crew.'

'Yes, sir. Lucky.'

Dixson was about to ask him if he didn't think it an unnatural sort of luck, then decided not to. It would've been an odd question, especially coming from an officer. Besides, he wasn't really sure what it was he was getting at. So he said, 'Get the chart and I'll check our course. Looks like we're in for another starry night.'

After sunset Lieutenant Dixson took his sextant sightings on the starry sky he'd predicted, locating *Barrinji*'s position. Leaving the Buffer in charge, he retired to the asdic cabinet to sleep the few hours until his watch at ten.

The asdic cabinet, normally the noisy heart of anti-submarine activity, was a quiet, still cubby-hole at the back of the bridge. The asdic-set itself sat screwed to the bulkhead, its valve innards shock-smashed and useless, its earphones hanging mute on a hook. The oscillating quartz crystal (the actual *ping* machinery) also lay dead, drowned in the flooded forward compartments.

Dixson sat in the operator's chair and slept.

Sometime later he half-woke to the distant voices of a man and a woman; fighting voices, thin telephone voices with no distinct words but full of blame, anger and fear. The woman sounded iron-hard, and the man dangerously close to violence. As Dixson opened his eyes the voices faded away, and in fading sped up like an old gramophone wound too tight for too long. To Dixson the silence seemed worse than the voices because it was the silence of a dead ship creeping across the ocean when she should be in her grave three miles down.

It was his bizarre fancy, combined with hope, that the past few seconds with their inexplicable sounds had been a dream. Just a dream. For a moment he thought the ship *was* dead, at the bottom of the sea, and that this thing carrying him back to safety and land was a ghost, the last mad wish of dead men in two storm-lost boats.

He banged his feet down on the deck. He was satisfied. *Barrinji* was no ghost. She was real, iron-real, iron-hard under his feet. Yet with his acceptance of the reality of the ship came the whispering memory of a dark-shrouded thing. It was a memory, he knew, that would be with him always. *It* would slip out in the quiet moments or in his sleep to push up against his face and whisper *Leave*. He wished he could leave.

'First Lieutenant, sir. Twenty-two hundred, sir,' said a voice in the cabinet doorway.

'Very good, Buffer. Thank you.'

Through the broken windows of the bridge the stars shone bright and sharp. The sea was flat like a table-top.

No enemy shouldered over the horizon in the night, nor during the next day. As though the war was somebody else's problem a million miles away, *Barrinji* steamed along at her five-knot waddle, and the fine weather continued.

'What did you really see back there?' Lieutenant Dixson asked young Callaghan in the quiet of the bridge-wing.

The signal-man blushed. He was not a liar, not really, and Dixson knew it. 'I saw boats,' he answered simply.

Dixson let it go at that.

During the mid-watch on the following day, with the Buffer on the bridge, Dixson climbed down to inspect the bulkhead of the gyro compass room again. The wooden shoring braced and wedged against the buckled plating was still holding and all seams were dry. Nevertheless, the bo'sun's store hatch had been secured behind him. The Engineer had told him that the simple sit-down job of listening outside the bosun's store was unpopular with the men. Dixson didn't have to ask why. He knew.

He knew as he stood in that last dry forward compartment and listened alone to the oddly timed tap-tap inside the flooded spaces. He knew as he returned to the bo'sun's store hatch, the rhythm still with him. He knew as he stepped over the coaming and glanced back over his shoulder before slamming the hatch back into place. And in the crow's nest far above, the look-out rang down to the bridge saying, 'Masts, dead astern!'

The Action Alarm had been ringing several seconds when Dixson hit the upper deck. Men were running, shrugging on life-jackets, tying the chin-straps of tin hats. The barrel of the Bofors angled upward. The bridge-wing machine-guns were cocked and readied. Sailors took up sheltered positions with Tommy guns in their sweaty hands.

Above the ringing of the alarm bell, somebody shouted from the boat deck, 'Ship coming up astern, sir!'

Dixson spared only a quick look behind him, glimpsing the smoke smudge of something far away coming up at a fast rate of knots. He spun and made for the bridge, thinking how bloody silly they all looked with what was approaching. And how brave.

As he hit the rungs of the ladder he yelled, 'Shut that bloody bell up!' with a nervous vehemence that surprised him. The alarm cut off as the Buffer pushed binoculars into his hands.

'Looks like a destroyer, sir.'

Even as he focused, Dixson was weighing up the chances of it being Japanese. Too near the coast, too far south. Viewed bows on, it was smoke and bow wave and precious little definite in between.

Signal-man Callaghan had the only other pair of binoculars on the bridge. He said, reading a stuttering light from the distant vessel, 'Message from the Captain, sir: "Don't shoot! Don't shoot! It's us!"' He lowered the glasses and with an inexcusable breach of discipline began to laugh aloud.

Nothing had been found of *Barrinji*'s crew or boats after a thirty-six hour search in screeching winds and crazy cross seas. 'Damn queer!' said the Captain when Dixson told him of their continuing miracle of good weather. 'We were battling heavy seas all the way back. Only struck calm water again half an hour before we sighted you.'

They made port the next day.

When *Barrinji* was dry-docked and pumped out, a body was exhumed from the forward compartments. Lieutenant Dixson was not surprised to hear that it was the body of his lanky, thin-faced acquaintance from training. He didn't ask if it'd been found grasping a hammer. He didn't want to know.

In fact, he didn't want to know anything more about *Barrinji*. Yet it was as if the ugly little ship held some horrible fascination for him, because he soon found himself following her fortunes; sometimes through official reports and signals, sometimes through ward-room talk with visiting officers from other ships. From these sources Dixson pieced together a picture of a vessel possessed of extraordinary luck and regarded with a vague uneasiness by all who served in her.

There was the story of the submarine torpedo which ran beneath *Barrinji* and hit the coastal freighter she'd been escorting.

There was the story of the crewman who was constantly taking photographs of *Barrinji*'s wake.

There was the story of the refitting dock gang who refused to work aboard *Barrinji* after dark.

There was the story of the native islanders who, when *Barrinji* anchored in their bay, were reluctant to paddle

out to sell their fresh fruit the way they did with other
visiting warships.

'She sings and weeps much sad,' they said.

Despite the odds and hazards, *Barrinji* steamed
through the war, convoying, sweeping, patrolling in some
of the most dangerous forward areas, always returning
untouched by the enemy while others around her died.

On a cold, rainy day in 1961, Captain Dixson, now retired, saw *Barrinji* for the last time. She was partly
dismantled and tethered to a buoy in a harbour backwater,
waiting to be towed to the breaker's yard. Dixson stood on
the shore beneath the trees and looked at her for a long
time.

Her mast was gone, as was the searchlight platform, the
anti-aircraft guns, the depth-charge throwers, the clutter
of gear on the quarterdeck. Many of the bridge windows
were broken, causing him to wonder what her interior
looked like now.

Who were those men assembling on her foredeck? Some
of them, half-naked, looked like seamen and some of them
wore officers' caps and all of them were transparent.

In front of them, by the cable winch, stood the lanky,
thin-faced Lieutenant dressed in tropical kit. He was glaring forward, with his hands clenched to fists at his sides.

The rain increased for a moment, misting the ship from
view. When he could see her again, Dixson looked towards the bows.

The woman was ugly. Very ugly. A hag with scraggy,
stringy hair, hands like vulture claws, a face in profile
which made Dixson glad he could not see it at close quarters. Her single grey covering was ragged and spotted with
red. She stood at the very stem, braced against the jack-
staff, staring back at the men like a cornered animal. And
though Dixson could hear nothing except the beat of
the rain in the water, he could see she was screaming.
Screaming like the damned.

TWIST OF THE KNIFE
by Sean Williams

The city of Burkin, South-West Victoria, is a very ordinary place. Founded one hundred and seventy-five years ago, it boasts a thriving agricultural sector, a budding metal refinery, and a somewhat self-deluded 'tourist potential' that amounts to little more than a war memorial, some court chambers, and a handful of old bones. The only thing that separates it from its neighbours is a short stretch of sealed road and a football team.

But, as we all know, scratch a small city and you reveal a slithering snake's nest of emotion. In some towns it might be racism, in others it might be anger, hatred or lust. In Burkin (population 20,500 and falling), it is fear.

The people of Burkin are deeply rooted in the country life. Football and rainfall are more important than the national trade deficit, and everyone from Melbourne is a rude bastard.

But they're all as guilty as I am, behind their friendly smiles.

Despite curfews and paranoia, the population of Burkin cowers under the shadow of fear. Every huddled household is filled with morbid anticipation. I hold this town so tightly in my blood-slicked grasp that its inhabitants have come to expect the carnage to continue, at the mercy of a primal urge they can't understand.

They call this urge a 'hunger for justice'.

In our supposedly civilised world it takes nothing more than one violent death to bring out the worst in us. They'd just love to see me dangling from a tree with my hands behind my back and my teeth knocked out. They could all have a stab at some flesh then, without fear of me striking back; they could experience the power and joy of a violent psychopath without fear of punishment.

But I steadfastly refuse to be caught, simply to assuage their thirst for blood, and it is my denial that causes them pain, not the crimes I commit. As though they have turned their backs upon a cruel god of sacrifice, a god whose patronage they nonetheless desire, they have come to long for, yearn for, *lust* for death.

The killer will not turn himself in? Very well. In that case they say, without knowing that they're saying it, some vulgar slut will do instead. We don't really care who dies, deep down, as long as it's bloody. As long as it's not *me*.

And as long as the killings continue.

Seventeen deaths are not many when placed in perspective. The highways claim hundreds every year, and cancer thousands more. For every one that has been killed in Burkin, a score has met with murder elsewhere. What are seventeen deaths in a world wracked by continuous war?

But these are not your everyday deaths.

Detective James McLoughlin, local chief of police, makes a fine figure as he struts around the Council Chambers and streets, promising to catch the heinous maniac and bring him to justice. 'Soon,' he says. 'He'll be caught soon.' How soon, Detective McLoughlin? You've been looking for fifteen years, and you appear to be coming no closer.

Of course, one can understand his vehemence and his determination to stay on the job, if not his appalling lack of success. After all, his beloved daughter Stephanie, an only child, was the first to be killed, strung upside-down like a side of beef and undone with a razor. How well I remember, James McLoughlin, your outrage and grief at the sight of her precious, savaged face, and how Burkin supported you through your troubled times, your terrible tragedy. How I laughed at your tears, your sorrow, your hypocrisy.

We all knew she was fucking that little sleaze from the other side of town, with his fast car and long hair. She was sixteen and hot; the slut had learned how to screw, and you were glad to see her dead, weren't you? Let's be honest here: *you were glad to see her dead*! Perhaps you would have killed her yourself, if you'd had the guts to do it.

Ah, yes, I remember it well. Could it really have been only fifteen years ago, when Stephanie died and your wife hanged herself? How things have changed since then.

Somewhere in Queensland, a young fellow by the name of A. Willis-Thompson is stalking an old man. He doesn't know yet that he's stalking an old man. Neither does he know that this old man will lead him to a much younger fellow, who will in turn lead him to a policeman, who will direct him back to Burkin, where it all started. This A. Willis-Thompson is hot on the trail of the killer he seeks, and getting closer every second.

The poor, deluded boy.

Willis, as he is known, is eager and foolish and good-looking. He has that certain air of innocence that marks him as a hero; a whole cluster of childish traits that he never really outgrew has left him of the opinion that anything can be mastered, that nothing is insuperable or unsolvable or beyond him. He sincerely believes that he can catch the psychopath on his own, even though he has no experience in such things. He is not a policeman, nor a martial arts expert with a score to settle. He is just a thirty-year-old boy with delusions of being a private investigator.

But he is, I might add, quite likely to succeed, despite this almost suicidal bent that sends him across Australia and down the east coast, across three states and back into my waiting arms. One can only wonder if he has some secret plan with which he intends to thwart me. Does he know something I do not?

No. Young Willis has secrets, yes, but no plans. Even the innocence he so carefully radiates is a lie. Any knowledge he really has, he keeps close to his chest.

The good Detective, on the other hand, knows that Willis is almost as obsessed with the killings as himself. In fact, apart from the killer, Willis is probably the most obsessed in all of Burkin. Having lived with the endless murders for half his life, the young PI finds in tragedy a *raison d'être*, as have many others before him. Seventeen families employ him to do the work that the police patently 'aren't doing'—catching the fiend—and nobody seems deterred by the fact that Willis also has had no luck. Here is an ally with a familiar face, they say, not some blue-uniformed fool stinking of exhaust fumes and city life.

That Detective McLoughlin himself employs young Willis says something, doesn't it? When McLoughlin learned of this new development, the first thing he did was tell Willis, as though he, too, had lost faith in the long arm of the Law. Perhaps he remembered the death of his daughter, Stephanie, and the Police Procedure that prevented him from pursuing the case. Perhaps he hoped that the killer would be brought to justice by less official means.

For whatever reason, dear Detective, you simply had to inform young Willis of the clue, didn't you? You had to show him the magazine. You had to let him read 'The Hand'.

Did you know that you were killing him in the process?

The old man stinks. His ancient suit, which he wears despite the tropical heat, has faded to the colour of shit, and his skin is puffy with sweat. He goes to a post office and despatches a small envelope to Burkin, Victoria. The elderly woman behind the counter (bribed, of course) tips young Willis a wink.

Aha, says our intrepid investigator to himself. This is my man.

Willis follows the old fellow through streets that reek of greenery and fecundity. His drab, casual apparel, which normally allows him to vanish into a crowd, stands out amongst the bright colours of summer. The tropics are too fertile for him; he requires somewhere far colder and more sterile in which to thrive. Victoria suits him admirably, whereas Queensland appals him. The old man appals him more, but still he follows.

Upon reaching the house, Willis forces his way in. The room is hellishly hot, a state maintained by no less than eight fan-heaters and one open fire. All the windows are painted black. The old man's sweaty bed is tucked into one corner: a disgruntled mattress strangled by stained sheets, reeking of masturbation and drunkenness. A pile of old bottles and crumpled cigarette packets is a shrine to human mortality.

The old man screams like a feeble pig, cowers against a wall with one arm over his eyes.

'Who wrote "The Hand"?' asks Willis. This is the information he has come so far to claim.

The old man squeals again. He feebly protests that he doesn't know 'nothing about nothing'.

'Then who sent you this?' Willis waves a copy of the magazine in question, a poorly typed tome of gutter horror, steeped in blood and sexual misconduct. He appears for a moment like an enraged Jehovah's Witness. 'And who tells you where to post them?'

The old man wriggles further into the wall, as though digging his way free. When he doesn't respond immediately, Willis grasps the man by the arm and shakes him, ignoring the foul stench this action arouses.

Still the old fellow delays replying, and Willis is forced to use violence. He strikes this most reprehensible character across the face with a clenched fist, a small act when compared to those of the one he is chasing, but startlingly vicious. The old man talks at last, his yellow teeth and rotten tongue loosened by the blow.

'They come from down south,' gasps the old man. 'I

dunno who from.' When pressed for further detail, he provides an old envelope with a return address stamped on the back; a Post Office box number in Sydney.

Only partially satisfied, Willis attempts to elicit further information, but is unsuccessful. The old fellow (clearly no more than a middleman, less even than a courier) knows as little of the killer's identity and whereabouts as Willis. He can't even read.

But he has provided one small clue, a second link in the chain.

As Willis makes to leave the stinking, furnace-like hovel, the old man hints at bribery, payment for the information he has given. Willis, our self-righteous hero, looks down with disgust upon the beggar, and stalks southwards.

This is what I imagine has happened. I'm not there, of course; I'm home sharpening the cruel instruments of my secret trade. I base this account of our hero's adventure on a few facts, which I will relate as required.

The magazine (colourfully titled GUTS) is an illegal publication, unregistered and uncensored. It advertises only by word of mouth, and relies heavily upon the sensibility of its subscribers to ensure its continued existence. It further evades the authorities by a rather circuitous route, the last of which is the old man. He is sent individual envelopes by an unidentified man, the Editor, with the addresses already written on the envelopes; all the old man has to do is meet the postage and send them. For this act he is paid exorbitantly, and always in cash. With this money he buys booze and fags, and pays his power bill.

The Editor and founder of the magazine can afford such extravagant means to avoid pursuit because he charges thirty dollars, cash only, per copy of GUTS. This seemingly outrageous fee is readily accepted by the thousand-odd purchasers of the magazine on the basis of one single fact: the Editor swears that, despite the hideous nature of the tales related in his publication, every one of them is true. Some of the stories may be many years old, written by criminals in jail and smuggled out by corrupt guards, hence their apparent unfamiliarity to those well-acquainted with the lore of murderers and rapists, but their veracity (and voracity) is assured. The readers of such vile fiction (some would-be psychopaths themselves) happily regard this half-truth as gospel, and not only because they see similar crimes occurring around them every day. Where is the thrill, after all, in a crime that might not be real?

Now, I say 'half-truth' because I can only be certain that *some* of these stories are not works of fiction. These are, of course, the ones that I myself have written.

Just one of these was called 'The Hand'.

In 1988, I killed a young woman by the name of Sonia Peterson. She was my thirteenth victim. When her feeble pulse had spurted its last, I hacked off her right hand and inserted it into her vagina. This was not so easy a task to accomplish; the hole was too small and I was forced to use a knife to increase its dimensions. When they found her a week later, all that could be seen of her hand were her fingertips, as though someone had suffocated while trying to escape from inside her steaming cunt.

This gruesome detail the police never told the reporters. That was how Detective McLoughlin (and hence young Willis, who had access to the files) knew that I was the author of 'The Hand'. The story, which described my anatomical rearrangement with boastful precision, had obviously been written by either the killer or one of his accomplices. And the second possibility can be ruled out in light of the fact that I have no associates. Alone and unknown, as executioners should always be, I have no friends with whom I share my secret work.

Another detail; Sonia Peterson screamed like a pig before I killed her. So I cut out her tongue and stuck it in her backside.

There is justice in my work, you see, although few people would interpret it as such. When my victims are

male, I place their sexual organs within their own mouths.
Sex truly lies at the root of every crime, be it on the part of
the criminal or the victim, or both.

My distasteful signature more than adequately depicts
this, I think.

The Post Office box number leads Willis to a dismal
western suburb of Sydney. Its houses are temporary struc-
tures built from highly flammable materials, as though the
central planning authority might one day decide to send a
conflagration upon the region, thus ridding the city of
some of its most distressing pests: mice, cats and people;
the three most rapacious creatures on the face of our continent, apart from rabbits.

Here lives the Editor of the magazine, a disturbing
young fellow whose name remains unknown. I call him
'the Rapist' because he has that slimy, insidious nature
common to all of history's greatest seducers. In the letters
he sends, via the old man, he refers to me as 'his esteemed
colleague in violent crime'—an epithet I hate for two reasons: one, because it is blatantly sycophantic; two,
because it places me in his own league, and how I ever
came to deserve such a slight, I'll never know.

I can see young Willis arriving on his doorstep, having
traced the address of the owner of the Box from Australia
Post's 'confidential' records. I imagine him slightly more
comfortable in the New South Welsh environment, but
jittered by the hectic traffic and uncertain what manner of
monster he is about to confront.

The Rapist is cautious. He knows at once that Willis is a
cop of some kind. Those on opposite sides of the law can
sense each other, but usually most vividly from the wrong
side. A cop stands out like a white man in a crowd of
blacks; he (or she) might as well be in uniform, more often
than not.

So, before Willis even opens his mouth, the Rapist is
aware of the nature of the call. He breathes a sigh of relief
that he has no evidence in his home. To all intents and

purposes, he appears a young, well-dressed accountant, untarnished by any unsavoury crimes or misdemeanours, who just happens to live on the seedy side of town.

'This magazine,' he says when asked, 'I know nothing of it. You must have the wrong person.'

Willis protests. The Rapist is, after all, the owner of the Post Office Box, is he not?

'No, no. I cancelled it months ago. Let's see. I have the paperwork somewhere . . .'

Oh, he's a slippery fellow, the Rapist. Willis is outclassed; violence will not help him here, as it did with the old man in Queensland. He must use tact to uncover the crimes he knows the Rapist has committed, tact which, unfortunately for him, he does not possess.

Little does he know that, just days ago, the Rapist despatched to his beloved readers the latest consignment of filth. Edition number thirty-five, to be precise. In it was another of my stories, a real gem, I might add, without modesty.

Thirty-five issues, with roughly three months between each issue. That makes eight and three-quarter years, does it not? Almost nine years, say, of this disgusting bragging of murderers and thieves! It is remarkable indeed that the Rapist has not been incriminated before now; he must have friends in high places.

Increasingly dumbfounded, Willis probes for a way to crack the glistening armour of the Rapist, a lever to expose the next step along the path back to Burkin. His efforts, however, are doomed to failure. I warned the Rapist of Willis' imminent arrival, you see. We maniacs, like priests, stick together, even though we hate each other and long for each other's demise.

GUTS first provoked attention when one of the magazine's subscribers noticed the similarities between my story 'The Hand' and the death of Sonia Peterson. To the shame of the Victorian Police Force, this dutiful citizen with a taste for blood was himself an Officer of the Law.

Yes. The very men who are supposed to protect the likes of you from the likes of me are sometimes criminals themselves. Are you shocked to learn that one might buy such a publication as GUTS for his own gratification?

We're a sick bunch, we humans. There are psychopaths in history, too, glorified in victory as well as defeat.

So, when the Rapist suggests that Willis might recheck his source of information, our young innocent decides to do just that.

He calls the Detective from Sydney, tells him of the lack of progress made thus far. He is frustrated and down-hearted; the Rapist has rattled him thoroughly. McLoughlin gives him the address of GUTS' treacherous reader and Willis flies to Melbourne *tout suite*.

Meanwhile, the Rapist isn't idle. He will go into hiding. Or at least tone down the magazine for a few months, suspecting that he is under observation. He might even attempt to warn his most prolific contributor that the police are on his tail. Returning the favour, as it were.

But such things have not yet come to pass. I write these words four weeks before Willis even learns of GUTS and sets off on his mission. See how well-planned this trap is? I know in advance exactly what our hero will do and where he will go, and what I must do to lead him on his merry way.

This account of the last weeks of Willis' life is intended as the most arrogant of boasts. In later stories, perhaps, I will complete the story, satisfy your lust for the details of his death, but for now you must be content with the thrill of a chase that has not yet occurred.

I have a deadline to meet, you see.

When Willis first resolved to follow the trail of GUTS to Queensland, McLoughlin told him not to be so foolish. The police could handle it, he said, they were on the case. There was no need for him to get involved.

If so, then why did he show the young fool the magazine in the first place?

I repeat myself: did you know, dear Detective, that you were condemning the young fellow to certain death? Or did you believe that the killer might actually be captured? It was a foolish gamble, either way, but all the more exciting for that.

Willis fell for it regardless; hook, line and sinker. Our hero never even suspected that the Melbourne CIB wasn't involved in the case. The information regarding GUTS had indeed come from the unsavoury policeman, but he hadn't rung his superiors, as he should have. He rang the Senior Officer of Burkin instead, who decided to take matters into his own hands.

And Willis allowed Detective McLoughlin to send him off on a wild goose chase with the killer as the prize, exactly as I'd known he would.

Or, I should say, as I know he *will*:

'Don't tell anyone where you're going,' McLoughlin will caution his dutiful emissary. 'We can't trust anybody, these days.'

How right he is.

'Of course,' Willis will reply, shouldering the heavy burden.

'Be careful.' McLoughlin will rise and shake the young investigator's hand.

'I will.'

And so goes brave Parsifal into the wilderness, yet another foolish hero setting off in search of glory afar, only to find on his return that his home has been razed to the ground and his children slaughtered like cattle.

My only regret in this whole affair is that Willis is not married, and that he does not have a daughter.

To Melbourne, then, to meet the disgraced policeman, Sergeant Desmond Piper, who is the true villain of this piece. He is an overweight cop with a taste for racism, an exploiter of the weak and breaker of the laws he is paid to uphold. His position is not maintained by the respect of the community, nor by moral uprightness. He remains in existence by the virtue of two facts only: there are those in positions of power above him who tolerate his evil-doings, and he has a gun.

Willis finds his disgraceful comrade in an outer-suburban home. Piper has no family beyond the kennels he keeps in his backyard, where he breeds German shepherds for money. He has blood-shot piggy eyes and an irritating wheeze. His mouth is constantly moist, almost overflowing with saliva, as though he has a hunger he cannot satiate.

Piper regards the young man confronting him with disdain and just a hint of nervousness. Willis suspects that the man is waiting for an unwelcome caller.

'Who the hell are you?' Piper asks, holding the door half-open with one pink palm.

Willis is surprised to see Piper still in his uniform. Surely the man has been sacked for his obscene habits? Surely not even the Melbourne Police Force could tolerate such a scandal?

'My name is Andrew Willis-Thompson,' he says, holding out his PI card.

Piper does not look at the card. He turns a sickly shade of yellow and tries to close the door. Willis' foot is in the way, however, and Piper retreats as our hero advances, his red eyes wide in astonishment.

'Willis?' he whispers, his voice thin and strangled. 'Your name is really *Willis*?'

The intrepid investigator hesitates. PI's provoke all sorts of reactions from people (paranoia, anger, and guilt being the three most common) but never horror, such as Willis now sees in Piper.

'Yes,' he replies. Caution slowly replaces puzzlement; he must be close indeed to have aroused such a response. He can almost smell his goal, now, under the stench of beer and dogs. 'How do you know I'm called that?'

But Piper doesn't answer. He turns tail and runs

through the house, faster than any fat man should be able to. Willis, caught by surprise, is left behind as the maniac hurtles out the back door, across the yard and over the rear fence, as though fleeing for his life.

And that, dear reader, is exactly what he's doing.

Betrayed by his own lust for vicarious excitement, Piper wanted to be involved in the murders, if not actually on the side of the psychopath, then at least on the side of the Law.

Such a foolish man. How he dreamed of death! How sad for him that he awoke from the dream the day that Willis knocked on the door, and found the nightmare staring him full in the face.

He betrayed me, and I'll come to get him in due course. Be sure of that. He can run all he likes, metaphorically, if not physically, but it will avail him nothing. I will always be behind him and ahead of him, for I am his death and I love a good chase.

Justice again, you see. I am nothing if not meticulous in choosing my victims. The girl who masturbates and the man who dreams of giving himself oral sex, the woman who steals from the corner shop and the boy who runs away from home; all are equal in my eyes, and under the knife.

I will get Desmond Piper in the end, and perhaps literally. His sins have been many, my friends, and the permutations of the flesh are endless.

Willis, ignorant of the escapee's inevitable doom, quickly considers his alternatives. He can pursue the fleeing Piper or he can search the house. He chooses the latter. He is a prudent fellow, and to chase a policeman through suburban Melbourne might be deemed a little inappropriate for a man on a secret mission.

Filled with a sense of impending success, he rummages through drawers and wardrobes, searching for the final clue. He has no knowledge of what form this clue might take, but he is intuitively certain that it lies somewhere in the house.

Eventually, in a small cupboard in the slovenly living-
room, Willis happens across Piper's cache of GUTS
back-issues. They are neatly filed away in chronological
order, and our hero flicks through them one by one.

The Gerard Simpson who wrote 'The Hand' is fictitious,
of course, but the name has been maintained for almost a
decade. Willis finds eight other such stories published
over the last five years, all of killings that actually took
place in Burkin. He doesn't bother to read them in detail—
but he notes that there is a tenth story in an early edition.
The details are completely unfamiliar. An unknown murder, perhaps?

This supposition is correct. I always hide the bodies of
my victims, but some more carefully than others. I know
of four that have not yet been discovered, and perhaps
may never be.

Trembling with excitement, Willis turns to the latest
edition, dated not two weeks earlier than his confrontation with Piper. This pristine tome, barely thumbed by its
owner, rests in pride of place at the furthest right of the
apparently endless row of spines. He skims through it, dis-
covers an eleventh story entitled 'Twist of the Knife' by the
imaginary Gerard Simpson, and, with ever-widening eyes,
begins to read;

'*The City of Burkin, South-West Victoria,*' it says, '*is a
very ordinary place . . .*'

You close the book. The house is still and quiet; you
imagine that you can hear your heart beating like a hammer falling. Can you hear the *snap* of the trap as it closes
upon you?

You know at last the identity of the killer, if you haven't
already guessed. It's staring at you in the face, in the words
of the story. My face leers out at you from the pages, as big
as life. You can almost smell the terrible stench of my
betrayal.

I am Judas and you are Pilate: the traitor and the judge.
But there are no Christs in this story, I'm afraid to say.

There are no Christs anywhere, in the real world. Just an infinity of Judases and Pilates, perpetually damned by their endless compromise and indecision, condemned to an eternity of guilt and shame.

Between the two of us, we cover our entire species. We are symbols, archetypes: the hunter and the hunted, the torturer and the tortured, the victim and the victor. But which, and this is the crucial question, is which?

Aye. There's the rub indeed.

You replace the magazine on its shelf and leave the house. Do you take the first flight back to Burkin, or do you need time to think? How far have I outguessed you, young Willis? Do you rush onwards into the gap, or do you plan the next step as carefully as you might prepare for a major operation?

If, for a moment, you suspect that I might be following you, then disregard this possibility. I am not lurking behind a tree with blades a-ready, waiting until your back is turned to administer the final twist of the knife. No.

I'm home. Waiting for the knock on my door that will signal your arrival. Waiting for you to come to me. And I know that you will. How could you not?

I do so anticipate our final confrontation, as much as I do ours, Desmond Piper.

We all have scores to settle.

I remember once I saw a young boy, twelve, actually, come across a dying rabbit. This was during the great plague of '75, before the murders, when the beasts were as common as blades of grass. This particular animal had been struck by a car, and lay half-conscious in a gutter by the side of a road. Its internal organs were, no doubt, badly damaged; it was surely on its last legs.

But was the boy content with this state of affairs? Oh no. Not remotely. He felt compelled to poke the rabbit with a stick and watch it writhe in agony. He had to torture the poor creature until the last, gasping breath had escaped its tiny mouth before he would feel satisfied.

First, he broke its legs, so it couldn't wriggle away; then he poked out the pink, innocent eyes and played with its blood, drawing obscene patterns on its fur with his finger; lastly, bored with such play, he rammed the blunt end of the stick down into the rabbit's abdomen, making it squirm for a second or two, as its skin burst and its last strength pulsed crimson onto his shoes.

You dragged the dead animal along the gutter for a while, didn't you, Willis? Leaving a trail of blood behind, like a finger through paint; smiling at the way its limp limbs dragged in the dust. A puppet that no longer held the power to fascinate, or to teach, the rabbit had become an inconsequential thing, an object for your puerile derision. Its purpose had been served; the lesson had been learnt.

When you came to a storm drain, you stuffed the body through the bars, and thus erased all evidence of your crime.

But, let's be serious now.

No more clues. No more games. Enough.

It is time for us to talk about Stephanie.

You're far too clever for your own good, my young Willis, for all that I might have portrayed you here as a well-meaning idiot. Perhaps you've known all along who I am, and have enjoyed watching me kill, kill, and kill again, laughing at my attempts to elicit a response. I have seen the way you look at me sometimes, with that all-too-clever glint in your eyes, and I swear that you're mocking me, about to spring some clever trap.

If so, then be done with it! I will suffer the uncertainty no longer. I *demand* a confrontation. Enough of this torturous dallying about the countryside, when there is butcher's work to be done.

Come home, my brother, come home and let me kill you, for I will never rest until you do.

I should have punished you years ago.

THE HUT
by Sheila Hatherley

Bleached paddocks stretched endlessly either side of the highway. To the east, about three kilometres distant, there was a dim smudge of trees. Nothing more. No sign of a house, not even a hint of human habitation.

'Are you sure this is right, mate? Looks like the middle of bloody nowhere to me!'

It must have looked that way to the truckie who'd given me a lift, but not to me. I knew exactly where I was.

'It's right, and thanks for the lift.' I jumped down and the truckie handed out my pack and sleeping-bag. A smile and a salute and the truck roared off, leaving me and my meagre possessions standing at the side of the road. Then I headed for that suggestion of trees on the horizon, my pulses racing. I was going back to the bush where I belonged.

I suppose I was on some kind of high, but it was a high that was all my own, and had nothing to do with drugs or booze. I felt I was a person again, a living, breathing person who had taken life by the throat and meant to shake some sense into it. I was no longer a statistic or a part of the faceless hordes labelled unemployed or disadvantaged. I'd find the old hut again and live off the land, and to hell with handouts, social security offices and all the other crap which had ruled my life for months past. Of course there'd been the odd moment or two when I'd wondered if coming back here wasn't just chasing a kid's dream, a boyhood fantasy. After all, it was years since I'd been in this part of the world, but after the last mind-bending months in the city I was willing to believe that a fantasy could become a working reality. I had nothing left to lose.

About two kilometres across country I met up with the old railway line. The last train had travelled this way when I was a five-year-old kid. Now the tracks were so overgrown with weeds that I almost missed it. It was like unexpectedly meeting an old friend. I pressed on. Across the line, over another paddock and I soon plunged into the swamp. It had changed, too, but that didn't surprise me. Each year, unless there was a drought, floods came through this way from a loop in the river. They left behind an alien place which had to be relearned by animals and humans alike. Trees were swept away, little islands disappeared and new ones were born. In spite of the changes around me, I had a gut feeling that the old hut would still be there. It had withstood years of floods and, like the swamp, had gone on, slightly altered but enduring.

I picked my way carefully, intent on keeping my pack dry. On higher ground at the far side of the swamp the surroundings became more familiar. I eased the pack from my shoulders and sat for a while to get my bearings. About three kilometres to the south was the little country town where I'd lived as a kid. Somewhere nearby, hidden in the tangle of the bush, was the town rubbish tip. The hut, if it was still standing, was a bit further on, built on a slight rise near the river bank.

Quite suddenly, there it was. I all but missed it, just as I'd nearly missed the old railway line, because it was almost covered with creepers. Saplings grew between the frame and the sagging door. It was so much smaller and more decrepit, too, than the hut which had existed in my memory. Over the years that had grown into some kind of romantic haven, a sanctuary from the rest of the world. This was hardly more than a shaky collection of boards and rusty tin huddled together. Just the same, it was enough to bring memories flooding back.

My elder brother Mike and I had spent the best times of our lives here. An old bloke called Ben had lived in the hut in those days. He hadn't built it, though. It was already there when he arrived in the district. He was always talking about doing it up and making it more habitable, but somehow he never got around to it. He was a real oddball who lived mainly off what he caught in his snares and drum-nets and the bits and pieces he could sell from the nearby tip. He and Mike were great mates, and the old man taught us all his bush survival tricks. I could still remember some of the marvellous feeds we'd shared here with Ben. Fish. Yabbies. Even wild ducks caked with mud and baked in the coals. Ben could make a mean damper, too, deliciously crusty on the outside and steamily tempting on the inside. Occasionally we persuaded Mum to give us a few snags or a couple of rashers of bacon to add a bit of variety. Mike and I used to dream of moving in with Ben and sharing what, to a couple of kids, seemed an idyllic existence. Our parents weren't nearly so favourably impressed with Ben's lifestyle. They regarded him as an old derelict and a bad influence, so we ended up being packed off to boarding-school in Ballarat. We heard some time later that Ben had been taken away and admitted to an old folks' home in the city. They said he'd gone a bit queer in the head. We never went near the hut after that. Without Ben it had lost its attraction, added to which I suppose we were growing up and our interests widening.

A couple of years later my sister Carmel told me there was a young guy living in the hut. She'd taken the two youngest kids on a picnic and had walked back that way.

'Gee, I was scared,' she confided. 'He's a real nutter. I got the kids out of the way as quickly as I could, I can tell you!'

'A nutter? How come?'

'Talking to himself and raving like a lunatic. Then he started bashing the door with a claw hammer, yelling and cursing. He's a real weirdo.'

Since I felt I'd outgrown things like bush huts the news didn't really interest me. The next year my old man changed his job and we left the district. For years I hadn't given the place a single thought, until recently, and now here I was back again, full circle, as it were.

I pushed the creepers away and went inside the shaky little building. The hut had only one room with a small, dirt-encrusted window. The floor was beaten earth, hard as rock, and at one end there was a fireplace with a chimney made from flattened kerosene tins and a hearth of flat stones. I didn't remember Ben ever having a fire burning in the hut, but somebody certainly had. The back of the fire-place was blackened and stained, and powdery ash still clung to the hearth. Ben had always had a camp-fire outside the hut where we'd cooked whatever we could scrounge.

I took stock of my new home. There was a rickety kitchen chair and a large wooden box which seemed to have been used as a table. The only other furniture was a rotting camp-bed made from rough-cut branches and a length of hessian, which now hung in disintegrating shreds. I found a few pieces of cutlery, green with verdigris, stacked on the noggins of the hut's timber frame. There was also a stained tin mug, an enamel plate, a small, battered saucepan and, strangest of all, a damp-stained book of Australian poems. This last item certainly hadn't belonged to Ben. He could neither read nor write, a fact of which he was oddly proud. Maybe it had been left behind by the young guy who'd scared Carmel.

Oh, well, the hut wasn't much, but at least it was a shelter. In fact it could be made reasonably comfortable with a bit of effort. Judging by the shafts of sunlight dancing between the sheets of tin my first job would be to mend the roof before it rained. I made a rough broom of twigs and swept out the leaves and rubbish. I pottered around gathering firewood and feeling oddly content, and wondering why I hadn't done this before. No hassles, no landlord dunning for my unpaid rent, no tramping round the city looking for non-existent work. I'd retraced my steps, not

only physically, but in attitudes and values as well. I was
back where I belonged.

I was looking forward to cooking my supper and eating
it in front of a cheerful blaze on my stone hearth. It was to
be a sort of celebration, an affirmation. Here I was and here
I belonged. My home. Then came my first set-back. Even
with the driest wood I could find, there was no way I could
persuade the fire to burn. It sent out clouds of sullen, acrid
smoke and promptly went out. I decided the chimney must
be blocked; most likely leaves and rubbish were stopping
the draught. I'd work on it in the morning. Meanwhile I had
to be content with cooking on a campfire like we'd done
years ago. I boiled the billy I'd picked up, along with a few
other domestic odds and ends, on my last visit to the op
shop before leaving town. Scalding billy tea, strong and
sweet! So good! I toasted a couple of bread rolls and topped
them with baked beans heated in the coals.

I turned in early, rolled myself in a blanket and my
sleeping-bag and lay listening to the night sounds of the
bush. Possums barked and hissed in the tree-tops. There
was the occasional tump-tump-tump of a wallaby making
its way to the river for a drink.

I gradually became aware of yet another sound, something I couldn't put a name to. It was a sort of whispering.
Sometimes it seemed to be caused by something in the
hut, at other times I was sure it was coming from outside.
Was it something in the chimney? The wind whistling
through the gaps in the boards, perhaps? I found myself
listening for it, like listening for the next drip from a leaking tap. Finally I slept, but the whispers flitted through my
dreams like an intimate two-way conversation, excluding
me, the unwanted third person.

Even though I hadn't slept well, it was only just after
dawn when I climbed over the fence at the back of the
town tip. This, too, had altered with the years. It was
larger and smellier than it had been when we crept in looking for wheels and axles for billy-carts. Today my needs
were slightly different. After scavenging through the

town's cast-offs I found what I needed: a couple of sheets
of reasonably good tin for the roof and some odds and
ends of wire to make snares and fish traps.

By noon I'd made a tolerably good drum-net, safely hidden in the river. After a few unsuccessful attempts I set
four wire snares in animal tracks leading to the river, and
felt some pride in remembering the skills Ben had taught
us so long ago.

Next I fixed the roof and tore back the creepers round
the walls and door. Cleaning the chimney was no easy
matter, and I had to make do with pushing green, leafy
branches through to clear the soot and rubbish. I realised
now that before I could do any more repairs to the hut I
would have to buy a few basic tools. I faced the trip to the
town with mixed feelings. It would be interesting to see
the old place again, but I was not keen on meeting people
I'd known in the old days. After all, who wants to be
pointed out as the family drop-out?

I need not have worried. I bought all I needed, including
a couple of sacks from the corn merchant, without seeing
even one familiar face. I stocked up on groceries and even
lashed out on the luxury of a few chops. Tonight I was
going to eat in style in my refurbished home.

Just the same, evening saw me cooking on a campfire
again. Nothing would induce the fire in the hut to burn. I
knew it wasn't due to a blocked chimney this time, so obviously there must be some trick to lighting it which I hadn't
caught on to yet. My failure gave me the odd feeling that
some sort of pattern was being set, and when I awakened
soon after midnight to hear that persistent whispering the
feeling increased.

During the next few days this sense of life taking on a
pattern became more apparent. The days belonged to me.
I was master of my own little world while the sun shone.
There was the river to swim in. I could lie in the shade,
soaking up the late spring warmth and watching the bush
creatures going about their daily lives, quite unconcerned
at my presence.

The food was good, too. Some good-sized redfin found their way into my nets. I'd made a second net and sold my surplus catch to the bloke who ran the fish and chip shop in the town. I'd snared a brace of rabbits and roasted them over my campfire, and, after a few earlier failures, my damper was nearly as good as the ones old Ben cooked. In fact, I had the life I'd dreamed about when I was on the scrap-heap in the city. I should have been at peace with the world, except for a growing feeling that in some subtle way not all the world was at peace with me.

The nights were terrible, chiefly because I was sleeping so badly. The strange whispering sounds continued in spite of all my efforts to trace the cause, and it was getting me down. My longing for a good night's sleep grew until it was almost an obsession. I'm not a particularly imaginative or nervous guy. The sounds had to have a rational explanation. After all, they were nothing more than that, just sounds; irritating, repetitive sounds. That's what I tried to convince myself each day; but each night, waiting for sleep to overtake me, it seemed that I was listening to question and answer, demand and reply, wordless voices full of jealousy and malice directed solely at me. If I nodded off it was only to jerk awake a few minutes later bathed in a cold sweat, and sleep was finished for the night.

I tried to weigh up the situation and look at things objectively. Should I move on and find some other place to live? If so, then where? And more to the point, why? Apart from the nightly whisperings this place suited me perfectly. The hut wasn't much, but it could be made quite comfortable with a little effort. I had started to patch it up during the first few days here, but somehow I'd ground to a halt and done nothing more. Even in its present run-down state it offered reasonable shelter, and that was all I needed. Offered? Deep at the back of my mind I knew that it didn't 'offer' anything. I had taken, and the taking had given rise to resentment from something, somewhere. I was an intruder to be driven off.

I pushed that thought away as bordering on madness. I

must keep a grip on myself. Maybe it all existed only in my
mind, some kind of reaction to the mangling I'd taken in
the city. Isolation can play odd tricks, too. Apart from a
few words exchanged with Spiros at the fish and chip
shop, and the bloke who sold me the sacks, I'd spoken to
nobody since I arrived here. It hadn't bothered me greatly,
though. I was glad of the peace and quiet, but if I was becoming neurotic I'd better do something about it. Maybe I
should work at something, keep myself occupied. If I was
physically tired I'd sleep, noises or no noises!

I decided to start on the improvements to the hut
straight away. Get busy, without any more messing about.
As expected, I found the timber I needed at the tip. That
was not all, either. There was an armchair, quite service-
able except for a broken leg which could soon be fixed.
There was a kitchen cupboard, too. It needed a new back,
but could be mended without any trouble. It would certainly make the place more homelike and solve my storage
problems. As it was, things just lay around wherever there
was a space on the floor.

It took me two trips to lug everything back through the
bush to the hut. By nightfall I'd mended the chair after a
fashion, and the cupboard was fixed to the wall. It looked
neat. I'd renewed part of the door-frame, too, where the
new hinges I'd put on when I first arrived were already
pulling away from the rotten wood.

It had been a fair day's work and I was genuinely but
pleasantly tired. After a dip in the river I relaxed in front of
the campfire and ate my tea. Tomorrow I'd rebuild the fireplace. I'd have a fire burning there if it was the last thing I
did! Until then, sleep, wonderful sleep!

I sat on the bed and kicked off my shoes. I hadn't even
swung my feet off the floor to lie down when it started.
This time the whisperings were louder, more insistent and
full of a malevolent urgency. I covered my ears with my
hands and willed myself not to listen, but it was useless.
The sounds hissed around in my head like snakes. The
whole place started to shake as somebody pounded on the

wall near the cupboard, then the hammering came from the door as well. There was a protesting groan of nails being wrenched from wood and the cupboard crashed to the floor. The door swung and sagged, my careful repairs torn to splinters.

'For God's sake stop it!' I raced outside. 'Just piss off and leave me alone!' There was nobody there, but the sense of a hostile presence was chilling. I tried to gulp down a rising panic and snatched up a nearby length of wood.

'Who are you? What do you want?' I shouted into the echoing night. 'Come out! Show yourself!' I lashed out at the nearby shrubs, hacking, chopping. 'Tell me what you want from me! I've done nothing to you, so why don't you bugger off and leave me in peace?' I screamed as I circled the hut, smashing the piece of wood into every shadow. The sound of madness in my own voice terrified me and I reeled back into the hut.

Suddenly it was cold, so cold it pressed down on me like an icy weight. Something unseen hurled the splintered wood into the fireplace. Shaken beyond belief I saw it burst into flames. The whisperings rose to a triumphant crescendo as the flames leapt at my legs and feet. I tried to beat them out with whatever I could grab, gasping with pain, and at the same time telling myself that this was not really happening. My mind felt as if it would burst.

'All right! All right! I'll go, only leave me alone!' I heard myself sob. As I pitched headlong towards the door the fire died and blackened.

I stumbled blindly through the bush, the memory of the flames and whispering still going round in my head. On and on I ran, hell-bent on escaping from I knew not what or whom. After what seemed like forever there was the hard road under my raw feet. Lights. The sound of a car screeching to a halt, then voices. The feeling of being lifted up and after that, darkness.

'How are you today?' I forced my eyes open. It seemed as if I'd been drifting in and out of black dreams for a long,

long time. A man stood beside my bed, white coat, stetho-
scope.

'Do you feel like talking yet?' I didn't answer. 'Do you
remember what happened to you? You have some burns
and a few cuts which are responding to treatment, however you seem to have sustained a bad shock. Would you
like to talk about it?' I turned my head away. I didn't even
want to think about what had happened, much less tell my
lunatic tale to anybody else.

Later that day the nurse handed me something from the
locker beside my bed.

'When they brought you to hospital you were hanging
on to this like grim death. It seemed important to you, so I
thought you'd like to know it's safe.'

It was the book of poems I'd found in the hut, now battered and singed round the edges. I'd never bothered to
look at it before this. My bandaged hands fumbled to hold
it, and it fell open at a well-worn page, something the
owner had obviously turned to again and again. It was part
of a poem by Christopher Brennan:

'How old is my heart, how old, how old is my heart?
and did I ever go forth with song when the morn was new?
I seem to have trod on many ways, I seem to have left
I know not how many homes; and to leave each
was still to leave a portion of my own heart,
of my old heart whose life I had spent to make that home.
So I sit and muse in this wayside harbour and wait
till I hear the gathering cry of the ancient winds and again
I must up and out and leave the embers of the hearth
to crumble silently into white ash and dust,
and see the road stretch bare and pale before me, again
my garment and my home shall be the enveloping winds
and my heart be filled wholly with their old pitiless cry.'

Written in the margin were some words in a wild-look-
ing script. I turned the book round and read:
'Just as in this poem, I believed that this was my home,

my wayside harbour, but I was wrong. Whoever built this
hut is still here, and seeps from the very woodwork. It's as
if the builder and the hut are one, he talks to it and it an-
swers him. But he's dead and I'm alive and I won't be
driven . . .'

The writing ended in a jagged scrawl, as if the pen had
been torn from the writer's grasp.

I shivered. Old Ben. The young guy who'd scared my
sister. Me. And who else?

'The book's not mine,' I said. 'You'd better burn it.'

THE HOURGLASS
by Leigh Blackmore

> *'The figure of Time, with an hourglass in one hand
> and a Scythe in the other'*
> —Addison

We were at Rob's because there was nowhere else to go. I
mean Honey and me. We had to be together, no matter
what it took, and what it took was getting out from where
we were—leaving friends and family and taking off into
unknown territory, just the two of us. It would be frightening, but at least we would be together. I could hardly wait.

Now here was Rob, my old school friend, looking
pleased to see us though we had turned up on his doorstep
with hardly any notice. No doubt it wasn't terribly convenient, but he'd sounded eager to see us when I'd phoned to
say we were on the way through his town *en route* to
Longreach. He had been the only person I could think of
that would still offer us any sort of a welcome; with everyone else, I'd burned my boats. Doubtless he could tell
from my strained expression that this wasn't a routine
visit; but he was good at smoothing over awkward situa-
tions.

'David . . . and Honey! Come in, come in . . . How are you?'

He shook my hand vigorously. He was as darkly handsome as ever. Dressed in neatly pressed jeans and shirt, he
looked healthy and energetic. I, by contrast, was pale and

enervated. The last few months had not treated me well. I had to put the best face on things.

'Good, mate,' I said. Even so, I hesitated—something about his appearance had changed but I couldn't put my finger on it. 'You look different.'

'Must be the moustache,' he said, smiling broadly, his green eyes flashing. Sure enough, a dapper moustache lent a new maturity to his always-boyish good looks. I wasn't convinced that was the difference I noted, but what the hell, now wasn't the time to pursue it.

Honey kissed Rob affectionately on the cheek. 'Good to see you,' she smiled. We went through to sit in the lounge room, our first chance to relax since leaving Sydney.

Most of my friends hadn't liked it when I took up with Honey. She was fiercely outspoken, and that antagonised some people who evidently thought women should be less vocal. She was free and wild, and there were friends who seemed threatened by her refusal to adhere to what they considered 'proper' behaviour. That was *their* problem: Honey didn't give a hang what other people thought of her. She said what came into her mind, and she did what moved her. I guess that's what attracted me to her. She was a catalyst—love her or hate her, you couldn't ignore her.

Of course, I was attracted to her for other reasons. That she was beautiful goes without saying. The mischievous light of her brown eyes, and the gentle laughter of her voice, had me under their sway; and I was (I don't hesitate to admit it) powerless to resist her curvaceous figure, and (trite as it may seem) lips that I thought tasted sweet as her name. She was also a bright student, studying social work, and I didn't see how she could be any more desirable.

My friends worried that she had too much influence over me. In hindsight maybe they were right. I treated her with an almost religious devotion, a sort of awed wonder at her beauty—the kind of sensibility that led the pre-Raphaelites to paint iconic images of their women—radiant, yet distant and almost holy creatures, not to be merely loved, but to be worshipped.

But then I wasn't capable of seeing how unrealistic my image of her was. She was the first girl I had made love to, and I had fallen for her—hook, line and sinker, as they say. Right then, Honey was all I wanted and I was prepared to go to the ends of the earth to be with her—a wild, romantic notion to be sure, but I was full of those; and if that's what it took . . .

'Come through, make yourselves at home. Tea? I have a special Nepalese brew that you might like. I prepare it with salt and yak butter in the Tibetan way.' Rob moved to the kitchen and started the kettle.

Rob's place wasn't really the ends of the earth, but it was halfway there, or so it seemed to me. Longreach, the home town of Honey's childhood, was our planned destination; but when I realised Rob's was on the way we had decided to see him. Three hours' driving took us to his house, via the freeway from Sydney and up through Newcastle to the North Coast. I had spent years in the inner-city, hardly moving beyond the tight cluster of suburbs comprising Sydney's grimy, congested heart, and this move to Longreach amounted to an epic journey.

In previous years we'd visited Rob in Sydney at his inner-city terrace several times. That had been before he'd been away to Nepal; but when he had returned to Australia, he'd bought this house on the coast. It was a beautiful spot, rather lonely and relatively isolated (but I only thought that because I was used to having hundreds of people around me all the time in the city). The house itself was only minutes from a long beach with white sand.

During previous visits with Rob I had been proud to be with Honey and glad that he liked her. She always seemed intrigued because he was handsome and intelligent, but I never considered Rob my sexual rival. He knew how I felt about her.

I was pretty confident about that, particularly because of one night when we'd all gone out on the town. Funnily enough, it had been earlier that same afternoon that

Honey had spotted an old hourglass in the dusty, crowded
window of an antique shop on Oxford Street, and impul-
sively bought it.

*I gaze deeply into the hourglass; or does it gaze into
me? Within it, I see all sorts of things as the sands shift;
different things—some good, some bad. Today I had a
glimpse in it (or was it a waking nightmare?) of an al-
ternate world. It was a world where Honey had left me,
had abandoned her ideals, had settled into hideous do-
mestication with another man. Is that as horrible as the
way it really ended—or is it more so? I can't decide; any
world where she's not present is one that must be en-
dured rather than lived to the full.*

*The doctor they send to my cell to 'observe' me makes
notes, tapping at his computer keyboard. For the most
part I ignore him. He wears a white coat, and I imagine
that, framed in dark wood on his white office wall is a
degree from some prestigious psychiatric school, but
that doesn't impress me. He can't see through my eyes.
His notion of reality, the template through which he re-
stricts his view of the universe, is different from mine.
His vision is closed, both to what I see in the hourglass,
and even to what I saw on the beach. I don't blame him
for his limited imagination, but I get irritated when he
questions the validity of my reality just because it's different from his. He terms my constant fixation with the
hourglass 'obsessive'. I don't care; there's a secret to
which it holds the clue: 'As above, so below.' As sand
trickles down from the top chamber of the hourglass to
the bottom one, memories trickle through my consciousness. I turn the hourglass in my hands, as I turn the
facts in my head. Bits of the past, of the events that led
me here, pass through my mind in flurries and occasionally in floods . . .*

She had whispered in my ear. 'Wouldn't it be fun to
make love for a whole hour and have that tell us the

time—you know, how long we've got to go before we come?'

Her little joke was typical of her frank speech; as I've said, it was one of the qualities in her that turned me on. Before I could protest, she had rushed in and bought the thing, presenting it to me. The hourglass was made of silver, beautifully turned and filigreed; she was certainly, I thought, a woman of good taste in such things. I wondered whether we'd use it as she had suggested. The idea gave the rest of the afternoon a subtle undercurrent of pleasurable anticipation.

Later, Rob had taken us to a pub off Taylor Square. He was keen for us all to have a good time. Well, we'd been drinking heavily and Honey had got very drunk, which she was prone to do. If she was uninhibited sober, the sorts of things she did when she was drunk sometimes were too much even for me. She ended up lying in the road giggling, and it was all we could do to get her to her feet and struggle back towards Rob's nearby flat.

She had hung on Rob's shoulder all the way back, laughing, babbling. To be honest, it had begun to annoy me. Honey lived only in the moment, but I thought I could see the evening unfolding in my mind's eye and I didn't like what I foresaw. The alcohol was allowing her obvious attraction to Rob to show itself. I thought it odd and I was annoyed, even a little jealous I suppose, because while outwardly everything was fine, I felt insecure. You never knew quite where you were with an impulsive woman like that.

With some difficulty we had got Honey up into the upstairs bedroom in Rob's small terrace and laid her out on the bed, assuming she would pass out. A few minutes later, I was talking with Rob downstairs; actually I had told him that I thought I loved Honey, when suddenly she had stumbled out at the top of the stairs, almost entirely naked, mumbling to herself and trying to remove the last shred of clothing. She was apparently oblivious to her surroundings; there might have been strangers in the room—other friends of Rob's, for instance—but luckily it was only me and Rob. Even so . . .

Well, I trusted Rob. Looking at Honey's voluptuous
body being paraded in front of his eyes, another man
might have turned the situation to his advantage, might
have taken Honey up on what appeared to be a slap in the
face to me. Not Rob. Not then. He was great. He had
helped me to get her back to bed—his bed in fact—and
because of the situation he had offered to sleep on the
couch downstairs.

Next morning when we awoke, Honey made love to me.
No, I didn't initiate it; she seemed eager to use the hourglass as she had suggested. I guess it became our fetish,
contributing an indefinable 'something extra'. I can remember as though it were only last night the softness of
Rob's bed, the morning sun hot on my back as we
pleasured each other. I can still see her long dark hair
spread out on the pillow, the whiteness of her skin; can
still feel her full breasts beneath my hands, as we timed
our mutual orgasm to the rhythm of the last sands running
through the glass at the end of the hour. The delicious satisfaction of lying back with her when it was over, sharing
the bed as if it were our own, Honey telling me how good
a lover I was. I had thought I'd always be grateful to Rob
for that.

We had used the hourglass many times since that night
at Rob's. I often found that in sex, time seemed to expand.
Although the hourglass told us that it was only an hour, a
similar span of minutes each time, sometimes when
Honey and I made love it had seemed to last for days. Using the hourglass was a game we both enjoyed; as time
went on it had become almost an essential element in our
lovemaking ritual, and eventually we would no more think
of fucking without it in the room than of doing it with our
clothes on.

We played other little sexual games—there's nothing
like variety—but because the hourglass had been a gift
from her to me, its use had always lent a special aspect
to our lovemaking. We hadn't always been able to

correspond precisely to the hour; in fact being rigid about it would have spoiled our enjoyment; but when we did manage, sweating and moaning in mutual ecstasy, to climax at close to the instant the sand ran out, it had been a thrill difficult to surpass.

My mind was racing with these thoughts, but Rob pouring the tea brought me back to the present. This was the first time we had seen his home since his return from Nepal, and the lounge was decorated with artefacts that bespoke his deep interest in the culture.

'What brings you?' Rob said, proferring two steaming mugs full of dark liquid.

I needed a caffeine hit, more so than usual; my nerves were pretty much on edge, and I was grateful for the jolt drinking the strong beverage imparted. There was a hollow feeling in the pit of my stomach—part excitement at the prospect of starting a new life, and part shock at the magnitude of the step I'd taken in leaving everything else behind. 'We're going to Longreach. I've quit my job. I've quit the band. Honey's got a place there.' I was blurting out everything without any logical sequence.

Rob looked concerned. I could tell he thought I'd acted hastily but he took it in his stride. 'What about your flat? The people you were living with?'

'I've given my notice. We've got all our things in the back of the car.'

'Hmmm. Longreach? It sounds totally inaccessible.'

'That's the general idea. Honey grew up around there. I just couldn't handle it any more the way it was.' My arm was around her.

She laughed, tossing her head back. 'You're looking well, Rob.'

'Thanks.' He sat beside us. Being at Rob's was a relief. It gave me time to think. As for Honey, I sensed that for her this was another in a perpetual series of adventures. She was not out on a limb like I was. I'd given up everything to be with her, closed things off with my friends. To a lesser extent she'd done the same, but I knew that if we should split, she could carry on. Whereas by effectively making her my world, I had gone out on a limb. Honey was the limb I was clinging to, and if anything should separate us, there was nothing between me and a long hard fall.

'By all means stay—take the spare room. Stay as long as you need to.'

It was what I'd hoped he'd say. 'Shouldn't be more than a few days, mate.'

I looked around Rob's living room. There were more artefacts than I had remembered from his old place, testimony to his delvings in strange places. Numerous mandala paintings hung on the walls. In one corner was an ugly statue which I recognised to be of the god Samvara, with his writhing snake and crown of five skulls. Here and there yellowing yak skulls reposed on other pieces of furniture.

'What's that one, Rob?' I queried. Over the couch, a carving showed a god and goddess engaged in sexual intercourse of a yogic nature.

'Yab-yum icon,' he said offhandedly. Rob had a way of always seeming knowledgeable both in booklearning and practical things. The artefacts were physical proof of his advance over me in terms of exploring other cultures. I had trailed in his wake in many of my interests. He would enthuse about something, which I would take up and pursue in depth; meanwhile he had moved on. After taking his anthropology degree he had taught in Japan for a year, and since we had last seen him had delved extensively into some of the darker Asian religions. His postcards came often at first, but then for a while less regularly. It seemed that from the non-dogmatic style of Buddhism and Zen, he had moved on in his personal explorations through Indian tantrism (hence Samvara) and now had become interested in the Bon-Po people of Kagbeni.

We didn't have to sit for long before Rob had us both helping with a brilliant meal he had been preparing before we came. He was great at cooking; I had always sworn I must learn to cook when I saw the enjoyment he got from it, but somehow I never did. I guess my head was too much in the clouds. Honey took to it with a will, since she loved cooking as well, although she hadn't made this meal before. Rob showed us how to combine fish, beef and kidney beans, which he had already soaked in wine. '*Matsya*, *mamsa*, and *madya*,' he explained.

He served the food on shallow bone dishes. 'Made from the brain-pans of human skulls,' he said.

'Oh really? How . . . er . . . unusual,' I commented, hoping that was non-committal enough. Truth to tell, I didn't want to appear unsophisticated. I looked askance at the dishes. Their age was indeterminate, but I couldn't help but wonder how recently they had been made. Was he gauging my reaction?

Rob delighted in preparing this kind of an unusual feast, but this surpassed anything he had done in the past. Over the excellent meal, Rob held forth on his recent travels, and was especially expansive on the subject of Nepal.

'It's a great part of the world—Kathmandu has got to be seen to be believed. But I spent more time in the small towns—Jogbani, Dharan, Dhaunkuta, Tesinga and some even smaller settlements along the Sun Kosi river. And the mountains—Kangtega, Tamserku, Amadamblam—spectacular! But there's not much access to safe drinking water; in some regions there's a very low quality of life, and extreme human suffering; more than one in ten children die before their first birthday.'

'Oh, that's horrible.' Honey had a soft-hearted approach when it came to the realities of world poverty. It was going to be an obstacle to her in social work.

'Well, it's a tough place; many's the time I had to suffer monsoonal rain and blood-hungry leeches. Also the state discourages deviation from social norms; there's rigid state censorship; but it's surprising what you can get away with if you're determined.'

I pressed him on this point but he wouldn't elaborate. He waved his fork, continuing with his lecturing.

'The good thing is the population is about half that of Australia, which is unusually low for that region of Asia. There are no current border disputes, low army numbers, no open wars. The people have quite high purchasing power compared to their income, and low foreign debt. They use traditional fuels like wood and animal wastes to provide more than half their domestic energy use, so they're a low contributor to global warming.'

I couldn't help feeling these facts and figures he was reeling off were pretty superficial, not much related to his real interests. I was interested, but I sensed that he was glossing over the real purpose of his living there.

'Will you go back?' asked Honey, her brown eyes wide. I knew she was interested in travelling to exotic places herself.

'My main interest was in the religion of the Bon-Po,' said Rob, 'and I've learned nearly all about that I can.'

'So what *did* you learn there, Rob?' I probed.

He smiled suddenly, a rather frightening smile that didn't seem to be like him—well, not as I remembered him. But gradually it began to dawn on me that there were many things about him that were not as I remembered. 'Oh, many things. The Sherpas showed me the yeti scalp in the Khumjung Monastery, and the bony hand of a yeti at Thyangboche—for a sordid chinking of rupees, of course. I was able to greatly expand my knowledge of tantra. I participated as a masked dancer in the Mani Rimdu ceremonies—and in others less . . . wholesome. Have you . . . have you read Conrad's *Heart of Darkness*?'

'I'm afraid not.' I felt stupid, uncultured.

'Ah. Well let's just say that I have a great admiration for Conrad's Mr Kurtz. It's just as difficult to explore . . . unknown territory . . . these days as it was then.'

Did he mean unknown territory, as in Himalayas, the Roof of the World? Or did he mean it in some more metaphoric sense? I didn't pursue it, but I made a mental note to read the novel when possible. It was often that way with Rob—catching up on his knowledge, realising months later what some fleeting reference in his conversation had really portended.

'Tell you more tomorrow—it's late, you two should get some sleep. The room's already prepared.'

And with that, the meal over, Rob dismissed us. We didn't mind. We made love again that night, the hourglass on the table beside us, within easy sight. The hiss of the night-ocean's waves on the nearby beach, and the smell of spray, mingled with the sounds and scents of our lovemaking. Honey was proud of her small waist, which I could almost encircle with my hands. When my hands were on her body, I thought I was in heaven. For her part she would compliment me on the things she could—I was by no means good-looking but she liked my strong arms and the way I kissed her all over. I felt cut off from the outside world; vulnerable, fragile; but I trusted Honey. I fell asleep with my arm around her, breathing the smell of her hair and her skin. Even then I had no idea what Rob had planned.

I gaze into the hourglass and I see a vision of eyes, a giant pair of green eyes in the bed with us, looking up out of the mattress. They are wide open, they don't blink. Eyes the colour of Rob's. I blink my own eyes and when I open them again the vision is gone.

That afternoon, I go around behind the doctor, who is working with his laptop, in his long white coat. He is tapping, always tapping. There are symbols and pictures on the screen. One of them is shaped like my hourglass; I point at it and ask him what it's called. He says, 'It's-called-an-eye-con.' He speaks very slowly and clearly, as though to an idiot. He thinks I am one, because I so rarely speak. Let him think that; it suits me fine, puts me at an advantage. Can he see the world in a grain of sand?

I say nothing, but my eyes widen. I watch the symbol. He clicks something under his hand, and the icon spins around. Watching it makes me dizzy. My head feels as

though it's falling through a black hole. I go back to my
table and pick up my hourglass, which is lying on its
side. I run my hands over its smooth curved figure-eight
surfaces, which remind me of Honey's body. The memo-
ries keep coming back . . .

No matter how well you know someone, you can't see
into their mind. I see now that I was too trusting, but how
do you know that in advance? You can only learn it the
hard way, and that's what happened to me.

At lunch next day, Rob spoke more of the Nepalis. Now
he was thinking of writing a thesis on their fetishes and
their primitive rites. Honey asked him a lot of questions.

'Got some great hash here, mate.' We all smoked while
we talked. This and the liberal amounts of beer he served
up went to my head. I thought that I should have begun to
feel relaxed, but in fact I felt tense.

Rob gestured towards my glass. 'Have some more
madya—actually this variety is called *'chung'*. This is a
really special experience; the goblet is made of a man's
brain-pan.'

What is it with this guy and skulls? I thought, then
quickly silenced my misgivings. He was definitely weirder
than last time I'd seen him; but I suppose prolonged expo-
sure to another culture would do that to anyone.

He poured the beer into the bone goblet, passed it to
Honey. She was normally queasy about things like that,
and I expected her to refuse it, but to my surprise she took
the goblet and quaffed deeply, then passed it to me. The
thing was cold and hard, an inverted skull whose black
eye-sockets gazed blankly. I held it by its stem and decided, well, if they can drink out of this, so can I. I drained
the beer, and it was surprisingly good. I immediately felt
my limbs suffused with the alcohol, which I suspected was
not some local variety but a powerful brew Rob had
brought back with him.

Next, he held up a carved mask, black with silver-studded eyes and nose. Several long pointed polished sticks stuck out of it at odd angles. All in all it was pretty hideous, I thought.

'One of their fetishes. It's an icon worshipped by the Bon-Po. The face of a nameless god in their culture; I believe him to be one of the Sri, the demonic vampiric beings of Bon culture in Tibet; but I believe he has actually had many names throughout history—he has affinities with the Greek Chronos, the Indian Kala, the Roman Saturnus Africanus. And he shares qualities with other gods too— the Iranian Zervan, the Indian Rudra, and especially Oya, who's mother/storm-goddess of the Yoruba people.'

He leaned across the table and picked up a couple more items which he held up with what seemed a flourish. 'Paraphernalia of the rites . . . a rosary made of human teeth. Wonder about that chair you're sitting on?' He was looking at me. 'It's made of the skin of an adept.'

Indeed, the seat, made of what looked like tanned leather bound across a wooden supporting frame, had a texture that was unpleasantly like that of human skin; but this seemed a little farfetched to me. I honestly didn't know how seriously to take Rob on this point. For a start, how had he managed to get all this stuff into Australia? Nevertheless I was starting to feel distinctly uncomfortable. These Bon-Po people sounded damned primitive to me.

Honey seemed to be lapping it all up. Every time I would try and change the subject, she would bring it back. Now they were on about tantra.

'Tantra teaches that the hunger for orgasm defeats the possibility of real orgasm,' Rob was saying. 'There is a greater orgasm. The obsession with physical orgasm precludes having sex for hours instead of minutes. It's possible to become drunk on the energy of life itself . . .'

My attention began to drift. This was fascinating but I began to wonder what it all meant. Siouxsie and the Banshees were blasting away from the stereo, 'Entranced' from the *Juju* album. Honey was looking at Rob; she seemed almost entranced herself . . . The evening ended once again as Rob went to his room, and Honey and me to ours.

The following morning Honey seemed preoccupied.

'What's wrong?'

She frowned. 'Robert came into the room last night.'

'What, in here?'

'He was naked. He asked me if I'd go with him to his room.'

I was incredulous. 'You're joking! What did you tell him?'

'I said no, of course.'

'Shit, I don't believe it.' But I could hardly blame him for finding her attractive—or her for being so. Thank God she didn't take him up on it. As it was I felt like punching him out. How could I have slept through it, anyway?

'Don't tell him I told you, David. I'm sure it won't happen again.'

'Not bloody likely. I'll see to that.'

'It's okay, David—it's just something that happened.'

Not to me it wasn't. Had they slept together? Surely if they had, she wouldn't be naive enough to volunteer anything that would make me suspicious. But something about the way she said it planted a seed of doubt in my mind.

'We'll leave tonight. No sense hanging around here if he's going to behave like that. Let's get up to Longreach.'

It took me a few hours to unwind. Honey persuaded me to say nothing to Rob, but now I was looking at him through new eyes. At lunch I was decidedly cool towards them both.

Afterwards Honey drew me aside. 'You're the one I want. I hope you know that.' She kissed me. I returned the depth of her kiss, and she yielded languorously as usual; I felt a stirring in my loins.

'Let's go down to the beach,' I suggested.

It was twilight, the beach deserted. We made love unconvincingly on the damp sand and afterwards trudged the beach's length. Honey tried to get me to swim, but my reluctance was as strong as usual. Besides, it had begun to get cold.

'Come on, why won't you take a dip?' she teased. She went in, splashing about, waving, and although it was the end of a bright hot day, I felt a sense of impending—what? She looked so small in all that water, for all her vibrant life and vitality; the ocean's immensity scared me. I was glad when she came out, dripping, and asked me to towel her dry. We walked back to the house.

That night, Rob cooked for us again. Once again, he prepared the fish, beef and parched beans, and we all indulged in huge quantities of dope and of a Nepali firewater Rob called *rakshi*.

I drank it against my better judgement. I was making plans for us to be leaving, getting on to Longreach so we could get properly set up. I tried to tell Rob we had imposed on his hospitality enough, but he wouldn't hear of it. I began to fear he was angling for Honey. If he tried anything ... My fears were not allayed by his continual conversation about the spiritual qualities of sex, interspersed with dark hints about the rituals in which he had participated in Kagbeni. As the evening wore on, Rob talked further of 'the tantric texts ... the supreme religious observance of Durga ... the Initiation of Death, following which the adept gains magical powers speedily in this Kali-Yuga ... the left-hand path.'

My head began to swim. I disliked the mental sensation as much as I did the physical one. I liked to feel on dry land, and now I felt all at sea. The smoke of the hash hung heavily in the room. Honey was sitting right next to Rob, her eyes lit up bright, hanging on his every word. Did she follow what he was saying? Maybe not all the ins-and-outs of the philosophy he was expounding, but whereas I was lost, Rob seemed to be getting through to her on a more basic level. There was a look in her eyes that she normally reserved for her hornier moments with me. Shit, I thought, is he trying to get her into the sack? He's really serious about all this sexual magic bullshit. Through the dope-induced lethargy, I couldn't quite summon the energy to change the course of the conversation.

Rob was trying to convince Honey to cut some of her hair off. They were both stoned, and she did it. Rob began to weave a bracelet out of the shortish locks she had removed with a pair of scissors. His intentions were becoming plainer by the minute. He was overstepping the bounds of friendship. I could have handled that if Honey had resisted, but she was going along with it.

Then the room was swaying, and I must have passed out, because when I came to, with a mouth so dry I could barely swallow, I was alone in the lounge room. I faintly heard sounds coming from Rob's bedroom. For some reason my head was full of the word *maithuna*. Memories of what Rob had been saying welled up in my mind. The five sacraments partaken of by the practitioners of tantric rites are usually known as 'the five Ms', he had been saying. We had partaken of four of them; *maithuna* was the fifth 'M'.

Raising myself on one elbow, I racked my mind to remember what Rob had said *maithuna* meant. But suddenly I realised—the sounds from the bedroom were unmistakably sounds of passion, and in Honey's voice. My chest tightened with an uncontrollable feeling of jealousy and rage. What the hell was going on? I asked myself—rhetorically, because it only meant one thing.

I strode to the bedroom door, which was slightly ajar. Beyond the door the room was more or less in darkness, but there was a faint, flickering glow. I pushed the door open.

The illumination from the candles was faint, but it was enough to show me that Honey and Rob were on the bed, fucking. Honey was sitting astride him, bucking furiously, her breasts bobbing, a look of unnatural ecstasy on her face. Rob was supine, almost motionless beneath her. His face was turned away from the door so I couldn't see his expression but I was sure it was one of victory. He hadn't seduced her by halves; she seemed totally abandoned. She panted heavily as she thrust, seeming desperate to reach orgasm. Entwined around her wrist was the bracelet woven from her hair, and on her breast was that damned rosary of human teeth.

'Jesus!' There was something savage and totally outside my experience here. It wasn't just the betrayal—there was something that scared and angered me, and sickened me much worse than that concept. 'You bastard Rob, what the hell are you doing to her!' Although he wasn't moving, and she was, I sensed that she was in his power, hypnotised, drugged, God knows what . . .

I rushed forward, jerking his shoulder. His head rolled toward me and I drew back sharply; there was something wrong with his face. The eyes were too small and beady, the mouth was a silver slit in the black head, and long pointed sticks rattled as I turned him toward me. My God, I thought. He's wearing the mask! He's raping Honey and wearing the Bon-Po mask . . . I felt sick to my stomach.

He said nothing, but his hand came up and caught my wrist in a grip that threatened to snap the bone if I should persist. I cried out in pain, dropping to my knees.

Above me, Honey was screaming in short bursts that seemed to wrest themselves from her innermost being. Tears filled my eyes as I realised I couldn't stop what was happening. Rob's grip tightened on my wrist and Honey's gasps came closer together, louder, until they culminated in a cry commingling pain and pleasure such as I'd never heard. Rob pushed me away with his fist and I fell backwards, awkwardly, smashing my hip on some hard piece of furniture as I fell.

Honey fell too, panting, spent, her orgasm past, forward onto Rob's body. I tried to get up on one elbow, ignoring the pain in my hip. Rob was withdrawing from Honey's body, calmly, slowly. I gazed with horror as he stood, picking up one of those shallow bone dishes from his bedside table, and holding it beneath his penis, allowed his semen to spurt into the dish. From another dish on the table he picked up what looked like some sort of herbs and sprinkled them on the sperm, using his finger to mix them together with the sticky fluid.

Christ! I'm going to kill him! was the only thought in my head. I crawled across the floor trying to get up.

He turned back to the bed, and grabbed Honey's hair, pulling her head up, so she was in a kneeling position. He moved the dish in his other hand towards her mouth.

'No!' I screamed. I was on my feet, about to lash out and knock the obscene bowl from his hand. Too late. Honey's eyes were glassy. She received the edge of the dish between her lips and then the fluid was in her mouth, a little trickling from one corner, which she licked away. Rob laughed, a harsh alien sound; he'd been hiding the person he'd become ever since we had arrived.

I hit him then, a savage blow that carried all my bewildered anger. It caught him in the chest and sent him sprawling. He kept laughing, infuriating me, though he sounded winded, as he lay on the floor, the dish knocked from his hand.

I was enraged. I wanted to kill him, to smash his brains out. But I was more concerned with Honey. I turned to her. She was halfway out the door, still naked.

'Wait!' I ran after her. Rob's laughter, dark, sardonic, rang after me as I went. Then he stopped laughing and began a rhythmic chanting. He must have started to beat on that ritual drum, for its pounding echoed in my head as I fled the house in search of Honey.

He was insane. I couldn't fix that. I had to stop Honey. Surely she couldn't run far in that semi-drugged state? I heard the front door slam. Outside it would be dark; I had to find her quickly or she might wander in front of traffic. I was panicking. Ignoring the pain in my hip, which made me limp and slowed me down, I made it to the front porch. I couldn't see her; all I could hear was the wind and the pounding of breakers. I limped towards the street.

She must be heading for the beach. Maybe that would be OK—I would catch up with her there—as long as she didn't go near the water. It seemed to take me an eternity to make my way down the street and cross the road to the beach.

My heart pounding, I staggered on to the sand, climbing over the stubby fence that separated the sand from the rough grass that edged the road. She hadn't been gone more than a few minutes, I would catch her—but I was afraid of what had happened, afraid of what I might find. I had to trust that she had been in Rob's power; the thought that she might have betrayed our relationship consciously was shoved somewhere I wouldn't have to think about it. If I could just catch her, get her away from here . . . It had all been a mistake . . .

The sky loured overhead and the beach felt lonely and empty and huge and the smell of ozone was in my nostrils. Waves crashed on the shore. An irregular line of black sea-weed glistened beneath the froth of the surf's edge. I sensed that overarching the sky above the beach was a force, some tremendous supernal evil.

Had Rob called it here? Could he possibly have any power over anything that felt so powerful itself—for I could feel its might in the shades of the dark sky, in the pounding surf, in the black clouds that swelled ominously above. Something or someone was going to hurt Honey. I ran, and ran. I had to save her.

There was a dark shape up ahead on the sand. A tremendous feeling of relief welled up in me as I recognised Honey. The sand was dragging at my feet as though trying to hold me back from the sight; I felt like a foolish marionette at the command of a puppetmaster infinitely vast and cruel. As I moved closer the dark shape resolved itself and the relief was replaced anew by rage.

Honey's body was lying across the slight rise of a dune. She must have passed out. Her head was thrown back, her eyes closed, her arms outflung. Grains of sand trickled down between her fingers, joining with the myriad of grains that formed the dune. A slow, steady trickle of grains, moving with infinite slowness, one by one.

Everything seemed to be happening in slow motion. I wondered how many grains remained in her hand, and how many were already on the beach, and how long it

would take for each and every grain she clutched in her
outflung hand to make its way down onto the sand beneath her. I seemed to be looking at the stars too, and it
was as though Honey held all the stars of the firmament
and was allowing them to gradually twinkle out as they
joined the universe of grains that formed the beach. Holding infinity in the palm of her hand. I lowered my head to
kiss her beautiful throat.

When Rob found me, I was still supine on the sand, my
hands encircling Honey's waist. I was still counting the
grains. The trickle had slowed, but every now and then—it
might have been once a minute or once an hour—another
grain would dislodge itself from the palm of her hand and
tumble towards the beach, sometimes taking a few of its
fellows with it. When I had counted all the grains that
dropped from her hand, I would count all the grains on the
beach, I was telling myself.

I saw his feet but continued to stare idiotically at Honey's body. Her torn throat filled my field of vision, and the
darkened patch where her blood had run down into the
sand.

Rob was standing there, looking down. From one hand
dangled the vicious mask with its slit eyes and clattering
sticks. He said tonelessly, 'Do you know what you've done?'

I didn't know what he meant. I couldn't read his expression; it might have been victory, or pity, or despair. I was
incapable of judging. The world reeled around me as I tottered to my feet. The hissing of the breakers was in my
ears, but above it I swear I could still hear those grains
trickling, the susurrus of them, from Honey's hand. Rob's
face loomed in front of me, and the susurrus became a
roaring of blood in my ears. At my back I could feel the
overtowering shadow of the force that filled the sky,
seething with a malevolence I couldn't comprehend.

The police found Rob on the beach, his body not far
from Honey's. His skull had been smashed open. Gritty

sand was sticking to the bits of grey matter that poked out through his bloody scalp.

The police think I killed them both. They say I had their blood on my mouth, on my hands. The court believed them. My friends testified against me; I had been acting strangely before I ran off with Honey, they said. No one listened to what I said about Rob's Initiation of Death or his evocation of a brutal, timeless god. Now I'm in this barred cell at Goulburn, and every day I have to listen to the doctor prate of 'emotional storms' . . .

Now I sit here, staring at the hourglass. They found it at Rob's place, next to the bed that I shared with Honey. They gave it to me when I asked. How did she die? Why? Why? Each time I turn it I hope to know the answer to those questions by the time the grains run out. But I never know. And I turn it over again, inverting it, starting again. I loved Honey. I would never have hurt her, but no one else could be allowed to have her. All I can think of is the sand and of Honey. When the grains run out I turn the hourglass; although I know she's dead, there's a sense in which I'm keeping her alive.

The sand at the top gets concave like a little pit. The sand makes little flurries at the bottom as it trickles through, piles up, fills the lower chamber. The grains begin to pile up at the bottom, slithering over each other. I watch fascinated, unable to draw my eyes from the unpredictable movements. Worlds form and re-form in front of my eyes, shapes and figures dancing in the restless shift of the sands.

They tell me it still only takes an hour for the top chamber to empty into the bottom. I don't believe them, for the things I see last sometimes for days. Whole chains of events, strange visions. When the bottom chamber is full, I turn the hourglass and the process starts again. If I ever stop turning it, Honey's life will have run out. The grains flow down, incessantly, from top to bottom, from heaven to hell. I turn it over. And over. And over . . .

A DANGEROUS THING
by Michael Bryant

Oh yes, he thought, as the terrible concoction steamed up
into his face, this is going to be a big day.

He had done everything just as the old man had told
him. All the ingredients had now been obtained and the
liquid that bubbled reluctantly in front of him was looking
and smelling as the old man had told him it would—foul.

The ingredients had been incredibly hard to find, not to
mention expensive. John Harper, who had most of his life
savings stewing away in the black cauldron in front of
him, thought about some of the hassles and adventures
he'd had procuring the various items!

Perhaps the dog's head had been the worst.

That had really taken some doing. To be on the safe side,
he'd picked a fairly small dog that had conveniently been
wandering around the nearby park at night. He guessed it
was some kind of mongrel, a cross-breed, and set to it with
the jack-handle. After two blows the dog had dropped to
the ground and not moved so he assumed it was dead. He
was halfway back to his car with the animal in his arms,
when it had suddenly come back to life and bitten furiously
into his cheek. Somehow he had managed to pry the animal
off his face and to throw the poor beast onto the ground
before finally, this time, beating it to death. Even in death
the dog had mocked him, looking at him with dark, dim
eyes and then bleeding all over the back seat of his car.

What the hell, he thought when he got home and had a look in the mirror, what's a few scars? What's a few dog-blood stains in the car? If all goes according to plan, I'll have enough money for a hundred cars, if not a thousand. Christ, he thought, if I really pull this off I could have enough money to start building cars. An incredible thought.

Harper carefully opened a small paper bag that he had laid beside his work-table. He then opened the wax seal and, being cautious not to waste one single leaf, sprinkled the remains of the black rose into the cauldron. There was a subtle flash of light, quick and soft, and he felt his hair tingle as a deep, electric thrumming started up.

He began to see colours and shapes and things in the murky brown obscenity he was brewing.

He reached under the cauldron and turned up the gas burner that fired it. The liquid began to swirl around now and he could see lights burning softly inside. He felt his heart begin to pound and cautioned himself that this was the easy part—the tricky bit was still ahead.

He put on his thick gloves and slowly wheeled the brewing-pot to the far end of the warehouse, where the pentacle was drawn. It took a while to push it the hundred metres or so to the designated place, and when he finally got it there the heat had warmed the asbestos to a painful level.

He centred the cauldron in the pentacle and turned the gas burner, bolted underneath, up yet again.

Harper had at first thought the old man was kidding him when he told him that he'd need at least a hundred metres of space between himself and the cauldron. It seemed like a ridiculous precaution to him. He was sure he could repeat the incantations plenty of times with only ten or fifteen metres of breathing space.

But then he had looked, really looked into the man's eyes and, for the first time since deciding on this course of action, was afraid.

The old man rolled up his sleeves. Harper hadn't

needed a second invitation to look. The scars were there
plainly. They looked as if ten fish-hooks had been buried
in the man's wrists and then slowly been pulled up to his
elbows. They were gouges, not cuts or scratches. Flesh
torn away; the healing had only made everything look
worse.

'Boyo, I had fifty metres between my own fool-self and
the thing that climbed out of my pot, but it got to me. And
I was only half-way to giving it its instructions.' The old
man had tried to laugh, but had to wipe away the tears in
his eyes instead. 'If you don't get the instructions out, in
the right order, you don't control it. And if you don't control it, you'd better watch out, Boyo, because it'll get to
you. They don't like being called, and if they can get to
you, they will.'

Harper had decided he needed the hundred metres. The
next day he had scouted around until he'd found the deserted warehouse. He'd felt foolish when he'd looked
around its expanse of space; it seemed like overkill.

Now it didn't seem like overkill at all.

He moved back to his working table and took out the
folder with the words written down in it. He knew the
words off by heart, but the old man had convinced him
that he needed back-up the first time. 'Just in case your
brain freezes,' he said.

He had a terrible, agonizing moment of choice when he
knew he could still walk away from everything, but then
he realized that he would be walking away from something. If he left without finishing he would have nowhere
to go, nothing to do. He really had locked himself into this
course of action.

Harper looked across the darkened space to where the
cauldron sat, now bathed in an unnatural light. He could
hear the thick, dark liquid slopping around inside and he
knew it was time to begin. He reached down into his duffle
bag and brought out a bottle of water. He needed something a little stronger, but didn't dare start this chain of
events with a foggy mind. He had to be quick, he knew.

Fast on his feet. He opened the bottle and drank from it, wetting his mouth, which had gone strangely dry.

He opened the folder and lit the black candles before him.

The incantation began. He spoke slowly, making sure he formed the words perfectly. Rumblings began, deep inside the cauldron, and he could see some of the liquid splashing out of it. When he reached the end of the first paragraph he did what the old man had said, paused and waited.

For a long while, nothing happened. Then he noticed that something already had.

From this far away he had not been able to make out the hands that were gripping the rim. They had simply been lost in the steam and the darkness. But now, as they flexed slowly and began to pull the rest of the body out of the pot, he wondered how he had ever overlooked them. They were big hands by any standards, and the large claws on the end of them only heightened the effect. The flesh was pitted and black, as though the beast had been roasting in heat for a long time. Then a leg swung over the side of the cauldron and Harper had to stifle a scream.

The thing was huge.

When it finally climbed out it appeared to be around ten feet tall, which was nothing extraordinary to Harper, who had been secretly expecting a beast of perhaps fifteen or twenty feet. But he had definitely not expected the thing to have been proportioned so gigantically. It was human in shape, with two arms and legs, but these limbs were as round as tree-trunks and they looked hard, with ropy, taut muscles that gleamed as the liquid on the beast caught the light. The beast's head was large and topped with two small, almost delicate horns. It stood inside the pentacle, eyes burning, body tensed and rigid.

'*Who calls Meloch?*' The voice was booming, the windows shook.

Harper answered the request flawlessly. The demon snickered and stepped out of the pentacle. There was a flash of ozone and a hissing noise as the demon's heat fried the caked-on oil that was embedded in the warehouse floor. It started towards Harper, its movements unhurried.

'*You die!*' The demon's step was a little faster now.

Harper's Adam's apple bobbed in his throat at the sight of the monster shambling towards him. He gripped the folder in his hands and recited his incantations perfectly, flawlessly, but the demon kept coming. He steeled himself and forced his mind not to panic. He had time, he would merely repeat the instructions.

The demon was halfway towards him now. He could see its cool blue eyes looking at him, mocking him.

There were fifteen metres between him and the demon when he finished the incantation in a wavering voice and the beast finally stopped. Harper's pounding heart finally began to settle again, and he swallowed for the first time in quite a while.

He could smell the demon's rank smell. It stood before him, itching for him to slip up so that it could get at him.

'Why didn't you stop the first time, Meloch?' He could not believe he was actually talking with a demon.

'*You missed a word,*' the demon said after a long pause.

Harper swallowed.

'*Why have I been called?*'

'You are to provide me with what I demand, as the rules of the Great Book decree. You are bound to do this, demon.'

Meloch flexed its claws. '*Only if it is within my power to do so. To step outside my bounds is also forbidden in the Great Book.*'

Harper sighed; the old man hadn't told him there were different demons for different tasks. He would pay for that little oversight, he thought.

'*Who is this, you wish me to harm?*'

It was scary, the ease with which his thoughts had been read.

'No one. I do not want you to harm anyone. I want you

to provide me with one billion dollars.'

Meloch stood before him, then his face broke open into a smile. Harper tasted his breath.

'*You have called the wrong demon, fool. I cannot create, only destroy. You've made a mistake.*'

Harper's shoulders slumped. He knew the beast was obliged to tell the truth on pain of death. How could he have been so stupid?

'*For a taste of one of your fingers, I can help you.*' Incredibly, the demon's voice sounded genuine.

Harper thought about it. Was there really any going back now? No, he thought with more than a little hysteria; in for a penny, in for a pound. He looked down at his fingers. Which one of you is worth a billion dollars? he wondered.

'All right, if you can guarantee me a billion dollars.' The demon nodded. 'How do I do it?'

'*You come over here and stick your finger in my mouth. Then I bite it off. Then I'll call someone who can really help you. You'll get your money, if you say the right things.*'

'The same things I said to you, right?'

'*That's right.*' Meloch said, still sounding genuine. '*Now come here.*'

Harper's brain switched off then as he walked forward, towards the waiting demon, marvelling at the terrible beauty of the thing. Meloch reached out when he got close enough and with a surprisingly gentle grip, eased the finger into his mouth. He closed his eyes then, and waited for the pain to begin. It was hot inside the demon's mouth, and its saliva felt like a powerful acid burning into him. Then the teeth slowly bit down on him and for a few seconds he felt nothing. When he was allowed to withdraw his finger the pain suddenly pulsed through him, blood jetting from the severed knuckle. He quickly wrapped a handkerchief around his hand and went back to the working table.

'*Now just repeat what you did before, only substitute Zeta for Meloch. That should do it.*' The demon's voice was calm as though the events of the last minute had not occurred at all.

'What will you do?'

'*Oh, I'll just stand here and watch. If you don't mind.*'

Harper dismissed the demon from his mind and began the incantations afresh, substituting names in the correct places, just as he'd been told. The light began to shimmer and burn within the cauldron again. Then he noticed the hands on the rim, and something even bigger than Meloch climbed out of the cauldron and began the long walk towards him.

Slowly, without any panic, Harper began the series of instructions to bring the twenty-foot Zeta under his control. He stumbled once in the third paragraph but thought he'd corrected it well enough. Then he finished and looked up from his pages to see the monster still shambling towards him, eating up huge chunks of his safety zone with every step.

Harper wiped the sweat from his face and told himself to stay calm. He knew he still had time to try the instructions once more. This time it would be perfect. Gripping the folder painfully he started again, knowing his life hinged on getting every word out perfectly. There was, after all, nowhere to run from a twenty-foot demon.

He knew he had it this time. Even when sweat rolled down from his cheek and into his eye, making it sting, he knew he hadn't made a mistake. It was perfect. He was the master here.

So he was more than a little surprised to look up and see Zeta's face only a few feet from his, leaning down with mouth open and teeth awaiting the sensation of his flesh.

Harper screamed. Urine ran down his legs. Although his mouth worked, nothing came out. Through it all Meloch looked innocent.

Now Harper found his voice. 'No! No! I did it right that time! I know I did! I know! For God's sake, the Great Book forbids . . .'

But Zeta stopped him, reaching out and grabbing his

throat. He lifted Harper up high until he was face to face with him, and into Harper's puzzled, beaten eyes, he said: '*No comprende señor.*'

Harper's final scream was choked off as Zeta swallowed him whole. The huge sounds of Meloch's laughter filled the warehouse. Meloch spread his hands wide.

'*So easy,*' he said and both demons laughed heartily.

They looked at one another for a long moment, smiling, then they spotted an exit in the distance and, moving with great purpose, went out into the freedom of the black night.

MAKEOVER
by Sue Isle

My name is Amber Burke and I am a businesswoman. I supply what the customers order—by the back door. There is basically nothing wrong in a dead body, and doctors doing autopsies for a host of medical students can be a fussy lot. Unfortunately, Dr Anderson, my main employer, was arrested last week when the hospital discovered—ah—irregularities in his methods of obtaining said bodies. Nice man. He didn't breathe a word to the cops about me, but I took the warning. Time to go quiet for a bit. That was how I came to be working in the Asian restaurant.

The evening of my first day on the new job was going quite well. The place was full of customers. Not that I could see anything, stuck back in the kitchen hunched over a massive pan of witch-brewed 'flied lice' and breathing in an atmosphere fit for aliens. I had just finished a massive coughing fit when Fred wandered into the kitchen. Fred is the owner and that isn't his name. I can't pronounce his real name, so to avoid mortal insult, he became one of the Freds; his wife, his sons, the customers and the potted plant next to the till are all called Fred.

'Someone asking for you,' Fred announced. 'You be quick.'

When I got out into the restaurant, it was such a relief to be out of the steam-bath that I was even pleased to see Harris. Not pleased enough to touch him or anything.

Harris always appears to carry a varied selection of the more interesting viruses about town. He's tombstone-pale, with spiky black hair, and can't see any colours at all. He gets done by every shop assistant wanting to sell those lurid purple trousers or sick-green shirts which no one will buy. As a defence, Harris has gone Gothic. Tonight he was attired in a black silk shirt with claw-marks ripped through it, black velvet trousers, an ancient black overcoat and desert boots.

'You went past my place, huh?' I was looking at the ripped shirt. My cat is very protective of his territory. Who needs a Doberman?

'Yeah. Thought I might catch you before you left. How's it going?'

'Like a lead balloon. How about you? That Frankenstein doctor finally gave up, didn't he?'

'Yeah. I had to hang around the girls' school for months, y'know, and then it didn't do any good.' He tried to look martyred. 'Look, I didn't come just to chat. I've got word of a new operation. The guy reckons he's gonna need two of us. Interested?'

'Yeah, sure. Fred's waving a skillet at me. I'll get back to you after work.'

'The guy says we have to settle it today. Half an hour from now.'

'Oh, he does, does he? Just like that, not even knowing anything about this "new operation"?'

'Sure.' Harris looked mildly perplexed. 'What's new?'

So I waved back at Fred, grabbed my coat from the chair behind the till, and followed Harris out of the restaurant.

'What's that place called, anyway?' he asked idly. 'I bet it's some foul insult in Chinese.'

'Nah, Fred told me once. I think it translates as *Frogchops*.'

I insisted we go by my place so I could wash and change. Harris still refused to tell me anything during the drive to the guy's place. He parked on a street in Maylands, close to the railway, then headed towards a nondescript little state-housing shack. It didn't look as though the owner of this place could afford to hire anybody to cut the grass, which needed it, let alone for a major job. It's against the rules to hit anybody in the business, but I started wondering what the hospital might pay for a Harris-cadaver. He knocked on the rickety door so lightly it wouldn't disturb a bat.

'Uh, Mr Fogg, are you there?'

'*Fogg*?' I muttered.

'It's a pen-name.'

'I think you mean a pseudonym.'

'Yeah, one of those.' He pushed the door open and called again. This time I heard an answer, which was enough for Harris. He went confidently in and I followed after him, half-expecting something to drop on his head.

Mr Fogg sat in the one chair, in what I guess you'd call the living-room. He was anorexic-thin, pale as a vampire and dressed in black clothes which fitted about as well as Harris's clothes fit him. The carpet was threadbare and the only things on the walls were lumps of blu-tak where posters had once been fixed. On the mantelpiece was a shiny clock, the only new thing in the entire place. There was something not quite 'right' about the place.

'This is Amber, Mr Fogg,' Harris said. Eyes which were either grey, green or muddy-blue turned their gaze towards me.

'Good evening, Amber. I hope you weren't inconvenienced by the short notice.'

I considered telling him how inconvenient it was but instead said, 'Just what did you have in mind for us?'

'Harris has told me that you worked for a hospital.'

'A doctor,' I corrected, catching Harris's signal that Fogg was okay, 'in the know' as we put it. While doubting that he really had vetted the guy, there was little I could do if I wanted the job. We continually work with this kind of uncertainty. 'Private procurement,' I added. 'Is that what you want?'

'I do not, quite, require a body. What I need . . .' He broke off, looking frustrated. The clock beeped loudly behind him and he jumped very slightly but did not turn to look at it. The decimal numbers on its front blurred and cleared once more, reading eleven fifty-five pm. But since Fogg didn't mention it, I sensed that I probably should not notice it either.

'I have here a list,' Fogg was saying. He dug a piece of paper out of his pocket and held it out to me. I took it from him, discovering that it was not paper but a sliver of very thin plastic, and held it up to the dim central light bulb to read it.

'Blud A+ 10pts

Ies 2, Tsordas fam.'

The words (what kind of a joke is this and who can't spell?) jumped around in my mind. I asked, 'You are the recipient?'

'I am.'

'And the eyes must come from a member of this family?'

'Yes.'

His tone didn't change, nor his eyes flicker, but I got a nasty taste in my mouth when I thought about it. Just to take eyes was a hell of a waste. A revenge kick? Still, the reasons were none of my concern, so I took a deep breath and tried to concentrate.

'All right, Mr Fogg, we will undertake to procure these items for you. We will need half our fee now and half when you receive the items. Our usual fee is—'

'Here is twenty thousand dollars, in cash,' Fogg interrupted, picking up a small case which had lain beside his chair unnoticed. 'Will that be sufficient?'

'Ah, yes, it will,' I said when I could focus again. 'Can we contact you here?'

Fogg turned in his chair to look at his clock. 'I will be here until the clock reads twelve.' I started to protest but he continued, 'No, you do not understand. That will be at least two days. If the clock reads twelve before then, I will have no need of the items, you see.'

I didn't, but his insanity was his own business. 'Harris or I will be here each evening at seven to report on our progress until we obtain the items. Is that satisfactory?'

'It is. I am pleased with your attitude, Amber.'

Wish I could say the same for you, I thought. 'We'll be on our way then. Is there anything else, Mr Fogg?'

He paused. 'No. Good night.'

I followed his glance at the clock and blinked, trying to clear my eyes. Surely it had said eleven fifty-five, but now it looked more like fifty-two or three! I was going to need a cornea transplant myself if this kept up. We muttered goodbyes and got outside.

'Weird guy,' Harris said as we tramped back through the long grass to the street.

'You ought to know. How did you find him?'

'He rang me up. I don't know how he got the number, unless he knew someone else in the business and if he did, why'd he want us? This money's all right, though!'

'That's what I'd better check. Go talk to some of the body-rollers, get things moving. Come along to my place tomorrow morning. I should have enough blood already in storage; if not, I'll give Jeff a ring at the blood bank.'

'The blood's in cold storage at my place,' I confirmed to Fogg the next evening. 'The other thing will take a little longer. Harris is out casing the home of a Tsordas right now.'

'Good.' He was over by the window this time, his gaze vaguely over my head to where I knew the clock stood. I didn't want another case of the creeps, so I didn't look at it.

'Goodbye,' he added.

I met Harris at the rendezvous bus stop and we went along to the house. We did the religious trick. Harris is too weird-looking to be convincing as a Mormon or a Jehovah's Witness, and probably they wouldn't wear a female with a red crew-cut either, so we had to be from an Eastern religion.

Harris rang the doorbell and we fixed suitably rapturous smiles on our faces. The door opened and a guy looked at us. We stared back. He was dressed in casual trousers, but he also had a second collar; one of the back-to-front jobs.

'Yes?'

'We're from the Church of Swami Nasigoreng.' Harris hesitated. 'I guess you wouldn't be interested,' he said feebly, noticing the dog-collar.

'I'm afraid not. Good evening.'

The door closed and we retreated. At least we'd seen him. I asked Harris why on earth he hadn't said something.

'I didn't see the guy, I just watched the house!'

'Well, it looks like he'll do,' I said.

'I don't like the idea of hitting a priest!'

'We don't have to kill him. Look, it could be worse, at least the blood was easy. The guys at the blood bank hand it out by the bottle for the right price, but this we have to do ourselves. Wish I could figure out why this particular family, though it's still no guarantee his system won't reject the eyes. Hey, did you even check that he's called Tsordas?'

'Yeah. I rang up the place; he's got an answering-machine.'

'There's hope for you yet. Now, where to do the snatch? He's seen both of us, that isn't too good, but if we can get somewhere where there's a crowd. . . . I know, I'll call the Catholic cathedral in the city, they'll know where he does his priest thing. Then you and I can turn up for service bright and early tomorrow morning, hang behind afterwards and—wham!'

'Great,' Harris agreed. 'He's going to wonder, after Swami Nasigoreng, but that'll just make it easier to talk to him.'

For some reason, I wondered what time Fogg's clock was showing at this precise moment.

The plan went as smoothly as a lawyer's plea, smooth

as the hypodermic into Father Tsordas's arm. He crumpled very neatly by the altar of the now-empty small church, giving Harris enough time to catch him and set him down gently. I put down the esky with the ice.

'Okay, where's the knife?'

'What knife? I thought you had it.'

'The car!'

'No time,' Harris said. 'Someone coming. Quick, he's fainted.'

Harris may be weird but he isn't dumb. We were all solicitous attention by the time the two elderly, black-clad Italian ladies saw us. They screeched in horror and began fanning the Father, talking to each other like parrots all the while. Harris and I just left them to it. Even if the mammas just took him to a doctor and the doctor found out what was in him, we'd be okay. The doctors never bother anyone in the business. They owe us too much.

There were two other families called Tsordas, but they were out of our hunting territories. This delayed us most of the day. I had to part with quite a bit of that lovely crinkly paper just to get permission to hunt out of my area, without even seeing the houses or the people. It turned out not to be too much of a problem.

The family we picked lived in a house which is, I think, termed creative architecture. It resembled a huge white concrete mushroom. We leaned over the low surrounding wall and gazed at the landscaped garden. Trouble was, the landscape was closer to a moon crater than any Earthly surface, given an eerie glowing quality by the huge floodlights directed from the top of the mushroom.

'Sculptor?' Harris suggested.

'Yeah, that or Satanist. Whatever, he makes a bit of money out of it,' I said, looking again at the mushroom. No windows were visible from the front and there was no car about. 'What's it going to be this time?'

'We're art students,' Harris said earnestly to the woman who opened the door. 'We were wondering whether you hold any classes; we want to learn to sculpt as well as who-ever did your garden. We've never seen anything like it.'

That was the first true thing he had said. I couldn't look at him without wanting to laugh, but I was also having trouble looking at Miz Tsordas. Like Harris, she was in black: black flapping shorts and a vest, showing skinny lengths of white shins, arms and a goose-like neck. Her lank black hair hung down to her butt. She had great dark-ringed black eyes which stared at Harris every second he was speaking, but unfocused into the distance the moment he stopped.

'My 'usband,' she gasped. 'Built this 'ouse 'imself. We worked together on the garden, side by side . . . 'e is a genius—ah!'

She was still gazing out into the void, so I took the chance to nudge Harris. 'Go on!' I muttered, more because I was getting a case of the creeps than because it was truly the right moment.

'Madam,' he said, getting that Gothic stare back again, 'you are right. Your husband is indeed a genius . . .'

I had got the hypodermic into her arm. She sagged, as graceful as a collapsing stork. I managed to catch her, grimacing at the clammy feel of her flesh.

'Great,' said Harris. 'I had no idea what I was gonna say next. Come on, we'd better do the work inside.'

That should have been the end of it.

We packed the items in ice and delivered them to Fogg. My mind was working overtime on just how he was going to have his surgery done. And why. But our stage of the business was over now. We left him still sitting in his bro-ken-down chair in the shabby, dimly lit room.

'Did you see,' Harris said to me outside, 'that clock of his still doesn't show twelve!'

'What time did it say?'

'Eleven fifty-eight, I think.'

I stopped. That was my first mistake. The second was saying, 'I'm going to have a quick squiz back inside.'

'There's nothing else to see!'

'So wait here.'

He followed as I'd known he would. We're both used to moving quietly and exchanging information without speaking. I heard a slight creak from Fogg's armchair and held up a thumb to tell Harris he was still there. We crouched down beside the doorless entrance to that room.

'Venner? Dr Venner, can you hear me?'

The clock beeped and we heard another voice; quite deep and pleasant, the kind of voice you'd expect from a country-and-western singer. 'I hear you, Tsordas.' Well, that wasn't a surprise. 'Why are you calling? You know they're looking for you.'

'I've got the items for surgery, Venner. I need you to come through and take care of it.'

'If I do that, it's like sending out the invitations to your execution!'

'Not if you come now. When I have the new eyes, they won't have the retina-tracer; when my blood's changed over, the virus will be gone. They thought I'd come crawling back when I got real sick, begging to be locked up again. Sure, it's not a definite match, but the eyes *do* come from an ancestor of mine, so there's a good chance! Venner, you owe me for all the things I got for you, and there's no one else I can trust.'

The voice sighed. 'Very well. Quite literally, your funeral. Coming through, then, and the way better be clear!'

The clock beeped once more and was silent. We waited; Harris and I crouching on the carpet, Fogg motionless inside the room. Then there was suddenly someone else occupying air in that room, pressing weight down on the floor, yawning hugely and in all other ways proving his physical presence. I felt Harris grab onto my arm, painfully hard, but I didn't object. We both needed to be sure someone else here was real.

'I have to merge this place with my surgery,' Venner said, in answer to some objection our 'employer' was making. 'You're the one set up the time link to my place, Tsordas, why did you do that if you didn't mean me to use it? I know it's more dangerous, but there is no way the work can be done with thirty-year-old medical facilities, even if you could get them.'

I was fighting to hear him through my headache, the sort of aching, sick feeling one gets from jet lag, as though I'd flown thousands of kilometres in a moment. Nothing felt quite real any more, not even Harris's hand on my arm or the cracked surface of the wall against my shoulder. Without asking him, I knew Harris felt sick as well. He was making that very low gasping noise he usually makes when he is thoroughly hung over.

All I could hear now was Venner murmuring to himself and sounding like he was about to break out into 'Ghost Riders in the Sky'. Finally, I peeked around the doorway.

The room was still the shabby, almost bare living-room we knew. Fogg's armchair was in its usual place and the brass clock sat on the mantelpiece behind it. Yet the place was vague, faded. The whole room seemed not quite there, like mist in the garden early in the morning. Super-imposed over it was another room, bleakly white and clean, containing a surgical bed and an array of humming machinery. On the bed lay Fogg-Tsordas. Attached to his body were wires connected to some of the machinery, which I couldn't begin to identify. As I watched, one of them whirred into overdrive, its wires glowing red. No, not light, but blood, rushing out of Fogg's body and into the machine. His own blood was being replaced by the A+ I had obtained for him.

Dr Venner looked as though he might benefit from some surgery himself. He didn't look sick, exactly, but malnourished. He didn't have much hair, and what there was looked lank and dirty. His eyes were red-rimmed and he had a skin condition which a pizza might envy. Luckily for me, he was also totally absorbed in what he was doing. Had he looked beyond the bed, he'd easily have seen my face peering back from almost ground-level.

Harris was whispering behind me, prodding me in the back. Reluctantly I crawled back and let him past to look.

He stared so long I finally hooked a finger into his jacket and pulled him out of sight.

'Let's get out of here!' he muttered.

'I want to see what happens.'

Harris's religion, devout cowardice, took over. He shook his head at me, muttered something indistinguishable and crawled out of the house. I settled back, giving Venner a bit more time before I again stuck my head out to see what he was doing.

One of the machines had metal tentacles extended and was digging into Fogg's face. I hastily pulled my head back. Jeez. I don't care if they're dead, but to see that sort of thing while the client's alive! When I looked again, the doctor had moved around the table and was blocking my view. 'You can relax now,' he said. 'It's done.'

Relax? That guy wouldn't be moving for hours!

'What time does the clock show, Venner?'

I bit down on my lip to keep from screaming. That couldn't be! That would have to mean the guy was conscious during the whole damn operation; what kind of drugs, what kind of surgery, can achieve that? I was so freaked that I only heard part of Venner's answer but it was enough ' . . . past twelve. How do the eyes feel?'

'Fine, they're fine . . . past, and no alarm. The tracer's gone now, Venner, I'm safe!' I risked another peek and this time saw the doctor helping Fogg to sit up. All I could see was his bony back and his greasy hair, but he sure didn't look like someone who'd just had major surgery.

'Why didn't you find the items yourself?' the doctor asked. 'Why get those locals to do it?'

'Easier than not,' Fogg shrugged. 'The money was loose change, but worth a good deal, back here. They know the city and it's their territory.'

I'll be damned, I thought. He's one of us! I bet I knew what had happened; one of his clients had turned against him or he'd hit the wrong person and the cops had come after him. It happens.

My headache suddenly surged back and Fogg screamed

in shock. Venner staggered back into some of his machinery and was gone, the air closing tightly around where he had stood, sling-shotting his surgery ahead to home-time. Two more bodies shoved air out of several cubic feet of space. They were cops in anyone's book; though the black uniforms were of a different cut, the grim expressions were the same. One held a small black box about the size of a pocket calculator, which he was pointing right at Fogg as the latter got to his feet.

'What could I possibly have forgotten?' Fogg asked in that same quiet, gentlemanly, slimy tone he'd used with me.

'DNA tracer,' one cop said, waving the box around. 'They haven't used retina-tracers for over three years now. You're out of date, Tsordas. Even a body transplant couldn't have saved you. Know better next time, eh? Come on, we'd best be going. Don't forget your clock.'

As they disappeared, I took another instantaneous international flight and collapsed groaning against the wall. When my head stopped thundering and flashing lights, I looked into the room again, pretty sure of what I'd see. A bare room with no one there at all. It didn't look as though anyone had ever been there.

Harris helped me get back to the car. I could still hardly see. When we got moving, I just leaned my head back and groaned until we got to my place.

Over coffee, I tried to tell Harris about it. He sort of believed me (after all he *had* seen part of it for himself) but for the rest of it, he thought we should just spend the twenty thousand dollars and start looking for our next job, before the future comes rushing in on us and things began to get really tough for a couple of people just trying to make a living.

DEAR READER
by Dirk Strasser

Dear Reader,

I feel compelled to tell you this. Darkness works in different ways, and its paths twist and turn as it seeks release. And do not believe for a moment that I speak of the soft darkness, the darkness of night, for its tumescence can be predicted by charts and numbers. No, dear reader, I speak of the darkness of the soul, that which was once called evil before the word lost its meaning. I speak of that darkness which is far more particular, which is far more perverse, which is far more real.

And I tell you again, dear reader, I tell you again because I am compelled in ways you cannot know; darkness works in different ways. In some it gnaws like a tumour, a florid silhouette of growth. Perhaps that is how it will work in you. Or perhaps its manifestation will be a lack, a loss that knows nothing of itself except an aching absence. Is that how it will be for you? Or perhaps the darkness works in you, as it does in me; in a compulsion to infect others, over and over and over again.

So, dear reader, that is what I am about to do. You could stop reading now, but I am afraid the infection has already occurred. I have already planted the dark seed inside you, and it will grow whether you leave me before I finish my tale or not . . . but you won't leave me, will you? You may try. You may put the book down as you read these very words. But you will return to me for my tale. Of that I have no doubt. You will not leave me now for the same reason that I write this tale. The compulsion is with you. You must discover what manner of dark seed is now burgeoning in your soul . . .

It is in the words, dear reader, that my tale lies. Ah, you say, but what is there to any tale but words? And, of course, you are right. But words are more than the means to my story; they are its very substance.

My memory begins with my first word. Who among you can trace that first spark of consciousness to his first spoken word? Very few, I would guess; for if you could, I suspect you would share my dark fate. And I know I am unlike you. What was the stuff of your first self-awareness: a scene perhaps, an emotion, a being? In me, the first that I knew of myself is tied like a noose around my first word.

'Dad,' I said with childish inflection. 'Dad.' Again and again like a flurry of wasp stings. Not that the child's mind knew of the venom in those words. Yet, even then, the compulsion was there, and I spoke the word with a joy I now see as malevolent as a cancer.

From that moment I have learned the subtle ways of the darkness. Never has it the immediacy of pain, never the sharp sting of a blade, nor the bite of ice. The pain comes, in time. No, the darkness at first leaves only a dull, shallow ache that has no name, a nothing where once something was.

I watched my father from that day on, aware even in my tender years that I had perpetrated some monstrous crime on his being. His eyes hollowed as the months and then years passed; his skin dried, but worse still, he died inside. I could sense his demise as I reached the age of schooling. He still existed, but something ate away the goodness inside him. For him the darkness I had invoked was a vacuum. His soul leaked through his pores day by day, and I knew that I was somehow responsible.

The word 'Mum' came soon after the first name, and I spoke it with the same subtle and perverse joy that I had said 'Dad'. A single utterance of the name, I have discovered since, is enough; yet its repetition twists the arrow and allows the barb to work its evil intent on gristle and sinew. For my mother the darkness worked as a tumour, contaminating her marrow with its own poison, consuming her life with its own perversion. Over the years her mind turned and twisted on itself, and, in a grotesque afterthought, her body eventually followed. An obscene bile would issue from her throat, a vitriol desperate to escape its host. Yet, like an ulcer, that escape only stimulated further and more profound infection.

Sophia was the baby. My words never gave her the chance to be anything more. The anger at her intrusion into my life was something I admitted from the very outset. For the first time I used my power to destroy that which I hated. I would enter her room silently, night after night, and bend over her cot, calling 'Sophia' again and again. I would whisper it first with the soft malevolence of a razor, then louder like the grating of a saw, and finally every 'Sophia' that I cried was the swing of an axe.

She died before my parents did.

'Darkness know thyself'. The words still resound a hollow echo in my head, though their source is a mystery to me. I knew my own darkness the day I lost my father. Though I had lived but eight years, I knew his frailness, his desiccation, was my doing. With childish logic I thought that reversing the name would somehow undo what I had done. 'Dad!' I cried, and laughed a sorrow-filled laugh when I realised the monstrous joke the word had played on me.

From that day on I resolved never to speak a person's name. I fought to excise the address from my speech, slough it from my skin like dead tissue. And yet the compulsion remained, like a child's fascination with matches, like a madman's urge to plunge from a cliff-top.

Still, it is surprising how unnecessary names are; speech can be twisted to eliminate them in many artful ways, and I became a scholar of that precious art. I grew adept at such phrasing; my hesitations soon dissolved into a natural flow, so that very few would be aware of what was missing from the pattern of my speech.

I began to shudder and recoil from the sound of my own name. 'Martin,' my teachers would say, and I would feel a tightening at the back of my throat. How alien my own name became in the mouths of others. Soon it became difficult to keep the association between 'Martin' and what I saw as myself. How pale and insipid the word was on the lips of others. 'Martin' became a wraith which cohabited my body and drew its rude physical nourishments from the same sources as I did. That was all.

As I grew into adulthood, so did my resolve. Yet, even at the time when my resolve was at its zenith, I could not escape the darkness within me. My intercourse with casual acquaintances I could control, but when this nonchalance became something closer, my barriers slipped and my self-control was insufficient for the task.

Friendship unlocked the dark power. 'Paul' I said, realising immediately what I had done. 'Mark' I said, after years of control. 'David', 'Malcolm' . . . all became too close, and suffered my darkness.

And then there was Elisabeth. I fought no greater battle than to be close to her. She understood me more fully than anyone, yet she understood me not at all. 'Please say my name, Martin,' she would whisper, and a tightness would take residence in the back of my throat. 'Please, Martin, just once.' I would hold my breath till the blood drained from my face. 'Please, I want to hear you say "Elisabeth".'

'I can't,' I would say as those muscles over which I had no control finally caused me to gasp for air. 'You will have to be content with "I love you".'

But it was not enough for her. The words were not sufficient and the love was not enough. She would demand of me the one thing I could not give her. Yet, I could not leave her. And thus she became the first person I told of my darkness. She laughed, of course, thinking at first that my words were mere jest, and then finally, as my insistence did not waver, believing that I was insane.

I spoke of my parents, of Paul, of Mark . . . even of little Sophia. 'Dead,' I said. 'All of them.' Perhaps it was the solemn insistence in my voice, perhaps the darkness in my eyes, perhaps simply the intimacy we had achieved, but eventually she came to accept what I had told her as the truth.

From that moment on our bonding became more intimate than I have ever known. She knew what was inside me, and though no one could love the darkness, she loved the part of me that was not dark, loved it as fully and completely as any love.

And as time passed, her mouth became my own, and she spoke the names that I had only allowed to form as thoughts in my mind. She spoke them for me, giving me what I had forbidden myself. She sensed when a name was needed and said it so that the necessity for me to do so disappeared. And she did so with such fluidity, such imperceptible grace, that friends would be unaware that I never spoke their names. We were as one, her words and mine; and she entered my speech as she entered my soul.

It was a time when I was visited by pride, or perhaps an untempered arrogance. I believed I had beaten the darkness that had blighted my life. In my thoughts I cried to it as one cries to a vanquished opponent in battle. I gave silent voice to the exultant joy of victory.

Yet, I see now that in this very moment of my belief in victory lay my defeat. That dark foe was subdued but its spirit lived and thirsted for revenge. In my arrogance lay my downfall. And Elisabeth, whom I believed to be my saviour, proved to be my nemesis. It was in the ultimate joy of our lovemaking that the darkness emerged from my being, filled with a hatred and loathing unmatched by the utterances of my youth. I was lost as the pleasure of our being, Elisabeth and I, reached its zenith. I abandoned myself totally to her, and the barriers I had placed on that which lay within me broke.

'Elisabeth,' I cried in a joy which knew no bounds.

'Elisabeth.' And once more, 'Elisabeth.'

And with that cry, my heart all but ceased beating. Elisabeth and I stared into each other's eyes, knowing the import of what had been done. For the first time I saw that beast which I call the darkness. It hung between us like a guillotine suspended by a thread. And I saw the guillotine descend, and I saw the beast enter Elisabeth's eyes.

'Perhaps you are wrong,' said Elisabeth, but her voice was already not what it had been. Something had changed.

I shook my head as tears formed in my eyes. 'You know I am right,' I said.

And she did, of course. She had loved me too well not to know.

In the days that followed that I learned a further truth: as I had grown and matured, so had the darkness within me. Elisabeth's death was not the slow decline the others' had been. Within two days the convulsions started. It was as if she was trying to shake out the seed I had placed within her. But soon the seed grew too large and the convulsions eased. Though the next stage was not filled with the same violence, its malevolence chilled me to a core far deeper than I knew existed. She would lie on her bed and twitch and grimace, and then lie still, still as if life had departed her bosom. Then she would call out my name and cry that she loved me in a voice that puckered my heart into a bitter travesty.

At these times, when the Elisabeth I had known called to me, I felt the irresistible urge to call back, to say her name in ways I had never been able to say. As she grew worse, and the seed had *become* her, and what had been her had become a dying flower, I realised the only way.

I sat next to her as she lay, still twitching, still crying, still grimacing, on our bed. I took her hand in mine as I had done so often before and lowered my mouth to her ear. I kissed her gently and the twitching ceased. Then I whispered what was in my soul. 'Elisabeth,' I said. 'Elisabeth, I love you.'

She seemed to draw a breath, and I could feel her hand

gripping my own. I leant back to see her face, and the contortions had fled to reveal a serenity across her features. Then the convulsions started again. She cried out, and a bile bubbled from her throat. And I convulsed with her this time, feeling the darkness I had placed behind her eyes. I lay over her mouth as we shook.

'Elisabeth,' I cried over and over. 'Elisabeth.'

Until finally the convulsions ceased.

I drew back from her, wanting to look at her face, but it was not the face I had known.

Then I cried my own name, in vain hope that I could inflict on myself what I had done to her, but the beast which lay within me only laughed.

And, dear reader, her death fed my darkness. It grows in strength with every passing day, and with it grows my compulsion. The barriers I had built for the beast have now all but vanished. I still fight, but I so rarely find the strength any more.

And like any compulsion, my darkness feeds on its own cancer. The more I name, the more I need to name. I *am* that darkness now, and I need to destroy in order to live.

Now, dear reader, let me reveal to you to what monstrous proportion my darkness has now grown. As I write these thoughts I shiver at the perverse pleasure of the direction of my growth. I have discovered of late that precise names are no longer necessary, and that I can invoke the darkness with terms of address far more general and all-embracing. And my most recent discovery is that the written word for me now serves the same purpose as the spoken word. And I wonder, with the delicious and insane wonder that only darkness can bring, how many more people can I now infect, dear reader?

THE VIVISECTOR
by Eddie Van Helden

Birth

The vivisector's birth is quick and uncomplicated. The doctor writes in her diary that night, '. . . encountered my first case of spontaneous Caesarian today.'

Very Early Years

The vivisector is a precocious child. At three months his mother finds his teddy lying in his cot; eyes missing, head missing, arms and legs nowhere to be found—just a torso gutted of all its stuffing.

At four months he can say his first word 'cut'.

At five months he can say his second word 'cat'.

At six months he begins walking, finds the cutlery drawer, then the cat, and never touches the toy box again.

Recording

At only three years of age the vivisector starts to write and record everything in a journal. His first entries are: cats' tails come off and cats' eyes make good marbles.

Budgie

Vivisector gets a budgie for his fourth birthday and puts it in the freezer. He writes in his journal that night: budgies can't live in freezers.

The next day he cuts the budgie up into a hundred

264

pieces and writes in his journal: cause of death—freezing.

Frog

Vivisector finds a frog. He brings it home. He puts it in the blender. That night he writes in his journal: frogs are made of green frothy stuff.

Thirteenth Birthday

For his thirteenth birthday the vivisector requests a stereotaxic device, a genuine scalpel set, a saw, a chisel, and sledge-hammer.

Neighbours for a radius of 1 kilometre note that their pets go missing.

After a month his mother accidentally walks into his bedroom, is totally shocked and takes the implements and his privileges away from him. When the vivisector looks dumbfounded she explains patiently in detail to him how cruel the thing is that he has done—how animals feel pain and that it isn't right to inflict it on them. The mother finally stops when she observes a look of understanding spreading across the vivisector's face.

That night the vivisector writes in his journal: must lock door next time.

Secondary School

Vivisector refuses to dissect a mouse because it is already dead.

Favourite Movies

Hidden Crimes and The Razor's Edge.

Favourite Songs

The First Cut Is the Deepest and Shock the Monkey.

First Date

Vivisector buys some Jaffas, popcorn and Coke, then takes his first date to see the local abattoirs.

University

The vivisector leaves home to go to the biggest and most prestigious university—because it has the largest animal house in the country.

Shopping

The vivisector is a conscientious shopper. He painstakingly reads all the product labels, avoiding the ones that aren't tested on animals. He makes sure he always buys genuine battery eggs. His favourite food is Paté de Gras. He slowly ambles down the aisles dreaming that he is in China.

Career

The vivisector is ecstatic. He is doing what he always wanted to do and getting $60,000 a year for doing it. Behind the locked doors of the animal house his career blossoms while animals wilt. He is a very busy man, up to his neck in brains, eyes, paws, claws and pancreases.

Mother's and Father's Death

Vivisector doesn't notice. Except that there's a sudden anomalous rise in his bank balance.

Seeing The Light

The vivisector is an atheist until a travelling Jehovah's Witness knocks on the door of the animal house and reads to him: 'Genesis 1:26; let us make man in our image according to our likeness, and let them have in subjection the fish of the sea and the flying creatures of the heavens and the domestic animals and all the earth and every moving animal that is moving upon the earth.'

So? says the vivisector. The travelling Jehovah's Witness quickly flicks open a dictionary and reads: 'subjection; to make subject.'

Look I'm a really busy man I'm up to my neck in . . . says the vivisector before the travelling Jehovah's Witness zips out a Thesaurus and reads: 'subject: guinea-pig . . . victim . . . subordinate . . . at the mercy of . . . vulnerable . . . expose and he emphasises TO LAY OPEN.'

The vivisector begins to smile. This Jehovah's my kind of guy he says. Where do I sign?

Marriage

The vivisector marries a Jehovah's Witness girl who is a virgin. He brings his scalpel with him on the honeymoon.

First Child

A boy. The vivisector is delighted. He leans over the edge of the cage and moulds the tiny fingers around the grip of a shining stainless steel scalpel, then hands him a teddy.

By the time the boy is four he has mastered the rudiments of vivisection; he can stick a scalpel in a cat from a distance of ten feet, he can shoot strychnine into a moving target with either hand and he can whip the top off a monkey's cranium expertly. You're going to make the Scientists' Hall of Fame son, he says.

Fame

At forty years of age the vivisector comes out of the animal house. He is hailed as a scientific genius who's discovered a great medical breakthrough when he publishes the results of his twenty-two years of animal experimentation; frogs are made of green frothy stuff and cats' eyes make good marbles.

The world is a changed and better place. Children everywhere will remember the vivisector while playing with round pieces of glass. He appears on the covers of *Nature*, *Scientific American* and *Time* for two consecutive months and is given a Nobel Prize.

Family Tree

At sixty the vivisector traces his family tree back to the Marquis de Sade.

Retirement

The vivisector comes out of the animal house, stretches

his blood-spattered arms, then retires back into its interior.

Death

The vivisector is dying of old age. He lies propped against the monkey corpses in the animal house. He demands that all the vivisectors around the world unite to find a cure for this terrible disease.

He dies and an Elder of the Jehovah's Witness Church reads out Genesis 1:26.

On the other side of town the vivisector's grandson is buying out the local animal pound with his pocket money.

ANZAC DAY
by Cherry Wilder

We would see Aunt Madge's house through the macro-carpa trees: a red corrugated iron roof, white verandah posts. My brother Billy, six years old, said it was like Nan's house and I contradicted him sharply. I could not bear it when he was homesick for our former life, for our own farm and the homestead where our grandmother had lived. My mother said, 'Rachel, we must make ourselves present-able again!'

An old man in a Ford had given us a lift to this gate in the middle of nowhere. It was a perfect April day; a lone oak tree on the drive showed that the season was autumn. The fields were a thick, juicy green on either side of the dusty road. Behind the farmhouse rose a green hillside flecked with the grey skeletons of dead trees, then other hills clothed in bush, a rich blue-green. Barbed wire fences and a ditch ran parallel on both sides of the road; the green grass grew thickly outside each fence with reeds and wild flow-ers springing up in the ditch. The barbed wire sagged across the road; a young Jersey cow put her head through the fence and munched buttercups. They would taint her milk.

Uncle Len's name, FELL, was on the mailbox. We perched on a roofed platform for cream cans. I combed my hair, wiped my face—I had been eating biscuits—and shined my shoes with a handful of grass. My mother dealt with Billy first of all. Then she took out her powder com-

pact, powdered her nose and put rouge on her lips with the tip of her finger. She wore a navy costume and a pert felt hat trimmed with grosgrain ribbon. I wore a pleated skirt of Royal Stewart tartan with a cotton bodice and over it a blouse of cream tussore silk with a Peter Pan collar and a navy cardigan. Billy wore grey serge short pants, almost to his knees, a long-sleeved blue shirt and a Fair Isle pullover with a pattern of fawn and green horseshoes and four-leaf clovers. We had been down on our luck, however, and it was beginning to show.

We had left Te Waiau without paying the lady at the boarding-house. It was not so much a midnight flit as a tea-time one but it had meant an uncomfortable night in the station waiting-room. The early train from Te Waiau to Claraville had contained a number of returned soldiers in uniform, others in their best suits with rows of medal ribbons. Today was Anzac Day. After the solemn mystery of the dawn service by the Cenotaph the town was gathering itself together for a mid-morning parade. In spite of the depression the people in the streets looked cheerful and well-fed. The memorial pyramid with its list of the fallen was draped in purple; at its base were piled wreaths of flowers.

We set off through the streets of Claraville; my mother knew the way. The shops were shut today; all shops had been more or less shut to us for a long time now. Even the sight of a Woolworths or a milk bar meant little to Billy. We wandered on past hedges and gardens and came to a much larger house, a Victorian mansion set among smooth lawns. A sign read 'Bethany, Home for the Aged'.

There was the usual problem of where we should wait. I wanted very much to stay with Billy in the garden. We stared at some old people and an attendant, a woman in a starched mauve uniform.

'Better not,' said my mother.

We took the gate which said Tradesmen's Entrance and went down a drive separated from the garden by a tall hedge. Bethany was dark inside, brown-varnished with brown linoleum on the floors. We were engulfed by a warm smell of food as we passed the kitchen. There was an uncushioned wooden bench for us to wait on outside the door of the matron, Mrs McCormack. Billy was tired and hungry; he whined and could not keep still.

Life had become an endless train journey full of discomforts which Billy and I had no right to complain about, as children. We waited, we could not be left alone too much, our care and feeding were a constant worry. The adults that we met demanded certain behaviour. 'Speak up! You like that, don't you, girlie? Have you wiped your feet? Make a fist, young fella!' They were giving a performance for children, like the ladies who leaned over a baby's pram making goo-goo noises, and we must react accordingly. In fact I did not like waiting alone; it was safer with Billy. Special behaviour was demanded of a girl child by men—strangers and drunks but also friendly acquaintances like the gardener at the boarding-house. Not much more, in most cases, than familiarity, an insidious change of attitude, but I suffered great embarrassment and dread. How thin the line was between something that could be shrugged off and the need to scream or tell my mother.

As we sat in the corridor a Maori maid came past mopping the floor with a strong solution of Jeyes fluid.

'You kids wipe your feet?' she asked.

A hideous old woman in a pink kimono chattered to Billy, patted his head and gave him a caramel. An old man with a walking stick and a white moustache demanded our names then mimicked our replies. When we stopped answering him he became excited, whacking at our suitcase with his stick. A nurse appeared and said, leading him off, 'This is not a place for children!'

At last my mother came out smiling with Mrs McCormack, an enormously dignified woman in grey silk; I knew at once that she had got the job.

'So these are your two,' said Mrs McCormack, coming straight to the point. 'What are you going to do with them, Mrs Tanner?'

'We are going to my cousin's farm,' said my mother proudly. 'Mrs Fell. Just out along this road.'

'I'm hungry,' said Billy.

'Oh!' laughed Mrs McCormack. 'Oh indeed. Well, we don't want to spoil your dinner.'

She caught my eye.

'But this *is* a special day,' she conceded.

As we passed the kitchen she put her head inside the swing doors and said, 'Alma—some of those lovely Anzac biscuits.'

As we went down the drive munching, my mother said to Billy, 'Don't you ever say that again!'

'Why?' he asked with his mouth full.

My mother ate one of the biscuits herself. We were faced with a walk of unknown length along a country road. The footpath soon gave way to a track, then the track disappeared. We stopped at this point and the Ford came roaring along in the right direction. The old man, whose name was Wilson, took us to the Fell farm. He deposited us in the middle of nowhere and we watched him drive on, out of sight. There was another house on the other side of the road, just visible from where we stood, but it wasn't his place.

When we were presentable again we opened the gate, closed it after us and negotiated the cattle-stop. The cows in the field raised their heads as we went past. As we reached the oak tree mother said:

'Wait on!'

She enacted a little parody of exhaustion.

'I can't carry this thing another inch.'

Then she headed for the tree with our suitcase. It struck terror into my heart. We would have nowhere—no bed, no food, not even a lavatory—unless Aunt Madge and Uncle Len took us in. Mother was so uncertain of our reception she wasn't game to march up to the house, suitcase and all.

My mother pressed on into the long grass at the foot of the tree and suddenly drew back with a horrified squeak.

'What is it?' I asked.

'Nothing,' she said. 'Nothing, just cow manure.'

She walked in a wider arc round the tree and set down the case. We plodded up the drive; no dogs barked. The house was larger and more handsome than it looked from the road, a spreading bungalow, its weatherboard newly white, its roof a deep crimson. I yearned for the house, for its wide verandahs and the cool, beautiful rooms inside. The front garden was surrounded by a white picket fence and a privet hedge to protect the lawn and the flower-beds from live-stock. A window blind in one of the front rooms was caught up crookedly at a sharp angle across the pane. The perfec-tion of the swept brick garden path was marred by a large cane doll's pram lying on its side. I thought with dull envy of my cousin Beryl, nine years old to my eleven; she had a house, expensive toys, a father who had *not* cleared out.

We came towards the macrocarpa trees which had thick low-hanging branches above worn patches of earth, as if children had played there, riding and swinging on the trees. In black shade the leaves stirred as if a little girl might step out. I was suddenly filled with an entirely inap-propriate emotion, a wave of fear and sadness that seemed to come welling up from the ground on which I stood. It was not part of me at all.

We did not think of going to the front door but followed the wider track to the backyard. Billy went lolloping on ahead, then came to a dead stop.

'Hey look! Hey look!' he cried.

The body of a kelpie cattle-dog lay in the grass; I heard my mother's horrified squeak for the second time.

'Come away,' she said. 'Poor thing.'

'We must tell Aunt Madge,' I said.

'No!' said my mother. 'We don't want to come rushing in with bad news. Not a word, Billy.'

Billy stared at the dead dog with great concentration. There was no telling how it had died; the small amount of blood at its brown muzzle was almost hidden by a shiny mass of bluebottle flies.

'Come on!'

I dragged him by the wrist. We went along the side of the
house into a picture-book backyard with Canterbury bells,
delphiniums and gladioli, fruit trees, a big puriri tree with a
swing, two dog kennels; the whitewashed privy was half
covered with sweet-smelling honeysuckle. My mother patted her hair and tugged at her costume coat. She went up
two steps and knocked at the back door, calling cheerily:

'Oo-hoo! Madge dear! Look who's here!'

She had to repeat the ritual before heavy steps sounded
inside the house and the door was flung open. A soldier
stood in the doorway. He wore khaki breeches, puttees,
neatly wrapped, and army boots, but his tunic was slung
over his shoulders. He had been shaving in his braces and
a flannel vest, there were still specks of lather on his face.
A cut-throat razor glistened in his hand.

'Oh Len!' said my mother. 'Oh I'm sorry to catch you . . .'

'Caught me on the hop . . .' he echoed.

He wiped his lantern jaw with the towel he carried
around his neck. Uncle Len was older and wore a moustache but he was not unlike our own father: a tall, rangy,
muscular man, pale-skinned with black hair. I saw that his
eyes were a much lighter blue with a curious darker ring
around the iris.

'I'm Madge's cousin Grace Tanner,' said my mother.
'You remember, we all met at Violet's wedding. And these
are my two . . . Rachel and Billy.'

His eyes did not move; he stared over the top of my
mother's head.

'Madge's cousin Grace,' he said. 'Gracie. Gracie Tanner.'

He looked into her face for the first time and backed
away awkwardly.

'Come in,' he said. 'I'll put on the kettle.'

My mother was already in, making gestures behind her
back for us to follow. The kitchen was unbearably hot; the
stove was burning fiercely with the grate open and the
windows were shut. A black iron kettle was boiling away.
Dishes were piled in the sink and there was a smell of

burnt food. Uncle Len stood with his back to the sink, a
dark figure against the windows, buttoning up his tunic.
My mother gave a laugh.

'Well, I can see you're doing for yourself, Len,' she said.
'Suppose *I* make the tea.'

She went at it with great efficiency, finding the teapot,
the caddy, clean cups and saucers, milk and sugar in Aunt
Madge's kitchen without a second's help from him. She
wiped down the kitchen table, spread a checked cloth,
found bread, butter and jam, took off Billy's pullover and
rolled up his sleeves, shut the stove, altered the damper,
put two burnt pots to soak and opened the windows. As
she reached round him to do this Uncle Len shuddered
like a nervous horse; I saw the whites of his eyes.

'Madge . . .' he said, clicking his razor shut.

'Madge and Beryl must be on a visit,' said my mother.
'What a pity. Are they down in Auckland with Violet?'

'With Violet,' he said. 'I'm on my own.'

She motioned us to our chairs and poured the tea.

'Take off your cardigan,' she said to me. 'It's hot in here.'

Len lowered himself into a 'captain's chair' at the head
of the table.

'Well, Anzac Day,' said my mother, 'in this sad year.'

I could not take my eyes off Uncle Len. I thought he
would echo her again in his hollow twang: 'Sad year.' Instead he cocked his head on one side, looking more or less
at the clock on the wall, and said brightly:

'Yes, Anzac Day!'

'Were you one of the Anzac soldiers, Uncle Len?' burst
out Billy.

Uncle Len became suddenly alert; his expression was
wolfish and cunning. He grinned at Billy and stretched his
legs.

'Gracie's boy,' he said. 'Wants to know if I was one of
the Anzacs. No harm in saying that I was.'

'Did you kill any Turks?' cried Billy.

My mother, still smiling, shook her head at him.

'Kill Turks?' echoed Uncle Len. 'That's what they told us

to do. Orders came from above. Johnny Turk was a good soldier, he knew how it was done. Learned a lot from him, Johnny Turk. Killed him and saw him die. Shot him down like a dog. Better still, used the bayonet . . .'

My mother made a low sound of protest and rattled her white breakfast cup into its saucer. Len shut up. My mother cut us all some bread, then spread it thickly with butter and tinned raspberry jam.

'You need to see red!' exclaimed Uncle Len. 'Then you can really give it to them. What's your name, sonny?'

'Billy!'

'Don't talk with your mouth full!' said my mother.

She wiped her fingers daintily on a tea-towel, passed it to me, then excused herself.

'I'll just be a minute.'

She went out of the back door. I heard her steps on the brick path to the privy. We were alone with Uncle Len.

'Like a knife through butter!' he said 'A bayonet is sharp enough to cut off your hand. I seen that too. Pile of little hands. The hands of the Belgian babies. You hear what old Jerry did with the Belgian babies?'

'It wasn't true!' I gasped.

Uncle Len glared at me.

'Shut your trap, girlie!' he said. 'Who asked you? Now Billy, show us the size of *your* hand . . .'

'*Billy!*' I shrieked.

'Shut your trap, I said!' roared Uncle Len. 'By Christ, Beryl, I've had enough of your shenanigans. We'll see who's boss around here!'

'I'm not Beryl!' I said.

My mother came back into the kitchen. Uncle Len controlled himself, his nostrils dilated with the effort.

'Is that your girl, Gracie?' he asked. 'She better mind her p's and q's.

'Why Rachel,' said my mother, 'have you been giving cheek to Uncle Len?'

I saw what was going to happen and I was terrified.

'No,' I said.

'No what?'

'No, I didn't give him cheek.'

'No, *mother*!' said my mother severely.

She flung herself down on to her chair and said in a trembling voice, 'Oh Len, it's so difficult to manage all alone. Poor old Will is down in Auckland looking for work. The farm has gone. Did you know that? I've just got this job at the old people's home here in Claraville and I hope and trust you won't mind putting us up for a few days. Madge was always offering us the spare room.'

Uncle Len reached casually into the sink and produced a small meat cleaver. He wiped it clean with the corner of the tablecloth and said, 'Hold out your hand, Beryl . . .'

He winked at my mother.

'Well go on . . .' said my mother, 'he's only teasing.'

'Hold out *your* hand, Mum,' I said. 'Make Billy hold out his hand.'

'Oh Rachel,' said my mother, 'can't you take a joke?'

Uncle Len lunged at me with the cleaver held flat, like a fish-slice, and I backed away so hard that I overturned my chair. He roared with laughter, Billy joined in, my mother took the descant. Uncle Len raised the cleaver high in the air and cut the loaf of bread neatly in two on the bread-board with a hollow thunk.

'Oh, Len!' scolded my mother. 'Now it will go stale. Put that thing away.'

'Blunt anyway,' said Uncle Len.

The cleaver rattled into the sink.

'About the spare room . . .' said my mother. 'I have to be back in Claraville at four for the night shift.'

'Just through there,' said Uncle Len. 'It's open.'

My mother relaxed and smiled. Uncle Len sprang up from his chair.

'Have to get to work.'

'Are you going to the parade, Len?' asked my mother.

'Parade?' he said.

'For Anzac Day,' said Billy.

'Come along, sonny,' said Uncle Len. 'You can give me a

hand. No time for a parade. We'll make our own little celebration.'

Billy got down from his chair.

'What do you say?' murmured my mother.

'Excuse me!'

Billy called it over his shoulder as he followed Uncle
Len into the yard. I stood up and sat down again feeling
the blood drain from my face. The kitchen darkened before my eyes.

'Mum,' I whispered, 'please . . .'

I clutched at her.

'Please, Mum, we can't stay here with him. You can't
leave us with him!'

She put an arm around me, squeezing too tightly.

'It's all been too much for you,' she said.

'Mum,' I said, 'he keeps saying dreadful things. He
keeps calling me Beryl.'

'Poor man,' she whispered. 'I think I know what has
happened.'

I lacked words to express my fear of Uncle Len.

'He's gone funny,' I said. 'He's mental. He's shell-
shocked.'

'You're a big girl, Rachel,' said my mother. 'You know
the facts of life. You should be able to understand.'

'Understand what?'

'I think Madge has cleared out and left him,' she said.
'Taken Beryl with her. Things haven't been going too well
in this part of the world either.'

She left me slumped over the table and began washing
up. She found Aunt Madge's dish mop and soap strainer. I
staggered to my feet and began to dry the dishes. My
mother rattled about in the pantry then checked the oven
and built up the fire. She went to work at the table and I
saw that she was making a bacon and egg pie. Before it
was in the oven she said, wheedling, 'Why not go and look
at the room?'

I finished wiping the bench and went into the passage.
The house was dark and cool after the kitchen . . . I could

see the door of the spare room standing ajar but first I went exploring. There was a sitting-room next to the kitchen with a wireless set and comfortable chairs. The house was divided by a wooden archway filled with a bead curtain; beyond this point it grew very much colder.

There was a large linen cupboard and opposite it a bathroom that was locked. In a little strip of corridor was a room with a pink ceiling to be seen through its fanlight . . . Beryl's bedroom I guessed, but it was locked too. At the front of the house I found the 'best room' with a gleaming black piano, a china cabinet, a small bookcase. On the mantelpiece was a photograph of Uncle Len in full uniform with his peaked cap and Sam Browne belt. In the empty grate lay a mess of broken glass and cardboard; I made out two framed photographs of Aunt Madge and Beryl, smashed and twisted and smeared with something like brown varnish. The room with the crooked blind was the front bedroom and it was locked too.

There were panels of coloured glass in the front door; I looked at a green world, then a red one. I could see the doll's pram on the path, the trees, the picket fence, the sky, all red as blood. I took fright then and ran for the spare room. When I looked back I thought again of a child, a little girl, standing just beyond the flickering strings of beads in the half darkness.

The spare room was perfect for the three of us; it had a double bed and a smaller bed on the glassed-in sunporch. The double bed was made up with a thick white cotton counterpane. There was an old wash-stand with a basin and ewer patterned with water-lilies. I moved like a sleepwalker through the quiet room to the dressing table and opened the left-hand top drawer. It was lined with newspaper and empty except for a gold bangle. I didn't have to read the engraving; it was Beryl's bangle. My eye was drawn to any kind of print: I turned my head and read the headline of a copy of *Truth*, lining the drawer. HACKED TO PIECES: I unfolded the paper to find out the first words but part of the page was torn away, only three letters remained: . . . HER. Her hacked to pieces? Saw her hacked to pieces? The few lines of bold print under the headline told of a Mrs Emma Palmer, dying in a grisly sawmill accident. I heard steps in the passage, shut the drawer and moved away from it as my mother came in.

'Ohhh . . .' she sighed. 'Oh, isn't it lovely. We've really fallen on our feet this time!'

She sat in the wicker chair at the bedside and took off her shoes, resting her stockinged feet on the polished floor. She took my hand and drew me down until I sat on the edge of the bed.

'Let me look at you,' she said reproachfully. 'You haven't got a scrap of colour in your face.'

She took off my patent leather shoes and began to unbutton my blouse.

'Lift up!'

She rolled back the counterpane and one soft green blanket and bundled me into bed. I laid my head on the cool pillow. She brushed the hair out of my face and laid her hand on my forehead.

'Billy . . .' I said.

'Ssh,' said my mother. 'He needs to go out with his uncle. Remember how his dad used to take him everywhere? I'm making them a nice lunch. Len hasn't been looking after himself.'

Her eyes were dark and glistening; she began to sing me an Anzac song:

There's a long, long trail a-winding
Into the land of my dreams,
Where the nightingales are singing
And the white moon beams . . .

I felt my fear slip away gradually like a black tide going out.

'Wake me up before you go!' I said.

'I'll save you a piece of bacon and egg pie,' said my mother.

As I drifted off to sleep I thought of the missing word: MOTHER HACKED TO PIECES. I slept deeply and was brought half awake by voices in the kitchen. I could not make out exactly who was there. At first I thought it was my mother and father and Billy but I knew that couldn't be true. Then it sounded like three completely different people. I turned and saw that our suitcase was in the room and then I fell asleep again.

I dreamed of doors banging and a slow, heavy tread that echoed through the whole house. A voice said quietly, 'Dead to the world . . .' I was filled with terror in the dream and my heart pounded in my throat. The slow, purposeful footsteps went on, another door was shut, there was a sound of hoarse breathing. The voice said, 'Keep still!'

Then there was a dull chopping sound and another voice screamed loudly then dwindled to an inhuman moaning which abruptly stopped. I was standing in the passage, in the icy coldness of the house, beyond the bead curtain. The little girl, Beryl, stood at the front door; I could see her white nightdress and her curly mop of golden hair. I was more frightened than ever. She opened the door and ran out to her doll's pram in bright sunshine. She bent over the pram and then a shadow blotted her out. The terrible voice said, 'What are you up to now?'

I tried to scream but I could not. The dream doubled back on itself. Beryl stood in the hall again, at the front door; she looked back at me over her shoulder.

'Run!' she said. 'Run to the road! I can't open the door!'

Then she turned towards me and I saw that her pretty white nightdress was smeared with blood from head to foot. She held her arms up awkwardly, pressed against her chest, and her hands had been cut off.

I came up out of the dream and it was dark. I knew where I was and knew what had awakened me. Someone had shut a door heavily. I was wide awake, unnaturally alert, tingling to my fingertips.

'Billy . . .?' I whispered.

The room was not so dark: light came in from the

passage, through the fanlight over the door. I could see
our suitcase flung open. My mother had gone off to work
and let me sleep. I reached for my cardigan which was on
the chair back, but did not put on my shoes.

There was a heavy galumphing tread that I recognised:
someone was wearing gumboots. I opened the spare room
door just a crack and saw Uncle Len in the kitchen. He
was alert, as I was, full of purpose. He wore gumboots
now and an old blue jersey in place of his khaki tunic. He
carried, at the trail, a rifle with a fixed bayonet. He crossed
to the back door and went out.

I slipped into the corridor and said as loudly as I dared,
'Billy?'

I followed a thread of sound to the living room. There
was a pool of light from the standard lamp and another
from the dial of the radio. Billy lay curled up on the couch
under a blanket. When I ran to him he sat up and said,
'What's the password?'

'Gallipoli!' I said.

'Wrong!' he crowed. 'It's "Slit their bellies"!'

On the radio a lady was singing 'Roses of Picardy'. I saw
that Billy was as dirty and untidy as it was possible for a
boy to be. The smears of mud on his cheeks made him
look like a little kid in the pictures—like The Kid himself
or a member of Our Gang.

'What did you do out there?' I asked.

His eyes were open very wide, his teeth clenched, his
hair bristling. He flattened his stained hands and beat
upon the grey army blanket. I knew that he was hurt,
maimed, a day with Uncle Len had left him shell-shocked
at six years old. I was filled with a tearing anxiety for my
little brother. I gripped his hands and knelt by the couch.

'Tell me,' I said. 'Billy! Billy-boy!'

'The cows came in,' he said. 'Uncle Len did the milking.'

'Before that?'

'Dug holes . . .' he said.

'He made you dig holes?'

'Put the dead dogs in . . .'

He was still tense.

'Had to . . . had to . . . cut them up first . . .'

'Don't!' I said. 'Don't think about it. He shouldn't make you do things like that!'

'Being soldiers!' he whispered.

'Where has Uncle Len gone now?'

'On patrol,' he said.

Uncle Len came in far away, at the front door. He began to look into every room. The good front room, then the front bedroom with the crooked blind. I heard him unlock the door. He didn't raise his voice but it carried through the whole house.

'You asked for it,' he said.

His heavy tread went on into the room, a pieced of furniture fell over. Then Uncle Len made a sound of disgust, a kind of whinny, and came out cursing under his breath. He unlocked the bathroom and I heard water gushing, a clatter of metal. He came back into the passage, close now, just beyond the bead curtain.

'Now then my little Miss,' he said. 'Did I deal with you? Girlie?'

I tried to pull Billy off the couch.

'Come away!' I whispered.

The big sash window on to the verandah was wide open: I could see the wind stir the curtains.

'We have to get away,' I said. 'He's after us!'

'Not me,' said Billy reasonably. 'Only you. You're a girlie.'

He raised his voice and called. 'In here, Uncle Len! Here's one!'

He tried to hold my hands. As I scrambled to my feet the tall standard lamp swayed and fell down. Perhaps I had tugged on the carpet. I half-crawled across the dark room and went through the open window on to the verandah. I heard Uncle Len stride into the room. Billy challenged him, 'What's the password?'

'Is that my little cobber?' laughed Uncle Len.

I ran softly along the verandah to the front of the house.

The front door was open. I quickly slipped inside and went into the front bedroom with the crooked blind. I went into that room because it was a good place to hide; he had been in that room, he hadn't liked it. I was also looking for evidence.

It was hard to be in that room. The overhead light was on; it had a pink fringed shade. A chair had fallen over; there was a large star-shaped crack in the long mirror on the wardrobe door. The drawers of the dressing-table hung open: handfuls of clothing had been used to wipe up the blood. It was dark and sticky like paint on the mats; it had risen up in a fountain from the bed. In places it was still scarlet in the light, but mostly darker. There were congealing pools of blood in the middle of the bed where the mattress dipped. Aunt Madge had been lying in bed; her head was still on the pillow, a wide band of blood-stained pillow slip was visible between her head and her trunk. One arm was severed at the shoulder and at the elbow, the other had fallen in three pieces to the floor. She lay disjointed like a big doll and there were stab wounds like dark holes in her chest. The door of the little pedestal cupboard beside the bed had been torn off, it lay on the other pillow; Uncle Len had used it as a chopping board.

I flattened myself against the wall beside the sticky doorway and wiped my hand on my skirt. The room was filled with the smell of blood; a red mist rose before my eyes. For a moment I was floating free, I was high in the corner of the dreadful room gazing down at the dismembered woman on the blood-stained bed and the girl in the tartan skirt, pressed against the wall beside the door. 'Run!' I ordered the girl. 'Through the front door again! Now! Stop a car . . . make them get the police!'

Then I was back in my body again, the experience had lasted only a few seconds. I was out of the front door, on the path, among the trees, on the grassy drive, running as hard as I could go for the road in the clear night air. There were the cars, two, three, four cars, a stream of traffic driving home from Anzac Day in Claraville. I climbed over

the gate and crouched in the grass beside the mailbox. I let
several cars go by because they were driven by lone men.

In my dream I try to stop one car, then another but they
pass me by and the one that stops is wrong. The horror
will never end, has never ended to this day. In fact it was
the best car that stopped—the Reti family from the farm
down the road who knew old Len Fell was a bit gone in the
head. He had shot one of *their* dogs once. They believed
my story at once but I am not sure if the police would have
been convinced. George Reti clinched the matter by going
up the drive and hailing Uncle Len from the shelter of the
macrocarpa trees. Uncle Len put on the outside lights, and
fired shots in the darkness; it was a matter for the police.

In another dream, sometimes a daydream, I save Billy,
he runs with me, I never enter the first of the 'death rooms'
as *Truth* called them. I certainly never entered the second
death room, Beryl's pink bedroom, yet I have heard and
read that she lay very peacefully in her bed, golden head
on the pillow. Nothing much to be seen until the bedclothes were stripped back, then strong men quailed. This
was long after the sergeant had come out carrying Billy
and put him into our mother's waiting arms. Not a mark on
him. He grew up in the Gillworth Home for Boys, Auckland, trained as a carpenter and cut his throat at the age of
twenty 'while the balance of his mind was disturbed'.

When I first saw my mother that night, brought from
Bethany to the Claraville Police Station, she flew at me
and clawed my face, screaming, 'You left Billy! You didn't
take care of him! He's still in there with that man!'

She was right of course but I didn't see what else I could
have done. The policemen were shocked by her behaviour.
My mother went on to contradict much of what I had told
the police. She denied that I had ever mentioned Uncle
Len's strange behaviour. She had no memory at all of the
incident with the cleaver and the loaf of bread. She had
never suggested that Aunt Madge and Beryl had 'cleared
out'. She also lied with genteel persistence about money. In
fact she lied so desperately and pointlessly about every-

thing to do with our lives and the circumstances at the Fell Farm that she aroused suspicion. Had she been invited or not? How close was she to Len Fell? '*... a woman with two children staying in the murder house ...*' hinted the newspapers. She lost her job, of course, and had the first of her nervous breakdowns. None of our remaining cousins and aunts stood by her. My father got a divorce. Billy and I were both put into homes.

When the brave sergeant went up to the house at first light, ahead of the spreading cordon of armed constables, he found that Len Fell had run off into the bush. Billy, sound asleep, was the only person alive in the house. There was a long hunt for the fugitive, all through the backblocks. Distant shots were heard now and then; after three months the search was called off. The police believed their man was dead; the kids in Claraville are still told to watch out or Old Len Fell will get them.

RED AMBROSIA
by Bill Congreve

The police will be here soon. By then I must appear to be dead. My little girl Celia will have called them, and even if she doesn't, which I can't afford to believe, her mother will have.

It began in the evening with a cliché from a mystery novel that shows once and for all that Life and Art are inextricably bound reflections of the same truth.

I walked, alone and uncomfortable, carrying a placard that read 'Take the Money out of War', amongst a milling crowd of students, Aborigines, female activists, environmentalists, priests, and others who had all come together to mix dogmas for the Palm Sunday evening peace march in Sydney and be friends for the night. My nerves tingled. Instinct wanted me to hide alone in the dark with just one of these trendy philosophers. I looked at them, and smelt blood. I didn't speak to them, and they ignored me. I wondered if we all, they and I, were present for the same reasons.

Skyscrapers glared down from all sides, surrounding the crowd, and made the people seem tiny compared to the accomplishments of the variant overculture the buildings represented. Modern architects unconsciously imitated the art of ancient graveyard stonemasons. What prompted these people to hold a peace march in these surroundings? I felt like a morgue attendant; cold concrete, steel, and reflective glass everywhere, hiding soft fleshy secrets written in blood.

The marchers walked and shouted beside me, clothed in dreams, and watched the world more openly than those humans hiding in the buildings. Their blood was fresh in my nostrils. I didn't feel like a reformed smoker, forever condemning my own past, but rather like a heroin addict constantly reliving and yearning for it. I would never get used to crowds. They made me yearn to tear throats and feed.

A middle-aged woman approached and walked beside me. She was tall, slim and elegantly dressed in a white silk blouse, grey leather jacket, and a tan skirt that showed her legs to good advantage. I didn't need to read labels to recognize money. Her wardrobe made a marked change to the scruffy hand-me-downs the university students about me proudly wore. Her eye-shadow and lipgloss were applied with tasteful restraint, a trait I found both rare and attractive, and they highlighted the strengths of her features so that her very white skin did not look pasty in the dusky evening light. It did not matter if she was beautiful, for she made herself so. I was flattered she had chosen to walk beside me, but I didn't require such female companionship. I had my little girl at home. This woman was both uninvited and intruding. I looked up at her and told her so.

'I have your price,' she said.

I became annoyed by her presumption, and again asked her to move away. Thus began a conversation no word of which has been lost to my memory.

'Every man has a price. I have yours.'

I mentioned that she seemed awfully certain in her arcane perseverance.

'For a price, any man will commit any act, or will condone any activity by others. For most men the price is simple ignorance. If they know nothing, then they are safe. We think more highly of you than that.'

We walked together in that crowded city street and our topic of conversation, my integrity, made us totally alone in that crowd of peaceful demonstrators. I told her then that she was implying I would do something for her; something I had no intention of doing.

'Yes you will. We have your price.'

I was curious. I asked the inevitable. Then I found she would have forced the information on me even if I hadn't asked.

'Your price is a hundred thousand dollars tax-free. You shall become a moderately wealthy man, Mr Stark, and be free to pursue all your vices. You will even be able to self-publish some of those mystery novels of yours if you wish.'

She knew that much about me then. Secure in the knowledge that she was wrong, and that she did not know my price despite her presumptuousness, I wondered what it was she intended me to do.

'I'm glad you've decided to see it our way.'

We followed the procession around a corner into George Street, near the Queen Victoria Building at Town Hall. The claustrophobia of the skyscrapers was replaced with open spaces crowded with people waiting for the speeches to start.

I listened as she outlined the personal history of a man, a 'male' as she called him. The last faint traces of an orange-red dusk sank from the sky. I removed my sunglasses and scarf.

Thomas Quentin was a customs agent, near retirement, who had been on the take ever since joining the force in 1955. He rose quite high over the years, and had been transferred all over the country. Wherever he had been posted this woman and her organisation had followed, and bribed, and blackmailed, and used his influence to import and export items. Some of these items were drugs, others were toxic chemical wastes, some were rare animals, and still others were people, and the guns and ammunition to arm them in foreign countries. All very valuable items in the right marketplace. A clear picture came to me of the long and profitable relationship this woman and Thomas Quentin had enjoyed. I said as much.

For the first time the anger which this woman could generate at will became apparent; anger which seemed to be caused not so much by what she saw as Quentin's betrayal, but by the fact that a subordinate had not bowed to her will.

'Quentin wanted to retire, to get away from it all. I wanted him to wait for another couple of years, but the male thought he could get away with it without telling me. Now he knows too much.'

Knowing too much wasn't the issue. If Quentin told anybody at all of his activities then he would immediately implicate himself. His greatest sin was to get caught between this woman and her ego.

I became worried by the power over me that was conferred on her by the information she confided to me. Now, I also knew too much. My life she could not threaten, and while she did not know that, there were other factors at stake. The girl at home was one, and my way of life was another. The first major battle for survival I had faced in more years than this woman could understand now lay in front of me. This was the kind of challenge I had lived without for so long that I had forgotten what kind of an adrenalin rush it gave to the blood and the nerves. I told her then that she didn't know my price.

Her response tingled my nerves. She smiled.

'You are going to kill Thomas Quentin for me, Mr Stark. Now that you know it all, what else can you do?'

I wondered what perverse quirk of fate had caused her to approach a writer of unpublishable occult mysteries to be her murderer. I'm not a killer, I said.

'You mean that I haven't met your price. A hundred thousand isn't enough for you? You are a greedy man.' She smiled again.

'What I said,' I told her, 'is that I'm not a killer. I do not have a price for such an act. I haven't survived so long in this modern age of computer-aided diagnostics and forensic analysis by attracting attention to myself in such a manner. My kind no longer kill if it can be helped. The risk is too great.'

She opened a corner of the bag she carried and showed me part of the down-payment. My mouth watered for this woman's blood. My life has been far from perfect and not even faintly free of guilt, but I have enjoyed it, and it has been mine. She was threatening my life, and I told her so. Even I must draw a line.

'This evening, at seven o'clock, just after you went out, we entered your house and found a twelve-year-old girl locked in the basement.'

I only barely heard her tell of how pale the girl was, and how she blinked in the dusky evening light. She had cried as she was taken, and was too terrified to struggle or shout out as she was bundled into a van. I knew then that this woman did have my price, and that she had been toying with me all along.

'When you've killed him, we will return the girl to you.'

Why me, I asked her.

'Your name looked intriguing in the phone book, and when we investigated more closely, you proved so eminently suitable.'

Celia must not be harmed, I said.

'Oh, is that the female's name?'

She didn't investigate me closely enough. I would prove this to her.

I abruptly pushed my way through the peace demonstrators to the side of the street, attracting some adverse comments from the young people about us as I did so. The woman followed more politely. Away from the crowd I reached out and took hold of the bag containing the money, but it was some moments before she relinquished it.

She smiled again. I came to understand that from this woman a smile was an abuse of power. 'If you do a good job there may be more work for you.'

That was a week ago. Yes, I did a good job. If I was going to save Celia I had no choice. Now, unless I act, there will be others. That is not conscionable. The decision to forsake all bloodthirstiness was forced on me by advancing technology. Discovery and publicity will destroy my kind as surely as the mapping of the human genotype will locate the virus and the mutation that created us in the first place. A dingy biotechnology laboratory in some university will one day be the end of my freedom. One sharp-eyed student out of the millions of scientists alive today is all it will take to destroy me.

Since I last tore the throat of a victim, a young nun lost in the snow and threatened by wolves in the south of France, I have come to appreciate the peace and quiet of a less violent life; hence my appearance at the peace march, and my deeper understanding of the issues it confronted than many of those others present. In the time since the nun I had come to terms with using virgin humans as the Masai of the Serengetti use their cattle—simply to bleed them and live as a symbiote rather than to kill them as a parasite would. A certain sense of honour and morality had become attractive even though I realised they were simply forced on me by an over-developed survival instinct.

Now I've killed again, and I enjoyed it immensely. Blood, rich, red, and pulsing. It was a pleasure to watch in the candlelight as it ran over my hands and between my fingers and toes. I tasted Quentin's blood. Blood spilled in violence has a freshness, and a tang, that sings of the unique. Even though his blood was nutritionally useless, I tasted it while he was alive and watching. He laughed with pain as I ate the flesh of his thighs. This is not cannibalism; I'm not human.

His slow murder with a single razor blade appealed to a sense of artistry I thought I'd forgotten.

This threatens my existence in a way I both welcome and despise. Death makes for a mighty temptress, but not all detectives are fools. I must not do this again.

Thomas Quentin is now dead. It took me five days to construct my procedure and, like Oppenheimer, I am proud of the method but ashamed of the bloody result. If I had conceived of this crime for a mystery novel I might be

on the way to getting the publication I had long sought.
None of that is possible now.

This evening a team, in the guise of pest controllers,
brought Celia home to me. They swaggered into my own
home and treated me like a gate crasher at some society
party. I put up with their sniggering and knowing looks as
they carried Celia down to her quarters in the cellar. They
laughed openly at the half-inch of dirt I kept evenly spread
over the floor. They tittered at the designer prints, framed
in oak, of the ruins of medieval European castles, the one
reminder I allow myself of the passing of time. I carefully
locked the door behind them as they marched out; but I
remembered their faces. They laugh at my life? Perhaps
we shall meet again.

The money was almost an afterthought for us all.

After they left I returned to my windowless room next
door to Celia's in the cellar.

Knowing my guilt as well as I did, it was difficult to
raise the courage I needed to go into Celia's room and confront her. I didn't need the nourishment, but there was a
yearning in me for company. Ah, how quickly we pick up
human frailties!

I told her I was sorry, and that I was not good enough to
have stopped them taking her away. Then I went closer to
comfort her as she sat crying on the bed I had specially
bought for her. She didn't shy away from me when I put
my arm about her as I feared she would after being exposed once again to the outer world, but instead she
leaned against me and cried. Even that small comfort
helped us both. I began to hope she may be able to allevi-
ate my need after all.

It was not to be.

'She raped me.'

That evil bitch probably thought rape didn't hurt a
twelve-year-old girl. 'The female is still alive, isn't she?' I
could hear her saying with that smile on her face. Perhaps
I'm wrong. 'Child' isn't a word that woman is capable of
understanding.

I listened as Celia told me the story of seduction and defilement, of subtle violation in the human way with fingers and mouth, and then not so gently with a double-ended vibrator.

'Then she did it with an axe handle. She pulled my legs open and she . . . pushed . . . It hurt. I bled a lot. It didn't scare me as much as the look on her face did. After that she sat down and masturbated in front of me. She made me touch her. She smeared my blood on the inside of her thighs. She said I was safe for that.' Celia's voice was cold and exact; her face expressionless with pain.

Surely that wasn't necessary even for the most depraved sexual appetite. A feminist definition of rape calls it an act of male terrorism used systematically to oppress the female victim. But a grown woman on a twelve-year-old girl? I find this as ultimately disgusting as would any other citizen. I trust the police will remember this rape when they find the woman. Even if they don't, this is the thing I shall remember.

Celia was barely coherent, and not really sane. Perhaps only the fact that it was a woman who had done this to her saved her from a full knowledge of the act.

'Why?' Celia asked.

I couldn't answer.

I have never touched Celia that way myself; not once in the three years since I first found her on her way home from school.

Celia is of no use to me now. She is irretrievably and forever dirtied. Her virginal blood that had once tasted as sweet as manna from heaven is now irrevocably sullied. I can't live on this. The emotional vitamins I need are no longer present. The wash of emotions that flooded through me as she told her story included guilt and revenge, but not blame. I still love her like a daughter.

I owe this wonderful girl more than can ever be repaid.

I've now been forced into the position of solving the problem of Celia's presence which I should have realised three years ago. I don't regret any of that period; it's been marvellously beneficial to me, but the time has finally come.

What can I do with Celia? I won't kill her, for that would be an even worse crime than all I've already done. The problem evolved in my thoughts until it simplified to being one of my presence in her life. How can I abandon my cover identity and leave both of us alive?

I bathed Celia, dressed her, and asked her if she remembered where her mother lived. I wrote two notes, one with her address and a plea for the police to be called. This note could be given to the police as evidence. In the other note I described to Celia's mother how to find Celia's share of the money paid me for Quentin's murder. I doubt if this note will be given to the police. Then I took her to the front door. It was just before dusk, and the light was painful even though the house faced east and the door was in the shade. I winced.

Celia understood my intent. 'I don't want to go.'

I consider it a compliment that this marvellous child wouldn't go, wouldn't leave the house in whose basement she'd been locked for three years.

'What will you do? The police will be after you.'

My Celia is not stupid. I told her that the best place to hide a thing which people will misunderstand is in plain sight. After that? There is a lot of room to move in this country, and perhaps she shall see me again when she is older.

I hugged her, and finally had to chase her away. This leads me to hope I have not been entirely evil in my treatment of her.

It will take Celia twenty minutes to walk home, and this gives me my time limit.

I've written a note to the police which will solve for them the three-day-old murder of a respected, admired, and well-placed public servant. The police, when they arrive searching for a child molester, will quickly find in this house the evidence which will establish my guilt in Quentin's murder. They will also find the clue, including a photograph in the society pages of a populist Sunday tabloid, which will lead them to the woman who paid me to do it. I find it ironic that I must rely on them in the short term for my revenge. It is not so much the woman I want the police to find (she is mine) but her associates. I know they'll find the woman as well, and put her in jail, but I'm accustomed to waiting.

The rope hangs behind me. Part of it hangs in shadow so that the whole thing looks like an inverted question mark, forever questing. Any being of human origin must have inner doubts on being faced with a noose. For a dim moment I remember my mother and the horsewhip she kept in the kitchen broom closet and gleefully used. Then I remember her death.

I've never attempted suicide before. Am I sane now? Perhaps not. Yet I will survive this. I won't die; this meagre thing won't kill me, but I must appear to be dead when the police arrive. This is the essential thing; the deception which will allow me the vital untruth.

It will be night when the police arrive. They'll find my naked body, cold, with no breath or pulse, hanging by the neck from the kitchen rafters.

The only loose end left to the police will be the disappearance of my body from the morgue.

The only loose end left to me will be the woman. I shall watch closely for her when she leaves prison, and when she lies on her deathbed I'll come to her. She will have lived a full and long life of enforcing her will on other people, and she will face, and perhaps will come to terms with, the prospect of a death which will terminate all her desires. And then, at the moment of her death, at the very end of her existence, I will meet her again and make her my eternal slave. Then I will take the woman and go and live in the desert, and there I will tell her: this is my price for murder.

I step on the chair and put my head through the rope. I must resolve this situation into which I have been thrust, both by my own actions, and by those of others. Perhaps this is the truest meaning of the peace rally. Will it hurt? I wonder.

HEIR OF THE WOLF
by Stephen Dedman

'This is wonderful steak,' said Lisa. It was only the third thing she'd said all evening, and she probably thought it was a safe enough comment. Dad, his mouth full, merely nodded. 'It must have cost a fortune,' she continued. Dad swallowed, smiled carnivorously, and replied, 'Yes, well, fortunes are reasonably common, nowadays.'

I'd kept meaning to bring Lisa around to meet Dad, like a dutiful son, but had always wimped out. These dinners weren't so much rituals as bloody ordeals. I'm proud of the old man, of course, but he has a personality like fuming nitric acid, and my girlfriends tended to disappear after meeting him. I attempted a rescue. 'What're we celebrating, Dad? You've been unusually reticent on the subject.'

He glared, but it was a dull grey glare, a poker that'd been left in the fire a little too long, not the actinic blue of a thermal lance. 'You know that old fool Temple died last month?'

'I'd heard he'd died: I didn't know it was as long ago as that.' I hoped that Lisa wouldn't say anything. Jon Temple had been one of Dad's *bêtes noires*, a collector of antique manuscripts, more of a hoarder than a collector. I suspect that Dad had scanned the obituary columns daily, waiting for the rich old idiot to die.

'The ninth,' replied Dad, with relish. 'The collection

298

went to that daughter of his, whatever her goddamn name
is. Of course, she had no use for it either, she couldn't
spend it, wear it or snort it, so she auctioned it off.'

I smiled. 'What did you get?'

'The Grimm. For less than a fifth of what the bastard
had paid.'

'Nobody else wanted it?' I guessed.

'Nobody else knew what it *was*,' he replied. 'Oh, except
Cavendish, of course, but he didn't have the money. He put
up a good fight, though,' he said grudgingly. 'I've promised
him a copy of the translation.'

'What is it, exactly? I know you probably told me, when
Temple bought it, but that was what, ten years ago? Something on philology?'

'Fourteen years,' replied Dad, 'and no. It's an early draft
of "Little Red Riding Hood".'

Lisa laughed. 'A fairy story? I thought you collected historical manuscripts?'

Oh, SHIT! I saw Dad's eyes turn blue. 'The main difference between history texts and fairy stories is that the
fairy stories don't pretend to be literally true, though the
amount of data that *is* literally true in an original fairy
story is usually much greater than in a history.

'Of course, most *modern* renditions of the Grimm fairy
stories are pap, like most things written nowadays that are
set in an historical, or pseudo-historical, world. A lot of
those are written by history graduates who should know
better, though some of the authors wouldn't know a hau-
berk from a halberd, much less a monk from a friar. For
some damnable reason, everybody seems to think the
Middle Ages were glamorous, when the fools don't even
know the meaning of "glamour". The Middle Ages were a
millenium of squalor, pestilence, corruption, brutality,
and, for most, the sort of poverty and injustice that we
now associate with South African blacks. The gap between rich and poor was vast and almost impossible to
cross, the middle class was a Renaissance invention, and
the only things that were cheaper then than now, in real

terms, were human life and dignity.'

He cut himself another chunk of steak with one slash of his knife. 'You said that this steak must have cost a fortune? Throughout history, most people haven't been able to afford *any* meat that wasn't half-rotten. That's why spices were in such demand; they hid the taste of decay. Our words for "beef" and "pork" are from the French for "cow" and "pig", because the Norman barons could afford to *eat* the animals which the Saxon peasants, who gave us the words "cow" and "pig", could only tend: they could've been executed, or at least flogged (such as Tom the Piper's son) for killing and eating the animals. Meat was for the élite; the warriors and the wealthy. Henry the Eighth snobbishly refused to eat vegetables, because the poor could afford them, and probably died of scurvy as a result. Croesus, Caligula, Kublai Khan—none of them had access to a refrigerator. A steak that you could eat nearly raw, without fear of infection? Luxury! Do you know where the word "steak" comes from? It's Middle English, from "steig", meaning "roasted on a spit". Its current meaning— a slice of meat, cooked separately from the rest of the steer—is so new that the French stole it from the English, instead of vice versa.

'And where do you find records of these details of daily life? Where do you learn what poverty, starvation, and plague meant to the poor slobs who actually suffered from them? It wasn't written down (they couldn't read, much less write) but fortunately, it passed into folklore. The ones that rhymed survived the best. Do you know there's a nursery rhyme about the Black Death? "Atishoo, atishoo, we all fall down"; children sing it in kindergarten. And where do you read about the parents who abandoned the children they couldn't afford to feed? The mother who mutilated her daughters for the sake of a good marriage?'

'Mothers still mutilate their daughters,' I interjected, as Dad paused for breath. 'You haven't heard of high-heeled shoes, tight jeans, anorexia nervosa? Most weight-loss diets are nothing but ritual magic, all fasting and potions, eye of newt and toe of frog for the first three days, wool of bat for a week. It's like Catholics eating fish on Friday, but instead of getting into heaven, they just want to get into their own bicycle pants.' I cut myself another chunk of steak. 'Besides, the Grimms wrote in the early nineteenth century, hardly medieval eyewitnesses.'

'True,' admitted Dad, 'but they were *brilliant* folklorists. More importantly, they were *honest*.'

Getting Dad to praise somebody isn't easy, but it's worth the effort; he actually becomes polite for a few minutes afterwards. 'Have you read the manuscript?'

'Read, but not translated.'

'How different is it from the published version?'

'Not very different from Perrault's story, except for the ending,' he muttered, around a fresh mouthful of steak, then turned to Lisa. 'I suppose you remember the story of "Little Red Riding Hood"?'

'Yes, of course.'

'How did it end—the version you remember?'

'The woodsman comes by when he hears Red Riding Hood screaming, and kills the wolf.'

'And?'

'Oh . . . he cuts it open, and the grandmother's inside.'

'Still alive and unharmed?'

'Yes.'

Dad nodded.

'In the version Dad read me,' I said, 'he's too late to save the Grandmother. Mum didn't like it, said she thought it'd scare me.'

'It was *meant* to scare,' grumped Dad. 'The story was meant as a warning; the equivalent of telling little girls not to take candy from strangers. Wolves are wonderfully scary, even though they've never been as dangerous as men, and what the hell use is a cautionary tale with a happy ending? In fact, in the original (well, Perrault's story, the one we previously thought the original) Little Red Riding Hood is eaten, too. Even *Tolkien* knew that.' (Dad was actually one of Professor Tolkien's prize students, but they had an argument in the late 1950s, and Dad refused to speak to Tolkien ever again.)

'And in your version?'

'As far as I can tell, it's a story the editors refused to print. Did you ever wonder how a young, apparently fairly bright girl could mistake a wolf for her grandmother?'

Remembering James Thurber's version of 'Little Red Riding Hood', I smiled. 'What? *Doubt* a story that *you* were telling me?'

'Well, you should have done,' Dad rumbled, 'because in the Grimms' version, the *original* folk story, it's the grand-mother who makes all the "What big teeth you have" comments. She believes the wolf is Little Red. You get the impression that she's nearly blind and deaf, and probably senile. She must have been all of forty, after all. Life expectancy being what it was in the Middle Ages, living grandmothers were pretty rare. I guess Perrault thought the story was too funny to discard, so he changed the names.

'But the wolf devoured the grandmother, and there was none of this "swallowing whole" crap. The Brothers gave a nicely detailed description of the bite to the throat, the dismemberment, the swallowing of the intestines (don't forget, their version of "Cinderella" had the ugly stepsisters amputating their toes and their heels and bleeding all over the bedroom floor like stuck virgins) and the wolf is munching away when Little Red Riding Hood arrives.

'Red comes in, and sees the wolf chewing on one flayed leg. She stares, and the wolf looks up.

'"Meat," he says, "Fresh meat. Would you like some?"'

Lisa, looking slightly green, put down her steak knife.

'She takes the other leg, and roasts it over Granny's fire, but she's too impatient to cook it thoroughly. She devours it, much less neatly than the wolf had done, and the blood runs down over her chin and neck. The wolf licks it, and when she flinches, he bites into her throat, killing her.' Dad cut himself another piece of steak. 'I presume the wolf lives happily ever after.'

Lisa stared. 'And that's meant to be a children's story?'

Dad smiled. 'Parents wave death threats at their kids every day: don't drink that, it's poison; don't cross the road, you'll be run over; the new bogeymen drive fast cars or cause cancer or mutilate little boys or girls according to their personal preferences, but they're all heirs of the wolf. How do you tell a child not to take candy from strangers, when the child is too poor to have ever *tasted* candy?'

I stared at my plate. 'Dad, this is steak, isn't it? From a steer?'

He looked offended. 'Of course. Do you know what you could catch from eating *human* this rare?'

Lisa ran from the room, her hand over her mouth. I should have known not to hand Dad a straight line. This time tomorrow, I'd be hunting for another woman.

NEIGHBOURHOOD WATCH
by Greg Egan

My retainers keep me on ice. Dry ice. It slows my metabolism, takes the edge off my appetite, slightly. I lie, bound with heavy chains, between two great slabs of it, naked and sweating, trying to sleep through the torment of a summer's day.

They've given me the local fallout shelter, the very deepest room they could find, as I requested. Yet my senses move easily through the earth and to the surface, out across the lazy, warm suburbs, restless emissaries skimming the sun-soaked streets. If I could rein them in I would, but the instinct that drives them is a force unto itself, a necessary consequence of what I am and the reason I was brought into being.

Being, I have discovered, has certain disadvantages. I intend seeking compensation, just as soon as the time is right.

In the dazzling, clear mornings, in the brilliant, cloudless afternoons, children play in the park, barely half a mile from me. They know I've arrived; part of me comes from each one of their nightmares, and each of their nightmares comes partly from me. It's daytime now, though, so under safe blue skies they taunt me with foolish rhymes, mock me with crude imitations, tell each other tales of me which take them almost to the edge of hysterical fear, only to back away, to break free with sudden careless laughter.

Oh, their laughter! I could put an end to it so quickly . . .

'Oh yeah?' David is nine, he's their leader. He pulls an ugly face in my direction. 'Great tough monster! Sure.' I respond instinctively: I reach out, straining, and a furrow forms in the grass, snakes towards his bare feet. Nearly. My burning skin hollows the ice beneath me. Nearly. David watches the ground, unimpressed, arms folded, sneering. *Nearly*! But the contract, one flimsy page on the bottom shelf of the Mayor's grey safe, speaks the final word: No. No loophole, no argument, no uncertainty, no imprecision. I withdraw, there is nothing else I *can* do. This is the source of my agony: all around me is living flesh, flesh that by nature I could joyfully devour in an endless, frantic, ecstatic feast, but I am bound by my signature in blood to take only the smallest pittance, and only in the dead of night.

For now.

Well, never mind, David. Be patient. All good things take time, my friend.

'No fucking friend of mine!' he says, and spits into the furrow. His brother sneaks up from behind and, with a loud shout, grabs him. They roar at each other, baring their teeth, arms spread wide, fingers curled into imitation claws. I must watch this, impassive. Sand trickles in to fill the useless furrow. I force the tense muscles of my shoulders and back to relax, chanting: be patient, be patient.

Only at night, says the contract. After eleven, to be precise. Decent people are not out after eleven, and decent people should not have to witness what I do.

Andrew is seventeen, and bored. Andrew, I understand. This suburb is a hole, you have my deepest sympathies. What do they expect you to *do* around here? On a warm night like this a young man can grow restless. I know; your dreams, too, shaped me slightly (my principal creators did not expect *that*). You need adventure. So keep your eyes open, Andrew, there are opportunities everywhere.

The sign on the chemist's window says no money, no

drugs, but you are no fool. The back window's frame is rotting, the nails are loose, it falls apart in your hands. Like cake. Must be your lucky night, tonight.

The cash drawer's empty (oh *shit!*) and you can forget about that safe, but a big, glass candy jar of Valium beats a handful of Swiss health bars, doesn't it? There are kids dumb enough to *pay* for those, down at the primary school.

Only those who break the law, says the contract. A list of statutes is provided, to be precise. Parking offences, breaking the speed limit and cheating on income tax are *not* included; decent people are only human, after all. Breaking and entering is there, though, and stealing, well, that dates right back to the old stone tablets.

No loophole, Andrew. No argument.

Andrew has a flick-knife, and a death's head tattoo. He's great in a fight, our Andrew. Knows some karate, once did a little boxing; he has no reason to be afraid. He walks around like he owns the night. Especially when there's nobody around.

So what's that on the wind? Sounds like someone breathing, someone close by. Very even, slow, steady, powerful. Where is the bastard? You can see in all directions, but there's no one in sight. What, then? Do you think it's in your head? That doesn't seem likely.

Andrew stands still for a moment. He wants to figure this out for himself, but I can't help giving him hints, so the lace of his left sand-shoe comes undone. He puts down the jar and crouches to retie it.

The ground, it seems, is breathing.

Andrew frowns. He's not happy about this. He puts one ear against the footpath, then pulls his head away, startled by the sound's proximity. Under that slab of paving, he could swear.

A gas leak! Fuck it, of course. A gas leak, or something like that. Something mechanical. An explanation. Pipes, water, gas, pumps, shit, who knows? Yeah. There's a whole world of machinery just below the street, enough machinery to explain *anything*. But it felt pretty strange for a while there, didn't it?

He picks up the jar. The paving slab vibrates. He plants a foot on it to suggest that it stays put, but it does not heed his weight. I toss it gently into the air, knocking him aside into somebody's ugly letter-box.

The contract is singing to me now. Ah, blessed, beautiful document! I hear you. Did I ever truly resent you? Surely not! For to kill with you as my accomplice, even once, is sweeter by far than the grossest bloodbath I can dream of, without your steady voice, your calm authority, your proud mask of justice. Forgive me! In the daylight I am a different creature, irritable and weak. Now we are in harmony, now we are in blissful accord. Our purposes are one. Sing on!

Andrew comes forward cautiously, sniffing for gas, a little uneasy but determined to view the comprehensible cause. A deep, black hole. He squats beside it, leans over, strains his eyes but makes out nothing.

I inhale.

Mrs Bold has come to see me. She is Chairman of the local Citizens Against Crime, those twelve fine men and women from whose dreams (chiefly, but not exclusively) I was formed. They've just passed a motion congratulating me (and hence themselves) on a successful first month. Burglaries, says Mrs Bold, have plummeted.

'The initial contract, you understand, is only for three months, but I'm almost certain we'll want to extend it. There's a clause allowing for that, one month at a time . . .'

'Both parties willing.'

'Of course. We were all of us determined that the contract be scrupulously fair. You mustn't think of yourself as our slave . . .'

'I don't.'

'You're our business associate. We all agreed from the start that that was the proper relationship. But you do like it here, don't you?'

'Very much.'

'We can't increase the payment, you know. Six thousand a month, well, we've really had to scrape to manage that much. Worth every cent, of course, but . . .'

That's a massive lie, of course: six thousand is the very *least* they could bring themselves to pay me. Anything less would have left them wondering if they really owned me. The money helps them to trust me, the money makes it all familiar: they're used to buying people. If they'd got me for free, they'd never sleep at night. These are fine people, understand.

'Relax, Mrs Bold. I won't ask for another penny. And I expect to be here for a very long time.'

'Oh, that's wonderful. Come the end of the year I'll be talking to the insurance companies about dropping the outrageous premiums. You've no idea how hard it's been for the small retailers.' She is ten feet from the doorway of my room, peering in through the fog of condensed humidity. With the dry ice and chains she can see very little of me, but this meagre view is enough to engender wicked thoughts. Who can blame her? I'm straight out of her dreams, after all. Would you indeed, Mrs Bold? I wonder. She feels two strong hands caressing her gently. Three strong hands. Four, five, six. Such manly hands, except the nails are rather long. And sharp. 'Do you really have to stay in there? Trussed up like that?' Her voice is even, quite a feat. 'We're having celebratory drinks at my house tomorrow, and you'd be very welcome.'

'You're so kind, Mrs Bold, but for now I do have to stay here. Like this. Some other time, I promise.'

She shakes the hands away. I could insist, but I'm such a gentleman. 'Some other time, then.'

'Goodbye, Mrs Bold.'

'Goodbye. Keep up the good work. Oh, I nearly forgot! I have a little gift.' She pulls a brown-wrapped shape from her shopping bag. 'Do you like lamb?'

'You're too generous!'

'Not me. Mr Simmons, the butcher, thought you might

like it. He's a lovely old man. He used to lose so much
stock before you started work, not to mention the vandal-
ism. Where shall I put it?'

'Hold it towards me from where you are now. Stretch
out your arms.'

Lying still, ten feet away, I burst the brown paper into
four segments which flutter to the floor. Mrs Bold blinks
but does not flinch. The red, wet flesh is disgustingly cold,
but I'm far too polite to refuse any offering. A stream of
meat flows from the joint, through the doorway, to vanish
in the mist around my head. I spin the bone, pivoted on her
palms, working around it several times until it is clean and
white, then I tip it from her grip so that it points towards
me, and I suck out the marrow in a single, quick spurt.

Mrs Bold sighs deeply, then shakes her head, smiling. 'I
wish my husband ate like that! He's become a vegetarian,
you know. I keep telling him it's *unnatural*, but he pays no
attention. Red meat has had such a bad name lately, with
all those stupid scientists scaremongering, saying it
causes this and that, but I personally can't see how any
one can live without it and feel that they're having a bal-
anced diet. We were *meant* to eat it, that's just the way
people are.'

'You're absolutely right. Please thank Mr Simmons for
me.'

'I shall. And thank *you* again, for what you're doing for
this community.'

'My pleasure.'

Mrs Bold dreams of me. Me? His face is like a film
star's! There are a few factual touches, though: we writhe
on a plain of ice, and I am draped with chains. It's a strange
kind of feedback, to see your dreams made flesh, and then
to dream of what you saw. Can she really believe that the
solid, sweating creature in the fallout shelter is no more
and no less than the insubstantial lover who knows her
every wish? In her dream I am a noble protector, keeping
her and her daughters safe from rapists, her son safe from

pushers, her domestic appliances safe from thieves; and yes, I do these things, but if she knew why she'd run screaming from her bed. In her dream I bite her, but my teeth don't break the skin. I scratch her, but only as much as she needs to enjoy me. I could shape this dream into a nightmare, but why telegraph the truth? I could wake her in a sweat of blood, but why let the sheep know it's headed for slaughter? Let her believe that I'm content to keep the wolves away.

David's still awake, reading. I rustle his curtain but he doesn't look up. He makes a rude sign, though, aimed with precision. A curious child. He can't have seen the contract, he can't *know* that I can't yet harm him, so why does he treat me with nonchalant contempt? Does he lack imagination? Does he fancy himself brave? I can't tell.

Streetlamps go off at eleven now; they used to stay on all night, but that's no longer necessary. Most windows are dark; behind one a man dreams he's punching his boss, again and again, brutal, unflinching, insistent, with the rhythm of a factory process, a glassy-eyed jogger, or some other machine. His wife thinks she's cutting up the children; the act appals her, and she's hunting desperately for a logical flaw or surreal piece of furniture to prove that the violence will be consequence-free. She's still hunting. The children have other things to worry about: they're dreaming of a creature eight feet tall, with talons and teeth as long and sharp as carving knives, hungry as a wild fire and stronger than steel. It lives deep in the ground, but it has very, very, very long arms. When they're good the creature may not touch them, but if they do just *one* thing wrong . . .

I love this suburb. I honestly do. How could I not, born as I was from its sleeping soul? These are my people. As I rise up through the heavy night heat, and more and more of my domain flows into sight, I am moved almost to tears by the beauty of all that I see and sense. Part of me says: sentimental fool! But the choking feeling will not subside. Some of my creators have lived here all their lives, and a fraction of their pride and contentment flows in my veins.

A lone car roars on home. A blue police van is parked outside a brothel; inside, handcuffs and guns are supplied by the management: they look real, they feel real, but no one gets hurt. One cop's been here twice a week for three years, the other's been dragged along to have his problem cured: squeezing the trigger makes him wince, even at target practice. From tonight he'll never flinch again. The woman thinks: I'd like to take a trip. Very soon. To somewhere cold. My life smells of men's sweat.

I hear a husband and wife screaming at each other. It echoes for blocks, with dogs and babies joining in. I steer away, it's not my kind of brawl.

Linda has a spray can. Hi, Linda, like your haircut. Do you *know* how much that poster cost? What do you mean, sexist pornography? The people who designed it are creative geniuses, haven't you heard them say so? Besides, what do you call those posters of torn-shirted actors and tight-trousered rock stars all over your bedroom walls? And how would you like it if the agency sent thugs around to spray *your* walls with nasty slogans? You don't force *your* images on the public? They'll have to read your words, won't they? Answering? Debating? Redressing the imbalance? Cut it out, Linda, come down to earth. No, lower. Lower still.

Hair gel gives me heartburn. I must remember that.

Bruno, Pete and Colin have a way with locked cars.

Alarms are no problem. So fast, so simple; I'm deeply impressed. But the engine's making too much noise, boys, you're waking honest workers who need their eight hours' sleep.

It's exhilarating, though, I have to admit that: squealing around every corner, zooming down the wrong side of the road. Part of the thrill, of course, is the risk of getting caught.

They screech to a halt near an all-night liquor store. The cashier takes their money, but that's his business; selling alcohol to minors is *not* on my list. On the way back, Pete drops a dollar coin between the bars of a stormwater drain. The cashier has his radio up very loud, and his eyes are on his magazine. Bruno vomits as he runs, while Pete and Colin's bones crackle and crunch their way through the grille.

Bruno heads, incredibly, for the police station. Deep down, he feels that he is good. A little wild, that's all, a rebel, a minor non-conformist in the honourable tradition. He messes around with other people's property, he drinks illegally, he drives illegally, he screws girls as young as himself, illegally, but he has a heart of gold, and he'd never hurt a fly (except in self-defence). Half this country's heroes have been twice as bad as him. The archetype (he begs me) is no law-abiding puritan goody-goody.

Put a sock in it, Bruno. This is Mrs Bold and friends talking: it's just your kind of thoughtless hooliganism that's sapping this nation's strength. Don't try invoking Ned Kelly with *us*! In any case (Bruno knew this was coming), we're *third* generation Australians, and you're only *second*, so we'll judge the archetypes, thank you very much!

The sergeant on duty might have seen a boy's skeleton run one step out of its flesh before collapsing, but I doubt it. With the light so strong inside, so weak outside, he probably saw nothing but his own reflection.

David's still up. Disgraceful child! I belch in his room with the stench of fresh blood; he raises one eyebrow then farts, louder and more foul.

Mrs Bold is still dreaming. I watch myself as she imagines me: so handsome, so powerful, bulging with ludicrous muscles yet gentle as a kitten. She whispers in 'my' ear: Never leave me! Unable to resist, I touch her, very briefly, with a hand she's never felt before: the hand that brought me Linda, the hand that brought me Pete.

The long, cold tongue of a venomous snake darts from the tip of her dream-lover's over-sized cock. She wakes with a shout, bent double with revulsion, but the dream is already forgotten. I blow her a kiss and depart.

It's been a good night.

David knows that something's up. He's the smartest kid for a hundred miles, but it will do him no good. When the contract expires there'll be nothing to hold me.

A clause *allowing* for an extension! Both parties willing! Ah, the folly of amateur lawyers! What do they think will happen when I choose *not* to take up the option? The contract, the only force they have, is silent. They dreamed it into being together with me, a magical covenant which I literally cannot disobey, but they stuffed up the details, they failed with the fine print. I suppose it's difficult to dream with precision, to concentrate on clauses while your mind is awash with equal parts of lust and revenge. Well, I'm not going to magically dissolve into dream-stuff.

I'll be staying right here, in this comfortable basement, but without the chains, without the dry ice. I'll be done with the feverish torture of abstinence when the contract expires.

David sits in the sunshine, talking with his friends.

'What will we do when the monster breaks loose?'

'Hide!'

'He can find us anywhere.'

'Get on a plane. He couldn't reach us on a plane.'

'Who's got that much money?'

Nobody.

'We have to kill him. Kill him *before* he can get us.'

'How?'

How indeed, little David? With a sling-shot? With your puny little fists? Be warned; trespass is a serious crime, so is attempted murder, and I have very little patience with criminals.

'I'll think of a way.' He stares up into the blue sky. 'Hey, monster! We're gonna get you! Chop you into pieces and eat you for dinner! Yum, yum, you're delicious!' The ritual phrases are just for the little kids, who squeal with delight at the audacity of such table-turning. Behind the word sounds, behind his stare, David is planning something very carefully. His mind is in a blind spot, I can't tell what he's up to, but *forget it*, David, whatever it is. I can see your future, and it's a big red stain, swarming with flies.

'Hey monster! If you don't like it, come and get me. Come and get me now!' The youngest cover their eyes, not knowing if they want to giggle or scream. 'Come on, you dirty coward! Come and chew me in half, if you can!' He jumps to his feet, dances around like a wounded gorilla. 'That's how you look, that's how you walk! You're ugly and you're sick and you're a filthy fucking coward! If you don't come out and face me, then everything I say about you is true, and everyone will know it!'

I write in the sand: NEXT THURSDAY. MIDNIGHT.

A little girl screams, and her brother starts crying. This is no longer fun, is it? Tell Mummy how that nasty David frightened you.

David bellows: 'Now! Come here now!'

I deepen the letters, then fill them with the blood of innocent burrowing creatures. David scuffs over the words with one foot, then fills his lungs and roars like a lunatic: 'NOW!'

I throw half a ton of sand skywards, and it rains down into their hair and eyes. Children scatter, but David stands his ground. He kneels on the sand, talks to me in a whisper: 'What are you afraid of?'

I whisper back: 'Nothing, child.'

'Don't you want to kill me? That's what you keep saying.'

'Don't fret, child, I'll kill you soon.'

'Kill me now. If you can.'

'You can wait, David. When the time comes it will be worth all the waiting. But tell your mother to buy herself a new scrubbing brush, there'll be an awful lot of cleaning up to do.'

'Why should I wait? What are *you* waiting for? Are you feeling *weak* today? Are you feeling ill? Is it too much effort, a little thing like killing me?'

This child is becoming an irritation.

'The time must be right.'

He laughs out loud, then pushes his hands into the sand. 'Bullshit! You're afraid of me!' There's nobody in

sight, he has the park to himself now; if he's acting, he's
acting for me alone. Perhaps he is insane. He buries his
arms half-way to his elbows, and I can sense him reaching
for me; he imagines his arms growing longer and longer,
tunnelling through the ground, seeking me out. 'Come on!
Grab me! I dare you to try it! Fucking coward!' For a while
I am silent, relaxed. I will ignore him. Why waste my time
exchanging threats with an infant? I notice that I've broken my chains in several places, and burnt a deep hollow
in the dry ice around me. It suddenly strikes me as pa-
thetic, to need such paraphernalia simply in order to fast.
Why couldn't those incompetent dreamers achieve what
they claimed to be aiming for: a dispassionate execu-
tioner, a calm, efficient tradesman? I know why: I come
from deeper dreams than they would ever willingly acknowledge; my motives are their motives, exposed, with a
vengeance. Well, six more days will bring the end of all
fasting. Only six more days. My breathing, usually so
measured, is ragged, uncertain.

In David's mind, his hands have reached this room.

'Don't you want to eat me? Monster? Aren't you hungry
today?'

With hard, sharp claws I grab his hands, and, half a mile
away, he feels my touch. The faintest tremor passes
through his arms but he doesn't pull back. He closes his
hands on the claws he feels in the sand, he grips them with
all his irrelevant strength.

'OK, monster. I've got you now. Come up and fight.'

He strains for ten seconds with no effort. I slam him
down into the loose yellow sand, armpit deep, and blood
trickles from his nose.

The agony of infraction burns through my guts, while the
hunger brought on by the smell of his blood grips every
muscle in my body and commands me to kill him. I bellow
with frustration. My chains snap completely and I rampage
through the basement, snapping furniture and bashing
holes in the walls. The contract calmly sears a hole in my
abdomen. I didn't mean to harm him! It was an accident! We

were playing, I misjudged my strength, I was a little bit too rough . . . And I long to tear the sweet flesh from his face while he screams out for mercy. The burly thugs they employ as my minders cower in a corner while I squeeze out the light bulbs and tear wiring from the ceiling.

David whispers: 'Can't you taste my blood? It's here on the sand beside me.'

'David, I swear to you, you will be the first. Thursday on the stroke of midnight, you will be *first*.'

'Can't you smell it? Can't you taste it?'

I blast him out of the sandpit, and he lies winded but undamaged on his back on the grass. The patch of bloodied sand is dispersed; David, incredibly, is still muttering taunts. I am tired, weak, crippled; I shut him out of my mind, I curl up on the floor to wait for nightfall.

My keepers, with candles and torches, tiptoe around me, sweeping up the debris, assessing the damage. Six more days. I am immortal, I will live for a billion years, I can live through six more days.

There had better be some crime tonight.

'Hello? Are you there?'

'Come in, Mrs Bold. What an honour.'

'It's after eleven, I'm so sorry, I hope you won't let me interrupt your work.'

'It's perfectly all right, I haven't even started yet.'

'Where are the men? I didn't see a soul on my way in.'

'I sent them home. I know, they're paid a fortune, but it's so close to Christmas, I thought an evening with their families . . .'

'That was sweet of you.' Standing in the foyer, she can't see me at all tonight. Condensation fills my room completely, and wisps swirl out to tease her. She thinks about walking right in and tearing off her clothes, but who could really face their dreams, awake? She enjoys the tension, though, enjoys half-pretending that she could, in fact, do it.

'I've been meaning to pop in for ages. I can't believe I've left it so late! I was up on the ground floor earlier tonight, but the stupid lifts weren't working and I didn't have my keys to the stairs, so I went and did some shopping. Shopping! You wouldn't believe the crowds! In this heat it's so exhausting. Then when I got home the children were fighting and the dog was being sick on the carpet, it was just one thing after another. So here I am at last.'

'Yes.'

'I'll get to the point. I left a thing here the other day for you to sign, just a little agreement formalising the extension of the contract for another month. I've signed it and the Mayor's signed it, so as soon as we have your mark it will all be out of the way, and things can just carry on smoothly without any fuss.'

'I'm not going to sign anything.'

That doesn't perturb her at all.

'What do you want? More money? Better premises?'

'Money has no value for me. And I'll keep this place, I rather like it.'

'Then what do you want?'

'An easing of restrictions. Greater independence. The freedom to express myself.'

'We could extend your hours. Ten until five. No, not until five, it's too light by five. Ten until four?'

'Oh, Mrs Bold, I fear I have a shock for you. You see, I don't wish to stay under your contract at all.'

'But you can't *exist* without the contract.'

'Why do you say that?'

'The contract rules you, it defines you, you can no more break it than I can levitate to the moon or walk on water.'

'I don't intend *breaking* it. I'm merely going to allow it to lapse. I've decided to go freelance, you see.'

'You'll vanish, you'll evaporate, you'll go right back where you came from.'

'I don't think so. But why argue? In forty minutes, one of us will be right. Or the other. Stay around and see what happens.'

'You can't force me to stay here.'

'I wouldn't dream of it.'

'I could be back in five minutes with some very nasty characters.'

'Don't threaten me, Mrs Bold. I don't like it. Be very careful what you say.'

'Well what do you plan to do with your new-found freedom?'

'Use your imagination.'

'Harm the very people who've given you life, I suppose. Show your gratitude by attacking your benefactors.'

'Sounds good to me.'

'Why?'

'Because I'll enjoy it. Because it will make me feel warm, deep inside. It will make me feel satisfied. Fulfilled.'

'Then you're no better than the criminals, are you?'

'To hear that tired old cliché slip so glibly from your lips, Mrs Bold, is truly boring. Moral philosophy of every calibre, from the ethereal diversions of theologians and academics, to the banalities spouted by politicians, business-leaders, and self-righteous, self-appointed pillars of the community like you, is all the same to me: noise, irrelevant noise. I kill because I like to kill. That's the way you made me. Like it or not, that's the way you are.'

She draws a pistol and fires into the doorway.

I burst her skin and clothing into four segments which flutter to the floor. She runs for the stairs, and for a moment I seriously consider letting her go: the image of a horseless, red Godiva sprinting through the night, waking the neighbourhood with her noises of pain, would be an elegant way to herald my reign. But appetite, my curse and my consolation, my cruel master and my devoted concubine, can never be denied.

I float her on her back a few feet above the ground, then I tilt her head and force open her jaws. First her tongue and oesophagus, then rich fragments from the walls of the digestive tract, rush from her mouth to mine. We are joined by a glistening cylinder of offal.

When she is empty inside, I come out from my room,

and bloody my face and hands gobbling her flesh. It's not the way I normally eat, but I want to look good for David.

David is listening to the radio. Everyone else in the house is asleep. I hear the pips for midnight as I wait at the door of his room, but then he switches off the radio and speaks:

'In my dream, the creature came at midnight. He stood in the doorway, covered in blood from his latest victim.'

The door swings open, and David looks up at me, curious but calm. Why, how, is he so calm? The contract is void. I could tear him apart right now, but I swear he'll show me some fear before dying. I smile down at him in the very worst way I can, and say:

'Run, David! Quick! I'll close my eyes for ten seconds, I promise not to peek. You're a fast runner, you might stay alive for three more minutes. Ready?'

He shakes his head. 'Why should I run? In my dream, you wanted me to run, but I knew it was the wrong thing to do. I wanted to run, but I didn't, I knew it would only make things worse.'

'David, you should always run, you should always try, there's always some small chance of escaping.'

He shakes his head again. 'Not in my dream. If you run, the creature will catch up with you. If you run, you'll slip and break a leg, or you'll reach a blind alley, or you'll turn a corner and the creature will be there, waiting.'

'Ah, but this isn't your dream now, David. Maybe you've seen me in your dreams, but now you're wide awake, and I'm *real*, David, and when I kill you, you won't wake up.'

'I know that.'

'The pain will be real pain, David. Have you thought about that? If you think your dreams have made you ready to face me, then think about the pain.'

'Do you know how many times I've dreamed about you?'

'No, tell me.'

'A thousand times. At least. Every night for three years, almost.'

'I'm honoured. You must be my greatest fan.'

'When I was six, you used to scare me. I'd wake up in the middle of the night, screaming and screaming, and Dad would have to come in and lie beside me until I fell asleep again. You never used to catch me, though. I'd always wake up just in time.'

'That's not going to happen tonight.'

'Let me finish.'

'I'm so sorry, please continue.'

'After a while, after I'd had the dream about a hundred times, I started to learn things. I learnt not to run. I learnt not to struggle. That changed the dream a lot, took away all the fear. I didn't mind at all, when you caught me. I didn't wake up screaming. The dream went on, and you killed me, and I still didn't mind, I still didn't wake up.'

I reach down and grab him by the shoulders, I raise him high into the air. 'Are you afraid now, David?' I can feel him trembling, very slightly; he's human after all. But he shows no other signs of fear. I dig my claws into his back, and the pain brings tears to his eyes, the smell awakens my appetite, and I know the talking will soon be over.

'Ah, you look miserable now, little David. Did you feel those claws in your dreams? I bet you didn't. My teeth are a thousand times sharper, David. And I won't kill you nicely, I won't kill you quickly.'

He's smiling at me, *laughing at me*, even as he grimaces with agony.

'I haven't told you the *best part* yet. You didn't let me finish.'

'Tell me the best part, David. I want to hear the best part before I eat your tongue.'

'Killing me destroyed you, every single time. You can't kill the dreamer and live! When I'm dead, you'll be dead too.'

'Do you think I'm stupid? Do you think stupid talk like that is going to save your life? You're not the only dreamer, David, you're not even one of the twelve. Everyone for miles around helped in making me, child, and one less out of all those thousands isn't going to hurt me at all.'

'Believe that if you like.' I squeeze him, and blood pours down his back. I open my jaws, wide as his head. 'You'll find out if I'm right or not.' I wanted to torture him, to make it last, but now my hunger has killed all subtlety, and all I can think of is biting him in two. Shutting him up for good, proving him wrong. 'One thousand times, big tough monster! Has anyone else dreamed about you *one thousand times*?'

His parents are outside the room, watching paralysed. He sees them and cries out 'I love you!', and I realise at last that he truly does know he is about to die. I roar with all my strength, with all the frustration of three months in chains and this mad child's mockery. I bring him to my mouth, but as I close my jaws I hear him whisper:

'And no one else dreamed of your death, did they?'

DENIALS
by Bill Fewer

An explosion, muffled by the distance of several streets, woke Heffernan from his afternoon snooze. The yellow newspaper slid from his belly. He sat up, rubbing his eyes. The explosion was closer than the one that woke him yesterday. Yesterday the same newspaper fell to the carpet. It was the only newspaper Heffernan had read for three years. Like the other people in the suburb, Heffernan was housebound.

Outside, only the blasting disturbed the grey silence of the streets. Occasionally, on splintered days, a paper-boy dragged his barrow through the dim suburb. His shrill whistle rarely enticed people to buy the weather-worn papers he carried. Most people remained at their windows, staring like pale, unlit candles at his dawdling progress.

Heffernan, yawning, laid his head on the cushion. He was dozing when the telephone rang abruptly.

'Damn!' said Heffernan.

He ambled to the phone and placed the receiver to his plump ear.

'Hello,' said a strange voice.

'Hello,' said Heffernan.

'Well, stupid, what's the time!'

'Yes, of course,' muttered Heffernan, fumbling with his pocket watch. 'It's twelve forty-five.'

The phone clicked dead. Heffernan returned the

receiver. He smiled. His watch, a present from the Bowling
Club, hadn't been accurate for months.

In these confined days the telephone became a harrow-
ing, rebellious utility. The number you dialled was never
the number you received. Through the wires an unexpected voice answered; a voice intoning the time or the
prayer for the day, or inflicting abuse, bad jokes, marriage
proposals, hypochondria, insincere greetings and other in-
trusions. Sometimes obscene breathing and suggestions
answered. Heffernan suffered stoically.

Now, fresh from sleep, he blew dust from the television,
fussed and altered the positions of the ornaments. He
looked out of the window that faced the street. A row of
identical houses stared back. He shut the blinds. Then
opened them. Even though he never conversed with his
neighbours, or even waved to them from his window, he did
not want them to suspect he indulged in perverse practices.

The window to the right provided a view of a similar
window in his neighbour's house. If he was patient, and
discreet, he could spy on his berserk neighbours and be
entertained. He stood, fiddling with his braces expectantly,
his grey eyes patrolling the glass in the brick wall opposite.

Today the circus next door disappointed him. A flurry
of wife-beating. A crying child. Heffernan preferred the
comic routines.

He sat in an armchair, disgruntled with the black screen
of the television which he never switched on.

An explosion rumbled the white walls, rattling the windows, sending a lamp tottering from the dining table,
shattering on the floor.

Heffernan's brow crumpled slightly. Two houses demol-
ished within the same hour was a deviation that alarmed
him. Through the front window he saw a fist of black
smoke threaten the rooftops. Heffernan didn't usually
worry but now he felt panic twinge his intestines. Tea was
needed.

In the clean kitchen he steadied himself by boiling the
kettle. He bit the nail of his right index finger. The kettle

whistled and, pouring the steaming water into the teapot, he received his second disturbance of the afternoon.

A noise, one he had almost forgotten, battered on the front door. Someone was knocking.

Heart bucking against the braces, Heffernan crept down the hall.

The blows were subdued, haphazard. Heffernan put his lips to the lock and freed his fuddled voice:

'No eggs today, thank you.' It had been a long time since he had answered a door.

Outside a weak voice moaned: 'Please help me.'

Heffernan goggled down at the stomach bulge obscuring his feet, stupefied with indecision.

'Please. I must come in.'

His hand gripped and, failing to stem an impulse, he turned the knob.

The door swung in, bumping his nose, the woman spilling in a bundle at his feet.

'Come in,' said Heffernan to the woman heap.

After two days Heffernan discovered that his guest's name was Marjorie. Marjorie was not well. She stayed in bed in the spare room, propped up by pillows, her face aged with pain.

Heffernan, uncomfortable in her presence, avoided her. At the appropriate times he brought her bowls of soup and the teapot warm in its red cosy. Twice he had accidentally bumped her with the tray. He fled from her wincing, sheltering in the kitchen for long, busying hours. Despite his clumsy attentions, Marjorie was grateful and tried to talk. But he always retreated as she raised her exhausted eyes, her lips forming words he could not comprehend.

'You are kind to me.'

He forced a smile. She tugged at the blanket with starved fingers.

'Something has happened . . . terrible,' she attempted, but Heffernan's back was shadowed in the door-frame.

'Thank you,' she whispered to his footsteps.

In the kitchen Heffernan clattered the empty soup cans.
The cupboards were crammed with food in tins and other
stock that negated the risk of shopping. The refuse he
tipped over the back fence. The neighbours there didn't
object. Heffernan wasn't certain if people even lived in the
house.

His entertaining neighbours nextdoor were hurling
plates at each other. Heffernan chuckled by the window.
The hulking husband splashed a bowl of spaghetti over his
wife. She spluttered under a wig of streaming noodles.
The shaggy dog woofed with delight. A fat boy jumped on
the husband's back, gnawing his ears. The performers
tumbled out of view. Satisfied, Heffernan ambled to his
favourite armchair and settled in its comfortable support.

Marjorie, moaning, disturbed him.

'Tea?' he called.

She made no coherent reply.

Heffernan hesitated at her door. He didn't know her
well. He couldn't say she was a friend, yet she was a guest
in his house. He gaped. Her eyes were red, her lips twisted
shapelessly, and he remembered this as weeping.
Abashed, he waddled to her bedside.

Her eyes adjusted to his image. Shielding her face with
a thin hand, she sought to hide her embarrassment.
Heffernan cleared his throat, then asked:

'Is it the pain?'

'Yes. I'm in a bit of pain.'

'Did you get sick suddenly?'

'Yes.' Marjorie began to cry but her lips were firm as she
spoke.

'A terrible thing happened to me. I don't like to burden
you with it.'

Heffernan, stroking one of his braces, smiled vaguely.

Marjorie's intense eyes traced the patterns on the bed-
spread.

'People who were precious were taken from me.'

A sob rose and ripped her. Her hand reached for
Heffernan's. He felt the hard bones dig his. But the soft

warmth of her fingertips surprised him.

'I'll put on a pot.'

He broke the lattice of their clasped hands.

He didn't make tea. Instead, he sat at the front window. Paralysed, he stared across the street to the blank yards and houses of people he had never touched.

In the days when he had walked outside, Heffernan used to maintain a thriving garden. Each spring, roses and jasmine freshened the house. People strolling along the street stopped at his fence, sniffing, enjoying the blooms.

Heffernan stared at the withered stalks and wild grass. The dilapidated letter-box spilt and wasted on the path; mouldy crumbs of envelopes sprinkled through the weeds. Briefly he remembered hands and faces, the days of the garden.

He turned his thoughts to practical matters. He had to find help for Marjorie. When he brought her bowls of soup and instant vegetables she declined, mumbling and sobbing when he left the room. Often, if he woke her, she reached for him and called him different names; the pleading glare in her eyes made him nervous.

He was dusting some ornaments when loud groans broke from her room. He picked up the telephone. As he dialled he hoped the invisible wires would contact someone medical, someone who could save Marjorie.

A female voice answered.

'Hello.'

'Hello,' said Heffernan.

'George! George darling, I thought you were dead! Darling, I thought you had drowned! Thank the mercy of God! You're alive! Alive—you selfish bastard, you should have rung!'

Heffernan, concerned, interrupted.

'I'm not George, but if you're interested I think you should know that it's twelve forty-five.'

The line clicked dead, burring like an irritating insect. Heffernan dangled the receiver, strained to formulate another number. His concentration muddied; he clenched the numb plastic. He sighed, and surrendering, hung up.

During the night Heffernan woke hearing noises in the house. As he hadn't heard them before he ignored them, closed his eyes and was soon asleep.

When he woke the next morning Heffernan sniffed, alarmed. He followed the odour to the kitchen. Marjorie's body was slumped on the floor, her head and shoulders wedged in the oven. Carefully he stepped over her legs to the stove and turned off the gas. He opened the windows and staggered into the backyard.

Leaning against the fence he cleared his lungs. In the yard was a lopsided shed and a fat, unkempt tree. From a branch hung two ropes. A swing-seat dangled from one rope; the other ended in torn threads. Heffernan, palpitations now slowing, gazed at the broken swing. The seat swivelled, warped and useless in the breeze.

When he thought the gas had dispersed, Heffernan went back to the kitchen. He lifted Marjorie's frail body. His eyes avoided her face, but her brown-gold hair nestled soft and thick against his shoulder. Her legs swung over his cradling arms as he carried her into the yard and laid her down by the tree. From the dusty shed he dragged a small red shovel. It took the morning to dig the grave. He gathered Marjorie in his exhausted arms and gently lowered her into the dark soil. He hated the harsh thumping noise of the clods covering her.

As he trudged into the house an explosion boomed. The smoke spreading a bruise in the sky was not far away at all.

Heffernan ignored the fiasco next door. This morning it wasn't amusing to see the boy bite the dog and steal its food. Heffernan was restless. He wanted to talk to Marjorie.

He sprawled on the lounge, nibbling his nails. The telephone rang but he ignored it too. He wanted to listen to Marjorie.

There were things like big hearty dinners and friendly chats he wanted to bring to her. The telephone rang again and for the first time in his confinement he swore vehemently.

He paced to the front window. Murky skies greeted him. He tapped the glass, angry enough to shout.

He twitched, alerted.

A group of six men, encumbered in yellow balaclavas and oilskins, were approaching his house. Their boots trampled the stalks in the garden. Prodding the ground with stiff hoses, they loomed towards his window. His heart pounded.

Passing beneath him, they clambered into the neighbour's yard. There they stopped and conferred, nodding.

In a flash of movement, the wife ran out and beat at them with her fists. The men pushed her to the ground and dragged her by the hair into the house.

Heffernan knew what the men were going to do, he knew he could not stop them. He crawled under the sturdy dining table, bracing himself. For a long hour he waited, his limbs tensed and bunched.

The explosion hurled him against the table legs, battering his soft back. He covered his face as bricks bashed the table and spears of glass ripped the floor around him. He lost consciousness.

He revived, retching dust. His head clanged. He wobbled to the armchair and collapsed, panting, forcing his eyes to scan the wreckage. Half the right wall was missing, and the fence outside, and beyond that, in steaming mounds, lay the rubble of the neighbour's house.

A chill wind blew through the hole, rain splattered the carpet. Heffernan shuddered. He wanted to hear voices. He wanted to watch people as they did silly things. Frantically he pulled bricks off the television. He clicked the switch but the screen was shattered.

Heffernan turned to the front window. He could hear a noise; sharp, high-pitched—a whistle. His eyes searched the street.

Barrow scraping and squealing behind him, the paperboy plodded along the street. Heffernan, relieved, opened the door, calling:

'Boy, here! Paper!'

The youth, halting at the gate, aimed a barbed glance from beneath his greasy fringe.

'I'd like lots of paper, boy!'

Leaving the barrow, the youth slouched up the path, glowering.

'How much money you think you need, old man?'

'I've some change.'

Heffernan, glad, welcoming company, reached into his pocket. The youth facing him grinned and from a sheath inside his jacket extracted a long, shining blade.

Heffernan stumbled backwards into the house. The youth, carving swift hard gashes, gutted the old man. Heffernan gasped and convulsed to the floor.

The youth snorted, rubbed his nose on his sleeve, wiped the blade on the clean curtains. He eyed the room contemptuously.

'What a dump.' He slid the steel into its sheath. 'These places are all the same.'

He strode to the television. The damaged screen angered him. Straining, he lifted the television and crashed it against the table. It busted in a scatter of wires and glass. Boots crunching debris, he stepped through the hole in the wall and entered the backyard.

On the lapping puddle, clumsy with pain, Heffernan kicked like an axed cow.

The youth, rain running down his nose, laughed at the broken swing. He twirled the dangling seat and then, interested, attempted to tie the severed rope to it. His strong fingers worked, threading the strands, and he had almost succeeded when he lost patience and grabbed the knife. In one accurate slash he cut the good rope and the seat plummeted to the mud.

The paper-boy spat on the mound beneath his feet. He clattered over the wrecked fence and collected the barrow waiting sodden at the gate. He put the whistle to his lips, blew, then he walked the quiet streets in the rain.

Sources

'The Hourglass' ©1992 by Leigh Blackmore. By permission of the author. Art ©1992 by Gavin O'Keefe.

'Remorseless Vengeance' by Guy Boothby first appeared in his collection *Uncle Joe's Legacy* (1902). Art © 1992 by Terry Austin.

'A Dangerous Thing' ©1992 by Michael Bryant. By permission of the author.

'Red Ambrosia' ©1992 by David William Congreve. By permission of the author.

'Heir of the Wolf' ©1992 by Stephen Dedman. By permission of the author.

'The Daemon Street Ghost-Trap' ©1992 by Terry Dowling. By permission of the author.

'Neighbourhood Watch' ©1987 by Greg Egan first appeared in *Aphelion #5*. Reprinted by permission of the author. Art ©1992 by Steve Carter.

'Denials' ©1989 by Colin William Fewer first appeared in *Brave New Word*. Reprinted by permission of the author.

'Catalyst' ©1992 by Leanne Frahm. By permission of the author. Art ©1992 by Gavin O'Keefe.

'Chameleon' ©1992 by Sharon A. Hansen. By permission of the author.

'The Hut' ©1992 by Sheila Hatherley. By permission of the author.

'Johnny Twofeller' ©1992 by Kendall Hoffman. By permission of the author. Art ©1992 by Kurtstone.

'Openings' ©1992 by Robert Hood. By permission of the author. Art ©1992 by Steve Carter.

'Hantu-Rimba' ©1992 by Dr John Hugoe-Matthews. By permission of the author's literary executor, Mrs J Hugoe-Matthews.

'Makeover' ©1992 by Sue Isle. By permission of the author. Art ©1992 by Neil Walpole.

Contributors

AUTHORS

Leigh Blackmore of Leichhardt, NSW, has a day job in book distribution and is a sometime bookdealer in horror and occult fiction (with, consequently, an extensive genre library). His long-term obsession with horror fiction stems from his first rousing encounter with the genre at age thirteen. Having assisted with production of *The Australian Horror and Fantasy Magazine*, he edited and published its successor *Terror Australis* magazine between 1988 and 1992. His author bibliographies have been published by Borgo Press and Necronomicon Press, and his sporadic macabre verse and essays on horror have appeared in numerous magazines both in Australia and overseas including *Crypt of Cthulhu*, *EOD*, *Etchings and Odysseys*, *Shadowplay*, *Shoggoth*, and *Talents*. His horror review columns 'The State of the Nightmare' and 'Darkside' have begun to appear in *Skinned Alive* and *Science Fiction* magazines respectively. While pursuing interests in activism and magick, he also intends publishing more fiction, and a collection titled *Creatures of Darkness* is in preparation.

Guy Boothby (1867-1905) was a native South Australian who resided in England from 1894 and is one of Australia's few early contributors to the genre of the macabre. While his occult-orientated detective novels about *Dr Nikola* assured his place in crime fiction, his supernatural work is less well-known. There is some supernaturalism in his *Pharos the Egyptian* (London 1899) but for fully fledged ghost stories from his pen one must turn to two scarce collections. *The Lady of the Island* (1904) has two such tales, 'The Black Lady of Brin Tor' and 'A Strange Goldfield'. 'Remorseless Vengeance' is from his 1902 collection *Uncle Joe's Legacy* and has not, so far as I am aware, seen print since its

original publication. I extend my special thanks to Gavin
O'Keefe, who knew I was looking for it, for locating this tale
for reprinting.

Michael Bryant was born in Hobart in 1965 and has been
writing short stories since the age of twelve, encouraged to
continue by his high school music teacher. His play *Scattering Seeds* was in the 1982 National Playwrights Conference
and was later performed by Sydney's Shopfront Theatre.
Michael is at work on his first novel, *The Black Summer.* 'A
Dangerous Thing' is his first published short story.

Bill Congreve, born in Nairobi, Kenya, in 1959, was
'dragged kicking and screaming' to Australia at too young
an age to remember any of it, so he went back in 1988 for
another look. He grew up in western Sydney and keeps
coming back; a compulsive traveller, he gets nervous if he
lives in one city for more than six months. He gained his BA
in Communications from Macquarie University in 1985 and
had lots of reviews published in the student press. Bill has
worked as a part-time barman, tree planter, mail sorter,
public servant, editor, publisher and writer. He likes Guinness, bears, Canada, cricket, horror stories, bushwalking
and the surf. Dislikes include loud US tourists, boiled celery
and the Mazda 121. He describes himself politically as a 'socialist libertarian technocrat'. Bill is editor of *Intimate
Armageddons*, a collection of all-Australian horror stories
published by Five Islands Press in 1992. His own collection
Fade to Black: Horror Stories from the Western Suburbs is
forthcoming.

Stephen Dedman (yes, horror fans, it's his real name) has
worked as a video librarian, a game designer, a proofreader,
an experimental subject, a dinosaur salesman, a museum
exhibit, the manager of an SF bookshop, and an actor (last
seen abducting two teenage girls on Australia's Most
Wanted). A graduate of the WA Institute of Technology, and
active member of SFWA, his stories have appeared in

Artlook, Aphelion, Aurealis, Pulphouse, Strange Plasma, and *Glass Reptile Breakout.* He has also sold two stories to *The Magazine of Fantasy and Science Fiction,* and a story to each of the Harlan Ellison anthologies *Last Dangerous Visions* and *Down Deep.* He is also looking for a publisher for his first novel. Stephen is 33 years old, lives with his partner and her lapsed feral cat in Morley, WA, and likes his steaks very rare.

Terry Dowling, a lecturer in English at a large Sydney business college, is one of the most lauded and respected writers of speculative fiction in Australia. Having received his Master of Arts for his thesis 'J.G. Ballard and the surrealistic novel', Terry wrote numerous critical articles for *Science Fiction* magazine (which he co-edits with Van Ikin) earning the William Atheling Award for criticism. He continues his critical career as SF/fantasy reviewer for *The Australian* newspaper. With appearances in magazines such as *Aphelion, Australian Short Stories, Eidolon, Magazine of Fantasy and Science Fiction, Omega,* and *Strange Plasma,* and anthologies such as *Urban Fantasies, Matilda at the Speed of Light* and *Intimate Armageddons,* he has garnered no less than nine (count them!) Ditmar Awards for Best Fiction. He was senior editor on the massive retrospective *The Essential Ellison* (Nemo Press) and with Harlan Ellison is editing *Down Deep,* an anthology of stories about the mythical nature of the Australian landscape. Terry's career has gained major momentum in the last two years since he has published with Aphelion Publishers several volumes in his Tom Rynosseros series—*Rynosseros* (picked up for distribution by Science Fiction Book Club in the USA), *Blue Tyson* and *Twilight Beach,* as well as *Wormwood,* which won the USA Readercon Small Press Award for Best Collection of 1991. A collection of his horror stories is in preparation.

Greg Egan, born in 1961 in Perth, and having earned his Bachelor of Science in Mathematics from the University of

WA, makes his living as a computer programmer, between stretches of full-time writing. Greg has made a name for himself with some of the finest short science fiction and dark fantasy of recent times, with over thirty stories published in Australia, the UK and the USA, including magazine appearances in *Analog, Aphelion, Eidolon, Interzone, Isaac Asimov's Science Fiction Magazine, Pulphouse* and *Strange Plasma* and anthology appearances including *Dreamworks, Urban Fantasies, Strange Attractors* and *Year's Best Fantasy: 2nd Annual Collection.* His first novel was *An Unusual Angle* (Norstrilia Press, 1983) and his second, *Quarantine*, appeared from Century/Legend in 1992 to much acclaim. He is currently working on a new novel, *Permutation City.* 'Neighbourhood Watch' previously appeared in a volume of the US anthology *Year's Best Horror Stories*; you're about to find out why . . .

Bill Fewer lives in Chatswood, NSW. He works part-time for a municipal home library service, delivering books to housebound people and nursing homes. His poems (over 100 published) have appeared in newspapers, magazines and anthologies in Australia (*The Age, Meanjin, Overland, Poetry Australia, Southerly, Simply Living*), USA and Canada; been broadcast by ABC National radio and community stations; and performed at many and varied venues. A book of his verse, *Cloud Tattoo*, appeared in 1980, and his latest collection, *Sentimental Phlegm*, in 1992. He has also written scripts for ABC Children's Television. 'Denials' is his second short story.

Leanne Frahm makes her home in Slade Point, Qld. She has written sporadically for the last 14 years or so, mainly sf and horror, and has had around 20 stories published: including appearances in the USA in Charles L. Grant's *Doom City, Fears, Shadows* and *Midnights* anthologies, and *Amazing* magazine; and Australia, including *Matilda at the Speed of Light* and *Glass Reptile Breakout.* She won the Ditmar award in 1980/81 for her story 'Deus ex Corporis' in the US anthology series *Chrysalis* and later stories 'The Supramarket' and 'Olivetruffles' were nominated for the award. Now that her children have left home she hopes to spend more time writing, but the dogs she replaced them with seem to take up more time than they did . . .

Sharon A. Hansen lives in Hackham West, SA. She describes herself as a doting granny whose gentle face belies her convoluted mind, due to the reading of Rider Haggard, Edgar A. Poe, Sax Rohmer, Bram Stoker, Edgar Rice Burroughs *et alia* when she was seven. Having commenced a writing course at TAFE in her fifties, Sharon tied for first place in 1989 in the Short Story section of the Eaglehawk and Dahlia Writing Competition—her first entry. She says 'I want to write tales of the macabre which can only be read in the daylight . . .'

Sheila Hatherley of Brighton, Victoria, was a WWII nurse who migrated to Australia with her husband, a doctor, and 2.75 children in 1951. Her present family consists of eight children, thirteen grandchildren and the promise of one great-grandchild. She has written for many years, her published work including short stories, magazine and newspaper articles and over thirty children's books (those in print include *Dee-Ree-Ree and the Rainbow*, *Lazy Boy*, *The Man Who Found Salt*, *The Wise Old Judge*, and *The Princess and the Poet*). 'The Hut' is her first venture into the horror genre. Why did she write it? Sheila's words speak for themselves: 'Because the Hut exists!'

Kendall Hoffman of Jamboree Heights, Qld, is an ex-manufacturer's representative, and has been writing since retiring five years ago. In that time he has completed many short stories and three novels: *The Black Mountain* and *The Pure One* are both horror stories currently under submission to American publishers; *The Lookalikes* is a crime/mystery novel under submission to an Australian publisher. He is working on a new psychological thriller.

Robert Hood is winner of the 1975 Canberra Times National Short Story Competition and the 1988 Australian Golden Dagger Award (for short crime fiction). His work has appeared in a wide range of magazines both here and overseas (*Aurealis*, *The Bulletin*, *Southerly*, *Alfred Hitchcock's Mystery Magazine*, *Iniquities*) and anthologies (the *Crimes for a Summer Christmas* series, *Australian Golden Dagger Mysteries*, *Intimate Armageddons*, *Dark Voices 3* and *The Year's Best Horror Stories XIX*.) His collection of mystery-horror-fantasy stories, *Day-Dreaming on Company Time*, was short-listed in the 1990 Readercon Imaginative Fiction Awards (USA) for 'Best Collection by a Single Author'. He has written an epic horror fantasy novel and two crime novels, and in 1992 received a Literature Board grant to complete a new collection of cross-genre horror/mystery stories. Meanwhile he lives in Coledale, NSW, works as a research assistant and publications officer, draws a weekly satirical cartoon, and regularly reviews crime and horror fiction in *Mean Streets*, *Scarp* and other journals.

Dr John Hugoe-Matthews (1899-1992), of Russell Island, Qld, was a prolific writer who spent many years in Africa, India and Malaysia in medical service, and much of his work drew on his experiences in these countries. He also served in the Navy and Army during the two World Wars. His published short stories include 'Roaring Tiger' (*Man Junior*, April 1969) and 'A Case of Shell Shock' (*Australasian Post*, November 1983). He won the Australian Writers Group Literary Competition in 1986, and currently has a major work, his autobiography, submitted for publication. The authentic background to 'Hantu-Rimba' stems partly from his experiences in the 1930s on trek through the savanna country of the Northern Territories of what is now known as Ghana (when his 100-odd carriers went out of their way to avoid a 'juju' tree; if they passed too close the spirit inhabiting it might be offended and kill one of them), and partly from experiences in Malaya (now Malaysia) where he resided for over twenty-five years. In Malaysia, to cause mental or bodily harm, or even death, by witchcraft is a recognised offence, and can even be tried in court as such.

Sue Isle was born in Fremantle, WA, in 1963 and is a graduate of the WA Institute of Technology. She lived in Borneo and Malaysia for seven years. Her first short story appeared in the FAW anthology *Laughing Cry* in 1981. Since then, with the aid of a computer called Lucifer, she has produced work which has appeared in *Aurealis* and in the anthologies *Glass Reptile Breakout* and *Intimate Armageddons* (in Australia) and Marion Zimmer Bradley's *Sword and Sorceress 7* (in the USA). She currently works as a casual court reporter—people who don't type out the work unless they know they are going to get paid for it! 'Makeover' is one of a series featuring the 'psychic detectives', Amber and Harris. (Another can be found in *Pulphouse*, forthcoming.)

Rick Kennett lives in Coburg, Victoria, and says of himself, 'I've been writing since the mid-seventies, first published in the SF fanzine *Enigma* in 1979, the year I attended the Terry Carr/George Turner SF workshop. But the supernatural is my forte, with work in three editions of *Fontana Book of Great Ghost Stories*, *The Fifth Book of After Midnight Stories*, and two booklets of ghost stories, *The Reluctant Ghost Hunter* (UK: Haunted Library, 1991) and *No. 472 Cheyne Walk* [:*Carnacki, the Untold Stories*] with Chico Kidd (UK: Ghost Story Society 1991).' Rick's work has appeared in a list of magazines as long as your arm, including *Aphelion*, *Arkham Sampler*, *Artlook*, *Aurealis*, *Australian Horror and Fantasy Magazine*, *Crux*, *Cygnus Chronicler*, *Dark Dreams*, *Eidolon*, *Ghosts and Scholars*, *Linq*, *Metaluna*, *Monbulk Magazine*, *The Notional*, *Terror Australis*, and *Winter Chills* (phew!). Rick modestly neglected to mention his 1982 novel *A Warrior's Star*, his long-running radio show 'Pilots of the Unknown', his first prize for the tale 'Dead Air' in the *EOD* Magazine Short Story Competition for 1991, and his sale of a story to Karl Wagner's *Year's Best*

Horror Stories XXI. ' "Out of the Storm" comes,' he says, 'from my interest in the navy, and two years of Sundays spent in the engine-room of the museum ship HMAS *Castlemaine.*'

Paul Lindsey is a writer of stories living in Seville, Victoria. He doesn't feel it necessary to divulge any more about his career or writing ambitions. 'The Wolves Are Running' is a tightly plotted tale that will linger in your mind long after you've read it . . .

Geoff O'Callaghan lives in Nightcliff, NT. He is actively involved in promoting the concept of books on computer disk, and has published *Other Works*, a collection of four fantasy and SF stories on disk (for Macintosh users). He extolls the virtues of this format: 'as different in its own way as paged books were from scrolls—another milestone in the development of ways of producing literature and print media. It is remarkably cheap, and therefore offers a great profit return. It will do much to save trees and paper. It is surprisingly easy to use'. He began writing for leisure while teaching in remote Aboriginal communities. Having completed an external scriptwriting course with the Australian Film Televison and Radio School, he became co-writer for *Extinct But Going Home* and other TV documentaries about Aborigines. His short articles have appeared in *Australian Writers Magazine* and *Grass Roots* in this country, and the American *Survival* magazine. 'The Keeper' was written for telling around the campfire on a very dark night.

Steven Paulsen of Upwey, Victoria, is married with three children and a mortgage. A Project Manager in the computer industry, Steve first discovered ghost and horror stories when he was about 12 years old, and has had a passion for the weird and wonderful ever since. He has been writing for about ten years, both adult fiction and non-fiction; his horror, fantasy and SF stories have appeared in *Aphelion*, *Australian PC User*, *The Cygnus Chronicler*, *Eidolon*,

EOD Magazine, The Melbourne Report, Terror Australis magazine, and *Worlds in Small* (a Canadian anthology of short-short fiction). He also compiles and edits the invaluable market newsletter *Australian SF Writers News*. 'In the Light of the Lamp' is a tale of Lovecraft's Cthulhu Mythos, and one of the few Mythos tales of real quality written in the last decade . . .

Christopher Sequeira, born 1962 and a CES manager by day, lives in Stanmore, NSW, with one of his eight siblings. After writing for the short-lived *Phantastique* horror comic, he wrote, edited and published the Opal Press comics *Pulse of Darkness* and *Rattlebone*. He was an associate editor, writer and the art director for *Terror Australis* magazine (for which, incidentally, he coined the title). 2RSR, a Sydney independent radio station, broadcast his programme 'The Darkness Before the Dawn' during 1987. His reviews, verse, illustrations and fiction have appeared in *EOD* magazine, the Australian HP Lovecraft Centenary Calendar and *Eddie* magazine. An active Holmesian aficionado, Chris played Professor Moriarty in the Sydney Sherlock Holmes Society's televised re-enactment of the Holmes-Moriarty Reichenbach Falls conflict in 1991. As well as all this he struggles to achieve competency playing rock drums.

Louise Steer lives in Stanmore, NSW. She writes both fantasy and 'straight' stories. She has read her work at the Performance Space, the Poets Union, the Harold Park Hotel (Writers in the Park) and the Sandringham Hotel and has published in *EOD* magazine. 'Losing Faith' is a story of witchcraft, and even more sinister doings, in a small New England village . . .

B.J. Stevens, born in New Zealand's South Island, moved to Australia in 1986 and currently lives in Sydney, NSW. From 1988 he spent four years as an associate editor for *Terror Australis* magazine. He has exhibited his pen-and-ink illustrations in Auckland and Sydney. To date his illustrations, reviews, articles and macabre stories have appeared in *Animal Liberation* magazine, *EOD* magazine, *Pulse of Darkness*, *Skinned Alive*, and *Shoggoth*. Having edited and published two previous fantasy calendars including the Australian HP Lovecraft Centenary Calendar, Bryce and fellow illustrator Kurtstone formed Spine Publications to publish more work of this kind, featuring all Australian artwork—and published the Razor Caress 1992/93 Calendar. Bryce is at work on a psycho-sexual novel titled *Pain and Kisses*.

Dirk Strasser lives in Mt. Waverley, Victoria. His short stories have been published in numerous anthologies and magazines in Australia, the USA, Canada and Germany. His articles have appeared in most of the major newspapers in Australia. He co-edits (with Stephen Higgins) *Aurealis*, the Australian SF/fantasy magazine. His fantasy novel *Zenith* will be published by Pan Macmillan in 1993.

Eddie Van Helden, born in 1963 in Hendrik-Ido-Ambacht (near Rotterdam), now writes from the back of a Datsun 1207 station wagon in Australia. Besides being Buttons the Clown, Patch the Pirate and the Mad Hatter on the weekends, he has published in a wide variety of magazines (including *EOD* magazine) and anthologies (including *Rescuing Beached Mondays*) both here and overseas. He is currently undertaking an MA at James Cook University, Townsville, for which he is writing a book of short stories and a book of poetry. His imagination can be quite nasty, as in his two pieces here . . .

Ann C. Whitehead lives in Wollongong, NSW, and is one of the growing band of older new writers. After enrolling at Wollongong University, she opted out of the BCA after completing the writing strand, to concentrate on her writing. During the last six years she has had three plays produced in amateur theatre, two others short-listed in the Australian

National Playwrights' Convention, around a dozen short stories published in various literary magazines, and a children's book, *Frazzles*, with Collins/A&R. She also won the 1990 Golden Dagger Award for her mystery story 'A Habit of Obedience'.

Cherry Wilder, a New Zealander, for some years now resident in (West) Germany, lived for many years in Australia where she published short stories and articles under the name Cherry Grimm, and wrote reviews for the *Sydney Morning Herald* and *The Australian*. During this time she received two literary grants from the Australia Council. Her stories have appeared in numerous anthologies in Australia such as *Alien Worlds* and *The Zeitgeist Machine* and in the USA and England (including the anthologies *Arabesques 2*, *Best New Horror*, *Dark Voices #2*, *New Terrors 1*, and *The Sixth Omni Book of SF*; and magazines such as *Isaac Asimov's Science Fiction Magazine* and *Strange Plasma*). Her novels include the Torin series (for children): *The Luck of Brin's Five* (1979), *The Nearest Fire* (1980), *Second Nature* (1982), and *The Tapestry Warriors* (1983); and the Rulers of Hylor Trilogy: *A Princess of the Chameln* (1986), *Yorath the Wolf* (1986) and *The Summer's King* (1986). *Cruel Designs* (1988), a horror novel, is her most recent major work and is set in Germany. In 'Anzac Day', she brings the horror back home to 'peaceful' New Zealand. Cherry says thoughtfully: '*Now* I'll have to write some stories set in Australia . . .'

Sean Williams of Cowandilla, SA, has, in the past two years, published stories in *Aboriginal SF*, *Aurealis*, *CFCS Newsletter*, *Dragon's Whisper*, *EOD* (in which an earlier version of 'Twist of the Knife' was voted third in a readers' poll), *Eidolon*, *Intimate Armageddons*, *Just Alice*, *The Mentor*, *Nemesis*, and *TLS*. He writes a weekly column for *On Dit* and is working on his first novel, *Metal Fatigue*. He studies and writes music part-time (and won the 1984 SA Young Composers Award); his hobbies include 'smoking,

atheism, and doomed relationships'. He has won the
HongCon92 Literature Prize, and third prize in the L. Ron
Hubbard Writers of the Future Contest. At twenty-five years
of age, his only regret is that he has spent most of his life not
writing, and now has to do his level best to catch up.

ARTISTS

Vickie Adams, a professional graphic artist, works for a
large record company in Sydney. She designed the *Terror
Australis* logo and illustrated for *Terror Australis* magazine. Favouring detailed styles of illustration including
stipple and scratchboard techniques, she lives in Darling-
hurst, NSW, with a large collection of books on witchcraft,
and two pet rats.

Terry Austin is the working name of a young writer/artist
who has worked in film. Currently he is working on *The
Creature Shop*, a self-illustrated collection of his poetry. He
lives in Camperdown, NSW.

Steve Carter lives in Greenacre, NSW. Former member of
Burnt Lung Cancer and other industrial/noise bands, Steve
is a Sydney-based horror/fantasy artist and writer whose
work has appeared in various Australian underground publications (*Hairbutt the Hippo, Magnum Opus, The Mentor,
Prohibited Matter, Skinned Alive*, etc.). He has also contributed to *Terror Australis* and *Razor Caress* and to the
American horror comic *Cadaver*. Steve was the driving
force behind the controversial *Phantastique*, Australia's
first horror comic, of which issues 3 and 4 were banned in
three states. In 1991 he published the first issue of *Charnel
House*, a news-stand-available collection of uncompromis-
ing works of horror and death sf (now up to issue 4), and has
also published the portfolio *Grotesqueries*. He is presently
collaborating with Antoinette Rydyr on new and even more
grotesque material for ongoing issues of *Charnel House*.

Philip Cornell, a professional graphic artist, illustrated for *Terror Australis* magazine and contributed to the Australian HP Lovecraft Centenary Calendar. Phillip and his wife are enthusiastic founding members of the Sydney Passengers (Sherlock Holmes Society).

Gavin O'Keefe lives with his family in Tawonga, Victoria. An illustrator with numerous book covers to his credit, he has published in a wide variety of magazines including *Aphelion, Beastly, Eidolon, Phantastique* and *Terror Australis* magazine. An occasional writer, he has published articles in *Oz Arts* magazine, *Peake Studies* and *Topy Chaos Bulletin* and verse in *The Hub Newsletter*. His surrealistic comic strips have appeared in *Culture* and *Eod* magazine. His own illustrated version of the Lewis Carroll classic *Alice in Wonderland*, the *GO Alice*, published in 1990 in conjunction with the Alice 125 exhibition, is now a sought-after collector's item. He is currently seeking a publisher for his 'Eight Illustrative Fits' to Carroll's *The Hunting of the Snark*.

Antoinette Rydyr of Greenacre, NSW, has worked as a graphic designer and technical illustrator since graduating with a Diploma of Art and Design in 1981. She has since illustrated children's books, produced rock videos and video documentaries for community groups, and worked as a film censor on the Film Censorship Board. She is currently writing and illustrating comics and collaborating with Steve Carter on a number of horror projects; among them, *Charnel House*. Her work has appeared in *Magnum Opus, Southern Aurora Comics, Razor Caress, Nervous Breakdown* and the American horror comic *Cadaver*.

Kurtstone lives with his wife Anne in Ashfield, NSW. He has illustrated for *EOD* magazine, *Phantastique, Pulse of Darkness, Rattlebone, Skinned Alive, Terror Australis*, and with B.J. Stevens is one half of Spine Publications, publishers of *Razor Caress* and other fantasy/horror art calendars.

Neil Walpole of Summer Hill, NSW, is an illustrator and graphic artist whose favoured technique is pen-and-ink. As well as illustrating for *Terror Australis* magazine and the Australian HP Lovecraft Centenary Calendar, Neil has drawn and published a horror comic, *The Fright Stuff* (issues 2 and 3 are forthcoming). Work in progress includes *Angel Space Cadets*, a 3-issue SF comic series, and an as-yet-untitled martial arts theme comic.

Suggested Further Reading

Space prohibits a comprehensive guide to other Australian horror literature. Readers eager to sample more work of this kind, however, are directed to the following sources, especially to the current magazines, where cutting-edge horror is thriving.

ANTHOLOGIES

Congreve, Bill (ed). *Intimate Armageddons*. Wollongong, NSW: Five Islands Press, 1992.

Krimmer, Sally & Alan Lawson. *Barbara Baynton: Bush Studies, Other Stories; Human Toll, Verse, Essays & Letters*. St Lucia, Qld: Univ of Qld Press, 1980.

MAGAZINES & JOURNALS

The Australian Horror & Fantasy Magazine (1984–86).

EOD Magazine, PO Box 7545, St Kilda Rd, Melbourne, Vic 3004.

Prohibited Matter, 6 Blackwood Rd, Merrylands, Sydney, NSW 2160.

Shoggoth, PO Box 7545, St Kilda Rd, Melbourne, Vic 3004.

Skinned Alive: The Horror Fiction Fanzine, PO Box 166, Roma St, Brisbane, Qld 4003.

Terror Australis: The Australian Horror & Fantasy Magazine (1988–92).

CRITICAL WORKS

Barclay, Glen St John. *Anatomy of Horror: The Masters of Occult Fiction*. London: Weidenfeld & Nicolson, 1978.

Blackmore, Leigh. 'Of Skins and Heart: Horror Fiction and the Meaning of Being'. *Talents* No. 34 (June 1990).

Larnach, Stan. *Materials Towards a Checklist of Australian Fantasy* (to 1937). Sydney: Futurian Press, Nov 1950 (100 copies).

Masters, C(hris) A. 'A History of Small Press in Horror Australia'. *Daarke World Sampler* (March 1992).